THE HALF-LIGHT

Katori Chronicles Book 1

A. D. Lombardo

*I dedicate this book to my son Connor and all the
parents and children who spend countless hours
reading stories and sparking memories.*

ACKNOWLEDGMENTS

Writing a book was more exhilarating than I ever imagined. From one idea sprouts another. One lesson I learned, never go to sleep mulling an idea. Night fairies whisk them away never to be recalled come morning.

I especially want to thank my awesome son, Connor. What started as a simple story, I told him as a toddler developed into a full-blown book series after a restless night's sleep. None of this would have been possible without the delight on his face when he read the first few pages in our grocery store parking lot. His writing contribution brought Rayna's character to life and kept her from becoming just a girl at the beach, effectively altering Kai's future and the story entirely. Beyond his insightful instruction, Connor spent hours reading and rereading every draft.

Encouragement came without limits from my supportive husband, Richard. Most days, I spent every waking hour, I was not at work—writing. When I felt frustrated or doubtful, he stood beside me and told me not to give up. He was essential to this book getting done. Thank you so much, my dear husband.

Special thanks to my two editors—Edwina, you helped me realize I don't need to color everything. Keith, you pushed me to punch up the story, reveal more and not resolved every fight within two paragraphs. Together you both taught me not to fear the delete key.

I would be remised if I did not thank my little sister, Rachel, for some early suspense advice, Ingrid for constant encouragement and downloading a very rough draft, and Karen for early proofreading and at times daily moral support.

One very important honorable mention, I must thank my dog, Buddy. While he will never read this, he spent hours downstairs beside my desk, ensuring I was not alone into the wee hours. His loyalty gave real strength in the creation of Smoke.

Finally, to all those who have been a part of my getting here: every friend, coworker, and relative who listened to me talk about my story over and over again, often braving the question: How is the book coming? Thank you.

The Katori Chronicles Book 1
A. D. Lombardo

This work is a work of fiction. Names, characters, organizations, places, events and incidents are either products of the author's imagination or are used factiously. Any resemblance to actual persons, living or dead, or actual events is purely coincidental.

Published by Angela Lombardo
ISBN 978-1-7333376-0-1 (Paperback)
Cover design by Rob
First Edition 2019

www.ADLombardo.com

CONTENTS

Chapter 1 Bonding
Chapter 2 Drew
Chapter 3 Routine
Chapter 4 Bad Dreams
Chapter 5 Betrothed
Chapter 6 Green Eyes
Chapter 7 Gianfranca's Secret
Chapter 8 Landon's Anger
Chapter 9 Half-Light
Chapter 10 Spellbinding
Chapter 11 Trapped
Chapter 12 Duplicity Born
Chapter 13 Real Proof
Chapter 14 Bonds Are Forever
Chapter 15 Entitlement
Chapter 16 Thade Forest Burdens
Chapter 17 Who's That Girl?
Chapter 18 Winter Storm
Chapter 19 Wicker Basket
Chapter 20 The Gift of Time
Chapter 21 Testing Limits
Chapter 22 Moon Blindness
Chapter 23 Cheese Pie
Chapter 24 Kodama
Chapter 25 Hamrin Bound
Chapter 26 Three Wolf Night
Chapter 27 Men or Monsters
Chapter 28 Childhood's End
Chapter 29 Town Hope
Chapter 30 Homecoming
Chapter 31 Future Predictions

CHAPTER 1

Bonding

Three days after Prince Kai's thirteen birthday, he found himself face-to-face with a Nebean black wolf pup. A spring chill whipped through the air of the Diu palace courtyard. Kai watched the pup hop and roll in the grass before him. Its feet were massive—in fact, everything about him was bigger than even the largest of dogs.

The pup's mother hovered near the young prince, her blue eyes fixed on Kai. Kai gulped at her intimidating height. Haygan, the new stablemaster, stood firmly beside her, his feet set wider than his broad shoulders. With him was Kendra, the children's governess. "Haygan, are you sure?" she asked.

"There's only one way to find out," Haygan responded. "Let him try."

The prince tilted his head. "Why can't I give him a name?" Kai inquired.

"Do you want a pet or a companion?" Haygan countered.

Confused by the question, Kai asked, "What's the difference?"

"Freedom. Pets are tame, dependent creatures. Companions, however, are bonded to you. There's mutual respect between you." Haygan looked to the enormous Nebean wolf-mother. "Shiva is not my pet, she is her own master. We are equals. My people, the Katori, believe a shared relationship is stronger."

"My mother was from Katori." Kai smiled. "Maybe you knew her, her name was Mariana."

Kendra knelt in the grass. "We both knew your mother, Kai. You can do this," she assured him.

Haygan's expression remained serious. "Focus, Prince Kai. Focus on the wolf. Find the connection between you. Sense his nature with your own. The point starts in your soul and reaches for his. Introduce yourself, but not with words. Use your mind. All you must do is ask and listen."

Kai let his hand stroke the pup's fur. The wolf settled in the grass. Kai thought about what Haygan had just told him. He wanted a shared connection. They were the same—they both wanted freedom. Emotion surged into Kai's heart when he thought of his mother. Since her death, he cherished any connection to her past and the traditions of her homeland.

Caught up in the moment, Kai felt a spark ignite his heart. A flood of energy flowed through his mind. Power tingled down his spine. The hair on his arms stood on end. They stared at each other. Mentally he reached out to the wolf—*I am Kai. Would you be my companion?* He offered himself to the pup and thought of how they would spend their lives together.

The wolf's eyes conveyed a sense of wisdom. Strength and loyalty echoed in his ears. Kai continued to listen. Visions of them older flashed through his mind. A campfire crackled, smoke from the fire floated into the sky, and he heard— SMOKE.

Astounded, he looked to Haygan. "Smoke, his name is Smoke," he announced proudly.

"You heard something?" Kendra whispered, surprised.

"It can't be possible..." Haygan knit his brow and stroked his chin. "He's a Half-Light."

Confused by their comments, Kai looked to them both. Had he done something wrong? He only did what they asked. Even now, he could still feel a tiny thread between him and the wolf. A spiritual tether linked them together.

Haygan knelt next to Kai. "Don't get me wrong, Kai. This is wonderful. We are just a little surprised you did it so easily. You've been blessed by Alenga with a gift. And we will help you develop your ability, but this is very dangerous. From one Katori to another, we must keep this a secret. If anyone found out, you would be taken away from your family. Your power puts everyone at risk; you, your family, other Katori, even Smoke. Horrible people could take you, use you as a weapon or tool to trick others."

Kendra placed her hand on Kai's shoulder. "I see the concern in your eyes. We are proud of you, of course, but we cannot stress enough the danger of others learning about any of your gifts. You are thirteen now, and any other gifts you may have will begin to manifest as you get older—potentially very soon. Being only half Katori, we were unsure you'd demonstrate any power."

Kai turned to Haygan. The new stablemaster had only been in Diu a few weeks, but he came highly recommend. "Is this why you came to Diu? To test me?"

Haygan looked at Kendra and nodded. "Yes."

"It's complicated, Kai," she added. "You are Mariana's son, and I, for one, wanted to meet you. But now, given your bonding with Smoke, it is important we teach you how to control your gifts."

"Imagine someone wanted to attack Diu fortress." Haygan gestured to the security guard and his canine patrolling in the distance. "With your ability, they could force you to turn the Mryken guard dogs against Diu. Consider the devastation those dogs could do. Two of those dogs are capable of killing a bear. While they are not as large as Shiva, they are formidable beasts. The devastation to the people would be catastrophic."

"I would never help them," Kai insisted. "I would never hurt anyone here in Diu."

"You wouldn't have a choice. They would leverage your feelings for someone else to force you," Haygan countered.

"Even if you trust the person you tell, it is not their burden to carry. They will not understand the risk and could accidentally tell another."

It was difficult enough to process his bonding, but now he had to grapple with the risk behind his gift. While Kai wanted to be excited, he was confused by the dangerous secret. "I would have never thought about it like that. I understand the risk. Can all Katori do this?" Kai asked.

Haygan pulled Kai to his feet. "Not every Katori can bond with animals, and even if they can, only a select few can communicate outside of their direct bonds. The more you practice with Smoke, the more attuned you will become. Only time will tell if you can interact with other creatures. Wild animals, when attacking, are the most difficult to reason with."

Kendra smoothed the front of her apron. "We can talk about this later. Let's get you inside. I must check on your little brothers."

The stablemaster motioned to Smoke. "Bonds are forever, Your Highness. Smoke is not a dog; he is a wolf. Respect him and his wild nature. You must promise to work on your bond. We are both proud of you."

The weight of their fear pressed on prince Kai's chest. Respectfully Kai nodded, "I will practice every day. And I will keep the Katori secrets," he promised.

Spring and summer were over in the blink of an eye. Kai sat cross-legged on the floor, and his wolf faced him. No longer a pup, Smoke's stature loomed over the young prince. Committed to strengthening their bond, they had practiced every morning since spring. Kai listened. Smoke sat. But since their very first day, he'd heard nothing. Desperate to hear the wolf speak once more, Kai pushed his thoughts—nothing happened. *What am I doing wrong?*

No matter how hard he tried, the result was the same. Had he imagined the words, the feelings? *No, they were real.* No matter how impossible the idea, he'd felt the connection and heard his wolf. Training Smoke to come when called, to sit and stay on command was the easy part. Hearing his wolf was proving to be more difficult.

Even the *Mryken* became his test subjects. He visited the kennels and attempted to force his will on the royal guard dogs. No luck with them either. Frustrated, he laid back on the floor of his room. Smoke's bark brought Kai upright to see Landon Maxwell blocking the door.

"Poor little prince," the older boy mocked as he stuck his head in the room. "No friends but your little mutt."

"I have friends," Kai protested. "Get out of my room, Landon."

"Or what?" Landon challenged.

Before Kai could respond, Amelia Maxwell entered. "Cousin Landon, leave Kai alone," she insisted. "Kai, some of us are going outside to the courtyard, do you want to come?" she asked as she petted Smoke.

Hanging out with everyone was never Kai's preference. All too often, the afternoon became a competition. The older boys showing off or picking on the younger children. But the alternative was being alone, and he didn't like that either. Kai reluctantly followed Amelia outside. Diamond Run was often the game of choice, only he hated being hit with the ball when it was his turn. He never ran fast enough or dodged at the right moment. Today would be no exception. The boys would play, and the girls would cheer.

Tolan and Landon were the eldest. They made up the rules and dictated everything. Tolan was the son of Admiral Roark Raebun, stationed at Diu's Fort Pohaku, and Landon Maxwell was the nephew of Regent Lucas Maxwell from the country of Milnos, but both of his parents were deceased. Both were bullies as far as Kai was concerned.

When Kai reached the courtyard, Tolan bounced a round

ball made of leather strips sewn together and stuffed with cotton and seeds. Tolan's gaze followed Amelia. "Everyone in for a game of Diamond Run?"

The rules of the game were simple: kick the ball, run, tag all three points in the yard, and cross back over the home line to safety—all before you were struck by the ball. They played every kid for themselves, one point each if you cleared the line.

Amelia was the only girl to ever play, and she never got hit. Nobody would dare hit her with the ball. She commanded a gentle respect that no boy would challenge. Plus, Tolan threatened anyone who considered it. Her blonde hair glistened in the sun as she stepped up to kick first.

Tolan's smile softened, and his usual fast pitch rolled even and slow across the grass. Everything Amelia did was graceful, even kicking a ball in a dress. The toe of her shoe struck the ball, and Kai watched it sail toward Landon, his arms outstretched and ready.

Tolan yelled, "Don't you dare catch that ball!"

Landon batted the ball to the ground with a huff. "Why do we let her play if we can't…"

Tolan was in Landon's face in an instant, his fiery red hair matched his temper. "We let her play because I said so. And she is the only girl brave enough to try."

Amelia skipped around the yard, happy as a clam. Tolan spun on his heels. His eyes followed her movements, and a smile curled the side of his mouth. She crossed the home line and curtsied, then found a place in the yard. Far enough away, she would not get hit by the next person kicking, but close enough that she could grab a grounded ball and toss it to a boy.

When Kai's turn came, he stood at the ready. Tolan's notorious fastball barreled in his direction. Kai charged the ball. His kick was good, low along the ground. He ran around the yard, he tapped the first marker. Gideon, his cousin, scooped up the ball and fired at Kai. The shot was high, and Kai tapped the second marker. After touching the third, he rounded the yard and headed for home. Landon grabbed the ball and beaned Kai in the back.

Landon whooped with pride. Kai gasped at the sting and stopped to catch his breath. *Why do I play their stupid game?*

Next Tolan stepped up to kick, and Landon launched the ball. Tolan's kick sailed the ball into the orchard, so hard that the force pinned it between two branches. One point for him.

The game continued with Gideon catching Landon's ball. And he got punched in the arm for the effort. The next boy got tagged out with a hit to the face by Landon. The next boy shot a line drive right back at Tolan, who dove to make a knee-scraping catch.

Luckily Gideon managed to kick his ball into the orchard and sailed around the yard without challenge. Three kicks later, Amelia came up to the line. As always, Tolan offered an easy roll, and she trotted around the yard with delight, Tolan pleased to watch her go.

It was Kai's turn again. Scanning the positions of the other players, Kai prepared to kick. *I need to try something different. Everyone always aims for the orchard...*

Landon stood at the ready. Kai angled his body; he shot his kick as far from Landon as possible. Perfect placement sent it rolling toward the kennel fence. Landon raced for the ball. Kai ran. He looped around the yard. Out of the corner of his eye, he noticed Landon zero in on the ball. This would be close.

Kai raced toward the home line. Everyone cheered. Kai's heart pounded. Fifteen feet, ten feet, five...he was almost there. Smoke barked, and a warning rippled through Kai's senses. He saw the ball sailing towards the back of his head. At the last moment, he ducked, and the ball whizzed by. His foot crossed the home line. Score one for Kai.

"Cheater!" Landon yelled.

"How?" Kai challenged. "You missed."

"Your wolf... I don't know how but he... you..." Landon stumbled through his objection. His expression was as though he'd smelled something foul.

Everyone stared. Landon glared at Kai. Kai held his breath on the outside, but his heart delighted with the connection he felt between him and Smoke. A thread linked them together.

The game ended the way it always did, Tolan won. This time, four points to his favor.

CHAPTER 2

Drew

Rain pelted the large arched windows of the palace library. Trapped inside, Kai yearned to escape the confines of Diu palace. Thick stone walls protected the fortress, and its upper and lower ward. The Diu stronghold sat atop a large rock and overlooked the city below, divided into three natural tiers—Hightown, Midtown, and Rimtown, all protected by the second set of walls.

When the morning's rain ended, Kai and Smoke climbed the palace walls to peer over the sprawling city below. The streets in Hightown Proper buzzed with people. Shopkeepers opened windows and doors to welcome the fresh air and patrons alike.

Kai inhaled and lifted his blue eyes upward. The storm clouds had passed. He turned his gaze to the white and gray stones of the palace where moisture still clung to the surface and highlighted flecks of silver in the granite, giving it a magical appearance in the light. Sunshine and promise overwhelmed him. He released a slow breath. The anticipation of his plan bubbled to the surface, and he chuckled.

To leave the palace, he needed his guard. Kai set off toward the southeast watchtower across the wall. The warm autumn wind blew across his face. The smell of wet stone and earth lingered. He held his chin high as he passed several guards in search of his escort Drew who should be completing his shift. Kai hastened his pace.

At nearly fourteen, Kai no longer spent his day with a governess. He had more freedoms to venture out. So why did he need a guard? The citizens of Diu paid him no mind, bowing, or stepping aside if they even noticed him. He longed for an adventure, the kind he would create today with the unsuspecting Drew.

When he reached the watchtower, a different guard stood at attention. He offered a slight bow to Kai. The prince furrowed his brow and nodded. Had Drew forgotten? No. He was not one to neglect his duty.

Kai rested a hand on his wolf's back. "Where could Drew be, Smoke? He should have been waiting for us in the palace courtyard, and he is not at his usual post."

Smoke's head cocked to one side. At ten months, his Nebean black wolf was already the same size as the Mryken guard dogs; the largest breed in the land. Big paws were an excellent indicator Smoke would be huge, even bigger than Shiva, his mother.

One guard swore he saw Drew go to the stables, while another said he went to the dining hall, and still another who saw him heading toward the courtyard. If Kai followed their advice, he would waste half his day searching. He needed to think, not wander.

Where would Drew go? He headed to the training yard. Keeping to the perimeter to avoid the bustle of activity, the prince scanned the area while voices and weapons rang through the air. A loud whistle broke through the noise. Soldiers formed lines and stood at attention. Their captain barked orders, directing men to pair off and practice maneuvers. The yard once again filled with the sounds of grunts and metal clanging against metal.

With the men spread apart, Kai caught a glimpse of three captains speaking with a small group of guards. One man stood out. His broad shoulders and muscular arms stretched the limits of his dark blue guard's uniform. A smile lifted Kai's mouth. He'd found Drew.

Thrilled, he ran the length of the fence and waved until he caught Drew's attention. Drew offered a quick smile and a sharp nod before he refocused his attention on his captain. Kai stopped a short distance away and waited.

Finished, Drew approached and bowed. "Good morning, Your Highness. My apologies for not meeting you in the palace courtyard. My captain's training duties took longer than expected."

Noticing Drew's tired eyes, Kai wondered if his personal guard had overextended himself. "Good morning, Drew. Please call me Kai or Prince Kai if you must."

"It is of the utmost importance to show respect, especially in front of my superiors. I would not presume to show anything less around the other men."

"Around others, I guess I understand. But in private, please consider my request. We are friends, right?" Kai huffed. "I mean, over the past six months, you are the only guard left who was originally assigned to me. The others never last more than a few weeks before they get bored."

"I am your guard, first and foremost. I cannot speak for the others. I signed up because I have Kempery-man ambitions. I stay because I enjoy your company. Although you are ten years my junior, I think you need the influence of someone who won't treat you, forgive any disrespect, like the spoiled little prince the others think you are."

Drew's words felt harsh. "I know the others call me little prince. You're the only one that takes me seriously. The only one who even talks to me, really."

"I treat you the way my father would, like the young man I expect you to become. Like a future King. Besides, I don't have any brothers, you're all I've got." Drew smiled and bumped Kai's arm.

They passed under the inner gatehouse into Hightown

Proper. The colored warehouses, shops, and homes were all four and five windows wide and four levels high. The streets bustled with carriages and high society ladies and gentlemen in their overdone hats and frilly clothing.

Standing in front of a clothing shop, Kai laughed at the absurd styles. "They call this the latest fashion trends. Too ridiculous." With his reflection striking the glass, he lined up his neck with the young man's high collared shirt. "Too stuffy," he mocked.

"Oh, I don't know, the socialite ladies may find you rather handsome in that one," Drew joked.

Their camaraderie felt fluid and natural. While their titles separated them, Kai felt a real kinship with Drew. Everyone else entertained him out of duty or because someday they would want a favor. Not Drew.

When they reached Giardina's Bakery, Kai peered through the large arched windows. Sweets and delicate pastries, bread loaves, and cakes decorated the display. The smell of fresh baked goods wafted into the street. Kai's mouth watered at the yummy treats.

It wasn't every day he indulged in such desserts. He entered and purchased one bite-size orange blossom cake and one chocolate puff swirl pastry. He smiled at Drew, who was too busy studying the crowd to notice.

"You never eat sweets, do you?" Kai asked.

"Too frivolous on my salary," Drew countered.

The Hightown Proper's clocktower struck the hour. Kai's eyes widened. "Barnum's Clockworks. Let's go." Kai darted down the street and hooked the corner; Smoke kept pace.

Drew called after the prince. His long strides brought him back alongside Kai. They soon found themselves in the doorway of Barnum's Clockworks. "How many times must I tell you not to run ahead," Drew said.

Both doors leading into the shop were propped wide open. The sound of overlapping gongs and chimes flitted into the meandering passersby. Inside the shop, every clock chimed in unison. Some melodies were soft and delicate, while others were deep and soulful. The blended tones by the eleventh strike were nearly too much to take.

Kai covered his ears. "I wonder how the clockmaker manages all day listening to each mark of the hour?"

"It would not be enjoyable work. Clocks make too much noise," Drew replied, stepping back through the doorway. "I still don't see your fascination with them."

"Open a clock and tell me the gears and mechanisms are not mesmerizing. Did you know there are rubies inside?"

"I am not one for machines, Prince Kai." Drew merged them back into the growing crowd.

With one hand resting on Smoke's back, Kai continued to wildly direct them through the city.

Drew placed his hand on Kai's shoulder, bringing them to a stop, his chiseled features sharpened into a stern glare. "Prince Kai, you need to walk with purpose. We'll never get anywhere crisscrossing to whatever catches your eye."

Kai had walked them in a circle, twice. "Fine, I want to go to Midtown Plaza to see Elise."

In Midtown Plaza merchants haggled over wares while patrons bartered for value. Many found delectable treats from around the world. He hoped Elise saved something new for him. He and Drew crossed down one level into Midtown.

It was astonishing to see the change in color. The Midtown homes and shops were almost all yellow; and not the vibrant yellows used in Hightown, but a pale imitation. While the homes were still four levels high, most were only two windows wide. The most notable difference was the addition of wrought-iron scrolled bars over the lower windows.

Middletown Plaza carried row after row of colorful tents and merchant stands. Worming their way through the crowds, they neared the southeast corner where Kai spotted Elise working her merchant stall.

"Good day to you, sir. Would you like to try a piece of kiwi? They're new," Elise said to the man in front of Kai.

"Honestly, Miss. I'm a world traveler, a collector," the man said. "I've had them before, so they are not new. I will take three kiwis, six red apples, and four peaches."

Kiwi? Kai glanced up at the plump man with his pointy nose jutted into the air. The fat man blocked his view of the fruit in Elise's hand. He tried again, but the crowd squeezed together around her. He no longer had a clear line of sight. "Drew, I can't see. Does it look good?"

"No, it does not. The fruit is brown and fuzzy, looks awful," Drew responded. "I say we head down two streets to Maggie's Tavern for lunch."

A few patrons parted, and Kai stepped up. Elise wore her usual puffy blouse, with a red and yellow rose-covered corset and a long black skirt, with her strawberry blond hair tucked under her hat. "Hello, Elise, I want to try a kiwi. Drew said it looks bad, but what does he know?" he chuckled, nudging Drew with his elbow.

Elise offered a soft smile and an awkward curtsey. "Hello, Prince Kai, it has been some time since you've been to see me. You know I'd never offer you anything bad."

At the announcement of the prince, a few bystanders turned to gawk at Kai. He instantly felt the pressure as people crowded around him, all trying to get closer. Strangers whispered.

"For a prince, he dresses rather common," an old woman blabbered.

"King Iver never comes into town anymore, outside of Kings Day or the Prince's birthday," her companion mocked. "This Queen keeps a tight rein on our King."

"Shhh, the poor dear, lost his mother." Sympathetic nods followed the woman's statement.

Kai's face felt warm. *How dare they mention my mother?* he fumed to himself. The crowd fell silent under Drew's stern glare. Kai focused on the kiwi. He'd never seen one before.

Elise split the fruit in half, and the faintest drip of clear juice dropped and splatted onto the ground. She placed half in Kai's open hand. "Don't eat the fuzzy brown skin, only the green flesh."

He took a bite, and sweetness exploded in his mouth. "It's wonderful. I will take three more, plus the other half of the one I'm eating." He held up the remaining piece. "Drew, you have to try this."

Drew clenched his jaw. The gathering crowd shoved toward Kai, and he stumbled. Smoke growled. Drew took in a deep breath; with outstretched arms, he used his long reach and pushed back the crowd. "Kai, we should get moving. Get to main streets where there are other guards on patrol." Drew placed his hand on the young prince.

Maybe coming into the city was not a good idea. "Thank you, Elise. We need to go." Kai made his purchase and quickly followed Drew through the crowd.

"Thank you, Prince Kai, come again," Elise called after him.

Kai followed his usual route to Castile Books. One street over and three intersections up. At the corner bookshop, Kai pressed his face against the window to peer inside. The owner, Jonah Castile, stood talking with Abram Denholm, the owner of Denholm Publishing. From his angle, Kai could see all the way through the two adjoining shops.

Jonah waved. Abram craned his neck. They had seen him. Today was not the day to live vicariously through a book, but he was tempted by his own routine, so he entered. "Gooday Mister Castile, Mister Denholm. It is a pleasure to see you both." Kai nodded, glancing over a new stack of books on the table. "Do you have anything I might be interested in, Mister Castile?"

"Your Highness, so good of you to visit us today." Jonah rounded the table. Both men bowed. "I do. A book called *Treasure in Bog Willows.*" He offered Kai the book.

The cover was deep emerald green with the title embossed in gold lettering. Skimming a few random pages, Kai considered the book. "Looks very good. Trolls, knights, and treasure."

He eyed Abram's printing press stamping out pages in the next shop. He yearned to watch the contraption. Still clutching the book, Kai took a step closer. Abram's apprentice wielded the machine and hung new pages to dry. "Mister Denholm, what are you printing?"

Denholm's bearded face turned toothy. "Your Highness. It's called *Bone Reader*, by a new Port Anahita author. You might like it. I should have his order completed within the week. I will hold a copy for you if you wish."

"Wonderful. Thank you, Mister Abrams. Mister Castile, I will take the *Treasure in Bog Willows*. I noticed the last page mentions a second story, *A King's Ransom*. Do you have that too?" Kai inquired.

"My apologies, Your Highness, I have not yet attained a copy. There is a new shipment due next month. The second part should be in that order. It will be my pleasure to secure volume two for you."

"Greatly appreciate your effort." Kai made his purchase and stuffed the book into his bag, careful not to squish the kiwi. "Good afternoon, gentlemen." With a bow and wave, he departed.

"Where to next, Prince Kai? Perhaps lunch?" Drew said.

"Yes. Let's go to Maggie's Tavern. I know my father would not approve of me exploring Rimtown, but I want to know every part of the city."

Drew nodded. "Rimtown is not a risky place during the day."

Along the way, Kai asked, "Any chance we could leave the city to explore the woods? I would like to hike through Thade Forest to Baden Lake."

"Prince Kai, it was a long night, I beg of you, can we go to Diu Central City Gardens instead?"

Although Drew was usually accommodating, Kai was not surprised. Drew led Kai down to the first street inside Rimtown where every window held iron bars. Men loitered on the streets. Small groups of children rushed through the crowds.

The majority of the Rimtown buildings were unpainted stone or weathered wood.

Kai stepped closer to Drew. Here in Rimtown, people kept their heads down and trudged about their business. They did not step to the side or bow when he passed. The idea of being anonymous intrigued Kai. It also made him wonder if being identified as the prince publicly was a good idea or a mistake on his part.

Maggie's Tavern—a clean establishment frequented by merchants and city guards—gave them their choice of seating with their early arrival. Kai and Drew took a small table near the window from where Drew waved to Miranda, the barmaid.

"Afternoon Your Highness. Drew. Same as always?" Miranda asked.

Kai nodded, and Miranda rushed off to get their food. Kai watched Drew's expression, noting his fondness for the young woman. He relaxed back in his chair. Every moment of today was meticulously planned to lull Drew into complacency. He hated tricking his friend.

Miranda approached with two plates of food. Her fiery red hair puddled about her shoulders. "Will there be anything else, Drew?" She batted her green eyes at the guard and smiled.

"Thank you, but no Miranda." Drew rocked back in his seat and watched her walk away.

The smell of beef and vegetable stew made Kai's mouth water. The steam kissed his face as he dipped bread into the sauce. Their meal was warm and satisfying. Drew spent most of the meal focused on Miranda, while Kai spent most of his anticipating his escape.

CHAPTER 3

Routine

Drew climbed the stone stairs into the Diu Central City Gardens. Kai noticed their pace was slow, and he wondered if his guard's numerous responsibilities were taking their toll. The Central City Gardens was a beautiful display of vibrant green lawns, colorful flowerbeds, and towering trees. White marble columns, statues, and fountains spotted the landscape.

The artist responsible for each unique garden left a small marker to notify the observer. Kai searched for his favorite gardener, a woman whose symbol was a shooting star. The best artist was given the centerpiece each spring to design for his birthday, and then for his father on King's Day.

He smiled when he saw that the royal garden marker was a shooting star. Linlou, his favorite, was still considered best gardener in Diu. Linlou's work came alive from an elevated perspective. Her autumn design was a myriad of swirling color; yellow, orange, and red. The overall shape was a horizontal banyark tree made of mulch, flowers, and grasses.

Through the sprawling gardens, they passed one of the many multi-tiered fountains. As Kai dipped his hand into the water, he thought of Baden Lake. What a great day for a swim. A mischievous smile formed across his lips. He grinned at the children playfully splashing each other to cool off from the heat.

On the east end of the park stood five large oaks growing along an extensive grassy area. Couples strolled into the shade with picnic baskets. Kai and Smoke joined the other children running and kicking balls. Drew nestled under a large tree. His tired eyes closed, and he sat up straight and wiped his face.

Before long, Drew's eyes closed again. Kai waited to be sure Drew was asleep. Pleased, he backed away and darted out of the gardens, wasting no time as he ran through the city with Smoke by his side. Grinning from ear to ear, he ran. The risk of his mischief was exhilarating.

Dressed in black and gray, he could pass as any other Midtown boy. With no royal escort, he would be dismissed. Ignored. He kept a keen eye out for other guards on patrol and stayed to the side streets when possible. Head down, he avoided eye contact. More than once, he had to hide behind bystanders or duck into narrow alleyways to avoid detection.

Two blocks from the gatehouse, he waited in the shadows. He needed a way through the city gatehouse. The chaotic streets of Rimtown brimmed with horses, carriages, and travelers. Kai waited.

Breaking through the street noise, Kai heard a familiar sound, the clip-clop of horse hooves. The sounds grew louder as the cart approached. His heartbeat increased in anticipation. He spied a large man perched upon a sturdy carriage, which was loaded with crates, bags, and barrels partially hidden under a canvas tarp. Perfect.

The supply cart clattered to an abrupt stop. The driver waited in line to exit the gatehouse. Kai leaped onto the back then whistled for Smoke. His wolf jumped up and allowed Kai to cover them with a tarp in time for the cart to lurch into motion once more.

Bouncing along the cobblestone streets, Kai peered through the slats trying to see the walls of the city gatehouse. He held his breath when Garrick the gatehouse guard spoke.

"Jordon, where are you going and what's in the back?" Garrick asked.

Through the slats, Kai watched Garrick approach. His long blond hair was pulled back taut, revealing a jagged scar along his jawline. Kai cringed. If discovered, Kai would lose all his freedoms. He closed his eyes, exhaled, and waited.

The cart shifted, and the bench creaked where Jordon sat. "Good day, Garrick. I'm northbound, through the Thade Forest. I have supplies for the Eagle's Nest outpost, the usual items, cheese, barley, salt, and figs."

With a wave from Garrick, the cart lurched forward. The bumping from the cobblestones soon turned into a smoother rock from side to side, indicating they had rolled onto the hard dirt of the north road.

Kai lifted the corner of the tarp and watched the gatehouse fade from view as they crested a small hill entering the Thade Forest. Pleased with himself, he snickered. The cart slowed at the top of the next hill, he and Smoke hopped out and darted into the cover of the forest. His heart pounded as he ducked into the underbrush, and the cart pulled away from view.

There was something exhilarating about breaking the rules. His escape had been so easy. Why had he not tried this sooner? Inside the tree line, he and Smoke ran toward Baden Lake. They weaved through the trees. The hilly terrain and the dense forest started to disorient him. Out of the corner of his eye, Kai caught a glimpse of someone watching him. He turned to get a better look. Nobody was there. He was sure he'd seen the silhouette of a man between the trees. The more he stared, the more nervous he felt.

The sound of water lapping pulled his attention back. Kai raced with Smoke to the water's edge. His four-legged companion ran through the small waves that licked the shoreline. Smoke's pitch-black fur glistened in the sun, and his white front paws a stark contrast against the dark mud.

"What a perfect day," Kai said as he stripped down to his undergarments.

Baden Lake was the largest lake in Diu, fed by the snowy peaks of the Katori Mountains. From the cove, he could see an island across the water; one of many speckled across the vast blue-green lake. Kai squinted at the gleaming water. In the distance, two fishing boats bobbed like toys on the water. South through the trees, two white sails unfurled in the wind; Diu fishing boats leaving the docks.

Hot from the autumn sun, Kai allowed the cool water to tickle his toes. He waded in and sank in the fresh water. Curious, Smoke swam up to him, pawing through the windswept waves before going back to shore. When Kai resurfaced, he ran his hands over his sandy blond hair and wiped the water from his eyes.

He needed this adventure. Time to free his mind from the reoccurring nightmare about the death of his mother. Here he felt at home. Free. The palace and the city felt restricting and loud. The responsibility and rules were gone.

Kai tossed a twig, it flipped end over end as it sailed over Smoke. His wolf bounded down the shoreline to retrieve it. Their afternoon alone was bittersweet. While it was good to get out of the palace, he wished he had a friend to share the day. He should have pressed Drew to come with him.

Baden Lake was vast, and the distant shore was impossible to see. While Smoke rested, he waded into the water. He wanted to see how far he could go on one breath. Neck deep, he dove under, and in his mind, he pictured the distant shoreline.

Stroke after stroke he swam, kicking until his lungs burned with the need for air. Once he broke the surface of the water, he gasped for air and looked out across the rest of the lake. He wanted to keep swimming. Onshore, Smoke barked, and Kai realized he was out much farther than he'd ever been.

Pleased, Kai rolled over to float on his back. Wispy clouds streaked across the sky. Two eagles circled overhead. *To be able to fly would be true freedom.* Kai watched them glide effortlessly above him.

Another eagle joined them. Its massive size dwarfed the

others. The smaller pair flew back toward Eagles Peak, the eastern summit of Thade Mountain. The bigger eagle remained, its golden tips sparkled in the sunshine. Its shadow blocked the sunlight from reaching Kai. He had the strangest feeling he'd seen this golden tipped eagle before.

Kai laid across a flat rock to dry in the sun. Again, the shadow loomed over him. The mighty eagle watched him. There was a visceral connection he could not explain. Was it trying to speak to him? Kai rubbed his temples.

It circled and turned toward the palace, disappearing beyond the trees. The bird's departure made Kai scramble to collect his clothes. Wet, he struggled to dress. Water from his hair ran down his back, soaking his once-dry shirt. Smoke shook, drenching Kai in tiny water droplets. Shielding his face with his hands, he laughed. "Smoke, stop!"

Along the North road, he realized he had no idea how to get back inside undetected. Voices echoed down the road behind him. He kept out of sight, crouched hidden in the brush. The oncoming group crested the hill. Men on horseback, covered supply carts, and walking stragglers. The walkers made it impossible to conceal himself as he'd done earlier, which would probably be unwise, as Garrick would most certainly search the cargo.

Head down, he worked himself closer and closer to the group, listening to their conversations. He envied their ability to come and go freely.

Near the north gate, everyone gathered around the carts for questioning. Kai moved Smoke into the shadow of the horses to hide his exceptional size. Garrick checked each cart against the lead driver's supply list. Kai kept his eyes down as he made his way between the second and third cart. Hidden beside the horse, he leaned into its neck and stroked her mane.

Smoke held his ground as one of the men on horseback sidled up beside them.

Garrick riffled through the various supplies while another guard mingled through the group; satisfied both men stepped aside, and Garrick motioned the all clear. Only a few more feet and Kai would be back inside the city without anyone the wiser.

Slowly the carts pulled onto the cobblestone road, and he heard the familiar clip-clop of the horses and the clicking of the cart's wheels on the stone. They moved through the gate one at a time. Kai waited for his opportunity to run. Each step was agonizingly slow. His stomach churned with anticipation. *Almost there.*

"Hold up. Stop. STOP!" Garrick yelled.

So close. Kai stomped his foot and dropped his head. He closed his eyes and waited for Garrick to apprehend him. He raised his head when the warrior passed him. Garrick ran up to the lead cart, tossed the cover back, and shifted through the merchandise. "One of your bags has a hole. You are leaking flour." Garrick placed the torn bag on top of the tarp. "Hope you didn't lose too much."

"Thank you, Garrick," the driver said as the horses jerked the cart back into motion.

The chance to run was upon him, and Kai edged away from the group. Clear of the horses, he ran. The fear of getting caught drove him faster. He embraced his speed. Buildings and people became a blur as Smoke raced at his side. Into the park, he sprinted. Between people and plants, he dodged. But then next corner came faster than he'd anticipated. His feet skidded out from under, and he tumbled into a bush.

What just happened? Kai wiped the dirt from his hands. With no time to waste, he hopped to his feet and kept going. Heart pounding, the east-end oaks came into view. He skidded to a stop. "No, no, no. Drew is gone." He stopped and fell to his knees. "We are in trouble, Smoke."

"Prince Kai, where in the world did you go?" Drew thundered from behind him. "I woke up and couldn't find you anywhere. I have been searching the park."

Kai spun around. Anger flickered in Drew's steel blue eyes. "I have been worried sick," the guard said.

Guilt welled in his throat. "What do you mean? We were playing in the fountains. We've jumped into them all. It was great fun. Sorry, Drew. Am I in trouble? Are you mad at me?"

"I am mad," Drew growled.

He deserved Drew's frustration. "Sorry, Drew, I didn't mean..."

"Prince Kai, I am not mad at you. I am disappointed in myself. This mistake could cost me my career. I should have never sat down, being so tired. You're soaked." Drew motioned for Kai to follow. "Let's get you back to the palace. I have things to do before starting the night shift."

They neared the palace before Drew said another word. "Your Highness, I will not be able to continue as one of your guards," he admitted.

"Drew. I would never tell anyone," Kai pleaded.

"I've let the King down, and myself, falling asleep. I know others have done it, but I wanted to be better. If anything had happened to you, I'd never have forgiven myself. I will speak with the Grand Duke Carmelo; as head of Diu security, my career is in his hands now."

Kai's head hung low. He had deceived Drew. "I'm not sure what to say. I will miss our talks. You will make a great captain and an even better Kempery-man one day."

His secret was safe, but it cost him a friend.

CHAPTER 4

Bad Dreams

Kai dropped his wet garments in a heap on the bathroom floor. Kendra, the children's governess placed a tray of food on the table near the bay window.

"Kendra, I spent the day swimming. My wet clothes are on the floor of my bathroom." He waved his arm to draw her eyes to the pile on the floor.

Her emerald green eyes squinted at the young prince. She readjusted one of the two silver combs and put a stray black curl back into place. "Prince Kai, you went swimming? Where?" She adjusted her apron as she crossed the room to collect his garments.

Did Kai dare tell her what he'd done? He fiddled with the cuff of his shirt. "Central City Gardens," he lied. "I jumped in the fountains and..."

"The garden fountains. Are you sure?" Kendra sniffed the clothing in her hands. "Smells very fresh. The herbs they use to keep the fountain water clean must be low after all the rain we've had," she added with a sly look.

Kai wondered if she knew, but how could she. A little apprehensive, he agreed. "Yes, we have had a lot of rain these past few days."

"I brought you a tray of food from the kitchen. Everyone is

eating privately tonight. Tomorrow will be a big day. Guests will arrive for the upcoming Master General's ceremony. I'll come back for your tray before bedtime."

It wasn't often he had an evening to himself. Kai sat down to eat his dinner. "Thank you, Kendra," he said, realizing he was famished.

Bowing slightly, Kendra gave him a quick wink. "My pleasure, little man," she added as she slipped out of his room.

The bowed window seat offered a view of the palace gardens below. The setting sun turned the sky a golden orange, while the valley below became enveloped in dark blue and purple. Lost in thought, Kai leaned against the wall and stretched to peer at the twinkling lights of Diu city.

The sunset brought thoughts of his mother. Little man, that's what she used to call him. Her absence still pained him. The last few moments of the day had been their time. The changing sky turned from shades of orange and red to deep blues and finally to black.

Millions of tiny pinpricks of light littered the night. The stars held all the secrets of the world. From his viewpoint, he could see a sliver of Baden Lake above the tree line. The full moon glimmered across the surface. He scanned the clear night sky hoping to catch a glimpse of a streak of fire; the sign of dragons flying from the Katori Mountains, across the lake toward Thade Mountain and back again. He saw nothing—it was too early.

Historical books claimed dragons were fierce creatures that attacked anyone or anything that got too close to their nesting grounds. For the most part, they avoided humans, keeping to the sheer cliffs and impassable glaciers of the Katori Mountains, above the Katori homeland and the only people known to interact with them.

Personal experience, however, reminded him they were vicious creatures that did not always keep to themselves. If dragons trusted the Katori people, why would a dragon kill his mother? Someday he would get his answer.

Thinking of his mother, he let his eyes drift down to the royal gardens below his window. An enormous banyark tree stood prominently at the center of the garden maze. Its dark red branches curved upwards like giant fingers reaching to the sky. Its autumn yellow leaves blazed in the bright moonlight.

Sadness welled in his heart. His mother's memory overwhelmed him. Near his feet, Smoke pawed Kai's leg. In his heart, he felt warmth, and he heard the word—*Live*. Overwhelmed by his wolf compassion, he joined him on the floor and buried his face into Smoke's fur. He no longer cried over her passing, now nine years past, but it still pained him.

"You're right Smoke, I need to live. I shouldn't be sad. I should be thankful. Thankful for Haygan, because he brought you to me. These past six months have been the best of my life." He hugged Smoke's neck.

Voices at the door propelled Kai back onto the window seat. Kendra entered his room. She tousled Kai's hair, and he turned to look at her. Startled, Kendra gasped. "Your eyes, they are green." She covered her mouth and stared.

Kai lowered his head. "I don't know why or how, but my eyes change when my emotions run high. It doesn't happen often. Mother found it frightening, but I don't remember why. It starts as pressure and heat in my head."

"She was afraid because changing your eye color is not natural. Even for full-blooded Katori. Half-Lights should not be able to do this. Kai, you must be careful. Control your emotions."

"You know so much about my mother, about being Katori. I miss her," he sighed.

"Do you want to talk about it?" She sat with him. "Talking may help."

Kai turned back to the tree. "What happened in the royal garden that day still haunts me. You are the only person who cares. Nobody dares speak of the day my mother was killed by a dragon. They think because I was only four, I can't handle talking about her death."

Kendra placed her hand on his knee. "Face her loss. Take your mother's memory into your arms as if you're protecting a small child. Allow the suffering inside, because with it comes all the love she gave. If you ignore your pain, you push her memory away."

"I will try." Kai tilted his head. "Kendra, why did my mother not have a governess when I was born?"

"Your mother Mariana was a strong-willed woman. Knowing her as I did, I cannot see her hiring a servant to do a mother's work. Sharing you with a stranger, no, that would not be her way."

"Then why did father's new wife demand a governess?" Kai questioned.

"Aaron and Seth are sweet boys, but twin boys are a challenge. Being an instant mother to you, well, not everyone is meant to be a mother. I suspect Queen Nola wants to give Iver children, but she's not the nurturing type. Governess Agatha did her best climbing the palace stairs in her old age, but I am thankful she chose to retire. So here I am. And I'm glad for it."

"Me too. You are much sweeter than Agatha." He smiled happily.

"I need to check in on your step-brothers. I will back before lights out." Kendra nodded.

"Thank you, Kendra."

When Kendra turned the dial to extinguish the lamp next to his bed, he watched the flame shrink into a thin red line before going out completely. It ended with a small stream of smoke rising above the flat wick.

Into the fading fireplace embers, she tossed two chunks of wood, and then she slipped into the small bed in the corner. The new wood caught fire, and Kai quietly asked, "Can you tell me another story about my mother? I want to hear about your country—Katori."

"Just one, and then off to sleep," Kendra replied. "Would you like to learn about our leaders?"

Delighted to stay up, Kai adjusted his pillows. "Yes, please."

"Alright, but remember, you must not repeat what I tell you. It is our little secret that I knew your mother before she became queen. The Katori way of life is a closely guarded secret. You would be in danger, all Katori would be in danger if anyone knew our secrets or about your gifts."

"Yes, I remember. Can you take me to your Katori homeland someday?"

The silence was a response within itself. It wasn't the first time he'd asked. He knew the answer. Kendra let out a breath. "It is very far away; the only way to get to Katori is by sea. I don't know. We do not allow outsiders. I would have to ask your grandfather Lucca."

"My mother was Katori, which makes me half-Katori," he added enthusiastically.

"Being proud of your parentage is wonderful. While the world knew your mother was from Katori, they do not know what that means. The truth of her, of us, would jeopardize us all. Please don't speak of it with anyone but Haygan or me."

It seemed nothing would change her mind. "I understand. Tell me about Lucca."

"There are four tribes. Your grandfather is one of four chiefs in the Katori nation. The mountain tribe is called the Hiowind, the highland tribe is known as the Matoku, the coastal people are the Kahoma, and the Mystic Islands are home to the Gemidi." Kendra paused to shift onto her side. Her thick hair flowed loosely around her face. "The chief serves the people of his tribe by representing their voice at the Agora —"

"What's the Agora?" he interrupted.

"The Agora is a spiritual place, located at the center of each tribe's territory, surrounded by gardens and fountains. It is a temple of white and gray marble, with stone columns that twist like vines, growing towards an open domed roof." Sadness echoed in her voice.

It was clear, Kendra missed her home. Kai continued to listen. "Eight arched entrances surround the perimeter. In the center, there is a sacred pool fed by a natural spring. Above, the roof swoops upward where there is a matching circle open to the sky, allowing the sunshine or moonlight to bathe the water."

Kai shifted to his side. "Is a chief like a king? If there are four, who is in charge?"

"A chief is like a king; however, no one chief or tribe is above another. Being a leader is a lifelong position. It means your dwelling is near the center of Katori, closest to the Agora."

"So, they make all the decisions, those four men?" Kai asked.

"Well, it's not just those four men. Beside each chief sits an Unie, again one from each tribe. Unie means to unite, a position held by a woman to ensure equality and compassion in the decisions made. My mother is the Unie for our tribe; which meant my home was next to Mariana's home."

"Were you best friends?" he questioned excitedly.

"Well, your mother is several years older than me; however, there was an attack in the Agora. Your mother protected me. It is that bond that brings me to you now. When I heard of your mother's passing, I was unable to come and care for you. Instead, I found a position in the palace of Nebea, tending the Cazier children. The new Master General, Adrian Cazier, recommended me for the position here when your old governess Agatha retired. I was happy to accept the position to be close to Mariana's son."

Kai sat up. "Wait. What? There was an attack on the Agora. By whom?"

Kendra shook her head. "I am sorry Kai. I should not have mentioned it."

Disappointed, Kai flopped back into bed. "You won't tell me, will you?"

Her voice was heavy. "You know I cannot."

Confused, Kai looked at her. "Why does it have to be a secret that you knew my mother?"

"I fear what others would think. I would hate to lose you because the King felt concerned about my motives."

"Motives?" Kai tilted his head. "I won't tell anyone. I would not want to lose you, either." Struggling to stay awake, he asked another question. "How long does it take to get from Katori to Diu?"

"Our lands are on tall white cliffs above the ocean, and there is only one decent beach. The harbor only allows shallow boats to get close. Dangerous rocks jut up from the ocean floor, like hidden spears below the surface. Ships dare not risk coming too close. Large ships must anchor and send in smaller boats with people and cargo."

"Can people come by land, over the mountains?" Kai asked.

"Not a wise choice," Kendra responded. "The Katori Mountains are treacherous, with jagged ridges and bottomless canyons. Not to mention they are home to all sorts of wild beasts: dragons, black shuk, ridgeback wolves, black panthers and more. Many of these creatures roam the Zabranen Forest. Nobody would dare try that route to get to Katori."

Kendra let her head rest on her pillow. "Enough talk, we both have a big day tomorrow."

"I want to hear about the dragons and why the Katori live so close or trust them..." Unable to continue, he closed his eyes, settled into his pillow, and drifted off into a dream.

In his slumber, Kai spun and spun under twin maple trees, making himself so dizzy he collapsed. From his bed of leaves, he watched the signs of autumn—red and orange leaves twirled in the air as they fell. Lifting up onto his elbows, he looked to his mother. Nearby Mariana sat on a small bench, her blue dress gently swaying in the breeze, her long mahogany brown hair blowing softly around her face. He watched his mother. She was completely engrossed in the pages of her book.

Mariana dropped her book, her pleasant smile lit up her brown almond-shaped eyes. She stood and approached Kai. The cool breeze and mid-day sun had turned her ivory skin to pink. "Want to race, little man?" Without another word, she grabbed the front of her dress and ran toward the entrance of the maze.

"Wait, no fair, wait for me," Kai called after her as he scrambled to his feet and ran to catch her.

There were multiple routes through the maze; the question was, which one did she take? The hedges were much taller than he was, and every turn revealed more green walls and choices. Each dead-end frustrated him because it meant he had to circle back and choose again. Kai's next decision led him to a small clearing with a sundial. He knew he was close because he could hear her laughing.

"I can see you!" His mother called.

He dashed along the hedge that he thought would be correct. Running to the end, Kai turned; he hoped to reveal her hiding spot. She was not there. Instead, it cut short as another dead end.

Disappointed, he looked down and stomped his little feet. Something landed on his head and shoulders. Pink and white flower petals dropped over the hedge by his mother's hand. A smile lit up his face—he knew that meant return to the sundial and turn at the pink and white flower bed.

Laughter filled the maze as they called to each other from different sides of the maze. He was close to finding the path leading to the center. While it had only been a moment or two when he'd last heard her laughing, now she was silent. The entire garden became eerily quiet. The wind ceased, and the air felt heavy on his shoulders. Even the birds fell silent.

Unsure of what else to do, he ran through the maze. The next sounds he heard were a terrifying mixture of screams and fabric tearing. His vision clouded and wind from the dragon's wings thrust his small frame to the ground.

Awake, Kai sat up in his bed, soaked in sweat and clawing at the covers. "No, no...NO!" he screamed.

Kendra burst through the door and wrapped her arms around him. She held him tight and rocked him back and forth. "Hush sweet boy, you're alright. I'm here now. You're not alone. I'm so sorry I wasn't here. I stepped out to check on your brothers."

No matter how many times he dreamed of that day, he still couldn't understand what had happened. He wiped the tears from his face. Then his stepmother Nola entered the room, followed by his father.

Iver Galloway was an intense man with pitch black hair, sharp brown eyes, and a thunderous voice. "Why can't you keep the boy quiet? Where were you? Why were you not with him?" he scolded Kendra.

Kendra hesitated, "Your Majesty, I..."

Iver held out his hand to Kendra and looked at Nola. "Maybe we need to start giving him his medication again?"

"No, not that," Kai begged. "I hate the medication. It makes me sleepy the next day."

Nola stepped between them and placed her hand on Iver's chest. Iver instantly softened at her touch. The queen was a noblewoman with long wavy blonde hair and green eyes. She placed her hands on her sizeable pregnant belly and sat on the edge of Kai's bed. "The boy has nightmares, Iver. Let me take care of this. Go back to bed."

Undaunted, Iver crossed his arms in frustration. "No. I've had enough. It's time he moved out of the nursery. I'm tired of his night terrors."

From the foot of the bed, Smoke growled.

"Hush," Iver thundered. "Why is he on the bed? If you can't train your wolf properly, maybe you shouldn't have him."

"Honey, please," Nola cried out. "Leave the boy alone. Let's talk in the morning."

"No matter. Get it done. Kai should have changed rooms six years ago when the twins were born. It's time we stop coddling the boy. Besides, the new baby will be here any day now, and we need the nursery. I want all of the new baby things moved out of our chambers and in here where they belong." Iver angrily stormed out, slamming the door behind him.

Kai cupped his face; fresh tears welled in his eyes. That was it, the King had spoken—he would be removed from his room, the only connection he had left of his time with his mother. His new sibling was coming.

"Don't worry about your father," Nola said softly. "I will speak to him. But unfortunately, he is right. It is time you move to a new room. I need the adjoining nursery for the new baby. Take your time moving. I know how much this room means to you." From the door, Nola offered a shallow smile.

Kai felt empty. Nola had such a way with father; an ability to calm the King with her touch. His father's moods recently were wildly unpredictable. One moment he was kind, the next angry or dismissive.

Kendra returned to sit beside Kai on the bed. "I am sorry I wasn't here."

"I thought I was doing better. For weeks no nightmares, but tonight something happened." He looked at her with desperation in his eyes. "My dream starts happy and clear, but the end becomes cloudy." He hesitated and looked away. "I'm sorry, I wish I could remember."

"I understand. Maybe I should not have talked so much about Mariana right before bedtime." Kendra shook her head.

"Oh no, please don't stop telling me stories about her," he begged. "I think it is the tree and the maze. It happened there, this time of year."

Kendra tenderly took his hands in hers. "While you may be able to navigate through the day-to-day, grief is not that simple. Certain triggers can bring all the emotions rushing back, reminding you of her absence." She paused for a moment.

She tapped her lips. "I want to teach you how to glean. Gleaning was something your mother often did to find focus. It is a cross between meditating and opening the mind. Done properly, it allows you to see things you otherwise could not. When you're ready, it may help you remember."

Learning anything that would bring him closer to his mother was something Kai wanted more than life itself. "I would like that."

CHAPTER 5

Betrothed

Kai and Smoke walked the palace grounds. Several small stones bore the brunt of his frustration. Drew crossed the courtyard and offered a wave, and Kai waved back heavyhearted. He missed Drew, but he was happy to know his guard was doing well without him as a distraction.

Ready for breakfast, Kai dashed into the hallway. Twins, Seth and Aaron, his younger half-brothers, walked down the hall with Kendra. Hoping they would not see him; Kai hesitated a few moments. A burst of hearty laughter bellowed, startling Kai. The king's chamber door opened, and he found himself face to face with his father.

Iver's smile faded. The shift hurt Kai. He felt insignificant standing in his father's presence. Lost in the moment, they stared at each other until Nola pushed Iver into the hallway. "Go Iver, I'm starving. I am eating for two."

Kai remembered the sparkle in his mother's eyes; Nola's eyes did not offer the same kindness. He felt she stood between them, while his mother had bonded them together. Uncomfortable, Kai walked away, mentally kicking himself for not knowing what to say.

"Good morning, Kai. I trust you are feeling better this

morning?" Nola called after him.

He turned and offered a pert smile. "Yes. Thank you for asking. Good morning, father. Sorry about last night."

"Yes, well, let's not talk about it now. We are eating in the great hall this morning. Everyone who matters came in last night." With a quick smile to Nola, Iver patted her hand in the crux of his arm, and they continued down the hallway.

Morning sunlight spilled through the wall of arched windows in the great hall. Kai stood beside his father as the king formally greeted their guests. The room was filled with familiar faces.

Iver offered a nod. "Good morning, Regent Maxwell. So good of you to make the trip. Lady Grace, you are looking well. Your daughter Amelia is a pleasure to have at the palace. She is a beautiful young lady." Iver glanced at Kai with a hint of pride, then back to Amelia, who clung to her mother's arm.

Kai's insides squirmed. Amelia curtsied to the royal family. The pressure of their betrothal overwhelmed him. While he was mostly ignored, left to lounge around the palace, this future responsibility loomed over him. He liked Amelia, but not in that way. For two years now she'd studied in Diu, and they had become close, but their connection felt more like brother and sister.

They were promised at birth to unite the old Bangloo kingdom of Milnos, far to the northwest of Diu. Amelia was the only child born to the aging regent, Lucas Maxwell. Kai knew their union made it possible to put a male Galloway heir on the Milnos throne and secure the final country on their continent. No more threats from an old enemy.

How he wished he could follow in his father's footsteps and marry for love, but Kai and Amelia's union would ensure that peace continued without future challenge. He would be sent away to a strange land far from his home to rule over strangers.

With no desire to rule, the responsibility felt like a burden. He wished Maxwell would father a son to free him from the obligation. Though the Maxwells had tried, the lack of a male heir had forced Maxwell and Milnos to accept Iver's offer.

The silver-haired Lucas Maxwell's distrustful eyes glared at Kai. The regent wore the Milnos badge, a black raven in flight on a field of blue. He offered a stiff bow to King Iver. "Good morning, Your Majesty. We are pleased to visit Amelia. We miss her dearly throughout the year. With your permission, we'd like to stay the month. I trust that my nephew, Landon Maxwell, gives you no trouble."

Lucas grasped Iver's offered hand. Kai noticed the sturdy grip and intense glances shared between his father and his future father-in-law. He knew they merely tolerated each other for the sake of peace.

"Certainly, Regent Maxwell, we would be happy to have you both," Iver said. "Landon continues to excel in his studies. Lady Grace, good morning."

Grace's half-hearted curtsy was barely noticeable. "Good morning, your Majesty. Queen Nola." Like Amelia, Lady Grace had golden blonde hair and large silver-blue eyes; which frowned when they reached Kai.

The conversation between the two men felt uncomfortable. Kai rolled his eyes towards his brothers. Amelia took his meaning and grabbed his hand—they joined Aaron and Seth to watch from afar. Kai caught an approving smile cross his father's lips. "Amelia, does your father really intend to stay in Diu an entire month?" Kai asked.

"He has business in Port Anahita along the coast. A shipment he is expecting. He is not here to see me," she insisted. "Our betrothal disgusts him. A Milnos highborn lady to marry a Diu-Katori underling. He says the only reason Milnos never crushed Diu was that Brandon Cazier, a Nebean prince, married Eden Galloway, a Diu princess, and the Nebeans defend you."

"Nebea is formidable," Kai chuckled. "And here I thought it was because the Katori brought dragons to protect Diu during the war."

She nodded. "My father hates dragons almost as much as

he hates Diu. Not to mention, he wanted to be king himself. Sorry, you know how I feel about him. My father has no use for a daughter. He is not an affectionate man. And he still hopes for a son, illegitimate or otherwise."

"I am sorry, Amelia. I am thankful we have the years to get to know one another, but I hope you understand, I am not sure I feel the desire to marry." He winced at speaking the truth.

She smiled. "No offense taken. You know I feel the same. We share a few interests, but I hope there is a way out of this union. They cannot force us to marry. Can they?"

Her smile faded. "I want to be with, well, someone I love." She twisted her fingers in her lap.

"They can," Kai said flatly. "Who are we not to do what is best for our people? I know you're several months older than me, but maybe when we are eighteen, we will feel differently about marriage." He had no idea what it would feel like to love another in such a way you were drawn to them permanently.

A tap from Seth interrupted Kai's thoughts. "When you go to Milnos, who will follow in father's place as king?" his half-brother asked.

"Well, Aaron, I suppose. He was born first. He would be the next Galloway King," Kai answered.

Aaron beamed. Seth slumped.

"I thought so." Seth's tone wilted.

Near the grand fireplace, Kai saw his father greet the new Master General. "Good morning, cousin Adrian. I trust you slept well and are finding everything to your expectations in the tower. It is most unfortunate the circumstances of your promotion, but I welcome you as my Master General. I will sorely miss your father."

Adrian Cazier wore the black and silver version of the Galloway family crest, a silver wolf with three spears in its jaws, worn by all the king's royal guard. With a bow, he accepted the king's offered hand. "Your Majesty. Everything is as it should be. Thank you for bestowing me this honor. I believe I will be of great use to you here in Diu."

Seth sharply elbowed Kai in the ribs and pointed across the room. "Cousin Adrian came in late last night. I miss his father, Aerin, he was nice." Seth's voice softened with sadness. "What does a Master General do exactly?"

"It is not nice to point, Seth," Kai whispered. "The Master General holds a seat on the king's council, he is second in command behind father, responsible for the Diu army, the king's champions—Kempery-men. He also sends spies on secret missions to other countries. Not that we should know about that part."

Aaron poked Kai from around Seth. The jab made Kai jump. "How do you get to be Master General?" Aaron asked.

Kai gently pushed Aaron's hand away. "The position is appointed by the king. Since Nebea is our ally and our cousins have sat on the throne for generations, it was natural to offer the position to the most qualified relative. Master General Aerin Cazier was Adrian's father and our second cousin. After he passed away, cousin Adrian requested the rank of Master General. He could have been the King of Nebea, behind his brother Andrew, but he is leaving that honor to his son Aden." Kai pressed a finger to his lips. "Shh."

Iver continued to greet guests. One important man was Admiral Roark Raebun. Who wore his midnight blue regimental surcoat, specially designed for his unit; the royal blue and silver Galloway crest was over his heart. A silver spear through a crescent moon, the symbol for Fort Pohaku on his left. Befitting his rank, Roark had the silver wolf above four silver stripes and four silver stars on his broad shoulders.

Roark stroked his well-groomed ginger beard and bowed. "Sire, my son Tolan has one year of academics left with Professor Greydon before he joins me at Fort Pohaku. Upon my arrival, I purchased a horse for him, with your permission, I would like to leave three men in your barracks. They will be his entourage between here and Fort Pohaku. He needs to learn the route and build on his skills as a tracker."

"Make whatever arrangements you need. I am happy to accommodate." Iver agreed.

Kai stretched to look around the room. Tolan was not present. And of course, if Tolan Raebun was missing, so was Landon Maxwell, Tolan's best friend. *They were probably at the stables spending time with Tolan's new horse.* Suddenly Kai felt jealous, he did not have a horse he could call his own.

Kai watched his father's expression lift as he approached his twin sister Helena. Iver wrapped her in a big embrace, sweeping her up off her feet. "Good morning, little sister! So good to have you at the palace."

Helena was a little shorter than Iver but had all the majestic presence of a queen. Her long black hair flowed like silk down her back and tiny braids on either side of her temples looped up and fastened with a silver seashell accented with blue jewels.

"Good to see you, dear brother. Do you mean to spin me like when we were children?" She laughed. "Put me down."

He let her down. Helena took her husband's hand. "Kaeco and I are very happy to be here for the Master General's ceremony. It gives us a chance to visit our son Gideon. We are looking forward to having him home full-time." She pressed a smile and curtsied.

Duke Kaeco bowed slightly, "Good morning, Your Majesty. Good morning, Queen Nola. Thank you for having us." Kaeco clasped a hand on his son Gideon's shoulder.

Both Kaeco and his son Gideon had long curly brown hair and olive complexion. Ever the businessman, Kaeco wore tailored clothes typical of the merchants in Port Anahita. "Sire, Gideon has two more years of formal education until he is sixteen—however, I would like him to start making trips home as well. I have yet to arrange for a horse, but if I may speak with the Grand Duke Carmelo and your stablemaster."

"Certainly, Kaeco. The Grand Duke can help find a proper horse for your son." Iver motioned his arm toward the other side of the room. "Dante, see here. How many unassigned horses do you currently have in the stables?"

Grand Duke Dante Carmelo was not an exceptionally tall man, but what he lacked in stature he made up for in brawn. He gave a small bow toward the king. His red hair was buzzed short, and his face shaved clean. "Your Majesty. Queen Nola. Sire, I only have nineteen now, with Roark's purchase for his son. I prefer to keep at least twenty spare horses on hand. I will speak with Haygan, my stablemaster. He can acquire two more this season."

"Dante, make that three. Stop by my study, and we will discuss this further."

"Yes, Sire. Thank you, Sire." The grand duke stepped back with a bow.

Envy was not a positive trait. Still, Kai was envious. His cousin, Gideon, and Tolan were about to embark on an adventure. They would both be moving on with their lives. For them, the world was full of choices, their futures undecided. Unlike them, he would follow a plan mapped out by others.

CHAPTER 6

Green Eyes

Four rooms set empty on the family wing, alternatively used as guest rooms during special occasions. The first was next to his father's study across the hall from his parents, a room with one window. Kai peered inside; this room would not improve his situation. The next room was on the other side of the nursery. He looked out the bedroom's window; it overlooked the great banyark tree and garden maze. Not a good choice.

The third room was small, with one window, nothing special. In the hallway, Kendra caught up with him. "Not impressed?" She motioned to the far end of the hall. "One room left."

Kai entered the last room on the right. He peered into the dim, shadowy space. It smelled old and dusty. Kendra stepped toward the windows and threw back the curtains. "What we need is light, so we can see what we have to work with."

Light poured into the room; a large four-poster bed set prominently between two large windows. The walls were ebony wood paneling halfway up with white-and-blue wallpaper the rest of the way. Kai opened a door beside a tall armoire—a large private bathroom.

Beside the grand fireplace were huge paintings. On the

other wall a great view of Thade Mountain, Eagles Peak jutted out of one side in the distance. Confused, he turned to Kendra. "I have never been in this room before." Around the corner, he found a large desk surround by dusty bookshelves.

Smoke sniffed with interest the chests and crates littered around the room.

"This room is incredible! But...but are you sure I can have it? This room should be for someone... I don't know ... someone important. Father will never agree to it."

Kendra pulled sheets off the furniture and folded them into a neat pile. "I already spoke with Iver about it. I assured him it was a good fit for a young royal who needs to find his independence. Not to mention, I reminded him just how far this room was from his."

Half listening, Kai looked out two large glass doors. He glanced down at the two handles. "Wait, is this a balcony?" He grabbed both handles, pushed the doors open, and stepped outside. "Have you seen this view?" he asked, mostly to himself.

He stepped back in the room and asked again. "How could you possibly know I would pick this room?"

Kendra grinned. "I believe you've answered your question. Now, go to class and let me get this room in order." She took him by the shoulders and directed him toward the door.

Late for class, he dashed out of his room. The family wing stretched out before him. He never realized how long it was before. He was now on the west corner, the opposite end of the palace from the others. There was no need to traverse to the east stairwell. Kai made an about-face; the arch of the west stairwell waited proudly in front of him.

On his way downstairs, a weight lifted inside of him. He leaped to the second-floor landing, Smoke right behind him. Darting around the corner, Kai nearly ran straight into a cabinet. He dodged and spun, his steps less than graceful. Mid-stumble, he stopped.

A woman dressed in all black stepped out from the

shadows, arms crossed. "Slow down, Prince Kai. Observe your surroundings. You might miss something important." Her dark green eyes glared at him.

"Riome Timika!" he froze in place, his mouth gaping.

Her dark auburn hair had been pulled into a tight bun, giving her features a fierce intensity. He knew who she was—Diu spy. They had never spoken more than a few words. Kai took note of her choice of clothing. *Is black the uniform of a spy, or is it the only color she owns?*

"Are you lost, Your Highness?" Riome interrupted his contemplation.

Snapped back to reality, it dawned on him. The west corner; his room was now beside the Master General's tower. Adrenaline coursed through his veins. The Master General and his spies always fascinated Kai. If he could choose his future, he would be a spy rather than a king.

No time to think about the tower, Riome or his new room. "Sorry, Miss Timika, thank you. Good day," he nodded politely and darted off.

Before Kai could enter the library, someone grabbed his arm. Sigry, the palace physician, glared down at him with his dark beady eyes and stern face. The man's grip tightened around his arm. "Not so fast, Prince Kai. Thought you'd skip out on seeing me this morning, did you? I spoke with King Iver. He informed me you need a sleeping tonic." Sigry's expression was sour.

"No, sir. Sorry, sir." Kai tried to hide his disdain for the old man with a smile.

Smoke hesitated by the library door, confused.

"Smoke, come." Kai patted his leg as he followed the physician in silence. He stared at the back of Sigry's nearly bald head, rimmed with snowy white hair. An uneasiness ebbed in his stomach.

When they reached the door to the clinic, Sigry stopped and pointed at Smoke. "IT stays out here!" he commanded.

Did the man ever smile? Kai twisted his brow. "Yes, sir.

Smoke, stay." Smoke obeyed and lay down outside the door.

The physician's room smelled of minerals, dried plants, and bubbling potions. Kai covered his mouth and coughed at the smell of the herb-covered walls. The back table was covered in crystals, ores, and powders. He'd never see so many varieties.

In the corner, there was a tall shelf lined with a variety of oil-filled vials, each bottle neatly labeled and facing outward. The arched fireplace on the opposite wall held curved metal arms with a dangling pot, frothing and oozing white steam.

"Have a seat on the table and take off your shirt." Sigry directed him to a narrow table in the center of the room.

Eye level with Sigry, Kai waited. The physician pressed a strange instrument against Kai's chest. It had a small funnel on one end and a metal piece which Sigry placed by his ear on the other. "Now breathe in deep and let it out slowly." Sigry continued moving the device around Kai's chest. "Again. Again." Then he moved to Kai's back. "And again. One more time. Good, sounds good."

"Now open your mouth wide and look up. Let's see how your throat looks this morning. No, redness." Sigry tugged on Kai's chin, turning his face left and right. "Your eyes look clear, not bloodshot."

Finished, Sigry opened his cabinet and selected various jars to hold up to the light. "Why have you stopped taking the tonic I gave you for sleeping? It will help with the night terrors."

Voice shaky, Kai tried to reply. "I, um…"

"Speak up, boy, I don't have all day," Sigry huffed.

"I used it all, and I don't like how I feel the next day. It is difficult to focus in class, and by the time it wears off, it's time to take more." Kai scrunched up his face and stuck out his tongue. "Plus it tastes awful."

"How much are you taking? Did you not listen to my instructions? Just three drops on the tongue are enough for a boy your size." Sigry replaced the bottles and closed the cabinet.

Embarrassed Kai wrapped his arms around his chest. "I... umm. Sorry sir, I..."

"Children, they never listen. I will make a diluted batch, and you can take a spoonful each night. Hopefully, you can manage to follow my instructions better this time."

He watched Sigry select dried herbs and grind them in a large stone bowl. He poured the dust into a black pot of boiling water, along with various drops from other vials.

While it cooked Sigry pulled a small gold box from his pocket and placed it on the table. The gold box had ornate vines and leaf embellishments covering the exterior. From the box, Sigry removed a long silver necklace and held it in front of Kai. "Here, I want you to hold this and tell me what you feel."

Kai accepted the chain and looked at the charm in his hand; it was an intricately designed silver crescent moon. Nested within the crescent shape dangled a round blue sapphire crystal. Unsure what he should feel, Kai looked at the charm, turned it over, then squeezed it tight in his hand. It was delicate yet durable; to his surprise, the stone warmed to his touch.

He took a second look. Located within the pendant, he noticed a hint of white at the heart of the blue crystal. Kai again grasped the necklace tight, and in his mind, he saw his mother's face. In turn, he saw the red dragon that killed her. Fear grabbed his heart. Why would this crystal make him think of his mother? Was this hers? Had he seen her wearing it that day? He couldn't remember.

Sigry was not the sentimental type. Kai didn't remember much, but he did remember his mother and Sigry were not overly fond of each other. The idea of discussing his feelings about his mother with this man made him uneasy. Kai handed the necklace back to the old physician. "It's a blue crystal, looks like something a girl would wear. I don't feel anything. Can I go now?" Kai squirmed.

A loud knock struck the wooden door. Kai turned to see his

father slipping into the room. "How's it going, any news?" Iver asked.

Sigry approached Iver and handed him the small box containing the necklace. "Your Majesty, nothing to report. I am sorry, you should take this back. I am not sure what we should have expected. I had him hold the crystal, and there seemed to be no reaction. I am brewing something for his night terrors; when ready, I will see it sent to his room. He will need to take it nightly to ensure an uneventful night's sleep," he assured Iver.

Iver took the box from Sigry, opened it, and placed his fingers inside. He took a deep breath and looked toward Kai. "Thank you, Sigry, keep me apprised of any developments."

"As you command, my King. Rest assured, I will continue to evaluate him as he matures, in case that makes a difference."

Iver nodded and left. Kai hopped down from the table, grabbed his shirt, and darted toward the door. He hoped to catch up with his father. "Thank you, Sigry. I will return to class. Thank you," he said, exiting the clinic.

By the time Kai reached the hallway, his father was gone. He wondered what Sigry intended by his comment—*I will continue to evaluate him as he matures.* What was the crystal pendant supposed to make him feel? The expression on his father's face told Kai it was special.

Disappointed, he tucked his hands in his pockets and shuffled toward the library.

Hesitant, he leaned into the tall library door. Faintly he overheard Professor Greydon speak to the class. "Good afternoon, class. Today we have the pleasure of meeting our new Master General, Lord Adrian Cazier, third son of the late Aerin Cazier."

After a loud round of cheers and applause, he heard his cousin Adrian's voice, "Good afternoon, class." Kai continued to listen. "Thank you, class, for the warm welcome. I would first like to introduce my son Aden and my daughter Alana who will be joining you in your studies. Children, please take a seat."

Kai was hot and fanned his face. His entire body was getting hotter. Head spinning, he pressed his hands to his temples. Kendra appeared on the stairwell, linens draped over her arms. Their eyes locked together, and she gasped. "Kai, your eyes are turning green." She squinted at him, and her eyes bulged wide. "You are so bright. We need to calm you down." She reached for his hand.

Behind him the large wooden door heaved, Kai stepped away. The library door creaked open, and Professor Greydon stepped into the hallway. The eccentric professor smiled and stroked the corner of his curled mustache. His long black robe with the Galloway crest embroidered into the lapel gave him a stately appearance.

"Your Highness, Prince Kai, I hope you are feeling better. Please join the class. Master General Adrian Cazier intends to escort the class on a tour of his tower's common areas and the Kempery-man training ground. I will be back shortly."

Kai kept his eyes down. "Yes, sir. Thank you, professor."

Kendra stepped forward. "Your Highness, Sigry has your first dose of medication ready. If you would, please, come with me." She eased Kai's shoulder toward the stairs. "Forgive me, Professor Greydon. I will see him back to class."

"Thank you, governess Kendra."

Sunshine and fresh air bathed Kai's head and shoulders. They stood enjoying the view from his new balcony. "What brought on this burst of energy?" She pressed the back of her hand against his forehead. "Your skin is hot."

"A necklace. Sigry gave me a silver necklace to hold. It warmed to my touch."

Frantic, Kendra spun him around. "What did it look like? The crystal. Was it blue?" she demanded.

"Yes, the stone was blue with a hint of white near the center," he stammered.

"Anything else? About the shape." Her eyes turned wild.

"A blue stone with a silver crescent moon. What does it

mean? Was it my mother's? I saw her face when I held the stone."

Kendra covered her mouth and stepped back. "It's here," she whispered through her hand.

"What's here? Please tell me," he begged.

"Your mother's necklace." She shook her head. "All this time, Iver's had it. I need to get word to Lucca. We need to find out what this means."

Kendra's gaze scanned all around until her eyes came to rest on one spot. Her eyes focused, and she nodded. She had found what she was searching for. Kai wished he could glean like her.

"Kai, if I could take you from Diu to Katori, I would, but Iver would never allow it. Your departure would create conflict between our two countries. And as a Half-Light, you would not be allowed to live in Katori."

"So, I have no place in either world." He could see the conflict in her eyes. "Why do you hesitate to teach me?"

"Fear. I am afraid our secrets will be revealed. Haygan and I were not technically given permission to come here. Your eyes concern me. Changing your eye color is not a natural gift. Without guidance, I am not sure what to do. There shouldn't be anything to teach. Half-Lights don't have powers." Her tone sounded frustrated, and she leaned against the doorway.

"One could expect speed and strength. Bonding, no. Maybe it is because Iver is part Katori too." She covered her lips with her fingers, lost in thought.

"What? My father is part Katori. How do you know?" Kai searched her eyes for answers.

"Your ancestor, Gianfranca, was Katori." Kendra pointed to the painting in Kai's room. "Iver's great-grandmother. None of this makes sense. Haygan will need to travel home to get answers. I will speak with him first chance I get. For now, Kai, you must learn to control your emotions." Kendra stepped behind him, her hands on his shoulders.

"I'm ready." He gazed over the palace grounds.

"Focus your mind on one image. Pick an inanimate object,

a rock, a cottage or a stone in the palace wall. Let go of your emotional thoughts."

Silent, Kai focused on a cannon atop a turret. Sunlight bounced off the metal exterior. His mind relaxed, and the tension in his body eased. The heat subsided. Kendra spun him around. "Better?"

"Yes, much better." Kai stepped around her. "I've missed too much of the day, and I must return to class. I want to talk more about the necklace," he insisted.

"I should get more information from Katori before I share too much. Please keep your emotions in check. If I didn't know any better, I'd say you are blooming into a full Katori."

Cutting across the courtyard, Kai saw Drew exiting the stables. They shared a brief nod, and Kai ran to rejoin his classmates at the training yard fence. A group of soldiers stood, feet shoulder length apart, hands behind their backs inside the fence. Kempery-man Farwick stepped forward.

The breeze blew through Farwick's long, straw-colored hair, revealing silver streaks near his temples. A long white scar cut through his beard on his left cheek, proof he'd seen battle. "Master General Cazier, the King's Kempery-men are ready to demonstrate some swordplay for the class upon your command."

"Thank you, Captain Farwick," Cazier responded. "You may begin."

Farwick motioned for them to begin. The men separated into pairs across the yard. Farwick turned to the students. "Class, today we are going to demonstrate for you how to attack your opponent, defend an attack, and even disarm your adversary."

The class watched as the opponents circled each other, shields raised and swords at the ready. Kai noticed how they sized up their opponent before attacking. Initially, they threw a few half-hearted thrusts and cuts that were quickly blocked by the defender.

The men circled each other again, landing several hard

thrusts and cuts from the shoulder toward the defender. The clang of the two metal swords striking was exhilarating. Kai watched the overall group and then the individual pairs, and realized they were each making an identical set of moves in a choreographed drill. Impressed, he stepped forward to get a better view.

The defensive person seemed to be cautiously retreating from their attacker, before suddenly stepping in, lunging, and throwing a few thrusts of their own. Skillfully the attacker blocked, held his ground as their two swords glided against each other. The defender closed the gap between them and slammed his opponent hard with his shield. The pair pushed away from each other and reset.

Again, the attacker took several steps toward the defender, circling, closing the space between them. The attacker, swiftly pushed his sword hand forward, leaning with his body, completed the motion by stepping into his opponent and landing a chest blow.

The entire class gasped. In response, the Kempery-men stepped back to reveal the blunt training blades and the mesh training armor. Relieved the children relaxed.

"I bet we could do that Landon, what do you think?" Tolan asked, jabbing his friend in the ribs.

Landon jabbed Tolan back. "Actually, I have already started solo training with a wooden training blade. You should come down and join me."

"Wait, you got a wooden waster training sword without me. When? Why didn't you tell me?" Tolan responded.

"Didn't know I needed your permission," Landon sniped. "I am on my own, and I do what I want. I need to be ready to fight for myself. Do whatever you want, I don't care."

Distracted by their argument, Kai watched Tolan stare at Landon, his mouth agape in shock.

Landon relented. "When your father arrived, I had to do something with my time. Garrick mentioned I should acquire a waster to begin weapon drills. Our hand to hand combat will only take us so far. Besides, all I did was beat on a training yard post."

Tolan kicked at the fence post. "I will join you tomorrow after class."

"Great. Sounds great, I will talk to Farwick about a second sword!"

As the class burst into applause, Kai realized he'd missed the disarming demonstration. "Thank you, Farwick and the King's Kempery-men," Cazier said, then he asked: "Class, one last question, who knows why we call them the King's Kempery-men?"

Several children raise their hands. Landon jabbed Kai in the ribs, getting him to drop his hand and grab his side. "Nobody cares to hear from you, little prince."

Tolan laughed and shoved Kai's shoulder. "Landon's right, we hear enough of you in class."

Kai never understood Tolan and Landon; they never made an issue with any of the other children. Why did they dislike him? Seth came to his brother's rescue and kicked Tolan in the shin. "Leave my brother alone, Tolan," Seth shouted.

Aaron kicked Landon. "You're both big babies." Aaron looked to Seth and Kai for approval.

Anger boiled in Landon's eyes at the Galloway twins. Before things could escalate, Amelia stepped between them, pushing them apart. "Tolan, please."

The sun highlighted her golden hair, and the breeze played with the soft waves. Tolan was caught in her gaze. "My apologies, Miss Amelia."

Gideon glanced at the commotion over his shoulder and hushed the boys with his hand still raised.

"Young Gideon tell us what you know," the Master General instructed.

Gideon dropped his hand. "Sir, to be a Kempery-man means you are a champion, a superior warrior for the king, one who fights with honor for others. You must be an honorable man, deserving of respect, and high regard. Your military record must be perfect."

"Well said, Gideon," Cazier stated, pushing into the middle of the group. He eyed Tolan and Kai as he stepped between them. "Let's go, everyone. We have a little time left. I would like to show you the common areas in the tower."

Outside the massive tower, Cazier held the door. "Young, Seth, can you hold the door for the group?"

Seth ran forward and took the Master General's place. "Yes, sir, happy to, Master General." Pleased with the honor, Seth stood tall, his back pressed against the door, holding it wide.

The entire group entered the tower banquet hall. Cazier directed them to find a position around the large wooden table. Kai marveled at the hand-carved Galloway crest in the center of the table.

Surrounding the table were tall, redwood chairs. Kai ran his hand over the chair back; it depicted the tree of life and carved within its roots was the surname of a Kempery-man. His chair read Henley. He knew the man: Kempery-man Marcus Henley. An honorable man.

Cazier motioned for the children to move around the room. "Children, you will notice all the family crests hung on the walls around the room. They represent each Kempery-man, the kings' champions, who have ever pledged fealty and service to Diu. It is a great honor to join this group of elite men."

Grand Duke Dante Carmelo burst into the room and approached Cazier. Cazier held up his hand to the students and then stepped away to converse privately. After Dante left, Cazier returned to address the group. "Sorry, class, matters of the kingdom. I will have to cut our tour short. You are excused. Captain Farwick, please escort the class outside." Cazier turned and left.

CHAPTER 7

Gianfranca's Secret

The first week in his new room was unexpectedly easy. He thought he would feel sad by the room change; however, he felt happy. The weight of his youth was gone. The memory of his absent mother no longer lingered like a ghost in the corner.

His first change was teaching Smoke to sleep on the floor. It took a few nights and a firmer voice to get Smoke to stay down, but Smoke obeyed. Kai felt proud. New room, new rules.

The door to his room slowly opened and Kendra entered. "Are you asleep yet? Sorry, it took me so long. Let me tend to the fire, and maybe we can talk about Katori before you go to sleep. Would you like that?"

"Yes, please," he responded, twisting around to adjust his pillow.

A rapid, loud knock interrupted his thoughts, and the door swung open, maid Mary entered. Kai observed her small frame. "Kendra, come quick, Nola needs you. She is in some pain. I have already sent for Sigry, and he should be on his way up now." Maid Mary pleaded.

Kendra tossed a log on the fire and dashed out the door.

Alone, Kai stared at the ceiling. He thought about what it

would be like to have a new baby around. Everyone fussing over him or her, as if they'd never seen a baby before. Secretly he hoped it would be a girl. He enjoyed being a big brother to Seth and Aaron, but every palace needed a princess.

No longer tired Kai hopped out of bed to have a look around his room. At the end of his bed, he wrapped his hand around the bedpost. His fingers slid down the spiral wood design. He stepped around the foot of his bed and a small bench with a blue and white seat cushion.

On his desk, he found sheets of blank paper, a brown leather journal, a few black drawing pencils, and a new book. The simple red leather cover read *The Invisible Thief. That could be interesting. I wonder where it came from.*

Startled by the sound of wood shifting in the fireplace, he turned to see sparks float up into the chimney. Mesmerized, Kai watched the flames dance and lick at the wood. Taking a more extensive view of the wall, he noticed the picture frame was not exactly flush against the wall on one side. The painting was a portrait of a woman with pitch black hair and dark brown eyes, his great-great-grandmother Gianfranca. He studied her features, fascinated to learn she was Katori.

First, he tried pressing the frame against the wall, attempting to straighten the picture. For some reason, it would not stay in place. It was then that he discovered the entire left side of the painting was not actually attached to the wall. Perplexed, he pulled on the frame and discovered a dark passageway hidden behind. The light from the fireplace was not enough to illuminate the corridor. He needed to light a lamp.

Excited about his discovery, he redressed and lit an oil lamp. Gianfranca's portrait hid a secret. *Spy tunnels. They must be used by the Master General's spies,* he fantasied. *I wonder where they lead?*

Smoke hopped up to follow, but Kai instructed him to stay with his mind. He smiled when his wolf sat without complaint. Their connection flowed naturally when he didn't force his thoughts or will on his companion.

Kai stepped over the threshold, leading into the narrow corridor and pulled the panel closed. When it did not remain shut, he inspected the wall and discovered a small latch to secure the picture in place. With the lamp held high, it illuminated the small space. Unlike the carpet in his room, he noticed the stone floor was cold on his bare feet.

Several steps into the passageway, there was a small opening to the right and stairs leading down. He debated but chose to go right. Within two steps, the space switched back to the right as if he was going back in the same direction as he'd started. Another twelve feet, it turned to the left.

Still making his way through the narrow passage, it finally cut again to the left, before it sharply cut to the right and opened behind what appeared to be a sizeable wooden panel. With his hands, he felt around where the built-in frame attached to the stone wall. He discovered a similar small latch to the one in his bedroom and released the pin.

Everything was the same: the stone threshold, the panel holding a painting, and a small latch. Kai stepped out to look at the artwork and noticed he was standing on a small landing between two flights of stairs. In front of him was a small door. Nervous and confused about his location, he stepped back inside the nook behind the portrait.

With the panel closed he took a deep breath. He had no idea where he was, but he loved a good mystery. And this mystery had to be solved. Not wanting to take the lamp with him, he placed it deep inside the secret corridor on the floor, dimming the light.

Kai stepped out onto the landing to look at the painting. It was of a large galleon ship on the high seas, riding the rolling waves. Quietly he pushed the picture back against the wall and secured the frame. He looked up and down the stairs. After a little deliberation, he went up. These stairs were smooth-cut stone, unlike the rough stone in the passage.

It didn't take him long to realize the stairwell had a bit of a curve to it. With the dimly lit wall sconces, it was difficult to see much detail in the stones. How had he never been in this part of the palace? As the wall curved around, he reached another small light next to a tall, thin window. He pressed his face into the glass to see what the view might reveal. That is when it hit him—he was in the Master General's tower.

Curiosity stirred his feet, and he sprinted two steps upward at a time. He had never been up to the top at night—at least not that he could remember. At the next landing, voices echoed down the stairwell. Kai froze. The sounds got louder. The men were getting closer. Would he be in trouble if caught here at night? He needed to retreat down.

He tried to be quiet, moving as fast as possible, again he took the steps two at a time. He was desperate to get back to the hidden passage before being discovered. At the next landing, voices billowed from below. Men were coming up the stairs. He still had another flight to go before his level.

How close are they? Can I make it? He stepped down and paused to listen. No, they were too close. He had to find a place to hide. One side offered two small chairs against the wall—on the other, a little dark alcove.

He stepped back into the arched doorway and held his breath as the two sets of voices closed in on him. His heart pounded in his chest. He closed his eyes and leaned back against the door, desperate to hide deeper in the shadows.

The door gave way, and he fell straight to the floor. Light from the room spilled over him, and a familiar voice behind him spoke. "You'd better shut the door before whoever you're hiding from reaches the landing."

As instructed, Kai stood, pushed the door shut, and leaned his forehead against the door. Of all the rooms he had to fall into, why did it have to be the Master Generals' office? *Now what?* He stood there facing the door as voices outside converged on the landing. They stopped, talked a moment, then faded away as they parted.

"Couldn't sleep I take it," Cazier asked casually.

Kai turned to see his cousin Adrian Cazier sitting at a large desk, going through stacks of papers. "No, sir. Sorry, Master General, I..." Again, frozen and unsure what to say, he stood there, staring at his cousin. The man was the second most powerful person in the realm.

Adrian placed his pen on the desk and shifted his chair to face Kai. "Sounds like you timed that well. It is the changing of the guard. I guess that is how you got trapped on my landing. Were you headed to the top?" Adrian scratched at his short beard.

Kai was afraid to answer. How could he possibly explain?

"It is a great view at any time—day or night. I'd say I like it at night the best. You know, if you are lucky you can see the hint of dragons flying and spraying fire above Baden Lake. It is amazing. Come in, boy, don't just stand by the door, sit down." He motioned to the two chairs on the other side of his desk.

Kai wanted to relax, but he wasn't sure he should, not yet. He stepped up to the chair and grasped the back rail. Adrian eased back into his chair, crossing his arms in front of his chest. "You mind telling me how you managed to get to the fourth floor of my tower without getting stopped?"

Stunned, Kai's held his breath. *Should I tell the truth?* In his hesitation, his cousin answered for him with a chuckle. "So, you found the secret spy tunnels?"

Kai looked to the floor. He wasn't ready to lose his new secret. "That's alright, Kai. Keep your secrets, keep them close to your chest. Remember, information is power. Just try to keep your expression calm. Don't let your emotions reveal something you're not ready for the other person to know. Although, in all fairness, your new room used to be mine. I used those tunnels to visit my father when I was young. Use them wisely, they are secret for a reason. Not even your father knows of their existence."

"Thank you, sir. I will remember that in the future," Kai responded.

"Sit, Kai," Adrian insisted again. "I noticed the tension today. I believe you could use some advice about Tolan and

Landon." His tone was serious.

"I would appreciate it. There isn't anyone I can ask. Father is, well, a king…and how do I ask him?"

"Tolan will be loyal to the crown like his father. Most of this foolish behavior will pass once he learns responsibility. And it couldn't hurt for him to be humbled by someone larger than himself. Right now, he's the biggest, and he's stretching his muscle." Adrian shrugged. "Landon, on the other hand, he's a loner. He seems to lash out at everyone and confide in none. Watch out for him. It is difficult to know where his loyalty lands since he is from Milnos."

Adrian's posture was apprehensive as he spoke of Landon. Kai had known Landon since they were children. His cousin was right—Landon was often mean and aggressive. Kai scratched the side of his face. "All I know is Landon moved from Milnos to the palace when he turned five. Landon is cousins with Amelia. Father felt we should take him in and provide a new life away from Milnos. I agree, he seems angrier recently. Tolan is the only one who can tolerate him."

Adrian cleared his throat. "Well, I do not believe it will get easier. You will have to stand up to them both at some point. I am not an advocate of fighting for fighting's sake. My advice to you, never start a fight, walk away if you can, and don't hold back if you have to defend yourself."

The Master General stood and gestured toward the door. "It's late, and I have work to do before I sleep. Let's take a quick walk to the top of the tower to see what we can, then off to bed with you, back the way you came."

Out on the landing, he motioned for Kai to follow. Kai stepped in line with his cousin. "Are you going to tell my father about my visit to the tower?"

"Tell him what, that you couldn't sleep, and you took a walk? No, I see no need to bother a king with something so trivial. Although, next time you decide to visit me, I prefer you knock before entering." Cazier said, reaching the next landing.

"Next time?" Kai asked. "You mean, I can come back?"

"Certainly. I may not always be free or able to talk long, but please feel free to come back. I believe we can help each other," Cazier added.

When they reached the top Cazier nodded to the door guard, who stepped aside, allowing them access to a small ladder that took them up to the top of the tower. Astounded, Kai climbed out and looked in all directions. It was very dark, but he could see a lot from this vantage point. The full moon beamed overhead.

Cazier pointed east. "The Katori Mountains and Baden Lake are that way."

Kai wished he could see even the faintest hint of their white peaks glowing in the moonlight. He had heard stories about them, yet their grandeur eluded him. Focused on the sky above Baden Lake, Kai waited. He had caught a glimpse once before, over the trees from the palace wall. From the tower, at this late hour, his chances were excellent.

"What a great view. You know, when I am old enough, I plan to hunt dragons."

Kai felt obsessed when it came to dragons. His only disappointment was he was never able to find a library book with details. Books always fantasied them as wise, benevolent creatures or mythical demons guarding treasure—all works of fiction.

"Well, is that so?" Adrian leaned toward Kai as they both continued watching the horizon. "Cousin, I am truly sorry about your mother. Only don't let your past dictate your future. You could be so much more, and I can help you."

"Kind of you to say, but my obsession is all I have." He looked from the summit of Eagle's Peak to Baden Lake.

"You have choices." Adrian touched Kai's shoulder. "You cannot blame the entire species for one bad dragon. They helped us in the past, and we may need them again someday. Would you have me put down every Nebean black wolf just because one attacked a citizen?"

"Never," Kai insisted.

Silence fell between them. He thought about his cousin's comparison. It was true he could not blame them all. But, could he forgive them? Adrian interrupted his thoughts. "Well, it seems no sightings tonight."

"Just five more minutes," Kai begged. His eyes strained and pleaded with the sky. Still, the minutes passed with nothing. Kai huffed in disappointment. "I guess tonight is not my night."

A hint of light flared in the distance, followed by a longer spray of fire streaking across the blackness. They were getting closer. Then another streaked the sky above the lake. Kai could see the reflection of the light. His eyes lit up, and he looked at his cousin. "That is amazing. I wish I knew their purpose," he whispered.

"They have no purpose. They live life in their way. Wild. Free. We need but to give them space. The Katori Mountains and the Mystic Islands are theirs, and that seems to be enough."

The Master General turned to the guard. "Keep a watchful eye. In the future, please admit Prince Kai to the watchtower any time he wishes."

One guard responded. "Understood, Master General. Your Highness." He bowed.

Silently, Kai walked with his cousin back to his office door. The thought of dragons only wanting to be free wrestled against everything he had decided about the beasts. The idea that he'd judged them unfairly poked at his heart.

"Well, cousin, this is where I leave you. Make your way back to your room. I am sure you know the way." He winked.

Unsure what to call him, Kai fidgeted. "Goodnight, umm Adrian... cousin... Master General Cazier," he stumbled through his response.

Adrian placed a hand on his door, his eyes softened. "Master General in front of your father. In front of others, Cazier will do fine. Cousin or Adrian if we're alone."

"Thanks, Adrian. I had a great time. Good night." Kai waved, darting down the stairs.

Tired, Kai made his way to the landing with the secret access. Positive nobody was coming, he released the pin and slipped behind the painting into the dark space. He secured the latch and retrieved his hidden lamp. He scurried back through the corridors to the entrance into his room. Still latched. Inside, he reset the panel securing the painting.

Smoke eagerly sniffed Kai's legs, and he knelt to pet his wolf. Smoke licked his face. "Thanks, boy, sorry I couldn't take you with me. I had no idea where that would go."

CHAPTER 8

Landon's Anger

Family meals were becoming a burden. All too often, Kai felt uncomfortable being on point to meet and greet visiting lords and ladies. Not that he did it on purpose, but once again he arrived late, and the doors were shut. Everyone was already in the great hall.

When Kai slipped inside the great dining hall, he was careful not to let the door thud behind him. He scanned the table for an empty chair, finding one between Tolan and Gideon. Eyes down, Kai took a seat. "Gideon, Tolan, good evening," he said shyly.

"You're late," Tolan whispered.

"Morning cousin," Gideon responded. "You haven't missed much. All they've talked about is the celebration, and what everyone is going to wear." He rolled his eyes.

Kai scanned the group; everyone was eating and deep in conversation. He dared a look at his father. His father gave him a serious yet reserved glare. Kai was thankful they were too far apart for his father to bother interrupting Nola's celebration planning to reprimand him.

The best thing he could do was keep his head down, eat, and get excused. He filled his plate and tried not to make it visible that he was rushing his meal.

Landon sneered around Tolan. "So little prince, why were you late? Busy playing with your mutt?"

Tolan chuckled. "Right…your stupid little…"

"Herrrhem." Roark Raebun, his father, interrupted, clearing his throat before Tolan could finish his comment. Roark gave his son a sharp look and then went back to listening to his wife Shannon and Queen Nola discussing the music for the celebration.

"Sorry, Kai." Tolan fell silent and poked at the food on his plate.

"Thank you, Tolan," Kai offered in return.

Gideon nudged Kai's arm. "Can you believe my father has me traveling back and forth between here and Port Anahita? I am only a year older than you. I am not sure I'm ready," Gideon confessed.

Kai nodded in understanding. "As I understand, it takes about four hours on horseback. Much faster than by carriage. It's not that far, really," he stated. "What I find exciting are the trips Tolan is about to take. He will go all the way to Fort Pohaku. I've never been there."

"Well, Tolan is nearly seventeen, and he rides better than me. You've seen him and Landon race around the track." Gideon argued.

Tolan piped in, "What are you two whining about?"

"Gideon is worried about riding all the way to Port Anahita. I told him it is an easy trip, and that your trips to Fort Pohaku are going to be way more adventurous."

"Tolan, ignore those two," Landon interrupted. "We've more important things to discuss, like swords and battle strategy."

Landon's raised tone caught the attention of the king. "Time for class children, you are excused. Time for the adults to talk." Iver waved them away.

Kai didn't have to be told twice. He ducked out of the great hall behind his brothers. Through his connection, he asked Smoke to follow. Partway above the second-floor landing, he heard footsteps behind him. He ducked behind the columned stone archway of the stairwell and hid. Landon emerged.

From his hiding place, Kai watched the boy. *What is he doing in the family hall?* Landon walked to the nursery, pausing in the doorway. After a few moments, he returned to the stairs and descended. Kai felt strange. *What was he doing? Was he following me?*

Maid Mary exited his stepbrother's bedroom, easing the door shut behind herself. Kai smiled. "Your Highness." Mary greeted him while smoothing the front of her dress and apron to curtsy.

He motioned for her to stop. "Please, Mary, Prince Kai is formal enough. You don't need to curtsy to me every time we meet." "New maids," he huffed in embarrassment.

She tipped her head and walked away. Kai studied her. Something was different. Her red hair pinned inside of her white cap was the same. Her freckled face was the same. Yet, her usual petite frame tonight, she seemed sturdier. Taller, broader even. He had to been mistaken.

Curious to know the truth, he followed her, keeping his distance. Through the hallway, down the spiral staircase. He slowed his pace to make sure she would not hear his footsteps on the stone steps. All the way to the kitchen, he stalked her. By the time he entered, she was gone. Escaped.

In the library, Professor Greydon looked up from his work. "Good morning, boys, you're here early. Everyone needs to complete their world map project. All of you have a math and history assessment, and a select few have a Bangloonese language exam. Kai, let me get the twins started, and then I'll hang up the reference map."

The professor motioned to the twins. "Over here, boys. Seth, I will start you with your math assessment. Aaron, you can work on history first. Work quietly and let me know when you are ready for your next assignment."

Kai retrieved his map and unrolled it on a large table near the back. The professor pinned the large reference map to the wall. "Remember this map is for outline reference only. Your completed project should include drawing the continents, major bodies of water, forests, and mountain terrains. Add in any palaces, forts, outposts, and towns. Neatness and spelling count, please take your time."

A squeak from the library doors announced the rest of the class had arrived. Quietly everyone took their places and waited for the professor to bring their individual assignments. Gideon, Kai's table partner, strolled around the table, visually critiquing Kai's map while he waited. Gideon scrunched up his face and took his seat.

Kai looked at his map and then the reference map. Carefully he reviewed every line. *What am I missing?* He counted the Mystic Islands, he had missed a small one. Grateful, Kai grinned at Gideon who sat happily waiting for Professor Greydon—that is until the professor placed a foreign language test on the table. Gideon's face fell in distress.

Kai finished the outline of his map and began to add the details. Nearly finished he heard Amelia approach Professor Greydon's desk. "All finished? Let me have a look." After reviewing her project, the professor handed her a math assessment.

Satisfied with his, Kai quietly approached the professor's desk.

"All finished Kai?" The professor took Kai's map and reviewed each location. "Well done, as usual."

Kai's math assessment took time, but he was confident. The history exam took much longer. Finished, Kai left the library. One mindful thought brought Smoke to his feet. Outside several other children were already in the courtyard.

Passing through the group, Landon stuck out his shoulder, clipping Kai as he tried to pass, send him to the ground. Smoke positioned himself between the two boys and gave a low growl toward Landon. Kai commanded Smoke with a glance, and his wolf backed off.

Not wanting to let it go, he stepped up to the taller boy.

"Sorry, Landon, I didn't realize you were so wide." He smirked, walking away with Smoke.

With a hint of anger, Landon chased after him. "Little Prince, did you just call me fat?"

"No, I didn't say fat—I said WIDE." Kai spun to face him.

With both hands, Landon pushed Kai hard in the chest and sent him to the ground with a thud. Again, Smoke positioned himself between Kai and Landon. Smoke's hackles raised along his back, a harsh snarl rolled through his bared teeth. Landon stepped back with a look of fear on his face. "Call him off! If he attacks me, I will see he is shot dead."

Smoke snapped at the air. Kai's heart pounded; fear rippled through his mind. He held his breath, and everything slowed. His mind quickly played out the scene; Smoke's teeth snapping around Landon's arm. With the shake of his beastly head, the wolf tore the boy's arm apart.

Snapped out of the vision, Kai lunged his hand forward. Time remained slow around him. In the next heartbeat, Kai reached for Smoke's muzzle. He focused his mind on their connection and asked his wolf to heel. With the release of his breath, time resumed.

In an instant, Kai's hand wrapped around Smoke's snout. The open jaws clamped shut, and the wolf bowed his head to the ground. Fear and shock wavered in Landon's voice. "How did you move so fast?" he demanded.

Still angry, Kai released Smoke and stood to face the taller boy. He balled his fists in anger. He felt himself get hot, but he held his ground. The two boys stood staring at each other, and everyone held their breath. Kendra's warning echoed in his mind. He could not risk losing control. Kai relaxed his hands and looked away.

Tolan laughed. "You're afraid," he addressed Kai.

Kai let his eyes wander up at the two boys. Tolan's smirk made his eyes dance. Landon's expression was curious. Kai sensed he made a mistake using his gift in front of others. He put his hands in his pockets and backed away.

Landon followed Kai. "We're not done, little…"

Amelia stepped in between them. "Kai, come with me. Tolan, deal with Landon." She grabbed Kai by the arm and led him away.

"You won't always be here to break us up, you know," Kai said, looking down at his muddy pant leg. "Well, thank goodness I have you, always coming to my rescue." He smirked. "You know, books show the hero being the man, not the lady."

Amelia feigned a blush and took Kai by the hand. "You want to be my hero?"

His eyes went wide. Wait no, that's not what he'd meant. "I umm, well I'm just saying that I, umm…" Red-faced, he stepped ahead of Amelia to open the chapel door.

Amelia entered laughing and pushed Kai on his shoulder. "You should see your face. That's hilarious. Of course, I am the hero in this story. Can't a girl be the hero?" By this time, she was laughing so hard she had tears running down her face.

An enormous smile crept across his face, then he too burst out into laughter. "Certainly, a girl can be the hero. Even if I must write the book myself. You are the best Amelia, where would I be without you?" His laughter echoed through the rafters.

Kai sat down next to her and asked. "Amelia, why are you so open with me, but around others, you act shy, even nervous?"

She gave him a little nudge. "I am supposed to be this weak little girl, right? Everyone tells me what to do. They don't expect…well, anything, really. I am playing the part they want. But you don't treat me like a precious little princess. Tolan can be nice when he is not trying to impress Landon. He is the only other person that treats me like I have an opinion."

She smoothed out her dress and crossed her feet. "I have ideas and desires. I don't want to be like my mother sitting in a palace, hiding. You know she didn't want to come. Please don't tell anyone I told you. She hates Diu. You'd think she'd miss me enough to make the trip more than once a year."

Her somber mood shift left an uncomfortable silence between them. They both glanced around at the chapel. He leaned into her. "Well, you always have me!" he said with a wink. "Come on, I have to change before mealtime. I'll never hear the end of it if I showed up covered in mud."

Amelia looked down at his pants and giggled. Her silver-blue eyes danced with delight. "You're probably right. Although it would be even funnier if we both walked into the dining hall covered in mud."

He snorted and laughed. "You're outrageous. I am glad we're friends. Let's go." From the aisle, he offered her his hand, and she accepted, sliding out of the pew.

CHAPTER 9

Half-Light

The smell of Lizzie's sweet almond cakes drew Kai to the kitchen. Lizzie was a short round woman with an infectious laugh and curly strawberry blond hair with hints of white streaks. From the door, Kai listened to what Lizzie called well-orchestrated orders.

Lizzie winked at Kai. "Hello, Your Highness. How are you today?" She dusted off her flour-covered hands.

"I am doing fine." He paused and rethought his answer. "To tell the truth, it was a late night—studying. Any chance I can have a hot almond cake?"

Lizzie stepped around the table and locked him into a hug. "My-my, how tall you are." She looked up to him.

Throughout his childhood, he'd spent countless hours around the kitchen. He trusted Lizzie. She was a good listener, and she made him smile when he needed it most. "I've been thinking about my mother. Nothing specific, just wishing she was here with me."

"I miss her too. Mariana was a great woman. I will never forget her kindness to me. I remember this one time she came to the kitchen and told me she wanted to learn how to bake a pie. Although I explained to her that the kitchen was no place for a queen, she wouldn't listen. She grabbed one of my aprons and a bowl full of apples."

"Did you help her?" Kai asked inquisitively.

"Of course, when your mother set her mind to something, it was best to give in. I can't say she was the best baker, but I enjoyed her company and yours." Lizzie leaned over the table, and her eyes glazed in reflection.

Kai's eyes wandered across the table, and his mouth began to water again. "So, the almond cakes, are they still warm?" He reached toward the platter of mini cakes and looked at her with a sly smile, waiting for her approval before snatching one.

"No. They're for tomorrow."

They stood there in a pleading standoff, her hands on her hips, and him perpetually reaching. "Well, just one, then go eat." She tossed up her hands.

Delighted, he reached for the sweets. "How about two?" he asked, wrapping his fingers around two.

Lizzie smiled and shooed him away. He grabbed the almond cakes, kissed her on the cheek, and darted out of the kitchen. Kai popped the first cake in his mouth, closed his eyes and the warm treat melted in his mouth. These were his favorite. His mother's too.

Later that evening a knock sounded and his door opened. "Good, you're ready for bed." Kendra closed his bedroom curtains. "Mary is with the twins; I hope we will have little time before she fetches me for Nola. I would like to teach you how to meditate, which is the first step in learning how to glean." She sat and motioned for him to sit beside her.

"First, you need to understand there are different reasons or outcomes. Meditation can help you find focus. Through discipline, you can invoke your mind; that is gleaning. Done correctly, we Katori see the world anew. The awakening of the mind for some brings other insights—visions. In rare cases, gleaning can help you find someone you've lost or remember a past event.

"The ability to glean allows you to see the energy within

all things. It gives everything a glow. With it, I can see the world around us. I can see the orchard outside. I see the guards walking on the walls around the palace, they look like tiny wisps of light until you focus on their form. I can see your brothers in their room down the hall."

"You mean I could do all that?" he asked excitedly.

Hesitantly she touched his hand. "I have to be honest. A few months ago, I would have said no because you are only a Half-Light. Now, I don't know. You must learn to be in the moment, focus your emotions, and discipline your mind." She turned her head to listen at the door before continuing.

"I am hoping eventually we can try reflecting on the past and help you see it more clearly. Tonight, we will start by learning how to be in the moment and free our minds—meditate."

A little concerned, he raised his eyebrows. "You keep calling me that. What do you mean by Half-Light?"

She looked down at her hands. "Everything around us has energy, a light within. The Katori are naturally more connected to Alenga. We shine brighter. Your mother was Katori but given Iver is only part Katori through his great-great-grandmother, you will only ever be half as bright. Your gifts should be limited to speed and strength. Your bond to Smoke makes no sense to me. Changing your eye color and feeling the power in your mother's crystal. None of this seems to fit with everything I have ever been taught."

"You mean I could see beyond like you?" Kai zeroed in on the one idea.

Kendra patted his hand. "We have little time, let's not get lost before we get started."

"So, what do I need to do?" Kai relented.

Kendra looked straight ahead and closed her eyes. "You need to sit with your eyes closed and breathe normally. Relax, let everything from the day leave your mind and be right here, right now. Allow your mind to focus on your breath; where it starts in your body, how it feels going in and out of your lungs."

Eyes closed he tried to focus and relax into the chair. In a much quieter voice, he heard her say, "Now focus on your inner self, go past your heart, deeper, connect to the spiritual energy within you—to your soul. Stay with the moment, let it build, like a light within your soul."

Kai sat and tried to focus, but he felt and saw nothing. Frustrated, he squeezed the armrests on his chair. He huffed in frustration. Kendra touched his hand. "I know this is new and strange. You must give yourself time to relax. Expect nothing."

"Why can't I do this?" Kai agonized.

"Children are taught to meditate as early as five. Their minds take years to gain focus. The attention span of most people is limited. The undisciplined mind is lost. Distracted by the chaos of day-to-day life, silence scares them. You must break through the noise. Learn to find comfort in the stillness."

"Do you think I can?" Kai asked.

"It doesn't matter what I believe. Your mind is ripe for learning. Open yourself to Alenga. She offers the truth. Understand the essence of all life is fundamentally the same. The power of creation can be seen in its simplicity. Raw power can be redefined. We can evolve, become more."

Lost by the depth of her words, Kai stared at her. She smiled. "This is a lot to learn, Kai. For now, sit with me in silence, slow your mind. Notice the clouds of each moment wash over you and let them drift away without allowing your emotions to take control." Her voice softened as she spoke, and the tenderness in her tone soothed him.

He refocused on his breath and watched the day drift by as fading stills in his mind. When old memories pressed on him, he observed, but he did not embrace them. By returning to his breath, they passed over him. After a time, one eye peeked open, then the other. He watched Kendra. She sat peacefully with her hands in her lap, back straight, and faced forward.

Although he tried to remain still, he let his eyes wander around his room. Smoke's feet twitched, and his wolf made bizarre noises as he dreamed happily near the balcony door. Kai imagined that his wolf was chasing something.

Still restless, he felt the pressure of sitting in one place. With a deep sigh, Kai shifted a little in his seat a few times. In a whisper, he asked. "How much longer do we sit here?"

She opened her eyes. "I suppose that is enough for tonight. We will practice again, I promise." She placed her hand on his shoulder. "I need to go see how Nola is feeling."

His mind reeling from the long day, he remembered that he wanted to explore the second passageway down the mysterious stairwell. Just as the night before, he grabbed the lamp and stood in front of the painting of Gianfranca. He felt for the latch behind the frame, released it, and heard a small click. He stepped back as the wall popped open. Curious, Smoke stood and approached. *Smoke, stay,* Kai thought. His wolf sat.

He stepped over the threshold into the narrow space. After one last look around his room, he pulled the panel closed and secured the latch. Again, he noticed the cold, coarse stone on his feet, unlike the soft carpet in his room or the smooth marble used throughout the palace. *This must be part of the original castle of old. A secret place for spies, an escape route for royals.*

With his lamp illuminating the dark passageway, he headed down the hall. This time when he reached the small opening, he went down the stairs. At the bottom, it switched back to the right to another set of narrow stairs continuing down.

At the bottom, he noticed a pile of large rocks blocking the path. He would have to remove those if he wanted to continue downward—but not tonight. Moving them could be noisy, and he would need the daily hustle and bustle of the palace to conceal the sound.

In the other direction, there was an angled wall narrowing the space in front of him. When he peered around the wall, he noticed a similar opening with a large indented panel. His lamp revealed the edge of a golden frame. Before he released the latch, he hesitated. He would need to learn to navigate these without the lamp; he could not risk spilling light into a dark room revealing the spy tunnels. He dimmed the light and left it in the space behind the angled wall.

Back behind the opening, he released the latch and stepped out to see which painting covered the passage. Moonlight poured in through the large windows of the library, filling the room, and he saw this painting was also his great-great grandmother. She was sitting under the great banyark tree in the gardens, reading a book.

Tall built-in bookshelves surrounded the panel around her portrait, and behind him, he saw the large red sofa and two brown reading chairs where he'd spent many an hour reading. Quickly he pressed the panel back into place and secured the latch.

This was fascinating—he'd never been in the library at night. He crept around the various tables and bookshelves, around Professor Greydon's desk and the rows of smaller desks he and the others sat in for class each day. The room smelled of wood, old maps, and books.

Up and down the aisles, he ran his fingers over the spines of each book. Down the next aisle, his hand caught on a book that was slightly pulled out from the others. It knocked over with a thump into the empty space left by several other missing books before it ultimately fell to the floor with an even louder thud.

Startled, Kai bent down and grabbed the book, and as he stood back up, he found Riome standing before him. He let out a small squeal. Illuminated by the moonlight, Riome wore her usual all-black clothing, and her dark auburn hair now flowed freely about her shoulders. "Are you sleepwalking tonight, Kai?" she grilled.

"Umm, no Riome," he responded with a bit of shakiness in his voice. "I didn't see you there."

"How did you get in here? I did not hear the doors to

the library open. There's no way you came in that way," she probed, glaring at him with squinty eyes.

Cazier's words filled his mind: *information is power, keep your secrets close.* He relaxed his face, hoping the shadows would hide any hint of deception in his answer. "Couldn't sleep, I came to find a book. I hope I did not disturb you."

If he ever intended to be a spy, he'd need to be able to convince people. He tried to sound carefree as he stepped away from her to a book covered table. "Please excuse me. I will head back to my room, have a good evening." Without looking, he grabbed the top book and turned to smile back at her.

Although she seemed to accept his response, she replaced her books in the empty space on the shelf and followed him. "I am finished for the night. I would be happy to walk you back to your room." She motioned for him to take the lead. "After you."

With her breathing down his neck, he walked in silence toward the doors—which he realized that he'd not be able to open quietly, just as she'd said. With a small sigh, he looked down at the book in his hands and realized he'd read the book already. *Great!*

"Ladies first," he said, offering Riome a pursed smile as he motioned toward the door.

She offered no reaction. She merely pulled open the door, and to no one's surprise, there was an ever so slight creak. Kai would have to talk with Dean Biorne, the palace carpenter, about fixing the squeak.

Once in the hallway, she pulled the door shut with a thud. Down the hall, one of the patrolling Mryken guard dogs turned and advanced on their position. Protectively Riome placed her arm in front of Kai, halting him. "Stand still and wait for him to register who we are—then he will turn and go. We've simply startled him."

Kai was not worried. Grand Duke Dante Carmelo, head of palace security, socialized the royal family with the Mryken as pups to ensure they knew and protected them. Anyone allowed to reside within the palace, or the tower, were introduced to the adult dogs. Otherwise, they would be attacked on sight.

Unafraid, he remained calm. He knew the Mryken would sense him and return to patrolling the halls. He reached out his hand to assure Riome he was not afraid. She pushed his hand back. Out of the corner of his eye, Kai spotted another Mryken dog approach. His stride was quick, his hackles raised.

Instinctively, Kai sat and closed his eyes. He slowed his breathing and relaxed. He could feel the dogs heightened concern. The dogs were nearing their position. In a breath, Kai released a sense of peace. The connection between him and the Mryken was strong.

"What are you doing?" Riome whispered.

"Sit," he whispered back, again instructing the dogs to relax with his mind.

Cautiously Riome sat beside him. The Mryken's pace slowed. Their massive frame hovered over him. Kai opened his eyes, tilted his head to one side and extended his hand, palm up. The Mryken studied the pair. One sniffed Kai's offered hand and nuzzled it with his nose.

Yates, the hall guard, came down the stairs. "Kai, you're up late. Miss Riome, did you have business in the palace this evening?" Calmly he approached them, glanced at both dogs, and gave a quick whistle and click with his tongue. The dogs returned to patrolling the hallway.

The tension in Riome's shoulders relaxed, and she stood to face the guard. "Thank you, Yates. I believe if the prince had been alone, they'd have ignored him; I think they perceived me as a threat to him. I was doing research in the library, and now I'm walking Kai back to his room."

One eyebrow raised, Yates looked at Kai and then back at Riome. "Security is extremely tight with so many visitors in the palace. I will see him upstairs, thank you. Please return to the tower, Miss Riome," Yates commanded.

"Thank you, I understand. Goodnight, Your Highness. I

hope your book helps you sleep." She bowed and left.

Relieved, Kai called out to her. "Goodnight Riome." Then he silently climbed the stairwell with Yates. At the top, Kai saw Beck, the next guard, walking down the hall toward them. "Thank you, Yates. I am good from here," Kai assured him. "Have a good night."

With a nod, Yates turned and went back downstairs. Kai continued to his room alone. On his way, another Mryken approached, recognized him, and continued past.

Inside, he shut the door and leaned against it with a sigh. *That was a close one.* Tired, he climbed into bed, and that's when it hit him. The lamp. It was still lit in the hidden passageway.

Eyes wide, Kai sat up straight. *I cannot risk leaving an open flame in a dusty old hallway.* He slipped out of bed, released the latch that secured the painting, and stepped into the secret passage.

Arms outstretched, he let his hand glide across the rough stone walls as he made his way downstairs in the dark. A small light illuminated the stairs as he got closer to the bottom, and he retrieved the lamp.

Relieved he turned, only to find Smoke standing behind him. "Smoke, what are you doing down here?" he said out loud. Smoke panted. Kai petted his wolf's head. "Well, in all fairness, I didn't tell you to stay."

A sense of dread welled in his chest. He dashed back upstairs and through the opening. After Smoke stepped through, Kai pushed the painting into place and secured the pin in the latch. That's when Kai heard Kendra clear her throat. Nearly dropping the lamp, he turned to see her sitting up on the edge of his bed.

Curiously she looked at him. "I wondered where you were. You mind telling me where that leads?" She gestured to the painting.

He was caught, no denying now. He hung his head down and pushed at the carpet with his toe. "Well, that all depends on which passageway you take. One leads to the Master General's tower—you pop out behind another painting of a large ship, and the other leads downstairs to the library. You come out behind another picture of Gianfranca. You aren't going to tell on me, are you? I didn't hurt anything. Although I kind of almost got caught tonight in the library by Riome. She didn't see me come through the passageway, but she saw me in the library. That's why I had to go back into the tunnel to retrieve my lamp." He babbled it all out so quickly he'd barely taken a breath.

Kendra seemed to be contemplating his question a little too long. But he waited. Finally, she spoke. "The palace is riddled with passages. How did I never notice before? I can only see them when I focus. Stone is much harder to see through." She turned and tilted her head.

He too stared at the painting, now sitting beside her. "There are many large oversized paintings. Nearly one in every room. There are so many spy tunnels to explore. You know, there is a large painting in my dad's study."

Not surprised, Kendra responded, "You're right." She looked as if she'd found treasure and he didn't understand why. She too seemed to realize she'd overstated her enthusiasm and her expression relaxed.

"You need to be more careful. Learn to listen before exiting, navigate without a lamp. This could be to your advantage to listen in on secret conversations or gain access to locked rooms. You cannot get caught. If you do get caught, act surprised, like you'd just discovered the tunnel. And no, I will not tell on you. I will keep your secret, as you've kept mine."

She patted his leg and stood. "Everyone loves a mystery, Kai. This is yours. You will have to tell me how you make out finding other entrances and where you end up. Just be careful and never leave one open behind yourself again."

Kendra squinted her eyes a bit and tilted her head. "If you end up in your father's study, don't linger there too long. That might not be a good place to get caught."

CHAPTER 10

Spellbinding

Kai stepped into Lizzie's kitchen and quickly caught sight of Dean, the palace carpenter, sharing his breakfast. "Good morning, Lizzie. Dean, you're just the person I was hoping to find this morning."

Dean's eyes lit up behind his round spectacles. Finished with his last bite, he nodded. "Good morning, Your Highness. What can I do for you?"

As far as Kai was concerned, the man could design and build anything. "I was wondering, can you look at the library door? It seems to stick when you go to open it, and it makes a rather annoying squeak."

"Certainly, I'll see what I can do. It has been on my list, but we are all working on completing the new bakehouse, so I've been a bit preoccupied." Dean reached into the pocket of his brown vest to retrieve his list. "Professor Greydon said that the doors stick, making it difficult for the younger children to open the large doors. Plus, we all know how he feels about unnecessary noises in his precious library." Dean chuckled.

It seemed to Kai that Dean had been working on the bakehouse forever. "How much longer will it take to complete it? It has been almost a year, what's left?"

"Building with stone takes time, lad. It should be complete

in the next few weeks. Most of what is left is finish work, building a mezzanine for supplies, installing shelves, hanging windows and making the doors. Plus, we have to finish the little adjoining home for the family."

Kai tilted his head and squinted at Dean. "So why do we need a bakehouse again? Lizzie is the best baker in the world. Lizzie, you're not leaving, are you?" Panic wavered in his voice as he consulted Dean.

"That's my boy," Lizzie winked at him. "Don't you worry, I will teach them all your favorites. Honestly, it will make things easier on me in the mornings. We won't have to get up so early to prepare the bread before starting on breakfast. We will also have more room in the pantry. All the baking supplies will now go to the bakehouse loft."

"Not to mention, who doesn't love a dedicated full-time baker?" said Dean, rubbing his chin. "It needs to be done before winter gets here, so the new family can get settled into palace life. They will be moving into the little adjoining house soon." Dean tossed Lizzie a wave. "See you at lunch, dear. Kai, stop by and see our progress. I'll check those library doors later today."

"Thanks, Dean. Bye, Lizzie." Kai headed to his room.

He wanted to spend the better part of his free day exploring the palace for more secret passageways behind large paintings—especially ones featuring other ancestors. He left Smoke in his room, grabbed a library book, and bounded down the stairs to the library.

Halfway down, servants slowed his progress. Hordes of staff carried tableware, flowers, and candles to decorate the great hall. Weaving his way through he reached the library entrance. Professor Greydon stood talking with Shannon at the opposite end of the hallway.

He tugged on the large door and slipped inside, hoping to inspect a second painting on the opposite side of the library and its surrounding panel without prying eyes. Satisfied he was alone, he ran between the tables, stopping only to drop his book.

Standing before the painting of his great-great-uncle... He couldn't remember ... but he knew it was a Galloway man, riding a horse. He checked the frame for the little latch. When he released the pin, the edge of the frame came free from the wall, and with a sly smile, he quickly stepped into the opening. Given all the daylight pouring into the library, he was able to see quite far into the empty space and instantly realized there was another hidden panel directly in front of him.

His eyes went wide, and he gasped. "The music room," he said out loud. One quick look down the passage and he could just make out stairs leading upward. He only had a few moments; backing out, he pushed the painting back into place and secured the latch. Confident it was closed, he raced back to the library doors.

Professor Greydon approached with several books in his arms. "Good morning, Professor Greydon. I returned a book I borrowed, let me hold the door for you," Kai offered.

Very pleased, Professor Greydon smiled. "Why thank you, Prince Kai, that is very kind of you. Do you need anything else this morning?"

"Thank you, but no professor." Not wanting the conversation to continue, he dashed through the door. "Got to run, professor!" Kai darted to the music room and pushed open the door. There sat Amelia on one of the sofas reading a book, her long blonde hair pulled back in a braid. Darn, he thought to himself. He had hoped the room would be empty. Amelia lowered her book. "Good morning, Kai, have you come to listen to me practice?"

He crossed to where Amelia sat, surveying both ends of the room. He took notice of the matching built-in bookshelves around two large paintings, one on either side of the room. Glaring at the one on the right, he thought, there must also be an access point in Dante's study. He was getting good at this. Pleased with himself, he took a seat beside her. "Good morning, Amelia. Honestly, I was just killing time. What are you reading?"

"*The Invisible Thief*. You know the one you gave me yesterday, about Benmar, the man who stole the crown jewels from Bangloo. I am at the part where he boards a ship to cross the Caprizian Sea. I kind of like how the author uses places we know," she said, closing the book.

Kai shook his head. "I knew you would like it. If you think that part is good, wait to till you get to the end when he…"

She gasped and gave him a little shove. "Don't you dare tell me anything, Kai."

Chuckling, he pushed her hand away. "Don't worry, I won't spoil it," he said with a grin.

Just then, the door to the music room opened, and Shannon entered. "Good morning, children. Sorry I am late, Amelia. It's been a busy morning. Are you ready to practice your piece for this evening's celebration?"

"Yes, Lady Shannon. Kai, please stay and listen to my piece. I will be playing first tonight."

Not wanting her to feel that he was disinterested, he agreed. "Happy to stay and listen." Although he secretly had the passageways on his mind.

Amelia took her seat on the piano bench next to Shannon and opened her sheet music. Ready she set her foot on the pedal below and her hands gently above the keys and began to play.

Kai loved the sound of piano music; her piece drew him in, and he closed his eyes to let it take him away. The music transported his mind to when he was young, to a time when his mother used to play for him. It was a beautiful piece, the notes all blended together like a happy story of two children dancing through the clouds. Each with their own personality blending harmoniously.

With his eyes open, he looked around the brightly lit room. He glanced upward and thought of the bedrooms above, wondering which ones would be empty. Which rooms could he explore?

Once she finished, she craned her neck to see him over the piano. "Well, what do you think? Beautiful, right?" Her hopeful smile waited for his reply.

Kai nodded. "Amelia, you play very well. I am sure your mother must be very proud. I can't wait to hear it again tonight. Thank you for letting me stay." With a nod to them both, he said, "Lady Shannon, Amelia." Then he turned and opened the door. There in front of him stood Alana, graceful as ever, holding her music. She smiled and stepped passed him.

"Uh, hello to you, Alana," he whispered as he entered the hallway. Sweet girl, but a little too shy for him. Besides the one time in class, when she gave her book report, he was sure he'd never heard the girl speak to anyone. Now was no exception.

Upstairs he made his way toward the nursery. He remembered all too well the large paintings in his old room. When he entered, he found Nola sitting in the window seat, staring outside. "Hello, Nola, how are you feeling? Better, I hope." Kai took the position across from her and looked past her shoulder to the painting of his great-great-grandmother holding twins, Eden and Anthony, in the nursery rocking chair.

Nola rubbed her hands over her bulging stomach. "I am well, thank you for asking. Did you need anything?"

Still eyeing the built-in bookshelf, he thought that there must be a correlating painting in his parents' room—not that he'd risk walking in there to inspect it, even if it were empty. "Not really, I thought I would come to see my old room. It has certainly changed with all the new baby things."

Nola gazed around the room. "Yes, it has really come together. I can't wait for the baby to be born, then I can have pink or blue ribbons added to all the white."

"I can't wait to be a big brother to him or her, although secretly I hope it is a girl. We need a princess in the palace." He reached over and touched her hand.

She placed her hand firmly on his, her green eyes looked deep into his, and she gave him a soft smile. "I agree, I would love a little girl." She said in a soft tone, tapping the back of his hand repeatedly. "You are such a good and loyal brother, Kai. You would do anything for your brothers." Her soft tone was more commanding than grateful. Still, she tapped. "You would even protect me over another."

Something about her eyes, her words, and her touch made him feel dizzy. His thoughts struggled to focus. Panicked, he wanted to free his hand. He could not move. Her words continued to bore into his mind. He felt his will bend to her suggestions. "You should watch out for Cazier," she instructed. "He cannot be trusted."

Her ideas pressed into his mind, mesmerizing him. He did not want to believe her words, but they began to take root. Trapped, Kai attempted to withdraw inside himself. Nola's words rang in his ears, confusing him. Kendra came to his mind, and he focused on his breathing. He heard his own heartbeat. The rhythm was comforting and loud.

At that moment, he closed his eyes and pulled his hand free. Kai rubbed the back of his hand, and then he shook his head and turned back toward the bookshelf. His mind fog cleared, and he looked back at her. "I don't feel well. I should let you rest. Do you need anything before I go?"

Nola's serious glare turned coy. "You should rest, dear. Can you get Kendra first? She is down the hall, making up a room for Lord and Lady Chenowith. They will be arriving around lunch." Her spellbinding eyes narrowed.

He cringed again at the sound of her voice. Her words sounded forceful. Even without her touch, his head began to swim. "Certainly, I will send her right over." He rubbed his temple and left.

In the hallway, he took a deep breath. His fog continued to clear. Down the hall, he found Kendra putting the finishing touches on some flowers. "Excuse me, Kendra. Nola needs you."

"Is she alright?" Kendra asked with concern and surprise.

Kai noticed the bookshelf and the large painting, and he ran his fingers around the frame, discovering the tiny latch securing it to the wall. "Yes, she's fine. Not sure what she wanted, just passing on her message."

Before Kendra could leave, he touched her arm. "Kendra, be careful. There is something about Nola I never noticed before. She touched my hand and spoke to me, and my mind seemed to cloud over. If you had not taught me how to withdraw and focus on my breathing, I…" He shook his head again. "I cannot explain it. Just be careful."

Kendra placed her hand on Kai's. "I too have noticed something. It's happened to me too when I touch her to check on the baby. She speaks to me. Questions me. It is not easy to break free from her hypnotic spell. I have no idea of her purpose. Fortunately, I am rarely alone with her. Sigry is usually in the room to monitor her progress, but I will be careful. Thank you, Kai."

CHAPTER 11

Trapped

The king's study was surprisingly empty. Near the door, a large ornate cabinet beckoned. Although it was probably locked, Kai wondered if the necklace was stored inside. If he were ever going to study it without Sigry, he would need to sneak inside and pick the lock. A skill he did not yet possess.

Along the back wall, a long display case and a set of bookshelves wrapped around a large family portrait. Kai pondered the mystery at hand, and he realized he needed to think more about the layout of the palace. If all the access points lead to a room directly above or below, it meant if there was a secret passage behind the painting in his father's study, it had to be accessible from the family room directly below.

They all utilized built-in bookshelves and large paintings to cover their entrances. Two such passages shared dual exits into adjoining rooms. Wanting to check one out, Kai entered one such access point from an unused bedroom between the nursery and his cousin Gideon's room. He knew he was taking a risk opening one during the day, but from an empty room, he hoped to go undetected.

After lighting an oil lamp, he entered the passage and replaced the pin in the latch. The dim light was just enough to reveal the path but not enough that it might illuminate any cracks around the panels. He wished he could walk them in the dark or glean them the way Kendra could.

There, as he figured, another panel directly across from the access point he'd just used. From his hiding point, he listened to his aunt Helena and Gideon talking on the other side. Kai's lamp illuminated a set of stairs leading down.

At the bottom, he found he was again between two panels —the one he'd opened just this morning, within the library and the music room on the other side. Quite thrilled with himself, he stopped to listen. No surprise, nothing was coming from the library. From the music room, however, he could faintly hear Alana playing the piano. He leaned against the wall to listen.

After she finished the piece, he could hear Shannon speaking. "You've done very well, my dear. I believe you are ready for tonight's performance." The muffled sounds of another voice interrupted Shannon. "Certainly, please clean the room, we are just leaving to have lunch."

Hungry himself, he picked up his lamp. When he reached the exit that would lead him back into the empty room, he heard voices. *Oh no, I'm trapped!* He panicked.

He had assumed the room would remain empty and that he could come and go. *Now what?* He knew the library would be occupied all day. Although currently silent, he did not want to risk using the panel to exit into his cousin's room. He would have to sit and wait for them to leave or risk exiting into the music room, something he was not prepared to do.

Kai sat on the stone floor for what felt like hours when he finally thought he heard the door close and the room go silent. Deciding his hunger was becoming more than he could bear, he turned the dial on the lamp completely out and waited for the smell of smoke to dissipate. On the wall, he felt for the latch to release the frame.

With one hand on the panel, he made sure to keep it from opening too far. The room was now filled with sunlight. The maids had opened the curtains and windows to let in light and fresh air. He quietly stepped out of his hiding place into the room, pressed the frame back into place, and secured the latch.

The room, he noticed, had been cleaned and prepared for an impending guest. Not wanting to stick around to see who might be using the room, he opened the door and headed straight to his room. *That was too close.* He slid down the back of the door with a thud.

Happy to see him, Smoke gave him a lick across the face and sniffed his dusty clothes. Relieved he'd not been caught, Kai decided that was too close. If he was to use these access points or hidden passages to eavesdrop, his knowledge of them needed to remain a secret. He would need to be more careful and consider only using them at night when everyone was asleep, especially considering the servants could come in on him to clean a room at any moment.

The next panel he wanted to confirm was the one in the family sitting room that inevitably would lead to his father's study. He would explore it tonight. For now, he was famished. Down in the family dining hall, Kai found lunch had long since been cleared. His best bet now was Lizzie.

On the stairwell he passed a long line of servants carrying linens, glass vases, armfuls of white dahlias and red roses for dressing the tables in the great hall. *How much decoration could one room need?*

When he entered the kitchen, he saw a flurry of workers cutting vegetables, others shaping dough, cutting it into small round rolls and placing them on a nearby tray. Lizzie shoved them into the oven and removed four large pies. The kitchen smelled like heaven, and it looked like a storm of activity he should probably steer clear of, but he needed something to eat.

Kai waved to Lizzie and caught her attention. "I am sorry to bother you, but I missed lunch. Do you have anything to spare?"

"Oh, honey, you've caught us preparing for tonight's celebration. We are really in between meals right now," she said, touching the back of her wrist to her forehead. "Come with me." She grabbed a plate, a small wooden board, and a knife. At the far end of the kitchen, she entered the adjoining pantry.

Lizzie set everything down on the large stone table in the center of the room. From the shelf, she grabbed a block of cheese and carved off three large slices, before placing it back and covering it with a towel. Then she reached into a box on another shelf, pulled out three thinly sliced pieces of dried meat, and pushed the plate toward him. "Start with this while I cut you a few apples."

Relieved, he stuffed the first piece of cheese in his mouth. "Thank you, Lizzie. You are the best."

Smiling back at him, she placed the two sliced apples on his plate. "Don't talk with your mouth full. When you are done, bring the plate to the kitchen for someone to wash. Now I really must get back to cooking, be a good boy and run along." Lizzie dashed back into the fray of the kitchen.

After setting his plate in the kitchen sink, he made his way upstairs to the great hall. The room had been transformed. They had already brought in Amelia's piano, decorated with a swag of pine branches, white dahlias, and red roses. In the center of the room, all the chandeliers had been lowered to hover just above the tables and servants were busy weaving green garland and white ribbons around the lamps.

On the dais, there was one long table set for the royal family and the guest of honor. Kai ran his hands over the intricately carved chairs until he came to his father's throne, which had been put at the center of the table. The throne was deep mahogany, and carved into the back was the Galloway crest: a wolf's head with three spears in its jaws brushed with gold and silver. The arms and seat were covered in thick blue velvet padding.

The rest of the room was filled with multiple tables covered in white linens and narrow dark blue runners, running the length of each table. Some of the tables were already decorated with tall frosted white glass vases overflowing with green garland and stuffed with the same flowers being used in the rest of the room. All the plants made the room smell of pine and roses.

Amelia burst into the room, heading toward the piano, and he darted over to catch up with her. Desperate to get fresh air, he asked, "Amelia, want to go outside?"

"Sorry, I can't! I need to go and get ready for tonight. Mother wants them to curl my hair, and I have to wear some fancy dress she had made for me. They just let me out for a few minutes while they complete some alterations. Seems I've grown more than she'd anticipated. I only came down to place my music before getting ready. See you tonight." With a sigh, he walked out behind her.

Later that evening, everyone gathered in the great hall to enjoy food and festivities to honor the new Master General, Adrian Cazier. The court herald had announced all the lords and ladies, most of which Kai knew already. He knew Lord and Lady Chenowith, Lord and Lady Albey, and Lord and Lady Hamrin very well.

After announcing the guest of honor, Lord Adrian Cazier, everyone took their seats, and Shannon motioned for Amelia to take her place at the piano. Kai was stunned to see Amelia; she looked beautiful in an emerald green dress. Her mother had indeed curled her golden blond hair, and it bounced as she walked. He rarely saw her dressed so formal.

She looked nervous, but she smiled as Shannon sat down beside her. One short nod from Shannon and Amelia began to play. It was just as beautiful as the first time he'd heard her perform. The music had such power and beauty. It could pull a memory from the past or paint a picture out of thin air.

When she finished, everyone clapped. Then Shannon and Amelia played a short duet together that sounded lively and complicated. After another loud round of applause, Amelia curtsied to the group and returned to her seat. Next Alana

Cazier approached the piano and sat beside Shannon. Alana played an exquisite piece. He could tell, looking at his cousin, that Adrian was quite proud.

Her selection made Kai feel introspective. He couldn't tell if he should feel happy or sad. The piece seemed to bounce back and forth between two moods. After another round applause, dinner was served.

The Master General leaned around Kai and whispered to the King, "Sire, thank you for the honor and this magnificent evening. You sure we couldn't have gone out on the town, just the two of us like when we were young?"

The pair burst into laughter. Iver sipped his wine. "You never were much for banquets, Adrian. I wish we could go back before all this responsibility. I wish our fathers were still with us; I wish our brothers were not lost to us. Thank you for remaining by my side and assuming the role of Master General. I know it was not an easy choice."

"Well, your only other choice would have been Ashwin, and we both know he is not up to the task. I just hope to live up to my father's reputation." Adrian took his glass and raised it to the King, and they clinked glasses and drank.

With a smirk, Iver responded, "I have every faith in you, cousin. Together we will set things right again. We will discover who sank your brother Andrew's ship. I only wish your father had been alive when they found him."

Cazier nodded. "I have my resources. My brother's body may have been lost at sea, but we will make someone pay for his death. Admiral Raebun is still searching the seas for clues. Someone will talk. Someday when they think nobody is listening, they will talk."

Kai shrank at the turn in conversation and the silence that followed.

After dinner, many took to the floor to mingle and dance. Near the piano, Kai saw Amelia and Tolan deep in conversation. In the archway to the great hall, Landon stood alone, glaring over the spectacle of the evening. Across the room,

Kendra escorted Seth and Aaron toward the door. This seemed like a good time to follow suit and slip out with them.

A loud knock announced Kendra entering his room. "I see someone is all ready for bed. I take it you would like to continue with your meditation lessons?"

From his balcony, he stepped back into his room. "Yes, Kendra, I would like that." He closed the large doors. "I know I didn't sit long last time, but I want to try, I want to get better. I need to get better. I need to move to the next step. I want to glean like you."

She sat in a chair near the fireplace, motioning for him to join her. "Come have a seat then. Please understand the outcome may not be what you want if you continue to pull at it."

"I can do this," he said with a wave. His heart bloomed with confidence, and he felt his body warm.

Reluctantly Kendra nodded at him and gasped. "Again, with your eyes. Are you learning to control their change?"

"I am," he acknowledged. "I feel the heat build, and I either let it happen or focus on something meaningless like you taught me."

Again, she gestured to the chair next to where she sat. "Let us start again by closing our eyes and breathing normally. Relax, let the day fade away and just be in this moment. Allow your mind to focus on your breath, how it feels going in and out of your body."

Kai sat there with his eyes closed as the silence enveloped him. Desperate to do better, he focused on his breath. He felt anxious after the previous attempt and squirmed in his seat.

In a quieter voice, he heard Kendra, "It is normal to have feelings about how you want this moment to unfold. Recognize them as the distractions they are and go back to your breathing. That is your anchor."

In his mind, he pictured an anchor, unmoving. His breath was his anchor, holding him steady, providing a focal point. The visual helped, and he relaxed. In the far reaches of his mind, he sensed a knowing. A light began to bloom. Excited, he reached and pulled on the moment. In his grasp, the light died.

Again he tried. Each time he relaxed a tiny light built inside, but it was quickly extinguished with his desires to control and force the energy. Frustrated, he sat waiting. The light never built again.

At some point, he relented and opened his eyes. "I believe I did much better tonight. I did not feel so jumpy, and it was easier to sit. The anchor visual helped, although I can't seem to hold onto the light."

Kendra placed her hand on top of his. "You are just getting started. Meditation cannot be forced; it needs to happen naturally. If you want to glean, you must give up your need to control the moment and just...BE in the moment. If you cannot fully relax, you will not be able to move forward."

"Thank you for your patience. You're right, though. I did try to force it. I will continue to practice."

"I should look in on Nola, see how she is this evening after all the excitement. Do you plan to go exploring again tonight?" she asked as she walked to the door.

"Maybe. I just need to find a way into the family sitting room to see if it does indeed access my father's study. The only thing—with all the extra guard detail, I'm not sure I will able to do it without being noticed."

"Whatever you decide, please be careful. Sleep well, goodnight Kai."

Casually he walked downstairs, passing Yates making his rounds on the second floor. His appearance late at night was not unusual, the floor guard paid him no mind. Once again, Kai noticed routine made people feel safe, relaxed, and complacent. Earlier in the day, he'd left a book on the sofa in case he needed to explain his presence in the family sitting room.

Fortunately, the room was empty, and he quickly made his way to the back corner and stood in front of his great-great-grandfather, Nicholas. With one of the oil lamps from the table, he released latch, the frame popped open, and he stepped over the small threshold.

Inside the passage, he pulled the panel closed behind himself and secured the latch. As the lamplight illuminated the space, he was not surprised to find narrow set stairs leading up; however, to the left, he'd expected a stone wall, but much to his surprise it was the back of a large panel. Quickly turning down the lamp to barely a glow, he placed it on the stairs behind him. He pressed his ear against the back of the frame, and he could hear servants talking and cleaning in the great hall.

How could this be? There were no built-in bookshelves, only large oil paintings. Kai knelt on one knee and inspected the wall along the edge. He found a sizable latch, different than the others. It was fastened much more securely. He would have to investigate this later when the room was not filled with people.

With the lamp in hand, he quietly climbed the stairs. Near the top, Kai stopped to listen for voices. Hearing none, he climbed the remaining steps and stood on the landing behind the hidden access panel to his father's study. He stood there frozen, wondering what he was doing. This was his father's study. What if he got caught? Unsure, he leaned his back against the wall and slid down to sit on the hard stone floor.

He contemplated his next move. If caught, he needed to have an excuse ready. This time he decided to take the lamp; he could not risk leaving it behind. Besides, if discovered, he could say that he was there to look at the trophy cases in his father's study. As a small child, he used to spend hours looking at everything. After pressing his ear against the panel, he listened intently for any sounds of movement or people.

How he desperately wished he could see inside to know if it were clear. He slowed his breathing and focused on the painting. In his mind, he saw his father's study, a bit aglow but empty. He opened his eyes and chuckled. If only he could really see through walls.

His hand on the latch, he released the pin, and as before he held onto the panel to keep it from opening too far. Slowly he let it open just enough to peer around the room. It was totally dark—no light from the fireplace or the door, only the small sliver of light from his lamp that spilled into the room.

Slowly he eased the panel open, but it quickly banged into something substantial. What had it hit? A small panic welled up inside him. The opening was just large enough for him to squeeze through. His hip bumped into the table in the corner of his father's study.

With the lamp through, he quietly pushed the panel closed and latched it in place. Blocked by the table, he stepped around to take a better look. Most of the maps and papers that usually covered the table during the day had been stowed on shelves.

He would have to make it a point to come back during the day while his father was there and move the table if he wanted to come and go through the painting. It was almost too tight of a squeeze for him.

I have apparently lost my mind. Sneaking into my father's office to search for my mother's necklace is insane. Kai took in a deep breath; he smelled whiskey and old paper. The memories of years past made him smile. The wall behind his father's desk brought him to a standstill. He froze in the dragon's skull glare. Kai had not noticed it earlier. It had been a while since he'd been in here; he had no idea his father had put it back up on the wall.

As a child, Kai could not stand to be near it. Although now, he could see that it was an impressive piece, considering very few dragon skulls were ever retrieved after the war. His father had told him that the dragon's head had been recovered by Iver's great-great-grandfather, Kronas Galloway.

Suddenly overwhelmed with emotion, he sat down in the middle of the floor, staring up at the giant skull. It had two protruding horns on the top of its head, a ridge of several smaller boney horns ran down the front of its head, and large sharp teeth. The head was nearly six feet tall. A chill ran through him, and he wrapped his arms around his knees and pulled them tight to his chest.

Light unexpectedly spilled into the room as the door swung open. Surprised Kai turned to and saw his father standing in the doorway. Lost in thought, he just stared at his father, and tears welled in his eyes. His father looked at the skull and then down at him. "I put it back up a few months ago. It fills me with rage, how we lost your mother, but it is proof they can be taken down. Cousin Adrian insists we cannot harbor ill will for every dragon." Iver sat on the floor and placed his arm around Kai's shoulder.

Kai bit his bottom lip. "I hope it is alright that I came in here. I noticed it was back on the wall."

Iver folded his hands together and leaned against the sofa. "I understand. I look at it sometimes, too. Although this one is not very large, compared to the live dragons I've seen. Feel free to come in here at any time you wish."

Surprised Kai sat up a little taller, folding his legs down in front of him. "You've seen one up close?"

"I have. It was all I could do to not run my sword through the beast's neck. Sigry convinced me I should not. He said we needed to use it for a greater purpose. Even though the beast was red like the one seen fleeing from the gardens the day your mother died, it could not possibly be the same dragon that killed her. And we can't blame all of them for one rogue dragon."

His father's words rang true. Astonished, Kai sat there listening, his eyes wide and mouth agape. "Use it? How do you use a dragon? I thought they were dangerous. Only the Katori live near them, don't they? I heard they actually protect each other."

Iver shook his head in agreement. "It is said the dragons live among the Katori. Though I have never been there. More importantly, when we needed help, the Katori brought dragons to defend Diu against Milnos. Dragons are fierce creatures. It's what made the Katori unbeatable and saved our kingdom."

Still curious, Kai persisted. "How can you use a dragon

without them attacking you?"

Iver lifted his head; his eyes shuttered as if he'd awoken from a trance. His hand drifted over his vest pocket. Kai saw the small bulge. He imagined his mothers' necklace was always kept close. "Son, it's late. I think we've talked enough for one night." Iver motioned toward the door.

CHAPTER 12

Duplicity Born

After the Master General's celebration, guests departed in droves from Diu, with each passing day the palace felt emptier. The few that remained were preoccupied with private conversations and gossip. Kai never understood why people relished in rumors, considering most of the stories were untrue. His only fascination was how the story evolved in the retelling.

Come evening, he noticed Nola was missing—again her chair remained empty. He wondered how she was doing. Lost in his own thoughts, he sat in a daze pushing the food around on his plate, until Seth poked him in the side and he nearly flicked a piece of meat across the table. "Kai, father has excused us, but you've hardly eaten. Are you alright?" he asked kindly.

He hadn't realized just how tired he was until now. "I have not been sleeping well, that's all. Come, I will walk you and Aaron upstairs since Kendra has not returned. I am sure Mary is upstairs getting your baths ready."

Ready for bed, Kai thought about sitting for a time to practice his meditation. He had gotten better, but tonight he was just too tired.

In the wee hours of the morning, Kai woke to the faint

sound of screams. Startled, he hopped out of bed and opened his door. There was nothing. Had he imagined it? Then he heard it again; it was coming from the other end of the hall. He approached the nursery, and the occasional screams got louder. For once, the screaming was not from him. Nola was in labor.

The four Galloway men lingered in the hallway, patiently waiting for news. Kai and the twins sat on the floor, stacking wooden blocks into towers and then knocking them down, while Iver paced up and down the hall. Each time the Mryken dogs passed, they would stop to listen and turn their heads. "What is taking so long?" Iver asked. "The twins came so easily."

Kai wished he could comfort his father, but he had no words. Every time that Mary came out to fetch something for Sigry, Iver would try to press her for details. The only words she would offer were, "These things take time, Your Majesty."

At one point, his father was tired of waiting, and he risked a look inside the nursery as Mary came out. Kai was not sure what his father saw, but he stopped asking questions and never went in again. Iver went back to pacing. At this rate, Kai was sure his father would wear a hole in the carpet. Eventually, he gave that up too and sat on the floor with the boys.

There they all sat huddled together on the floor, a father with his arms around his three boys. It warmed Kai's heart to have this time with his father. He was beginning to see that being a king—settling disputes, keeping the peace, and running a country—was stressful and time-consuming.

After what seemed like ages, Nola's cries finally stopped, and they were replaced with the short cry of a baby. All the men stood, waiting in anticipation. After what seemed too long, Kendra finally emerged. "Congratulations, Your Majesty, you have a baby girl. Mother and child are both doing fine."

Relieved, Iver knelt and wrapped his arms around all three boys. "Blessed be Alenga, the sacred mother, it's a girl. We have our princess, boys." He squeezed them so hard, and they all squealed to be free. "Kendra, may I go inside?" he asked wearily.

"Yes, sire, you may," she replied.

"Father wait," Kai called after him. "Does she have a name?"

Iver looked over his shoulder. "Her name will be Cordelia. Good night, son." Then he disappeared into the nursery.

The twins were now lying on the floor in the hall. Clearly, they were overtired. He too felt exhausted, but he stood there in a daze, unsure of his place. Before the door to the nursery closed completely, the other maid, Molly, stepped out carrying a pile of linens. "Kendra, Sigry is nearly finished. Mary and I remade the bed with fresh linens. I can come back once I take these to the laundry."

"Thank you, Molly, but you should get some rest. You can switch with me in the morning. I will see to getting the boys back to bed before returning to the nursery to relieve Mary." Kendra turned her attention to the boys. "Boys, why are you all still up? Let's get you back to bed. You need your rest. Kai, I trust you can find your own way."

"Yes, Kendra. Good night." Kai quickly scooted to his room and hopped into bed. Although he felt too excited to sleep, it didn't take long.

Kai woke exhausted. He could tell by the height of the sun he'd overslept. Several nights in a row staying up late to explore the secret passageways, and now the birth of his sister, was taking its toll. He needed a day with some fresh air, peace, and quiet, and he wanted to be alone.

When he finally made it to the kitchen, he could tell Lizzie was just finishing up from breakfast. He'd missed it. "Good morning, Lizzie. I suppose you've heard the news?"

"Oh, yes, dear. The entire palace is all aflutter with talk of Princess Cordelia. She sounds precious." She smiled.

"I am sure she is. Only now, well I hate to say, but when will they find time to spend with me? I remember when Seth and Aaron were born. I hope it is not that way for the twins." He felt a little sad, knowing everyone would fuss over the baby. "Lizzie, what do you think of Queen Nola?" he asked cautiously.

"Don't worry, honey. Your father loves you. Trust in him." She paused a moment. "Queen Nola, on the other hand… Well, you didn't hear it from me, but I don't trust the woman, not the way I did your mother. Something about her tells me she bewitched your father."

"I know I shouldn't say this," Kai whispered, "but she never leaves his side for long. When they are apart, he is more attentive to me and the twins, if you know what I mean."

Hands covered in flour, she dusted them off on her apron. "Here, honey, never mind me." She stepped around the table to grab a plate. "Sit, let me make you some food. I'm sure I have something that will make you feel better."

In a huff, he sat down. "Thanks, Lizzie. I'm sorry, I just woke up, and I feel miserable." Kai rested his elbows on the table and rubbed the sides of his head. "I didn't sleep well, and my head is pounding."

"Poor dear. I will be right back." Lizzie darted out the back door. She brought back a few small daisy-like white and yellow flowers. "Hold out your hand. This is feverfew; it will cure your headache." Kai slid his open hand across the table to her as she pulled off the little white petals and dropped them into his hand. "Now eat them," she insisted.

He pursed his lips as he brought his hand up to his mouth. He smelled a strong bitter, citrusy smell, and it made him turn his nose away. "Are you sure about this? They look like daisies."

"Yes, honey, I am sure. Working in a busy kitchen gives me plenty of cause for headaches. After enough visits to Sigry, he offered a plant for my herb box and instructions. You are about the same size as Tory, so I will give you what Sigry recommended for her. Don't linger on it. Just toss them in, chew, and swallow quickly."

Again, he lifted his hand to his mouth, and this time, he tossed in the flower petals. A quick chew later, he instantly knew why Lizzie said not to linger. "That is terrible," he said as he crinkled his face.

Lizzie handed him a glass of water and a piece of buttered bread. "Here, wash it down with this," she smirked.

He gulped down the water and tossed the bread into his mouth; it melted on his tongue, and he smiled. "Now, let me make you a proper breakfast. Plus, if you wait, I can send you on your way with some almond cakes once they are out of the oven."

"Lizzie, why don't you trust Queen Nola?" he asked softly.

Fear washed over Lizzie's face, and she sat down beside him to whisper near his ear. "Observe for yourself—her words, actions, and overall demeanor. When she came, you needed a mother, but she was not much of a mother. You and Agatha spent more time here in the kitchen than with her. The queen is always whispering and hovering. The king barely has room to breathe. I hear she has secret meetings with Regent Maxwell, but you didn't hear it from me. Besides, where did she come from? Your father loved your mother, and for him to take a new wife so soon... well, it's wasn't right. I feel it in my bones." Without another word, she stood and resumed her duties.

He ate, contemplating her words. It's was true—she was controlling. The queen hovered any chance she could. And she was very vocal about Aaron growing up into a position of power. How could he separate the woman who seemed to be kind with the person Lizzie warned was in their midst, possibly pretending to be good?

This had to be more than loyalty to his mother's memory. Although he knew first hand, Nola had a way of charming people, getting them to listen. He wished he understood more.

After breakfast, he made his way around to the courtyard with Smoke and over to the new bakehouse. Two men were going in and out carrying all sorts of metal brackets, long pieces of wood, and tools.

At the front of the bakehouse were two large openings, clearly meant to be windows once the glass was added. Kai stepped inside and admired the newly hung doors. The floor was made of smooth dark stone blocks, interlocked to create a zigzag pattern. Three of the walls were cream colored, but one wall was made from burnt red brick with two large ovens fixed with large metal doors. Most of the space was empty except for several metal brackets that had been attached to the walls.

Above him, he heard voices, so he called out. "Hello, Dean, are you in here?"

A voice from above shouted. "Prince Kai, come on up."

Kai climbed the small stairwell leading to the mezzanine and found Dean on a ladder installing some hooks into a large beam running the length of the loft. "I just came to see how things were going. Everything looks great. I love the large wooden beams and the metalwork."

"Thanks, lad," Dean said as he climbed down the ladder. "Please try to be careful. We've not added the railing on the edge of the loft or the stairs leading up here. Can't have you falling." He turned to a nearby carpenter, who was hoisting a ladder over his head. "Let's get the railing up next, then the shelves can be dropped on all the brackets. We'll have the loft finished by lunch." The burly helper grunted and marched down the narrow staircase, easily toting the hefty ladder.

"I hate to rush you off, but I've work to do and men to push about. Come back this evening, and I will have lots to show you." Dean picked up his tools and followed Kai downstairs just as two men came in carrying four long pieces of wood and several twisted black iron rods.

Kai stepped outside into the warm sunshine. Today would be the perfect day to go to Baden Lake; they could swim and watch the boats. At the first gatehouse, he noticed only a few people coming and going, but no carts. He would need to try something new. How about a direct approach? He walked straight up to the gatehouse, where he stood under the archway and opened the small pouch of cakes Lizzie had provided. "Hello, Wallis. Slow morning?"

The gate guard looked down at him. "Not too bad, but I think today is going to be a hot day. Probably one of the last." He spied Kai eating a small cake. "Is that an almond cake? One of Lizzie's almond cakes? Please tell me you have more."

Silently Kai snickered to himself. "Sure, would you like one?" He stood facing the road leading into the city and saw a group of soldiers riding toward them. He'd need to time this right if he were to make this work. He waited for Wallis to respond.

Wallis gasped. "Of course, I want one." Still trying to maintain his post, he watched the approaching riders without turning to face Kai.

Kai paused, waiting for the riders to get closer. "Well, I only have a few." He paused, popping another into his mouth. "I don't know. They are delicious," he teased as he continued to wait for the riders to get even closer. Wallis licked his lips, and Kai knew he had him.

Distracted by the delicious cake, he turned and looked down at Kai, who was still facing the road and the oncoming riders. "Come on, Your Highness, don't offer and then refuse."

Still, Kai held his ground, waiting. Finally, he replied. "You're right, here, have two." Slowly he handed Wallis one cake at a time, all the while watching the approaching riders.

Thrilled, Wallis popped one cake in his mouth and closed his eyes. Kai took the opportunity to step back against the stone archway just as the riders approached. Startled by the horses, Wallis popped the last cake in his mouth, looked up at the lead soldier, and mumbled, "Good morning, Amos. Your shift starts in about ten minutes, you'd best get a move on."

Blocked by the horses, Kai walked right out of the gatehouse and into the city with Smoke trotting behind. He made his way down the first side street, slowly zigzagging through the city, working his way to the next gatehouse. Fortunately for him, there was always a cart leaving the outer walls. Having found a reasonably large wagon with a covered tarp, he and Smoke hopped in. Right under Garrick's nose, they rode out of site along the northern road.

In the back of the cart, he finished the last of his almond cakes. Proud of yet another successful escape, he was thrilled to be free. Once the cart was out of view, he hopped out and ran through the woods toward Baden Lake.

The second he reached the shoreline, Smoke ran in and out of the water, and Kai pulled off his boots and clothes to go for a swim. Together they splashed around in the fresh water. As Smoke bounded through the water retrieving sticks, Kai realized just how much his wolf had grown—although he was still not quite as large as Shiva, his mother.

Ready to dry off, he stretched out on the warm rocks and enjoyed the apple still left in his pouch while Smoke rolled around in the grass. Across the lake, he watched fishing boats pull in their nets. Since the day was young, he dressed and walked through the woods before heading back to the palace.

He had not really spent much time exploring the woods alone. To get his bearings, he climbed a small hill and looked around. There were so many trees it made it difficult to see far into the forest, or up Thade Mountain. Kai knew Eagle's Peak loomed over Baden Lake to the east. In the distance, he could hear the trickle of a stream splashing against rocks.

Each step he took, he laughed—I've stepped on every stick along my path. The crunch of leaves and the snap of twigs echoed through the trees. At the top of the next hill, he could see down to the stream and was pleased he'd been able to find it. "Look, Smoke, we found it. I know where we are."

Together they ran down the two small rolling hills toward the stream. At the bottom, they hopped down the small slope to the rocks, and Smoke easily hopped across and jumped to the other side. As Kai stepped up on the first rock, his boot slipped just a little. He regained his balance and stepped to the next rock. The next step was over the water and looked farther.

He held his breath as he placed his right foot on the edge of the rock and leaned with his left foot reaching for the next. Halfway across, he pushed off with his right and landed safely on the other side. "Ha, ha. I did it!" he called to Smoke, who was up ahead through the first set of trees. With his eyes on Smoke, he confidently hopped to the last rock. Then he jumped down on the other side and fell into the loose leaves on his hands and knees.

Not shaken, Kai stood and brushed off his pants. Before he could take another step, a low growl startled him from behind. Fear rolled through his mind. He turned. A timber wolf stood atop the small slope on the opposite side of the stream. He had been utterly unaware of the wolf. It stared him down, bearing its teeth. It crept down the slope and onto the rocks and moved closer.

Smoke dashed back through the trees to stand in front of Kai, growling.

As he'd done with the palace guard dogs, Kai breathed slow and easy. He pushed a sense of calm at the wolf. The angry animal snarled. Its fangs looked sharp. The eyes were fierce and unyielding. It was not working. Kai's mind raced, and he felt the panic well in his chest. He was unable to calm the wolf.

Panicked, Kai wanted to run. Before he could think, he heard a man's voice. "Don't run, boy." Frozen in place, Kai stood stiff. "Step slowly backward and lean to your left... Call your wolf to follow."

Terrified, Kai heard his heart pound in his chest. He lifted his foot and took one slow step backward to the left, calling his wolf with his mind. "Smoke, come." Smoke still growled, but he stepped back with Kai. The wolf wildly hopped across the stream to the next rock, growling all the while. Kai took a second step, and the wolf lunged.

Kai turned his head away and raised his hands to cover his face. In his right ear, he heard an arrow whiz by his head, followed by a yelp and a loud thud. When he opened his eyes, he saw the wolf dead on the ground at his feet, an arrow piercing its chest. Smoke angrily barked and sniffed at the dead wolf.

"Come with me, Your Highness. Let's get you cleaned up before we take you back home." The man grabbed the wolf by its hind legs, removed the arrow and raised it up over his shoulder. "I'm Hunter Micha Marduk, I work for your father. You really should not travel into the woods alone unprotected at your age. If you come up here again, either bring a guard or become more aware of your surroundings. That wolf had been tracking you for a while."

Still in shock, Kai looked at the tall, rugged man. His dark, blond hair framed his face.

"You're alright Kai, come with me."

Focused on the kind blue eyes, Kai blinked. He could hardly think. Marduk rubbed his short stubbly beard and motioned up the hill. The pair walked silently through the woods with Smoke keeping pace behind them.

Hunter Marduk led him to a small clearing with a cabin, large fire pit, a barn, and a few small buildings. The first two buildings had taut lines connecting them—covered in animal skins. The third building had a large plume of smoke escaping from the top and smelled of meat. To the right of the cabin, there was a small barn with two white horses feeding on hay.

"Shane, can you come out here? We have a guest." The door to the cabin opened, and a young boy stepped out. He was the spitting image of his father, dressed in rugged mountain gear. There was a large hound dog with him. Paying no mind to Kai or Smoke, the dog picked a spot in the grass next to a large tree to lie down.

"Son, Prince Kai had a run in with a timber wolf. Make us some lunch while I tend to this wolf. Then we will walk him back home to the palace."

Kai stood there, staring at nothing, realizing he'd never thanked the man for saving his life.

Like his father, Shane had sandy brown hair and blue eyes. "Hello, my name is Shane. Nice to meet you, Kai. What's it like living in the palace?" the boy asked.

Brought back to reality, Kai stumbled through a response. "Oh, um, it's alright, I guess. There are a lot of academics most days, but occasionally I get time to explore the palace grounds, the city, and from time to time I go to the lake for a swim. Today I guess I just wandered farther into the woods than usual. Lucky for me, your dad came along." Still, in shock, he ran his hands over his arms and shoulders to calm his nerves.

"Tell me what happened," Shane asked intently.

Kai watched Shane prepare lunch. "I don't know, really. I was climbing over some rocks by this stream, as I jumped off the last rock I slipped and fell. When I stood to dust myself off the wolf growled at me. I just never noticed him, Smoke came in front of me. Smoke is my wolf's name.

"Anyway, out of nowhere, your dad shows up and tells me to step back, and the timber wolf jumped, and your dad shot the wolf with an arrow. It was amazing."

"Amazing, that's what you'd call it?" Hunter Marduk stood, blocking the sun from the doorway. He had one hand on the door, the other on the hilt of a large blade strapped to his waist. "Lucky is what I'd call it. You've no business being out here on your own. You've no sense of your surroundings, and you have no means to protect yourself." Hunter Marduk looked sternly at Kai.

In total shock, Shane motioned toward Kai. "Dad, do you know what you're saying and to whom?"

"Yes, I know exactly. All the more reason. The boy is a prince, and he knows nothing of being in the woods. In fact, why were you at the lake alone? This is not the first time I've seen you out of the city alone. Usually, you have a guard with you. Where is your guard today?" Hunter Marduk's eyes narrowed. "You think because you have that wolf, you're invincible?" Marduk's voice thundered louder and louder.

Kai sat there, afraid to answer. He was supposed to tell someone if he wanted to leave the palace, but having found a way around taking a guard, he'd gotten overconfident. He had not really thought about what could go wrong alone in the woods.

"Dad, please, he's upset. I am sure he didn't mean..." Shane said defensively.

"Ahh right, he didn't mean to get killed in the woods," Marduk shouted, pounding his fist into the table.

Kai jumped at the sound, and Marduk clenched his jaw.

Hesitant, Kai looked at the only man willing to stand up to a prince. "It's alright, Shane. Thank you, Hunter Marduk. I meant to say it earlier, but to be honest, I was at a loss for words. Thank you for saving my life. You're right. I was careless. I have been ditching my guards."

"You are lucky I happened along at the right time. I saw you come over the hill with your wolf. From a distance, you remind me of my boy, so I watched you for a few moments. It was then that I saw the wolf crest the hill not far behind you. I had to move quickly to get down the hill. I wanted to beat you to the stream. I figured that would be where the wolf would choose to attack you. I think your wolf was the only thing that delayed its approach."

For a few moments, they all sat around the table eating until Kai broke the silence. "How long have you lived up here? You seem well established... This is not a new cabin."

Marduk leaned back in his chair. "You're right, this cabin has been here for years. We've been here now going on five years this past spring. I rebuilt the barn and the smoker. The old man before us caught the smoker and the barn on fire one summer."

Looking out the window, Marduk realized the time. "We need to get going. I need to get you back to the palace and still have time to get us back home before sundown. Grab your gear, Shane. I'll close the barn and check on the smoker."

"Yes, sir." Shane attached his knife to his belt and picked up his bow and a quiver full of arrows, slinging them both over his shoulder. Outside they met Marduk as he let out a whistle for their hound dog, who trotted over to join them with

Smoke following behind.

All in line, they set out for the palace. The first thing Kai noticed was that they were taking a different direction back to the palace. They were not walking down toward the lake and the northern road. They continued to crossing hill after hill and stream after stream. As they crested the next hill, the trees began to thin, and he soon noticed the northern road coming around on their left and gatehouse up ahead.

When they reached the gatehouse, Marduk called to the guard. "Good afternoon, Garrick, just bringing Prince Kai back from a trip to the lake."

Garrick looked at Kai, cocked his head to one side. Kai knew he was surprised to see him outside the gates, especially once he noticed the prince had no guard. "Your Highness," Garrick said with a smirk.

CHAPTER 13

Real Proof

The first rule in accusing a person of a crime is to make sure you have proof to support your accusation. If that person is royalty, you better have solid facts, not subjective belief. Kai knew this as he wrapped his knuckles on the Master General's door and waited for a reply.

Riome answered. "It's Kai," she muttered, her eyes locked on the prince.

His cousin's voice echoed from inside. "We're all finished, let him in." The door swung wide, and Riome, Milton, Brannon, and Jarrod spilled out of the room. All dressed in black, all spies for Cazier. They glared at him as they departed.

Alone, Kai addressed Cazier. "I need to ask a question, in confidence. If I am out of place, I hope you can forget I even asked." He stood at attention like a soldier.

Cazier leaned back in his chair and gestured to the chair next to him. "I must stay I am intrigued, continue."

Nervous, Kai chose to stand. His observations of Nola worried him. Was Lizzie right, or did he see only what he wanted to see? His encounter with her in the nursery did not seem real. Her grip on his hand, the words she spoke, and the mind fog he experienced.

"I wanted to get your opinion about someone." He chose

his words carefully, not wanting to give the impression that his worries were not based on facts only the ramblings of a cook and a strange moment he could not explain.

"If I suspect someone of wrongdoing, how do I know if my concern is real?" There was something off about Nola, he knew it, as much as Lizzie felt it in her bones. "Someone told me… and I tried watching this person myself…" He'd said that all wrong.

"Well, you're clearly protecting someone and their second-hand information. Typically, my recommendation would be if you suspect someone has or is about to commit a crime come back when you have solid proof." Cazier looked sternly at him and then continued. "Tell me this: do you trust this other person giving you this information, and do you believe their suggestion has merit?"

Kai did not want to give a rash answer, so he took a moment to mull over the question. "There was a time, I would have said I trusted both the informant and the accused. No one has laid seeds of doubt in my mind—I have always felt there was something fake about the suspect and my own observances only confirmed their warnings."

Cazier nodded, and a smirk flicked across his mouth. "In your position, you have ample opportunity to observe. The young are often dismissed as distracted children, innocent and naive. I would like you to start spending time with Riome. There are tells people have when they are lying or merely hiding the truth. She can teach you to look for subtle clues, sense the tone of the room, and gather information without revealing your purpose. Her skill allows her to get information without ever speaking a word. Other times she must take a more…aggressive approach."

"You want me to become a spy? Yes, I would like that," he said with enthusiasm. To him, it had been an impossible dream.

Cazier chuckled. "A spy. Such a word." His expression turned serious. "Espionage is an art. The best start as young children. Riome was about your age when she started. She is actually the one who recommended you. She says there is something special about you."

Had Riome been watching him? He had always fantasized sneaking into castles, stealing secrets and evading capture. "Really? Why?" Kai asked, surprised.

"She said you notice things most do not. She did not elaborate, and I didn't question. I trust her judgment. Plus, as a king in a foreign land, you will need to discern friend from foe. This type of training will be beneficial."

"I agree. Milnos is so far from Diu, and besides Amelia herself, I've never heard of anything good about the country. Unless you consider it's formidable keep with iron clad walls and massive gate a good thing."

Adrian nodded. "I must also insist Professor Greydon expand on your Banglonese lessons. I know you've studied it in class, but I need you to become proficient with the accent, learn more than numbers and common phrases. If questioned, remind him of your future as the King of Milnos. Many there still speak it, and it would only be advantageous as a leader to know it."

"Yes, sir, I will ask tomorrow." Kai took the previously offered seat.

"Riome will teach you what she knows: weapons, hand-to-hand combat, and other implements of the trade. I will need to teach you our hand signals and our ciphers for sending coded messages. All this must remain a secret to everyone else. Yes, I want you to become a spy. There are secrets in Milnos, and so far, even my best, Riome has not discovered their truth."

A bit more seriously, Cazier leaned into him. "Now on the other matter at hand. Bring me proof or give me names, and I will set others to the task. Either way, our task is to protect the kingdom and our King, he comes first. Do you understand?"

Kai's smile slid off his face as he realized the gravity of

his situation. He held it tight in his mind—information was power—and he had to be careful what he did with it. "Yes, sir, I understand."

"Good, you can get started tonight. I will teach you how to decipher a coded message; you can practice here. Rule number one: never take messages outside of this office. Please don't practice creating any in your room. I burn them when I am finished. We never leave a note behind…ever," Cazier said firmly.

The Master General slid Kai a sheet of paper and three long slips of coded messages. "I have already translated these, and they are harmless. Now I want you to try."

Kai looked at the slips. Each one contained what seemed to be nonsensical letters, numbers, and shapes. "How? These are a mess. There are no real words here. Plus, there are symbols and numbers mixed in each line."

"Take the first strip. What shapes and numbers do you see?" Cazier asked.

"A triangle with a circle inside and a two on the end of the first line. The next line starts with a one, and it has a circle with an X inside."

Cazier smiled. "Good. That means the first line shift is ten letters, and the second line shift is three. The triangle is three, and the X is a ten." His cousin took a sheet of paper with the alphabet already written out and added a line of symbols with corresponding numbers. "Now decode all three. Let me know when you're done."

Kai sat there for a moment studying the gibberish, and he considered the hints Cazier had given him. Pen in hand, he set to decoding the notes. While he worked, he took a few moments to glance at Cazier, who was busy reading messages and writing letters.

This reminded Kai of his younger years, sitting in his father's study. It felt good to be here and work in tandem with his cousin. The last one was the hardest because it had ten lines, but he managed to finish. "I'm done," he said, sliding the paper back toward Cazier.

"Let's have a look." The Master General lifted the paper. "Looks good, Kai, well done." Cazier smiled, setting down the paper. "Now you need to memorize the symbols because not all messages come with cipher hints, and from time to time, we change the correlating numbers. Other things can be done to the paper or the style of the writing to tell you which cipher to use. We also use numbers for certain people, places, or actions that need to be conveyed quickly. I will teach those to you another time."

Cazier picked up the papers and handed them to Kai. "Now toss all these in the fire. Again remember, never leave any messages behind. It is better to destroy an unread message, then have it found by the wrong person."

"Yes, sir. I understand. May I be excused?" he asked, tossing the papers and watching them burn. "I should get back to my room before I am missed."

"That would be best," he said, shifting back toward his paper-covered desk. "Wait, one more thing. Be sure to take the stairs back to your room. I know you're coming through the secret passageways to get here." He grinned. "I had your bedroom back in the day. I am the one who left it open for you to find the other night."

Kai tried to keep his face composed, but a little grin slipped out. He couldn't help enjoying this secret with his cousin. Such an extraordinary man who made Kai feel important. "If you think it is important, I will. Should I always come up the stairs of the tower?"

"I am sending you that way because the others saw you arrive. They may be waiting to speak with me upon your exit. Or they may just decide to watch you, understand your reason for being here, as they know I will give them none. Once a spy, always a spy. I would advise using the stairs from time to time over the next several weeks. I will be sure the tower guards know you are privy to come to the tower."

"Thank you. Goodnight cousin."

Back in his room, Kai felt the need to sit with everything

he'd learned. He took a chair out onto his balcony. He relaxed under the stars before he closed his eyes and focused on his breathing. He took a deep breath and released it slowly, trying to feel each speck of air leave his lungs. He relaxed into the chair and let the day's events drift away into the night. Any thoughts that threatened his focus he released and refocused on his breathing.

Behind him, he heard a faint click and the whoosh of his bedroom door opening. With no sound from Smoke, he listened intently and realized Kendra had come in his room. She did not disturb him. He wondered for a moment why she'd come, but he let the concern go.

Again, he refocused his breathing and relaxed into the nothingness. Even though he was aware of the wind tousling his hair and caressing his skin, he continued to concentrate. He had been practicing, sitting longer and longer each night. Once he let go and stopped grasping at expectation, he found it easier to sit. His thoughts no longer jumbled about behind his eyes. He was comfortable in the silence. This peace took him deeper within, beyond his mind.

Focused deep inside, Kai felt his heart and mind connect. He sensed tremendous energy within. He felt his soul. As the moment built, he saw the light within him flow outward. His mind saw the world anew. His soul emanated in a wispy white form. Everything had a glow. The trees and the ground pulsed with life. Animals below, he saw them all. Birds in the trees, night creatures scurrying along the ground, men walking the perimeter—their wispy glows larger than their forms.

Behind him, he sensed Kendra sleeping on the sofa. A wisp of light, bright and robust. Her outline was very bright compared to the other men outside. Focused on her features, he noticed her face become clear. Bringing that same focus to mind, he was able to see the faces of the men below.

For the first time, he had achieved an open, clutter-free mind. *This is what it means to glean.* Threads of light woven into everything. At their core, they were all the same. Raw power molded into a shape. He let a smile creep around the corner of his mouth. Pleased with himself, he focused on the stars. They beamed with power.

A second click of his door handle opening broke his concentration, and he opened his eyes. Behind him, he heard tiny footfalls on the carpet, and he sat patiently as they got closer. "Kai, can I sleep in your room?" He heard Seth ask.

What had him up at this hour? "Seth, let's walk back to your room, and along the way, you can tell me why you are awake."

In the hallway, Kai noticed Yates walking toward them. "Is Seth alright?" Yates asked.

"He hasn't told me anything yet. Can you tell me why he is in my room, wanting to stay with me?" Kai held tight to Seth's hand.

"All I know is the prince came out of his room and went into your parents' room. When he came back out, he was crying, and he ran down the hallway. One of the Mrykens chased him. They were not aggressive, just curious why he was running and crying. I sent him into your room to calm him while I dealt with the dogs." Both Mrykens now sat at attention, focused straight ahead.

Kai looked at his brother, desperately clinging to his arm. Kai sensed the dogs were calm. "Seth, are you afraid of the Mryken?" he asked, kneeling beside him.

Seth looked at the large dogs. Their massive heads were eye to eye with his. "Maybe," Seth squeaked, leaning into Kai.

"Don't be afraid. The Mryken dogs are here to protect us. Your distress made them chase you. Understand their nature and purpose. They are extensions of the guards. Are you afraid of Yates?"

Seth's face brightened as he looked up to Yates. "Of course not. He's my friend."

"The Mryken are guards, too, only four-legged. They are the same. They cannot speak and ask you what you need. They must sniff and follow to learn. Do you understand?"

Kai reached forward, extending his open palm to the nearest Mryken. The dog lowered its head into Kai's hand. He gently ran his hand around the dog's face and over its ear. "Seth, now you try."

Seth extended his open palm to the Mryken and smiled as the dog lowered his head. "He does seem nice now."

Kai stood and looked at Yates. "Thank you, Yates, I will take him from here." Back at Seth's door, Kai noticed Seth staring at their parents' room. His brother's tiny hand gripped tighter around his and didn't relax until they entered the bedroom. "Can you keep a secret, Seth?"

In a small squeaky voice, Seth answered. "Yes. I like secrets."

"Sometimes at night, I wake up. I hear things. Since I am only half-awake, they don't always make sense to me. I find that if I talk with Kendra, she can help me make sense of things. Do you understand?"

"You want me to tell you what I saw, don't you?" Seth replied, climbing into his bed.

Kai pulled the covers over his brother. "I do. Only go slow and think of it as a picture book. You are retelling something from a book. Nothing can hurt you now." Kai tried to sound confident while Seth relaxed.

"Well, I wake up sometimes because Aaron snores and I thought I heard singing in the hallway. I went to check, and I heard chanting coming from our parents' bedroom." Nervously, Seth stopped and pulled the covers up to his nose.

"Remember, sleepy eyes can play tricks on us. It's alright, now." Kai lowered the blanket around Seth's chest and rubbed his hands gently with his own. "You're alright—I'm here."

Still, nervous Seth continued. "I went inside. Mommy was sitting on the sofa with father, holding his hand, and she was singing to him. When I tried to ask her if I could come in and sleep with her, she yelled at me." Again, tears welled in Seth's eyes.

Kai tried to soothe his brother by holding his hand while

he thought about everything he'd heard. He wanted an answer that would make sense to a little mind. "I am sorry you were afraid, and I am sure Nola didn't mean to scare you." He rubbed Seth's hand while he spoke and kept his voice calm.

From the corner of his eye, Kai noticed the light from the hallway waned. Someone had come into Seth's room. Thinking it might be Nola, he continued. "You know father has a lot of responsibility being a king. I am sure Nola was comforting him to help him sleep."

Seth's posture relaxed. "You're right, Kai. Mommy loves me. I probably scared her by coming in, upset."

"Exactly, she was just helping father. She has a lot of stress with baby Cordelia. Are you ready to go back to sleep now?"

"Yes, I think so. Thank you, Kai." A smile crept across Seth's face, and Kai felt a hand on his shoulder squeeze just a little.

"Yes, Kai, thank you. Wait for me in the hall while I talk with my son." Nola's voice sounded soothing in his ear.

Nervously Kai waited in the hall. His stomach twisted in knots. He did not trust the queen. The thought of being alone with her terrified him. *What could she get me to reveal? What could she make me do?* He feared observing her. There was a risk she would notice that she was losing his trust. At the very least, he knew he had to reassure her of his loyalty.

The door to Seth's room opened, and Nola stepped out. "Thank you, Kai, your words were very kind." Her eyes were soft but tired.

"It is good to see you are feeling better, and I was happy to help. I've had trouble sleeping most of my life—my father is lucky to have you." Kai reached to touch her arm, and she took his hand.

She rubbed the back of his hand in tiny circles. "I know I am not your mother, but you know I am here for you if you need me. We need to support each other." She looked deep into Kai's eyes. "Hear me, Kai. You must protect me."

Fog clouded Kai's mind. He'd felt this before—he should not have touched her. Alone she could say or do anything.

Nola sounded so reassuring, and Kai felt overwhelmed by her hypnotic tone.

"Aaron is our future; you must protect him at all costs." Trapped, he could not pull away. "I am your queen. Trust in me, confide in me. Tell me your secrets, Kai."

Her words felt like moles burrowing into his mind. Kai's insides squirmed. He knew he had to free his mind. Repeating his breathing mantra, he eased into a meditative state. The fog began to lift. Nola's words faded from his consciousness. The thump of his heartbeat drowned her compelling ideas, and his hand dropped.

He was torn between the mother he thought she was and this new duplicitous woman he found before him. "I will always protect you, Nola. I know you are here for me, and I am glad." He took a risk, stepping forward to hug her. She wrapped her arms around him, pulling him in tight.

"Goodnight, Kai," she said, releasing him. "You better get to bed, too." She ran her hand over his head.

"Goodnight Nola." He forced a smile and walked away.

Inside his room, he breathed a sigh of relief. He'd best not make that mistake again. With the warmth of his covers around him, he thought about his cousin's plan. Could he really become a spy and serve the Master General? The bigger question now was how he could find real proof the queen was trying to manipulate him and most certainly the king? Proof he could show. His word against hers was not enough.

Was this what he was meant to do? Questions exhausted what little energy he had left as he drifted off to sleep.

Once again, he was caught in a horror he couldn't face. Whenever he thought he was free, the nightmare returned— loud and intense and frighteningly detailed. Horrific sounds and vivid colors. His mother's face, there one minute, gone the next. The dragon's head loomed over him. He felt an unbearable loss. Again, he awoke, tortured by the death of his mother.

He hated his nightmares. Blocked by the mind of a child, he

was unable to comprehend the moment. There were times he wished he could see more, remember. Yet he was thankful his mind hid from him her final moments.

Stretched out on the floor, he joined Smoke lying in the moonlight that spilled through his balcony's glass door. Smoke's quiet breathing soothed his heart.

CHAPTER 14

Bonds Are Forever

The weeks of anticipation had been more than Kai could bear. He was up at dawn, pacing around the stables, nearly bursting with enthusiasm. Groomsmen Finlee and Weston offered him busywork while they finished preparing for the new arrivals. He gladly pushed a broom and folded blankets.

Normally new horses only came in the spring; however, today three new horses were coming into the stables, requested specially by his father. He only wished he could be down at the docks when the boat from Chenowith arrived. He'd asked Haygan if he could go, but he was told it would be unwise.

When Haygan crested the hill leading three new horses, Kai dashed in behind them with Smoke. Inside he watched Haygan take the measure of each new horse. The stablemaster checked their teeth before running his hands over their head, neck, and ears, and through their mane. Next, he went along the back of each horse, and down their back legs before putting them into the main paddock.

To get a better look Kai hopped onto the fence. Haygan smiled at Kai, eyeing the new stock. "Good morning, Prince Kai. What do you think? See one you like more than another?"

Haygan asked, nodding at the new horses. "Does one speak to you?"

Kai swung one leg over the top of the fence to study the horses. He was sure this was a test. After his bonding with Smoke, he knew today he would need to do something similar, but he was unsure how since he was not touching the horses. He looked at each horse and reached out with his heart to discover what they would share. After a few moments, he turned to Haygan. "I don't feel anything. Can I touch them?"

"You give up too quickly. Hop down, I will hold them while you get closer." Haygan motioned Kai over. "Just don't walk behind them. Which one would you like to look at first?"

Headed to the one in the middle, Kai pointed, "The chestnut brown with the black mane, please." He slowly approached the middle horse, held out his hand palm up, to allow the horse to sniff his hand. Then he turned it over to touch its soft nose, running his hand up the front of its head. Kai paused just between the eyes.

He stood there, sensing the horse, allowing it to see into his heart. In his mind, he began to picture riding him, the wind in his face. Again, as he'd done with his wolf, he opened his mind. *My name is Kai, I want to be your companion.*

In return, he sensed confidence, loyalty, and speed. In his mind, he saw himself sitting in the grass, leaning against a tree with Smoke by his side. Looking up into the star-filled sky, he saw the moon rising. In his mind, he saw his horse eating grass in the distance. As he observed him, Kai saw the cinders of his fire flash in the night ... and he heard the word *Ember*.

Thrilled, he stepped back with awe. "He is truly amazing."

"I am sure he is, but don't fall in love with the first horse you meet. Give the others a chance," Haygan insisted.

It didn't really matter, he'd already bonded. After spending time with each horse, Kai stepped back and leaned against the fence. "I think the best horse is the chestnut brown. If I could pick any horse, I'd pick him. He's perfect."

"Why did you pick him?" Haygan asked.

Kai wanted to be sure, so he looked again over all three. "He seemed to be the strongest in my mind, the most loyal. And he was the only one that seemed to reach back out to me."

"Well, in all fairness you spent the most time standing with him. So, I am guessing you bonded with him. What's his name?"

"Ember," said Kai proudly.

"Well, Your Highness, he is yours. Your father requested three new horses—one for Master Gideon, one to replace the horse purchased for Master Tolan—and he told me I was to get a horse for you. He believes it's time you had your own."

Surprise covered Kai's face faster than he could control it. "Father thought of me when sending for new horses?" he blurted.

Kai covered his gaping mouth as if he could wipe away the feelings before they were noticed. He took a deep breath and looked up at his horse.

Ignoring his comment, Haygan took the other two horses out of the paddock. "Ember is a good name. Grab one of those brushes. I need to teach you how to take care of your horse. Before you can ride, you need to brush out his coat. You want him to be comfortable because it means you will be comfortable."

"Isn't brushing a groomsman's responsibility?" Kai asked.

"It is their responsibility." Haygan's face became stern and serious. "Ember is your horse. Being privileged should not diminish your commitment."

Kai felt a little ashamed, thinking his rank was above hard labor. "I'm sorry. You're right. I can't take for granted the benefits my station provides."

With his hand over Kai's, Haygan put it on the back of the horses' mane. "Place one hand here on his mane, or here on the side of his neck. It will help keep him calm. Use the brush in your other hand, make long brush strokes along the grain of the horse. When you work with or ride a horse, they can sense what you are feeling. Their confidence comes from you, so there must be trust between you."

After brushing the horse, Haygan grabbed a brown leather riding saddle from the fence. "Grab a blanket from the crate," he instructed.

Kai approached with the horse with the blanket. The horse nuzzled and pushed him away. "Hey, why did he do that? I thought we were friends."

Nodding for Kai to try again, Haygan said, "You've got to earn his respect. You want him to be your horse, don't you? Well, you must prove. You must stand up to him, show him you are not afraid. Remain calm and confident."

"I can do that." Kai stood up tall and placed the blanket up over Ember's back, then Haygan tossed up the saddle and secured it in place.

Quick as anything, Haygan grabbed Kai by the waist and tossed him up onto the horse. Surprised to find himself in the saddle, he asked, "How did you do that so easily?"

Finlee escorted Misty into the paddock, a gray mare that looked like the morning mist in the valley. Her saddle already secured by the groomsman. Haygan climbed into the saddle and brought the horse up next to Kai. "Let's see how he handles. I will ride Misty alongside, you just keep pace with her."

"Can we ride out into the fields near the outlining farms to the west?" Kai begged.

"Not yet. I don't know yet if Ember is prone to spook. I've had no time to work with him yet. There are distractions enough in the stables and the training yard. I am not about to trust him with you in the open. We both know your father would have my head."

"I understand." Disappointed, Kai pushed forward slightly with his seat muscles and kept Ember even with Misty as they rode around the outside paddock. He wanted to argue; he'd been riding for two years now. Unfortunately, he knew Haygan was right. Kai had seen a horse spook at the sounds of the city and throw a rider.

Out of the corner of his eye, Kai caught Haygan squeeze Misty with his lower legs, right before she surged ahead. Mimicking the motion, Kai gave the same light squeeze, and pushed forward in his seat, encouraging Ember to burst into a trot. Beside Misty again, he settled back in the saddle, easing his horse's trot into a walk.

"I believe you are capable of testing Ember. Are you ready?"

"Me? Test Ember?"

"Time to practice your bond. Have confidence. It is the same as with Smoke. Trust him and yourself. Most of these tests can be done by any rider. I already have the groomsmen waiting. First, I want to see if loud noises will be an issue. If Ember bucks even in the slightest, I will stop the exercise."

Near the back of the paddock, Kai saw the men conversing. Haygan stood in his saddle, and the stablemaster pounded his chest with his fist twice. All three men mimicked the motion, banging their fists against blue and silver Diu shields, over and over. The clang of the metal rang loud across the open area, and Kai felt it pulse against him. Kai relaxed into the saddle and loosened the reigns. In his mind, he reached for Ember. *Stay calm.*

Ignoring the sounds, Kai turned Ember around the back end of the paddock. He focused on sitting square in the saddle. Maintaining his balance and looking forward. His calm demeanor washed over Ember. The pounding ceased when they made the second turn, leading back toward the stables.

Ember had done well. Kai felt a sense of pride well up in his chest. They had passed the first test. Remain calm amid chaos. Although he had seen this test done with other horses, this was the first time he'd been the rider.

Before Misty could surge ahead, Kai gave Ember a stronger squeeze with his legs, encouraging Ember into a trot. A second squeeze urged Ember into a gallop; Haygan and Misty kept pace. He felt alive as they lapped the paddock. Their pace was exhilarating. After the second pass, they eased both horses back to a walk.

Haygan motioned again as they rode toward the back of the fence. Kai noticed the groomsmen had spread out, two along the end, one around the side. Kai recognized the next test. Haygan pulled Misty to a stop away from the men.

"Again, remain calm for this test. Drastic changes in light can disorient both rider and horse. Your eyes will adjust faster than his. You must trust each other. The groomsmen need not know it, but you can try sharing your ability to glean, allowing Ember to see." Haygan gave the nod to the men and urged Misty into a walk.

The three men angled the shields. Bright beams of sunlight glared off the silver wolf design. They directed it at Kai and Ember; it was blinding. Unable to see, Kai closed his eyes and tensed his body. He pulled on the reigns. Below him, he felt Ember tense and pull right. Kai felt his leg hit Haygan's. They had collided with Misty. He felt Haygan's hand touch his leg.

"Kai, relax. See the paddock in your mind, listen to the sounds around you. Listen to the hooves beat against the ground. Trust Ember. Squint if you need to, most men do." Haygan's reassured him.

Ember's rocking motion calmed Kai. His body followed his horse's rhythm, and he felt Ember relax. Slowly Kai eased Ember away from Misty, her stride no longer guided them. Even with his eyes clamped shut, he could still see the sunlight blaze against him, and he sensed it hindered Ember's ability to focus.

He needed to see without his eyes. Kai thought of the threads of energy woven into the fabric of life. He needed to glean the world around him. As Kendra had taught him, Kai took a deep breath and cleared his mind. The sounds of the world faded. Within his soul, he sensed energy, he let the power build, and a wave of light flowed outward. Connected to the essence, Kai had a clear picture of the yard in his mind. The three men positioned around the fence glowed, but the reflected sunshine did not blind his mind.

He heard the beat of Misty's and Ember's hooves against

the hard dirt of the paddock. Their physical form pulsed with light. Kai was astonished that he could see each strand of hair on Ember's mane. Silky threads of light.

Confidently Kai made the turn at the back of the paddock and squeezed Ember with his legs, urging him into a trot. With his mind, he pushed his vision of the fence to Ember, and Ember made the second turn back toward the stables. When they passed the third man, the sunlight faded from his eyes. Pleased, he squeezed again, and Ember galloped around the yard.

Eyes closed, Kai noticed Haygan pull Misty to the center of the yard, waving off the groomsmen. Confidence surged through Kai into Ember. The bouncy rhythm of Ember's gallops warmed Kai's soul, and he felt their connection grow. Through their bond, Kai knew Ember could see in his mind what Kai saw in his. The open yard, the fence, and each barrel positioned throughout.

"Listen to my voice, Kai. Confident teams—rider and horse —rely on each other. Any rider can close his eyes and ride. They trust their horse to navigate through the blackest of nights. Horses see better than people. This is a good opportunity to build your bond. Don't worry about anyone watching us. This is common practice."

Pommel in hand, Kai steadied himself, directing Ember toward the barrels strewn through the paddock. Together they practiced switching between the different gaits and rhythms of each. After several switchbacks between the barrels, Kai felt the natural ease in which they blended together. Ember eased to a walk. Kai opened his eyes and rode to Haygan and Misty.

Kai felt alive. Connected. "That was amazing. In my mind, I could see everything, down to the smallest detail." Still reeling, he looked at Haygan. His look told Kai he too was proud.

"It's still impossible to understand." Haygan shook his head. "You, being able to see the ambient energy. I would never have believed it possible. You should see the real world in your mind, only with a bit of a glow. Everything with its own degree of brightness."

They both stared at each other. Kai pleased, Haygan bewildered. "How long have you been able to glean?" Haygan asked.

Kai thought back. "Only a few nights. Kendra doesn't know yet. She came to check on me and fell asleep on my sofa while I practiced. Baby Cordelia and Nola consume most of her time."

"Interesting. Very interesting. So much like Mariana..." Haygan mumbled under his breath.

"How well did you know my mother?" Kai wanted to know the truth. "Unlike Kendra, you won't speak of her. When she comes up, you close off and get quiet."

Haygan's face turned solemn. "You've done well today. I say we've done enough riding. We need to cool the horses off." Without another word, Haygan pressed Misty into a trot and rode to the gate.

Being brushed off hurt and confused Kai. *Why would Haygan avoid talking about her...unless? Unless they had been very close, and her loss hurt him a great deal.* Kai knew that it upset him to remember his mother was gone, so he let it go.

CHAPTER 15

Entitlement

Kai meandered across the courtyard, entering the back of the palace through the laundry. Inside he found Kendra collecting the day's wash.

Kendra looked him over. "Filthy day, I see." She looked down at his dirty boots. "Leave your boots. They can clean them for you tonight. I am sure you will want them back in the morning."

He untied the laces and realized his back was getting stiff. In the doorway, Kendra sniffed the air. "My, don't we smell of nature. Let's get you upstairs. You'll need a bath before joining everyone for dinner." Kendra leaned toward a young maid folding clothes. "Julia, please have hot water drawn in Prince Kai's bathroom."

"Yes, Miss Kendra," she replied before scurrying off out of sight.

With a huff, Kai dropped his shoulders and rolled his eyes. "Family dinner...tonight? I'm exhausted." He tried to dust off his hands on his pants and only succeeded in stirring up more dust.

When Kai walked past, Kendra got a renewed whiff, and she buried her face in the fresh laundry. Her eyes peered at him over the white linens. "Oh, my, you need a bath." Kendra gave a short nod toward the stairs. "Yes, you need to have dinner with your family tonight. I believe your father wants to talk to you."

A sense of dread welled up in Kai's throat, then he thought of Ember. He did owe his father a thank you. He silently followed Kendra to his room. As he slipped into the hot bathwater, it felt good on his sore muscles. Kai watched the steam rise above the water for a few moments, then he slowly slipped his head beneath the surface.

Before heading down for dinner, he took a moment. Outside on his balcony, he gazed over the city. Pinpricks of light dotted the hillside below. A chilling breeze blew announcing the change in weather. The air smelled of snow.

Dinner was the usual fair. All the adults sat around discussing matters of state and the pending winter festival, while the children kept quiet conversations with whomever sat near. He'd hoped to sit near Amelia, but she had taken to sitting with Tolan. The pair sat huddled together, whispering and laughing. Landon now sat alone, glaring at Tolan.

For Kai, it was all he could do to stay awake. Mostly he pushed the food around on his plate. He wanted to eat; he just didn't have the energy to bother. While most had finished and were now gathered around the fireplace visiting, he sat staring at his plate. Iver cleared his throat, and Kai looked up startled. They were alone at the table.

Iver put down his cup, leaned back in his chair and folded his arms in front of himself. "I spoke with hunter Marduk. Seems you've been out of the palace alone." He raised his eyebrows at Kai. "More than once."

With a look of concern, he tilted his head to one side. "Son, I don't like you going out on your own. You really should take someone with you. I know you're getting older and you think because you have your wolf you can go alone. I assigned a guard detail to you for a reason. You're a prince."

Kai glanced around the many faces trying not to eavesdrop; although he did notice Landon grinning from ear to ear.

Embarrassed, Kai wanted to shrink. He piped back in frustration, "But father, the guards never want to leave the city, the groomsmen are always busy, and Kendra no longer has time. I didn't mean to go that far. I am sorry. I won't..."

Iver held up his hand and motioned for Kai to stop talking. "I wanted to talk to you this morning in private, but you failed to show up at breakfast." The king glanced at Cazier. "Stop by my study after dinner, we will discuss this further." Iver turned to Cazier and began discussing other matters.

The walk to his father's study was agonizingly slow. He could tell by the document and map covered tables it had been a busy day. Dark circles under his father's eyes were something Kai was not accustomed to seeing. When Iver closed the door behind them a lump formed in Kai's throat.

"Let me get straight to the point son. There need to be changes. Cazier believes I have neglected your military training. Both he and I served, and it is simply expected of a royal. However, your mother wanted a different life for you. But since she is not here to advocate her position, it falls to me. To my recollection, she wanted you to be an ambassador.

"Your ruling in Milnos notwithstanding, the Grand Duke and Master General both think you should make trips each summer to our distant cities. You will travel with my authority to extend goodwill and represent the Galloway empire. This should provide a good foundation for your political education."

Kai could not believe what he was hearing. How could his father lay this burden on him? Still, his father continued. "To satisfy Cazier, I will allow him to arrange one-on-one training as he sees fit. I do not want you training with the other youths. They are often too harsh on a royal. Believe me, I took my share of hammering at your age to gain respect."

"Why all this now?" Kai tried to stand at attention. He knew his father was not pleased with his recent antics, but why did those choices have consequences now?

"I had hoped Smoke would teach you responsibility. I see

now he is not enough. Because you are a prince, you have certain luxuries; however, in turn, you have obligations. It is time you felt the other side of your birthright." Iver kept a stern face.

"Will you not go with me?"

"No." Iver held his head high. "I plan to resume my summer travels abroad. It has been a few years since Diu has made itself known outside of our continent. It is undecided who will travel with you beyond a guard detail. I will select a Kemperyman to lead, and he will select his squad. It is my hope that Marduk and his son will accompany you. Haygan the stablemaster could be useful. He sails back and forth to Chenowith's horse breeders quite often.

"These trips will be opportunities for you to establish your reputation. The friendships you forge over the coming years will benefit you in the future. These men and women will become your allies and advisors. Even the smallest gesture will solidify their opinion of your character. Choose wisely, my son."

"Do I have any say in my future?" Kai challenged. "What if I don't want to go?"

"Entitlement doesn't suit you, Kai. You can do better. What will be will be, only Alenga knows our fates. But unfortunately, duty commands you serve the people. This rebellious behavior has to stop." Iver clenched his jaw.

"Is that all?" Kai slumped his posture.

"One more thing. As I said, hunter Marduk informs me you have been secretly escaping the city. Since you seem determined to go, I believe you could benefit from a different type of supervision. I have asked Marduk to take you under his wing. His son Shane could use the companionship, and you could use a new perspective on the world."

That was the longest conversation Kai could remember having with his father in years. It was news to him that his mother did not want him to join the military. This explained a lot. All the other boys had started wrestling and archery, but not him.

Iver pulled two letters from the desk drawer and handed them to Kai. "One is for Marduk; to inquire about the summer trips. The second is for Professor Greydon, excusing you from class. I still expect you to excel in your studies, even with these new distractions. I have neglected you, I know; I hope this will get you back on track."

There was no doubt about it, life was about to change. Only Kai was not sure it was for the better. He took the letters. "Yes, father. I won't let you down." He straightened his posture. "And thank you for my horse. I spent today riding and learning how to care for him."

Iver stepped around his desk. "You're welcome, son. And tell those guards they are to accompany you wherever *you* wish. Be bold. Stand up to them. I will see about assigning you a Kempery-man to become your official guard. Where you travel, he travels."

"Thank you, father. Goodnight." Kai backed out with a nod.

Unable to sleep, Kai found himself wandering the halls. Voices echoed lightly down the corridor. Quietly he approached the corner. One voice he knew well: Nola. The other was a man's voice, not his father. Kai wanted to look, but he dared not risk being seen. He pressed his back into the wall and closed his eyes. In his mind, he reached for the light within and followed it outward. The palace walls came alive with illumination. Two faint wisps of light hovered around the corner. Kai focused on their forms. The smaller one was Nola. Her delicate form wrapped around a man. Fixated on the man, the face became clear—Lucas Maxwell.

No! Why would Nola be hugging this man? Kai edge closer to the corner. He wanted to hear what they were saying. He watched Nola release the regent, but her hands remained in his.

"Now is not the time. I need to discover where he is hiding it. How he controls it," Nola insisted.

"Right. Until we find a way around his dragon, we cannot

move against him," Maxwell seethed.

A dragon? Who's dragon? Kai was confused. Who could they possibly be referring to and why were they colluding together? None of this made any sense.

"Nola!" a man's voice shouted. "You would conspire with that man under my own roof? Take your hands off my wife, Maxwell."

Kai scanned the other end of the hall. Iver was storming in their direction. Nola dropped Regent Maxwell's hands and approached the king, her hands outstretched to greet him. "My darling," she soothed. "I'm merely assuring him for the future of our two kingdoms through the match of our children. Promising him of his daughter's happiness." She took Iver's hand in hers, and the king's expression softened instantly.

Maxwell bowed and ventured away. Realizing he was now in the regent's path, Kai searched for a place to hide. He ducked into an alcove, a small reading nook with tall wingback chairs and plants. Kai pressed his back into the stone archway behind the column, hidden in shadow as he waited for Maxwell to pass.

Maxwell's energy wisp descended the stairwell out of sight. Around the opposite corner, Kai noticed Nola and his father were gone. Satisfied it was safe to come out of hiding, he stepped into the dimly lit alcove. "What did you learn?" He heard a voice whisper from the shadows.

A face emerged from behind the opposite stone column— Riome. Dressed in all black, hair pulled into a tight bun atop her head. He studied her expression. She gave no hint of her own observations.

"Nola is meeting in secret with Regent Maxwell. Maxwell mentioned a dragon and moving against someone. I can only speculate on who they mean, but..." Kai hesitated to reevaluate his assumptions and fears. "This doesn't make any sense. Why would she plot against my father?"

Riome nodded. "Leave this with me, I will speak with Cazier. You did well, listening and hiding." She turned to go but stopped. "Next time be sure you're the only one listening."

CHAPTER 16

Thade Forest Burdens

Excited by his day with Shane, Kai grabbed the two letters from his father and scrambled downstairs. The first letter he dropped off to Professor Greydon, excusing him from class. Then he headed down to meet Shane and Marduk in the courtyard.

"Hello Hunter Marduk," Kai said as he approached. "Thank you for speaking with my father. I am excited about my day. Marduk, this letter is for you."

"Yes, well…do not be too excited. It won't be easy, and it's not meant to be fun." Marduk stuffed the letter into his coat pocket. "I need to go see the blacksmith. I will catch up with you two at the stables."

"Shane, you have to meet my horse, Ember." Kai ran to the stables.

Shane chased after him. "When did you get a horse? I was only gone a day."

"Yesterday three new horses arrived. One of them was for me, and I got to pick him." Totally elated, he started walking again. "And now I am going to spend the day with you and your father. Today will be exciting."

"I bet it is difficult, your lack of freedom. I wouldn't want to be trapped in the city. Although I don't go far without my dad, I still have a lot of independence. We used to live in Nebea before my mom died, but we were well outside the city."

Kai looked sympathetically at his new friend. "I'm sorry. It's hard losing a mother. What happened? If I can ask?"

Shane winced. "Right, your mom…sorry I have heard the stories. My mom died in childbirth when I was eight. My baby sister died too. It was hard at first, and I still miss her. I think that is why my dad decided to move here. To get as far from our life with mom." Motioning toward the stables, Shane asked. "Who's the warrior talking with Haygan?"

The broad-shouldered man in black wore a large hunting knife strapped to his hip and twin double-sided battle axes across his back. Although he had the same olive complexion as Haygan, this man's hair was long and black, and he was clean-shaven.

"I wonder if it would be alright if we went over to say hello," Shane asked.

"Sure, why not. Any friend of Haygan's should be a friend of mine. Let's go find out who he is." Kai bolted toward the stables.

Haygan nodded in their direction, and the stranger stared at them. His gaze froze the boys in their tracks. Kai noticed a jagged scar across the bridge of the man's nose and right cheek. Haygan clasped forearms and pulled the stranger into a quick shoulder hug. With a slight nod, they split and walked in opposite directions.

Able to move, Kai and Shane closed the distance between them and Haygan. "Good morning, Haygan," Kai said. "Who was that? Is he from Katori?"

Haygan crossed his arms. "Yes, he is from Katori. He's a good friend. We had news to share with each other before he left on a long journey."

Kai's eyes continued to follow the man as he walked toward the gatehouse. "He seemed…intense. What's with all those weapons? I thought the Katori were peaceful people now, not warriors."

"Yes, Ryker is intense. Great man, though. I'd trust him with my life. He is searching for someone, and he's asked me to do him a favor when I return home for the winter." Haygan turned back toward the stables.

Realizing what he'd heard, Kai whipped his head around. "Winter? Home? What do you mean home for winter?"

Headed inside the stables Haygan motioned for them to follow. "I leave in a few weeks on a ship out of Port Anahita to go home for the winter. I have obligations and people in Katori. I will return with new horses come spring. Spending winters at home was the deal I made when I accepted this position back in the spring."

Stunned, Kai was at a loss for words. Looking down at his hands, he remembered the two apples he had brought for the horses. Misty whinnied as he laid his hand open for her, and she eagerly took the apple. Two stalls down he offered Ember an apple. Kai ran his hand down Ember's neck to his withers. He wished he had more time for him today.

He wished a lot of things really but now was not the time. He was trying to flow with all the changes in his life, hoping he could keep pace. *See you tomorrow, Ember,* he thought through their connection.

Marduk exited the blacksmith and approached the court-yard. "Let's go, boys. We're all ready. We need to stop by the stables and borrow Shiva. Haygan has offered her help to teach Smoke what he should be doing for you."

Marduk led the way through the city. Outside the walls, Kai saw the Thade Forest trees were almost bare. As they entered the woods dried leaves crunched beneath his feet. Smoke and Shiva wormed through the undergrowth.

"First, we need to move through the woods in silence. Silence allows us to be aware of what's around us. I would like you to look for signs of animals. Step quietly, learn to listen beyond the sound of your own feet. Get to know the forest. Remember where holes, rocks, and embankments are should you find yourself traveling at night.

"Now for your wolf, it's time he did his job. By your side is not his place. He is a wild animal, and you're holding him back by keeping him so close. Shiva, go!" Marduk pointed up ahead. "Now send Smoke with her. Let him go."

"Smoke, go," Kai motioned, in his mind and felt his wolf connect with him.

Both wolves trotted ahead, and Kai watched them go. "What is his job, if not to be by my side?" he asked.

"His job is to scout ahead and then circle around behind. Hunt and protect. He is a wild animal—he needs to be wild. He uses his senses to become aware of what is around him and what is around *you*. He must learn what dangers are out there and how to fight them like a wild animal. Then he can protect you, just by his presence, by intimidation or fighting."

Between a cluster of trees, they jumped down an embankment. Kai was careful not to slip on the wet leaves. The smell of damp earth filled his nose, and he heard splashing water from a nearby stream. The chirping of birds echoed through the trees. While they walked, he heard sounds he never noticed before.

Eventually, Marduk found a rabbit in one of his small traps. "Kai, I want you to watch how I reset the trap. We will spend a good part of the morning checking and resetting all the traps. By the end of the day, you will know how to do it as good as Shane."

As the hunter reset the trap, Kai watched. "How do you know where to place your traps?"

Marduk stood and handed the rabbit to Shane. "We place our traps near their water source." He pointed to the embankment. "See the tracks and small paths where animals have repeatedly come to the river? Animal signs help me decide where to place a trap."

Marduk spent hours checking and resetting traps, and then they crested the hill to the huntsman's cabin. "Boys, take everything you're carrying to the shed. Be sure to close the door, and we will have lunch."

After lunch, Kai stepped outside to sit on the edge of the porch next to Smoke. He ran his fingers through the wolf's thick black hair. Behind him, Marduk stood with his hand on the railing and looked out across the clearing. "You ready for the next part of your day?"

"Yes, sir, what's next?"

Shane stepped out of the cabin. "Shane, hang today's catch. I'll be right there once I split the last of this wood."

Shane hopped down all three steps in one jump and ran around back. Marduk handed Kai a pair of brown leather gloves. "These are Shane's gloves. I need you to stack all of the wood I've chopped. Stack it on this side of the cabin. I have a bit more to split before I help Shane. When you're done, collect any small branches and kindling around the cabin. It goes there."

Kai looked at the pile of wood, and then over to Marduk. "Um, yes, sir." Not wanting to question, Kai proceeded to spend the next two hours stacking wood, collecting all the small branches around the cabin for kindling and placing it in neat piles. Finished, he found Shane and Marduk still working out back skinning the animals from the morning's traps.

Looking up, Marduk smiled. "All finished? Great. I have something else you can do. Shane, you can help, follow me."

Wiping his hands on his smock, he stepped between the two boys. He let out a loud whistle, and his hound dog came running, followed by Smoke and Shiva.

Behind the property, they walked deep into the woods. Kai observed everything as they walked down the hill. They leaped over hollow logs, weaved through trees, and crossed a small creek. Near a rocky cliff, Kai saw a pile of rubble. Above them, he could see the small ridge where the rocks had fallen.

"I need these rocks brought up to the stables. You won't be able to finish today, just move as much as possible and don't worry about the ones that are too big to carry. I need to cover the back of the stables before winter to help hold in the heat. Keep the hound dog with you, but let Shiva and Smoke wander. You two keep an ear out for animals in the area."

Marduk bent down, picked up a couple of rocks and waited for them to follow suit. They trampled back to the stables and Marduk set his stones down. "Place them along here. I will go finish in the shed."

Silently the two boys walked back to the rubble pile. Kai looked down at the rocks and then back toward the hill. "Forgive me, but how is this helping me learn how to hunt?"

With a small smile, Shane ignored Kai and grabbed two rocks. As they walked back, he finally responded. "There is much to learn. It is not just about setting traps and hunting animals. As dad said, he is teaching you how to be in the woods —quiet, observant, and ready. On our walk today, we saw rabbit, deer, bear, and fox tracks. What we did not see were mountain lions, wolves, big horns, cougars, and moose." Shane dropped his rocks and headed back down the hill.

Reluctantly Kai followed. When they reached the pile again, he paused. "That part I get, learning the woods, where the creeks and streams come together, and knowing which way is north." He grabbed another rock. "But what does stacking wood and carrying rocks have to do with anything?"

Shane turned to Kai. "No offense, but you don't get it. You don't know where they live, how they hunt, and if they are a threat. And honestly, you are rather…weak to be in the woods. Please don't be mad. It is just a fact. I like you. I want to be friends and friends are honest."

Mouth agape, Kai stopped. "What do you mean I'm weak?" Shane hadn't stopped, so Kai ran to catch up. "Well?" he questioned, tossing his rock on the pile.

Shane dropped his head and looked at his feet. "Let me be honest with you," he said, looking back up at Kai. "I spend my days tracking, hunting, resetting traps, skinning, and cleaning our stables. Half that wood pile, I chopped. I work hard every day. You spend your day reading books, playing in a park, and walking around the city. Hard work will help you build your stamina and grow strong." Shane motioned toward the bottom of the hill. "Come on, let's keep going."

Watching Shane walk in front of him, Kai wanted to be mad. He wasn't weak. Was he? All the way down the hill, he didn't say anything. They continued transporting rocks in silence. Still wounded by Shane's words, Kai bent to grab another rock. A loud thump thundered on the cliff above them; leaves fell from above. Somewhere to the right of them, he heard Smoke and Shiva let out a low growl. They'd heard it too. The hound dog sniffed the air and began to bark.

"Did you hear that?" Kai asked.

"I did." Shane backed away from the pile, scanning the ledge above. "There, do you see them? Grizzly bears. My father and I saw them a few days ago near the river. A mother and her two cubs. Kai, we need to go. That slope will bring them right down in our direction."

Shane dropped his rock, took his fingers, placed them in his mouth and whistled. Shane yelled. "Run. Run for the cabin," Shane shouted already in motion.

Kai heard the rustling leaves. Then a large dark mass followed by two smaller shadows strolled through the trees. Smoke and Shiva converged on his location. Kai calmed his breathing. With a thought, he instructed the wolves to stand firm. Without a sound, Smoke and Shiva were poised to lunge, their hackles raise into razors down their backs.

In his next breath, Kai searched his soul for the light within, let it build and flow out to illuminate the forest. The wave washed over the three bears; their essence bloomed with life. With a thought, he sent a feeling of peace into their minds. They continued to move in his direction. He felt their wild nature in his mind. The mother spotted him, and he felt her tense.

Eyes open, he could see them both with his natural sight and the highlights of energy through gleaning. They walked straight towards him. He kept calm. The grizzly sow glanced at her trailing cubs. Kai again offered peaceful thoughts, suggesting she pass him to go down the slope. He knew it was against her nature to come closer to him. His wolf guardians were as large as she was, and she would normally perceive them as a threat. Kai offered assurance that she was free to pass.

Kai took a step back and instructed Smoke and Shiva to do the same. Without challenge, they did as he asked. The bears progressed. When they reached Kai, the mother bear huffed. Kai felt her relax as they meandered down the slope. Pleased, he watched them disappear into the trees, gone from view.

Behind him, on the hill, he saw two wisps. One was bright—he focused on the energy and Shane's face became clear. The second was not as bright—Hunter Marduk. They stood at a distance in the trees. Kai gulped. He'd made a mistake by using his powers. But he couldn't help his desire to try again on a wild animal.

He turned to face them. They had seen and would now have questions. As he approached, Marduk stood with one arm across his midsection and the other grasping his mouth. Shane gawked in awe. There was no easy explanation for what he'd done—what they'd seen.

Together they stood in awkward silence. Nobody was willing to say the first words. Shiva and Smoke patrolled around them. Marduk cleared his throat. "That was foolish, Kai. You could have been hurt."

"How?" Shane interjected. "How did you do that?"

Shane's eyes were wild and confused. Before Kai could respond, Marduk answered. "Kai is like your mother—Katori. It was foolish of him to use his gifts in front of us. Now, my son, we bear the burden of knowing and keeping Kai's secret."

Marduk was right. Kai was foolish, and they were now at risk for just knowing. "I am sorry." Kai looked at them both. Marduk's hard, unforgiving glance told Kai all he needed to know. The man was angry for the reminder of his lost wife and the Katori burden he and his son now had to carry.

"As for the grizzly bear and her cubs, we need to be aware that this is a route she plans to take her cubs. Keep an eye out for them and stay clear when they pass. No more heroics Kai. We are not the only ones who hunt on the mountain." Marduk turned and walked back to the smokehouse.

Stepping between the two boys, Marduk motioned, "I think you've both done enough today. Let's get you back to the palace; I want Shane and me home before dark."

Shane collected his things and fell in line beside his father. Marduk motioned toward the woods. "Lead the way, Kai. Let's see what you remember."

Confident, Kai started down the hill. Before long he recognized a few rock formations and a tree bent at an odd angle. He turned toward a rotten stump. The farther down the hill they went, the louder the sounds of water echoed about the trees.

When he came to the slope leading down to the large creek, he smiled. On the way back, he looked for landmarks to guide him until he saw the palace walls through the trees. He had done it.

Inside the second gatehouse, he turned to Marduk and Shane. "Thank you. I hope I am still welcome. Besides, Shane and I still have a large pile of rubble to move."

Marduk put out his hand to Kai. They shook hands. "You are always welcome, Prince Kai. I am very proud of how you handled yourself today. Only be more careful. Not everyone would be as understanding. And many would take advantage." Marduk gave a wave to the guard and headed back through the gatehouse.

Kai headed for the stables with Smoke and Shiva by his side. Haygan was standing outside talking with Finlee and Weston. "How'd it go?" Haygan asked.

He didn't dare tell Haygan what he'd done. "It was a long day. They are good people. I am lucky to have them around me. Shiva spent a lot of time in the woods with Smoke. I hope he learned something today, given most of the time, they were circling the perimeter around us."

"It would be a good idea over the coming weeks to let Smoke out of the city with her," Haygan suggested. "Especially overnight before I leave."

Kai wanted to say no; he liked having Smoke nearby. He trusted the nature of animals over most people. But Smoke was a wild animal, and if he was to serve his real purpose, he needed training. "Let me know what nights, and I will send him to you."

"Why not start tomorrow night? Let him rest tonight, and they can go out every other night until I leave."

"That often?" Kai asked in surprise.

"Yes, that often. Smoke will be fine. It will be good for both of you. I will keep an eye on them the first night, don't worry." Haygan assured him.

Again, Kai wanted to protest, but he knew Haygan was right. "Alright. Can we go riding tomorrow?"

"Certainly. I believe Amelia and Tolan are also going for a ride. You are welcome to join us, or I can send Bram with them. We can go for a ride just us."

Kai thought about his offer. "Since you only have a few weeks before you leave, I want to spend as much time together as we can, if that's alright."

"I will speak with Bram about escorting Tolan and Amelia. Also, I think you should start running regularly. It would be good for you to build up your speed and control. You can run the inside perimeter of the wall—tomorrow."

Kai nodded in agreement.

CHAPTER 17

Who's That Girl?

Kai had been dreading this day. Winter was nearly here, and Haygan was leaving. Across the courtyard, he noticed Shane and Marduk approaching on horseback. The huntsman's horse was pulling a small cart. Inside the stables, guards loaded saddlebags. Finlee and Weston helped saddle the horses.

In the back of the barn, he saw Haygan pull out his black stallion. How would Kai manage the next three months without him? Over the past few weeks, they had spent every day riding, working in the stables, or running together. He wasn't ready for him to leave.

Arms crossed, Kai kicked the ground with his boot. "Good morning, Haygan. Are you ready to leave?"

"Nearly ready. How are you feeling after yesterday?"

Kai thought about it and realized he felt good. "This is the first morning I don't feel sore." But he was too disappointed to be happy, so he said, "I wish you weren't leaving. When will you be back?"

Haygan looked at Kai. "As I mentioned before, I will not return until spring." He placed a hand on the prince's shoulder. "You need to continue riding over winter. Please ask Weston or Finlee to help you and take a guard if you leave the city without Marduk."

With a nod, Haygan gestured toward Ember. "I believe he's trying to get your attention—or at least get that apple."

Kai looked at the apple in his hand. He held up the apple to Ember and ran his hands down his long neck, unable to shake how he felt. While he had other friends, it wouldn't be the same without Haygan and Shiva.

Unexpectedly, he heard Shane call him. "Kai, what are you doing today?" Wagging his eyebrows, Shane smiled. "Saddle up! We're going to Port Anahita this morning. Dad has more furs for your uncle Kaeco, and we need to pick up supplies like salt and oil before the snow comes."

Ecstatic, Kai ran to the tack room, along the way he grabbed Finlee to help him. This is going to be a great day, he thought. Brush and blanket in hand, he waited for Finlee to pull Ember from his stall. As he started to brush Ember down, out of the corner of his eye, he saw Hagan motion for him to step outside.

"You better get permission for the trip. I am sure Marduk has asked if you could go; however, out of respect, you need to ask your father. I need to speak with Dante about what he needs in spring for new dogs and horses. Hurry up, we need to get going! I don't want to miss my ship."

Fear welled up in his throat as Kai approached his father's study. His father stood between Cazier and Kempery-man Henley as they rifled through large maps on the corner table near the bookshelves. As Cazier tried to slip around the table, he looked up at Kai waiting in the doorway. Glancing from the table to the wall, he smiled and pulled it away from the wall.

Well, that's convenient, Kai thought. As he entered, Cazier nodded toward the door, and Iver turned. "Son, come in. We are looking over the maps discussing a new outpost near Milnos. Join us." Iver beamed with pride as he motioned Kai over.

With hesitation, Kai approached the table. "Actually, father, I wanted to get permission to ride with Hunter Marduk, Haygan, and Shane to Port Anahita." Worried he'd disappoint his father by not staying, he interlocked his fingers behind his back and looked down at the maps.

Iver clapped a hand across Kai's shoulder and smiled. "Is that today? Marduk mentioned the trip a few days ago. I had been waiting to speak with you. I have some letters for Kaeco, would you mind delivering them for me?" From his desk, Iver grabbed three letters and handed them to Kai. "How many guards are going with you?"

Shocked, he glanced at Cazier, who motioned him forward with his eyes. "Thank you, father. Yes, I would be happy to deliver your letters. I believe four guards are going."

The king addressed his Kempery-man. "Henley, since my son's taking his first trip to Port Anahita, I want you to see to the arrangements. Ensure that four designated guards are going both ways. Also, I want Kempery-man Dresnor, Albey, and Redmon assigned to my son going forward. Return when you're done." Then his father placed an arm around Kai's shoulders. "Have a good trip, son. I wish I could go with you, but duty commands my presence here."

"Thank you, father. I will see you this evening." He was so thrilled he could hardly stand still.

As the large group rode out of the southern gatehouse, Kai sat tall and proud in his saddle. He had been placed in the middle of the group, between Haygan and Kempery-man Dresnor. "How long will it take us to get to Port Anahita?" he asked Haygan.

The stablemaster scanned the road ahead. "On horseback at a quick pace, about two hours. But with Marduk pulling a cart, and the additional supply cart Captain Henley is sending to Kaeco, it will be four hours. Still enough time for me to catch my ship."

Feeling his heart jump, Kai's eyes doubled in size. "I've never ridden that long."

Shane let out a small chuckle ahead of Kai. "And that's one way. We still have to ride back," he said, shifting in his saddle to look backward. "Dad and I have made the trip in a little over three hours pulling our cart. We should not slow you down."

Then it dawned on Kai. "Can Shiva and Smoke really manage such a long trip walking?" He stretched his neck to find them ahead of the group.

Still scanning the area, Haygan replied, "They'll be fine. It may be hard on Smoke by the trip's end, but wolves can travel about forty miles or more in one day. We are going about twenty five this morning. We will stop twice to water the horses and take a break."

By the time they reached their second stop, Kai was quite happy to hop down and stretch his legs. He sat in the grass and rubbed Smoke's thick black fur, watching a cloud bloom across the pale-gray sky. The brisk wind whipped around him and he felt a bite in the air he'd not noticed earlier.

From the road, Shane approached the horses. "Time to go, mount up." With help from Haygan, he hopped back in the saddle. Again, Kai folded into the center of the group, and everyone rode on in silence, allowing the guards to survey the area and take their places around the group.

Breaking the silence, Haygan cleared his throat. "I wanted to talk to you about next summer. The Master General spoke to me about your trips around Diu. Your father made these trips when he was young. As I understand it, no one has been tending these towns over the last five to ten years. He wants you to learn the Diu territory and meet its people. You will travel to cities on the far side of Baden Lake."

Kai thought about the idea of spending his summers traveling. He knew it was a typical role for a prince, but he never thought he would be asked so young.

"While it would be easy to take a boat across the lake and we'd be to any city of our choosing," Haygan continued, "you need to be saddle ready for longer trips. It has been years since Iver has made time for some of his people, and you need to make yourself known. Earn their respect and offer aid where you can. Obviously, this is in preparation for when you move to Milnos."

Lost for words, Kai did not respond. He tried to process everything. Every time he went to speak, nothing came out. More thoughts came into his head. Sleep outside. Summer-long trips. Lead people. Move to Milnos... *I'm not ready!* His mind was spinning. Now he knew how Gideon felt.

Being adventurous sounded exciting when it was someone else. Now Kai owed his cousin Gideon an apology. Slumped in the saddle, he stared straight ahead. "Milnos. It takes over two weeks to get there. What are they thinking? I am not ready to..." Overwhelmed, he cut himself off.

Then he started again. "This is all too much. The bonding, weapons training, studying maps, language lessons, cipher codes, and gleaning...I just can't," he responded sharply.

Haygan held his hand out in Kai's direction, patting down the air. "One step at a time. I know change can be overwhelming. And at your age, things physically and mentally begin to change." He waited a moment for Kai to breathe easier before he continued.

"We'll be in Diu territory, camping on the far side of Baden Lake one night, maybe two. Cazier has recommended a few sites we can stop along the way. Most of the time, we will be within a small estate. Each summer trip we will go a little farther around the great lake. I have much to show you. And most importantly, we aren't going tomorrow."

"Who would be going with us?" The tone of concern in Kai's voice revealed his apprehension.

"Like today, we would have your Kempery-men, scouts, and guard escorts. Cazier said Hunter Marduk and Shane will go with us." Haygan answered.

As the idea began to settle, Kai found it easier to breathe and started to sit a little taller again. Craning his neck, he could just see the horizon. The sky came down to press against the dark blue sea. Cresting the hill, the full breadth of Port

Anahita city came into view.

His mind exploded with wonder. The last time he'd visited his aunt and uncle, he'd been six and he'd ridden in a carriage. Thinking back, he'd slept the entire way. He had never seen the view from this hill. The town was a mix of white, pink, and yellow homes with flat roofs.

At the stables, they were greeted by the local stablemaster. Marduk offered the man money to tend their horses.

After a quick goodbye, Haygan made straight for the coast with his horse to board a ship. Marduk and the boys walked the city in route to Kaeco's office near the docks. Along the way, they purchased candles, honey, lamp oil, and salt. At each stop, Marduk sent his order back with one of the guards.

Around the center of town, they passed a park and Kai looked down at Smoke. "I wish we had time to play." Kai's hand drifted across Smoke back.

Two buildings away from their destination, they stopped. Two men exited a store, and the smell of freshly baked bread spilled out into the street to fight with the salty air. Both boys stopped to eye the toasty brown loaves on display in the window. They licked their lips and pointed to the tasty treats. Hunter Marduk joined them. "I brought some dried meat and cheese for lunch. What do you say we get freshly baked bread too?" He grinned.

Smiles crossed both of their faces. "Yes, please," they said in unison.

Inside the small shop, they were overcome by the warmth from the ovens. Behind the counter, a short woman kneaded the dough into small round balls and then placed them on a rack under a towel. Her auburn hair twisted into a round bun on top of her head. Her round pale white face lit up when she spotted them. "Rayna, we have patrons, please see to their needs." The woman nodded in their direction.

As if by magic, a young girl popped up from behind the counter in front of them. "How can I help you today?" She smiled.

Caught in her honey-brown eyes, Kai stared at her across the counter. She had long brown hair swept neatly to one side and tan skin.

Marduk stepped forward. "Hello, dear. I'll take three round loaves. Please split one three ways, if you don't mind. Thank you."

Looking past the young girl, Marduk addressed the woman. "Hello, Dori. Where is Levi today?"

While the young girl went to split the bread, her mother collected two other loaves and placed them into a small cloth pouch. "Levi is busy packing up our home—we are moving into the palace bakehouse, you know." She helped the young girl place the three pieces into a pouch and handed it to Marduk.

"That's right, we'll be seeing you lot at the palace very soon." Marduk handed her a few small coins and smiled. "Thank you for the bread, Dori."

"Always happy to serve you, Marduk." Dori waved and turned back to her work.

As they all turned to leave, Kai continued to gawk at the young girl and stumbled into the back of Shane. "Oh, sorry. I didn't see you." A bit embarrassed, he stuffed his hands in his pockets and shuffled out the door.

Shane and Marduk smiled to each other without saying a word, as they took a seat on a bench outside of the bakery. Together they ate as they watched the busy streets ebb and flow with people.

"Boys," Marduk said once he was finished, "while I complete my business with Kaeco, why don't you two go down to the docks? Let's meet back at the stables in two hours."

Kai reached into his coat and pulled out the letters from his father for Kaeco. "I have my father's letters to deliver to my uncle first."

"His office is on the way to the beach." Marduk directed them to the warehouse.

When Kai delivered his father's letters, he felt a sense of

pride in completing his mission. "Kempery-man Dresnor, escort Kai and Shane wherever they'd like to go. Be sure all of you are back at the stables by two-o'clock." Then the huntsman pointed at two other guards. "You two can come with me." Marduk walked back inside the warehouse.

The two boys stood and glanced at each other. "We want to walk to the docks," Kai said, directing Smoke to follow. With a glance over his shoulder, he saw three other men fan out. Dresnor stayed about three feet behind while another guard made his way in front of them and the third and fourth took positions on either side of the street.

Once they reached the docks, the smell of the sea hit him in two waves—first the salty air, which smelled clean, and then the harbor's fish trade, which made Kai want to gag. Attracted to the smell, seagulls hovered everywhere, swooping to steal scraps and squawking incessantly.

Kai was amazed by the ship masts cluttering the harbor as their crews loaded and unloaded cargo. In the distance, he noticed a large man-o-war ship drifting in the wind; its name, *Discovery,* was painted on the stern. It pushed out to sea with confidence, breaking the waves on its bow. He wondered if that was the ship Haygan had boarded.

As they watched all the smaller fishing boats, the bakery girl kept drifting into the back of Kai's mind. "Shane, we should ask the bakery girl if she wants to go to the beach with us. I would love to watch the waves crash on the sand, and maybe wade into the water." Without really waiting for a reply, Kai addressed Dresnor. "We're going back to the bakery and then to the beach." His men nodded and followed.

As they approached the bakery, Kai saw a man on a ladder removing the sign that read "Kendrick Bakery."

That's odd, Kai thought as he stepped into the shop. He instantly spotted the young girl packing spice bottles into a large crate. "Um, hello, miss. We were wondering if you'd like to go to the beach with us."

Excitedly, she looked to her mother. "Can I go?" she asked

pleadingly as she looked at the crates and the long shelf. "I promise to finish this when I get back."

Dori placed her hands on her hips. "If they want to go, have them help you finish. Chores first, young lady." Smiling, her mother walked through a door at the back of the bakery.

The girl hung her head and glanced over her shoulder. "I have to empty this entire shelf first." She motioned at the expansive shelf of tools, spices, and baking supplies. She slumped her shoulders and reached for two more bottles on the shelf.

Kai looked at Shane. "What do you say? Together we can empty this in, what, ten minutes?" As he walked around the counter, he saw a smile bloom on her face.

"Leave the glass bottles for me. Everything else needs to fit in those five crates on the floor." She pointed.

Kai and Shane both took a crate and quickly began placing the contents of the shelf neatly inside. "We saw a man outside pulling down your sign, and now it looks like you are packing up the shop. Are you moving?" Kai asked.

Dumbfound, Shane looked at Kai. "Did you miss that conversation earlier? They are moving to the palace—they will be in the new bakehouse. You will be neighbors."

Without stopping, she added. "That was my father, Levi, taking down our sign."

Finished with all the glass bottles, she took a new crate and continued packing. "My parents have been hired as bakers for Diu palace. I will miss the beach, but it is a great opportunity for them."

The three of them made quick work of the shelves, and she darted through the back door to speak with her mother. As the door opened, she came through all smiles. "Mom said I can go, but only for an hour."

Still reeling from the idea she'd be at the palace, Kai walked behind her all the way to the beach. With his hands in his pockets, he hopped down the short grass embankment and landed in the loose sand. The sounds of crashing waves caught his attention. He stood near the surf's edge, watching the blue-green tinge of the water fold over before crashing onto itself and soaking into the white sand.

In the distance, the sun sparkled and tossed its reflection across the water as the distant waves crashed against the rocks around the lighthouse and leaped back to punch the sky. Mesmerized, Kai stared off into the blue. He'd always enjoyed his visits to Port Anahita.

As they stood by the sea, he'd noticed the increasing breeze rushing in to whip through his hair. Drawn forward, he felt something in the sea. It pulled him as if it called him into the deep. Without noticing, he took a few steps more into the sand and heard a small crunching sound beneath his boot.

Under his foot, he found a seashell, now broken. The beach was littered with shells of all sizes and colors. Glancing around, he took note of Dresnor and the other Kempery-men and guards holding their positions.

Smoke's bark brought him back to the present, and he ran to catch up with the others running along the shore. "What do you think about kicking off our boots and run through the water?" Shane asked.

Without waiting for a reply, Shane removed his boots and rolled his pants up above his knees. Kai and the young girl followed his lead, and they all ran up and down the water's edge, splashing each other. Before they knew it, the bottoms of their clothes were soaked through.

Sitting on the rocks to dry off in the afternoon sun, the young girl asked, "Now that we are all friends, what are your names?"

She had caught him by surprise, and Kai raised his eyebrows and nodded to Shane. "Uh, give us a minute." He held up his finger to her and stepped a few feet away with Shane.

Shane stepped off the rocks and joined Kai near water's edge. "Should we tell her who you are?" Shane asked.

Not sure what to do, Kai listened to his gut. "I say we can trust her. I mean, Smoke likes her."

Shane nodded in agreement. "True, but we are kids, what do we know?"

Kai turned back and faced her. She placed her hands on her hips, and her chin jutted out at them. "Stop whispering, you know I can hear you anyway—I'm right here. Name's Rayna Kendrick, and I'm thirteen years old, almost fourteen." She pointed to Shane. "I've seen you around town with your dad. He's the Huntsman, Micha Marduk, right. I've seen him selling pelts and smoked meats to my dad."

Caught by surprise, Kai blurted out, "I'm Kai Galloway from Diu. Nice to meet you."

Astonished he said it, Shane interjected. "I'm Shane Marduk. I live on the south ridge of Thade Mountain, and we're both thirteen."

Rayna crossed her arms and looked at Kai. "No, you're not. Really?"

He had expected her to be totally surprised and (he hoped) a little impressed; he raised his arm to slide back his coat sleeve revealing the arm ring with the Galloway wolf. With a funny bow, she laughed, and both boys laughed too.

Hands back on her hips, she scoffed. "So, if you don't mind me asking, why are you out of the Diu palace—alone? Shouldn't you have guards or something?"

To match her stance, Kai placed his hands on his hips. "Who says we're alone. There are six guards around us right now, no more than twenty paces from us."

As Rayna tilted her head, she looked behind Kai to the tree line just above them in the grass to see two men standing in the shade. Following the tree line farther to the right where it met the rocks, she spotted three others, and then another leaning against an upside-down stack of boats. Each had a sword fastened to their waist, a shield on their backs, and a Galloway crest on their coats—a silver wolf and three silver spears in its jaws.

Back on the rocks, they pulled on their boots. Rayna looked toward the docks as she climbed up the sandy embankment onto the grass. "How long do you think we've been out here?" She offered a hand to Kai and pulled him up, who in turn pulled up Shane.

With that thought, two boys look at each other with sheer panic. "How long have we been gone? If we don't make it back to the stables, we are both in trouble."

Dread consumed Shane's face. "You're right, my dad will have my hide if we're even a minute late. We've been gone too long, and we still have a long ride home."

Kai motioned to Dresnor and called for Smoke as he stepped up to the tree line. "We need to leave, which way to the stables?" Then he glanced at Rayna, and he reprised his comment. "Take us by way of the bakery, please. We should escort Miss Rayna home."

As they ran to the bakery, the wind blew, and the sky filled with fat dark clouds. Kai held the door for Rayna. She ducked inside and waved. "Goodbye, Prince Kai, Shane."

"It was a pleasure meeting you Rayna. I am sorry we cannot stay."

For the first time in his life, Kai felt moved by the presence of another person. Even now, his heart tugged at his feet to turn around. His mind replayed the afternoon. The memory of her smile warmed his soul in a way he never thought possible.

CHAPTER 18

Winter Storm

The boys set a fast pace towards the outskirts of town. Kempery-man Dresnor directed them back at the stables. Marduk busily adjusted the cart harness. "You're late, boys. We should have left already. There's a storm coming. If we don't hurry, we will be caught in it."

With a stern look at Dresnor, Marduk motioned to the other guards. "They've started on your mounts; please help them finish, we need to be underway." Frustration ebbed in Marduk's tone. "Given the impending storm, I am tempted to leave the cart, so we can make haste, but I fear we will be unable to come back any time soon."

Embarrassed, Kai looked around to see if there was something he could do. "Marduk, is there anything we can do to help?"

"Actually, yes. Shane, take this money and pay the stablemaster. Kai, grab those remaining supplies leaning against the cart and stack them tightly with the rest. Shane can help you finish when he gets back. Cover everything with our tarp, and I will tie it down."

Satisfied that he could be of some use, Kai helped place the small bundles securely in the cart. It didn't take long to get everything loaded. Once they were mounted, they headed out of town on the road north to Diu. As they crested the large hill above Port Anahita, Kai took one last look at the coastal city and the ocean as they entered the forest and descended the slope on the other side.

At their first and only planned stop, Kai noticed the temperature had dropped significantly. The wind had also increased, and the sky had darkened. How quickly the weather had turned. They were only at the halfway mark, and Kai felt chilled to the bone as he squatted against a tree near Smoke. On the other side, Shane sat holding himself, trying to keep warm.

Up near the road, Kai spotted Marduk untying the tarp over his supplies and sifting through everything. "What's your dad doing? Should we go help?" Kai asked.

Anxious to be doing something, Shane hopped up. "We should, yes."

Marduk worked free a few furs. "Here, take these. Higher up in the hills will be colder. This storm is moving fast, and the temperature is dropping. Your thin coats won't be enough should it begin to snow, and I don't want to stop again." Marduk handed three furs to Kai, and he and Shane quickly began resetting the load. "I believe the horses have rested enough. We need to go."

Underway, Kai felt warmer with the sizeable black fur wrapped around his back. It was so large that it even covered part of his legs. He rode between two Kempery-men, Dresnor and Albey. Neither man spoke, focused instead on the road and surrounding trees. Kai wished Haygan was still with them.

On his right, he saw Smoke sniff the ground and dart into the trees. Kai was glad Smoke knew what to do. When he returned, the wolf ran ahead of the group, sniffing the air. Finally, he circled the group and slowed to trail behind them, checking the other side of the woods.

It seemed like a lot of work for him without Shiva, but Kai kept silent. It wasn't long before he spotted a few snow flurries fly by his face. Each little flake fell like a delicate flower petal.

He opened his hand and let them fall on his open palm. They melted instantly.

The wind whipped the snow in the air. The few flakes that did land melted as if they'd never existed. As they rode, the flakes grew larger and larger. Then the snow began to collect on the ground, turning the grass and trees white.

Then it was as if the clouds opened and snow filled the sky. The muddy road quickly turned white. Worried Kai called to Shane. "We should be getting close, right?"

Before Shane could answer, huge flakes began to fall and whip around them. There was so much snow that the road and sky ahead had gone completely white. "We're close, yes!" He yelled over the wind. "Once we break through this line of trees, the walls of the city should come into view. I'd say two or three miles left."

Kai pulled the fur tight around his arms and then felt strangely anxious. He looked around for Smoke and noticed his guards riding on either side had closed in around him. As they continued, he could now barely see the two guards in front of Marduk's horse.

Shane circled back after checking with his dad. "We should be really close. It is hard to tell with all this blinding snow. Are you alright, you look pale?"

"It's Smoke. I don't see him. I'm worried." Kai craned his neck around to search for Smoke.

Marduk pulled his horse to a stop and turned in his saddle. He motioned for one of the guards to advance as he slid off his mount.

Before advancing, Kempery-man Redmon leaned over. "No matter what, stay on your mounts. If I give you a sign, ride for the palace. It's just beyond the edge of this forest. If you come into view at an all-out run, guards will come out. Once they know who you are, they will surround you. Do not stop until you reach them and the gatehouse." With that, Redmon slid from his mount to see what was wrong.

A lump came to Kai's throat, but he tried to remain calm.

What's going on? Straining to see through the snow and wind, Kai watched his man approach Marduk on foot, pulling his horse with him. The rear guards pulled up close behind. They could just make out that Marduk was instructing the two guards to pull a fallen tree from the road, while the third paced back and forth facing the woods.

Kai sensed his guard's concern, and he looked over to see Dresnor's stern face scanning the surrounding trees. With everyone around him, he could still not see Smoke. His wolf had been walking up front even with the cart, but in the commotion and the blinding snow, he could not see him.

In his mind, he searched for Smoke. Kai closed his eyes and focused; he pushed with his mind out to reach Smoke. *Smoke, what is it?* Then he waited. Nothing. *Relax, don't force it.* He chastised.

Again, he tried. *What do you sense?* Still, he felt nothing, so he tried again, this time pushing not just his mind but his soul toward Smoke. *What's in the trees, Smoke?*

Smoke pushed back a sense of warning to Kai. Blinded by snow, he used his nose to smell their surroundings. Instinctively he stalked, closing in on a mass that neither could see.

Eyes closed, Kai opened his mind to the energy within his soul. Threads of light wove up through the tree trunks and out their branches. Even the snow floating through the air contained life. He pushed farther through the trees, beyond Smoke.

Then he saw them. A large group of people hiding in the thicket. *Smoke, come back.* He pulled on the connection. His wolf responded. Kai opened his eyes and turned to Dresnor and shouted. "There are people in the trees! They have weapons, and they are coming."

Smoke bounded out of the forest and began to bark at the trees in front of them. As he pranced back and forth, he growled and backed toward the group. Dresnor pulled Kai out of his saddle and the other men slid from their horses. They drew their weapons and surrounded Kai.

Kai feared what was coming, so he called out. "Smoke, come." Smoke ran to the cluster of horses surrounding Kai. Shane ran to his father and the guards who worked to move the felled tree. Over a dozen men rushed out from the woods onto the road. Weapons at the ready, the bandits yelled as they charged.

There was nothing in his life that had prepared him for this. The men clashed swords, their faces fierce and angry. Kai studied their attackers. Men dressed in black, their heads were shaved, and the black armor they wore was embossed with a black star. A symbol he had never seen before. *Who are these men, and what do they want?*

Metal angrily clanged over and over. Men dropped to the ground. Blood splashed across the snow. Kai had never held a sword against another man with intent. With his men protecting him, Kai gripped his weapon. Its clean blade shone bright; its hefty weight made his arms begin to shake. A man broke through and slashed at Kai. With both hands, Kai held his weapon against the blow. The metal vibrated with fury.

Dresnor punched his opponent in the throat. In a backhanded blow, he sliced down the man who had charged at Kai. Redmon filled the gap between him and Dresnor. Above Kai, on the cart, Shane launched arrows. One struck a man in the leg; another hit a man in the shoulder. Smoke attacked men from behind. His ferocious fangs ripped arms and legs. Another man lashed at Kai between his protectors. The force of the blow shocked him. Kai pushed against the man's blade. A second blow aimed at his side; Kai turned his sword to block the strike. Dresnor and Redmon both stabbed the man.

These men were good, not your typical roaming bandits. They put up a good fight, but his Kempery-men were better. His men were turning the tide until a new group of men poured out of the woods. Outnumbered, Kempery-man Dresnor called to Redmon. "We need to get the prince out of here!"

Redmon charged through the horde. Dresnor grabbed Kai,

and they ran to the horses. Kai's blade fell in the snow. Unwilling to leave it behind, Kai stopped. Albey scooped up the sword and handed it to the prince. They mounted up, and Dresnor reached out, yelling at Kai. "Ride boy, ride hard." Then he smacked Ember's rump.

Ember lurched into a full gallop and Kai adjusted to the horse's rhythm. His first thought was of Shane and the others. When he heard the clang of metal on metal behind him, he feared for his friends who were fighting for their lives against these savages.

Kai kicked at Ember's sides. Knuckles white, he clutched the reins. Snow pelted his face. In his mind, he felt the warmth. Ember and Smoke were there. He was not alone. Ember could help him, he only needed to ask. Kai laid one hand on the side of Ember's neck, accessing the bond. *Ember. We need to ride, ride fast. Take us home.*

Ember lunged forward—the extra speed ripped Kai's fur wrap off his shoulders. Lost in the snow. Eyes focused on the road, he held on tight. Between Albey and Dresnor he raced. The snow melted down his head and shoulders.

Ahead the trees begin to thin; he could see a clearing through the snow. They were near the edge of the forest. Safety was within reach. Clearing the woods, he could barely see the white and gray city walls in the distance. From his side, Albey advanced, pushing his horse faster and faster.

Kempery-man Dresnor stayed at Kai's side. Diu city was in view. *Why aren't they coming?* Kai squinted through the blinding snow. The watchtower bells rang in the distance. The city gatehouse spewed a mounted horde of blue and silver, advancing on their location. Kai sighed with relief.

His hands and body felt frozen. Snowflakes soaked him through to the bone. At his speed, it was a matter of minutes before they were within the range of the riders. Albey met the approaching group and motioned for them to follow. He joined their ranks and raced back toward the forest.

They slowed and rode to safety within the twin towers

of the gatehouse. Dresnor's horse stopped and circled around Kai. Dresnor dismounted and informed the others what had happened, and more riders rode out into the storm. Kai thought of the others–Shane and Marduk.

Outside the gatehouse, Kai saw Smoke, watching and waiting for the same news they all held their breath for. Dresnor remounted and took Kai's reigns. "I will take Prince Kai to the palace and inform the King what's happened. Bring me news when you have it," he instructed the guard standing watch.

Quickly they rode through the city streets. The relentless snow fell, collecting on the homes and roads throughout the city. Once through the second gatehouse, they rode straight to the long stone bridge that led to the palace. Soaked through, Kai shivered.

He could barely see across the bridge to the palace. In the distance, two figures waited in front of the palace doors. Midway across the bridge, Kai was able to make out his father and the Master General Cazier.

Kempery-man Dresnor escorted him inside and stepped away with the Master General. Iver knelt to look at Kai, his expression a mix of emotions. His eyes were filled with concern, but his mouth revealed pride. "You look alright. What happened?" Not waiting for an answer, Iver took hold of Kai's shoulders. "My goodness, son, you're half frozen."

Kendra lowered her face to Iver's ear. "Your Majesty, let me take the prince. I will bring him to you once he's warmed up." Still, in shock, Kai followed with one hand on Smoke's back.

Warm, guilt pressed on Kai as he waited in his room. His friends fought for their lives while he was swept away, unable to help. Unwilling to wait any longer, he darted into the hall. Beck stood guard, two Mryken at his side. More guards littered the corridor.

He ran to his father's study. Shane and Marduk stood next to Iver's desk. Marduk had a white bandage wrapped around his left hand and wrist. Relieved everyone was safe, Kai took a breath.

Iver looked to Kai. "Son, I am very proud of how you handled yourself. Dresnor said you did well." He nodded and looked at the Grand Duke. "Dante, when the storm passes, I want the woods cleared out around the road. Once you've interrogated the survivors, I want to know their intent."

Dresnor interjected. "Sire, I have never seen men like this. Their fighting was different, reminiscent of an old style, it does not appear that they were after Kai, but they were not merely looting a passing cart either."

"A bold move given the number of soldiers in our group," said Redmon.

Kai turned to Dresnor, taken aback by his Kempery-man, seeing him for the first time. His stern green eyes, sharp cheekbones, and commanding presence. Dresnor's wet uniform emphasized his muscular build. The sides of his thick onyx hair trimmed to stubble, yet the top was left long and slicked back. His scruffy beard gave him a confident yet aggressive appearance.

Marduk stepped forward. "They were impressive fighters. Only one man ran once help arrived, and they were outnumbered. The rest fought to the bitter end."

"Sire, I will question the two prisoners with Kempery-man Farwick. We must find the one who escaped," said Cazier.

Iver raised his hand to quiet the room. "And we will find him, but my orders stand. Dante, clear out the woods. We cannot have the palace or the road south compromised. Cazier, give me a report when you have it. Marduk, let's get the boys something to eat." Iver motioned them out.

In the hall, Kai spotted Kendra. "Shane, you go on ahead, I need to speak with Kendra." Alone he whispered, "I need to talk to you about what happened with Smoke and Ember today. It was amazing. I was able to reach out to Smoke. I felt and sensed what he was feeling. I saw into the woods. In my mind, I saw people clustered together in the underbrush."

He looked into her eyes, and she shuttered. "Kai, your eyes are green. Control your emotions before someone sees you."

It was hard to control the barrage of emotions, but he reined in his mind. The temperature in his head cooled, and she nodded in approval.

"You did well today. Gleaning is difficult to maintain under pressure. Meditation will help you control your emotions." Kendra tilted her head toward the nursery. "I need to check on baby Cordelia. I have prepared an extra bed in your room for Shane. Marduk will be staying across the hall. I will see you later if I can."

"Thank you, Kendra," he replied.

It had been a long day, but they'd survived. Shane eagerly hopped in bed, covers pulled up to his chin. Warm in his own bed, Kai let his head sink into his pillow. Thoughts of his mother crept into his mind. Her Katori gifts—*his* gifts—had saved him today. He closed his eyes, and sleep took him. Dreams flowed freely. His mind drifted into memories of his mother, moments from the past.

Clear blue skies and sunshine. In the palace gardens, he laid in the grass with his mother. His baby blanket was tucked under his chin; it was soft against his skin. Sunshine spilled over his young shoulders. His little hand turned the pages of a picture book. He read the large print below each image. "Elephant. Cat." He turned the page. "Horse. Wolf." He touched the picture of the wolf. "I like this one." He flipped the page. "Whale. Dog." Again, he flipped the page. "Lion. Eagle. Eagles are so lucky to be able to fly." He looked at his mother, and she smiled.

"Keep going, you are doing so well!" Mariana encouraged.

He turned to the next page. "Bear. Dragon."

A warm summer's breeze blew against his face. The smell of roses filled the air. Mariana's hand smoothed the rustling pages. "Which animal would you like to be?" she whispered in his ear. "If you had to pick just one."

Her soft brown hair tickled his face. He stared at the animal forms of his children's book, flipping back through. The scenes were simple, yet beautifully drawn in pale watercolors, splashed against the pages. "I would pick a dragon. They are the strongest," he answered quickly.

He flipped to the next page and paused. "But maybe an eagle. People aren't scared of eagles." Proud of his answer, he looked at his mother.

"Wise choice Kai. Choosing an animal based on how others might feel."

He gazed at her smiling face, and she slowly faded away. He woke clutching his pillow; tears welled in his eyes. He was struck by her memory, a happy moment. He remembered that day. Pleasant and simple. Kai wished he could go back and linger with her in that instant.

CHAPTER 19

Wicker Basket

Uncomfortable, Kai sat upright in a chair placed beside his father's throne. King Iver Galloway stood below on the bottom step of the dais. The rest of the royal family sat enduring the winter festival announcements and the gift offerings. Dukes of Diu, lords and ladies, high society merchants, and the king's Kempery-men were all in attendance.

They came together to welcome the new year and exchange goodwill blessings. Each offered a gift and promised fealty to King Iver. Reaffirming their commitment, they ensured the prosperity and growth of Diu.

But the only thing Kai noticed was the long, endless procession. They brought everything from wine, jewels, gold, livestock, lumber, marble sculptures, and honey. They brought whatever they could offer, their regional treasure. Large and small the gifts came, each blessed in the giving. King Iver personally cherished and accepted each one.

Kai was proud, knowing the gifts were redistributed throughout the city and surrounding farms, used to repair or improve the lives of the people. Last year's collection provided new wells in Rimtown, and rebuilt homes and restored a library lost in a fire.

As kings went, Kai knew his father was a good man. He protected and provided for his people. Iver ensured that rich and poor alike had the basics; shelter, food, and clean water. No one in Diu was homeless or went without food if they were willing to work.

The end of the line delighted Kai. The last gift was surprisingly unique, and it was Kai's favorite. A glass harmonica. A series of glass bowls, one set inside another, large to small on a single shaft. Upon closer inspection, he noticed the rim of each had been painted a different color. This fragile treasure came from Lord and Lady Chenowith.

They were accompanied by a group of men carrying the large box with legs. They placed it near the far corner of the dais. The last man poured water into the large basin, and two women took their places. One stood by a wooden wheel and slowly cranked, spinning the shaft with the individual bowls. The other sat on a bench and dipped her fingers into the water basin below the bowls. As her fingers danced across the spinning rims, the individual bowls produced various musical tones.

The harmonica's musical splendor filled the air. Over the delicate tune, Iver announced: "Thank you all for sharing this winter festival and presenting these wonderful gifts for the betterment of Diu. I cherish them all and will ensure they are used to improve our great city." Cheers and clapping spread through the gathering.

Servers moved through the crowd, dressed in Diu blue and white, offering wine and fruit juice. Hands raised, Iver calmed the crowd. "Let us each give a moment of thanks for all that we have and remember those we've lost this year."

In a moment of silence, people bowed their heads.

After the moment passed, Iver took his glass and raised it to the crowd. "Family and friends. Blessings to you all in the coming year. Let's eat, drink, and bring in the new year. May Alenga bless you, one and all."

"Blessings to you in the coming year," rang out across the

room.

Kai watched as the crowd mingled. Music, gifts, food, and wine continued to flow freely between guests as the night progressed. In the background, the enchanting music of the harmonica was accompanied by two flute players and a piano.

Realizing the late hour, Kai slipped out of the great hall and out of the palace. With a gift in hand he anxiously stood in front of the baker's cottage, unable to knock. Twice he tried and stopped himself. *Come on, you can do this.* Not wanting to lose his nerve again, he knocked on the door.

The door swung open, and there stood Levi Kendrick. Kai swallowed hard. "Blessings to you in the coming year, Mister Kendrick. May I see Rayna, please?" His heart pounded in his chest.

Levi was a heavy-set man with curly brown hair and a gentle face. "Your Highness, please come in. You are most welcome in our home. Rayna, you have a guest."

Her father slowly backed away from the door, revealing their humble home. It looked warm and welcoming with all the personal touches of a loving family. Along one shelf he saw a row of large seashells from Port Anahita. They had been living as the palace bakers going on two months now.

"You have a lovely home, Miss Dorothy. Thank you for allowing me to visit." Kai bowed respectfully to Rayna's mother.

"Please, Prince Kai, call me Dori," she said shyly. Miss Dori's long auburn hair flowed freely down her back, and Rayna was skillfully weaving it into a braid with three white ribbons.

Kai could not help but stare at Rayna. From the moment he first saw her in Port Anahita, his heart felt connected to her. Tonight, her long dark brown hair was swooped softly over her shoulder, and her honey brown eyes sparkled in response to her laughter. "Blessings to you in the coming year, Prince Kai. So good of you to bless us in our home this night. Are you enjoying the winter festival? The parade of candles through the city streets was quite beautiful. Did you get to see it?"

Rayna smiled but focused on her task.

Kai felt that he could sit and listen to her all night. Transfixed on Rayna, he stood holding the gift, waiting for her to take a breath. Still, she continued. "We had a great view from the Central City Gardens. The winter blooming plants are wonderful. Did I mention the music? Flutes and violins were playing the loveliest tunes while people danced in the streets. I have never seen anything like it before!"

Dori interrupted her. "Rayna, honey. Prince Kai has a gift. Give him a chance to speak."

Ever polite, Kai responded to her questions. "I have seen the parade of candles. Every year it seems to be more enchanting." He had heard Shannon say that, and he wanted to impress Rayna. "I wanted to give you something. It's not big…I mean, it *is* big, but it is a…here." Kai stumbled over his words. Unsure what else to say, he slid the gift across the table.

Finished with her mother's hair, Rayna tied the ribbons into a bow. "All finished. You look lovely, mother." Rayna kissed her mother's cheek and looked at the package on the table. Her hands delicately traced the soft dark blue cloth and untied the bright pink bow. The blue fabric fell in a puddle around a large wicker basket.

Inside, Kai had placed three white winter roses on a bed of pink and purple heather. He desperately hoped she liked it. It had not been easy to convince Kendra to help him purchase a gift for Rayna. Everyone advised him it was unwise to spend time with the baker's daughter. Still, he wanted to get Rayna something. *What harm could a wicker basket possibly cause?*

"I love the basket and flowers. I am sorry I did not get you anything." Rayna pulled the flowers from the basket and placed them in a large vase in the center of the table. "I wasn't sure I could give a prince a gift." She looked at her parents for reassurance.

Kai instantly felt he'd made a mistake surprising her. "Please, don't feel bad. My gift will be knowing you enjoy the basket. Come spring, I will show you where the wildflowers grow outside of the city." Kai tilted his head, trying to lift her eyes. "In summer the palace gardens produce vegetables, and in the fall the apple orchard fills with fruit. A basket will come in handy."

Dori and Levi smiled at Kai. "Thank you for thinking of our daughter. Rayna, you bless him by enjoying his gift. Blessings to you Kai in the coming year." Dori rubbed her daughter's back.

Not wanting to overstay his welcome, Kai bowed slightly. "Thank you again for welcoming me into your home. I need to return to the palace."

Excuses made; he exited the small cottage. He was a bundle of emotions. *Why does this girl make my insides flip upside down?* He took a breath and felt a hand touch his arm. He glanced to his right; Rayna had followed him outside. "Thank you for the gift." She smiled. "It means more to me than you know."

"It was my pleasure," he nodded.

All the way back to the palace festivities, he worked to control his bubbling emotions. He could feel the heat in his head ebb. Clear-minded he returned to the party. The air was filled with bouncy music and laughter. Everyone was still having a grand time.

Roark had one arm clasped around Shannon's lower back and the other raised to the side, cupping her hand in his as they gracefully floated around the room. They danced into the center and out again, spinning apart and pulling back together.

Not far from them, Tolan twirled Amelia and pulled her back to him. Her dark blue dress flared slightly about her knees, and her blonde hair bounced on her shoulders. Even Iver and Nola had joined into the rhythmic choreographed pattern. Together they were a grand display of joyful color.

Kai approached his cousin Gideon, who was leaning against the wall. He was sharply dressed in a chestnut brown dress coat and peach vest, his curly brown hair free about his shoulders.

"Gideon, I am surprised you are not dancing with Victoria," Kai jested until he noticed his cousin's face turn red. "Tell me you've at least asked her?"

"I couldn't possibly ask her to dance." Gideon tried to back away, but Kai set his hand on Gideon's shoulder. Kai may have been a year younger, but he was nearly two inches taller than his cousin. "She's talking with Alana and Aden. I couldn't possibly interrupt. Besides, she's way too beau…" Gideon's clapped his hand over his mouth, muffling his words.

"You can, Gideon. I'll go with you. Now she is looking at us —we have to go over!" Kai insisted. "I will ask Alana, and you ask Victoria. She will have to say yes. Trust me." Kai pulled Gideon along, making their way across the room.

Kai bowed to the group. "Cousin Alana, you are looking nice this evening. Cousin Aden, I hope you're enjoying yourself. Have you danced any this evening?"

Aden smiled briefly. "Cousin, you know I don't dance. I like to spend the evening talking about politics and law. But I do not dance." Aden tugged at the lapel of his jacket.

"Right. You don't dance." A smile crept across Kai's face. "Shame to let the night waste away without at least one dance," he added, nudging Gideon's arm.

Nervously, Gideon cleared his throat. "Victoria. You are looking lovely this evening." Sheepishly he stared at Victoria's feet and then looked into her eyes.

Behind them, the music stopped with a burst of laughter and cheer as couples left the dance floor. The next tune was a slower melody, and it was their cue to find a partner. Kai bowed to Alana. "Cousin, would you dance with me?" he asked, offering her his hand.

Alana looked to Victoria and smiled. "Why, yes, I would love to dance. Thank you for asking." She took Kai's arm, followed him to the dance floor, and glanced over her shoulder at Victoria.

On the dance floor, Kai put on hand on Alana's waist and held her hand in the other. "Do you think Gideon will ask her?"

he asked.

A bright smile crossed Alana's face. "He did it! And she said yes. Here they come." She nodded excitedly over Kai's shoulder.

Kai spun Alana around in time to catch Gideon and Victoria glide past them, followed by Tolan and Amelia. He was surprised to see them together. He wasn't sure how to feel about their blooming relationship. They seemed to be together more and more.

"Alana, what do you know about Amelia and Tolan? They seem to have gotten rather close in recent weeks. Always together, whispering and laughing."

Alana tilted her head to see around Kai. "Didn't you hear? They have gone riding in the countryside or walked to the central City Park nearly every day since he returned."

Kai hesitated. Had he been so busy that he missed this? He and Amelia had always been close. It wasn't until the last year that either of them understood what their betrothal meant. Now they were moving in different directions. He wasn't sure how that made him feel.

Amelia was his best friend, but he had not made any time for her lately. Twirling Alana out one-handed, he brought her back and guided her around the outside corner. Slowly they followed Lord and Lady Chenowith, swaying with the slow, delicate music.

"Well, rumor has it you have been spending a fair amount of time with the baker's daughter. Is that wise? Seems to me, both of you need to remember who you are and your future obligations." Alana held her chin high, poised perfectly.

"Her name is Rayna," Kai insisted. "And I wasn't aware we were the talk of the palace," he added, a little sharper than he intended. Then he sighed and twirled her out and back again. "But you are probably right."

He couldn't help but wonder how different things would be if he could be who he wanted and with whom he chose. If only there were a spark between Amelia and himself—but she was more like a sister. The music slowly ended, and Kai stepped back from Alana with a bow. "You know, Alana, I believe this is the most we've talked since you arrived."

Alana curtsied in return. "Mother thinks I should be demure, quiet, and attentive." She took his arm, and they walked back to Aden. "Honestly, I am shy, speaking in front of groups. I prefer one on one. Thank you for the dance, cousin."

"My pleasure. Besides, it was worth it. Gideon and Victoria are finally talking." Kai motioned across the room.

How he envied their freedom. The right to choose. Their destiny was unknown, but duty commanded the structure of his life and fixed his future. Each lesson molded him into a king. How could he possibly live up to their expectations?

Back in his bedroom, Kai felt the cold air hit his face. He had forgotten to close the balcony doors. Newly fallen snow covered his balcony and a fair bit of the carpet inside the doors. With the large glass doors closed, he knelt to rekindle the fading fire. Warmth slowly pushed back the cold as he sat watching the blaze, Smoke at his side.

Nightly meditation had become his ritual to center his mind and connect to the energy that strengthened his awareness. He had learned that stone was the most difficult to see through in any significant thickness. People varied the most. The old and sick had the faintest light, while the young were very bright.

The few Katori he'd met all defied the rule. They were extremely bright at any age, although he had yet to meet anyone who looked old. Besides Kendra and Haygan, only a few lived in the Diu city. They were transient people who came through to sell goods before departing.

A knock at his door brought him out of his meditation, but he held onto the connection. Through the door, he gleaned Kendra, shining brightly. Her wispy light was intense. "Come in, Kendra," he called through the door.

Kendra entered, carrying baby Cordelia. "I noticed you were still awake. How did Rayna like her gift?" She stood, rocking his little sister.

"Fine, I guess. She was uncomfortable that she had no gift for me, but I still think it was the right thing to do," he said, trying to convince himself more than her.

"Understandable." Kendra rocked his baby sister. "What kind of future do you see with Rayna?"

Kendra did not sidestep the issue. She was always direct.

And unfortunately, he knew the answer. They had no future. She was the baker's daughter, and he was a prince, betrothed to another. Although Diu allowed royals to marry below their rank, the old tradition of betrothal defined his choice.

Still, he could not help but want a different life. "I see a soul mate. I felt a connection the moment I saw her. There is something tangible between us. I know I shouldn't, but I sneak out to see her any chance I get. Each moment we spend together deepens that bond. I wish you could understand."

"I understand perfectly, but we don't always get what we want." Kendra paused. "I know how you feel. I also know your duty commands you marry another. Connecting with Rayna is a mistake. It will only make it more difficult."

"You keep saying that, and I agree with it in principle. But my soul believes there is a future. Should I ignore that?" Kai couldn't help what he believed. Something told him his life would depend on her. Frustrated, he crossed his arms.

She pursed her lips. "You should rest. Goodnight, Kai." Kendra left quietly, closing the door behind her.

Settled in bed, Kai closed his eyes and drifted off to sleep. His mind flashed as slow, detailed images unfolded before him. The apple orchard; the smell of trees full of ripe fruit. Rayna sat beside him. She flipped through a book, the edge of the pages crisp and clear. Kai reached for her hand, but the wind blew through the vision, and she disappeared.

He grabbed for her, but she was gone, replaced with a new image. Cannon fire exploded in his ears. Two ships battled in Port Anahita. Men screamed. Kai ran through the streets behind Dresnor. The image faded into a man with fiery red hair wearing a Diu uniform; his shoulder displayed the rank of captain.

The man turned. It was Tolan, his face and chest slashed, dripping with blood. The smell of smoke and iron lingered in the air. Overwhelming sadness struck his chest. Kai resisted the image and pushed it away.

Relentless he moaned in his sleep. The vision changed, and Kai smelled pine trees. He had the sense of falling, tree branches pricked at his arms. He landed with a thud. He gasped for air. Darkness passed over his eyes. Kai blinked, his vision cleared, a gray wolf stood over him. Fear coursed through his body and he covered his face.

Tossing in his sleep, Kai fought the visions. He awoke, frantically ripping back the covers. Soaked in sweat, he left his bed. Grateful he no longer woke to screams, he opened his balcony doors. Cold air washed over him. His view was clouded by falling snow.

Eyes closed, Kai gleaned his surroundings. The power lit up his mind, and the snowflakes became tiny falling stars. He stepped out on to the balcony. Snow melted on his head and shoulders. Through his visions, he searched the night, looking for one small cottage. There, he found one light as bright as his own—Rayna.

The thought of her calmed his racing heart. Kai moderated his breathing to steady his mind. That was no regular dream, the images felt real. It was not a moment from his past. They were visions of things to come. Random moments twisted together. He didn't understand what everything meant, only that Rayna was his touchstone.

What did his future hold? Uncertain, he released the connection and let her fade from his mind. Were they right? Was bringing her into his life a mistake? Or was she indeed his future?

CHAPTER 20

The Gift of Time

Spring was always Kai's favorite time of year. The mornings were brisk, the afternoons warm. A time when life began anew. Four long months of winter weather had broken. The Central City Gardens were all newly planted on his birthday–the first day of spring. On the eve of summer two months later they would be changed again for Kings Day—Iver's birthday.

Today was Kai's fourteenth birthday, at two fourteen in the afternoon, the bells around the city would ring for him. The great hall was decorated in his honor, and a small gathering had assembled. From the head of the table, Iver raised his glass. "Fourteen years ago today, I became a father. Prince Kai Galloway, my son. I am proud to be your father. Blessed be Alenga, may she bless you in the coming year."

The group echoed. "Blessed, be Alenga. Happy birthday Prince Kai."

Kai raised his glass in return.

"Son, my gift to you this year is *time*." Iver handed Kai an intricately carved black walnut box. The lid's filigree carving was the tree of life, inlaid with five rubies set as apples within the tree. Inside the box, Kai found a golden pocket watch on a long thick chain.

"Time is a precious gift, my son. Use yours wisely and cherish the time others give."

Kai looked at the casing around the watch. The symbol of the morning star above the tree of life. He opened the timepiece and read the engraving. 'You will always be our son. Forever, Mariana & Iver.' The words made his eyes water. He wiped away the tears.

"Thank you, father. I will." He slid the watch into his vest pocket, letting the stylish chain dangle from its clip on his vest.

Together Kai and his family exited the front of the palace. Crossing the bridge, they climbed inside the royal carriage. Kai tilted his head when he heard the city bells chime. It was the hour of his birth, and today, thoughts of his mother were everywhere. He hoped she was looking down on him. *I wish you were here, mother.*

Kendra, Aaron, and Seth sat on one side of the carriage with Kai, and his father sat with Nola as she held baby Cordelia. Their carriage was surrounded by royal guards. Led by Kempery-men on horseback, they rode through the streets of Hightown Proper and Midtown. Well-wishers waved as they passed, hoping to catch a glimpse of the royal family.

Although Kai had once spent a great deal of time in the city, he had stopped openly traveling the streets as Prince Kai. Dresnor had begun teaching him how to safely move through the city, and they often walked in plain clothes to avoid attention. Though most of the streets were safe, there were still a few areas that could get loud and ruthless if enough ale was involved.

Riome, on the other hand, taught him how to navigate the rougher parts. She padded his shirt, dirtied his face and clothes, and took him to Rimtown taverns. She said, "Fear is not an option. Walk with purpose and awareness." Though little poverty existed in Diu, it still had its share of drifters and ruffians. Riome insisted in sneaking him out at night to experience their life firsthand.

They exited the carriage near the entrance to the City Gardens, next to the marble statue of King Nicholas Galloway, his great-great-grandfather. Tall and proud, King Nicholas sat on his trusty stead, Bashon.

Together they climbed the stone stairways winding through the terraced gardens; each tier bloomed with new spring flowers. The upper gardens were divided into three long rows, separated by decorative paths and evergreen hedges.

In the final bed at the very apex of the stacked gardens stood a large obelisk to honor his grandfather King Everette Galloway. It was also newly planted with pansies, hyacinths, tulips, and daffodils.

The garden's central showpiece was freshly toiled but empty. There a woman waited for Kai. It would be his choice of flowers that would fill this bed. Her design would be determined by his selections.

The rest of his family took the stone stairs leading up to the terrace. There they could relax and enjoy the view from a raised gazebo enjoying afternoon tea and food. Kai looked up to the other raised gazebo, where the terrace was lined with Kempery-men.

"Hello, Your Highness, Prince Kai," said Linlou. "I have been selected to create the spring centerpiece. Along the path, I have set a selection." She gestured to several groups of plants. "Some plants bloom with color, while others have colored foliage. Please tell me which you like from each grouping."

Linlou wore a broad-brimmed green hat, black pants, and a royal blue shirt. She carried a thick leather-bound journal embossed with her shooting star marker. Directing Kai through each group of plants, she noted his selections. Once finished, he turned and climbed the stairs, joining his family.

Perched on the stone railing, Kai watched Linlou wildly

sketch in her journal. He was surprised to see her scrap her first two designs. Three pages later, Linlou stood and approached her patiently waiting team.

After showing them her design and providing directions, there was a flurry of activity. Men dashed off, carrying away the unwanted plants and returned from the greenhouse pulling carts filled with plants, flat stones, bird baths, and a small circular wooden bench.

Briefly, Kai watched the flood of people join in the action. One group set out staking and stringing the area, laying out the plan. Their first lines were clean and straight, angled out from the center. The second lines didn't exactly make sense, each curving outward, more significant than the previous.

Finally, a few men began planting dense bushes covered with clustered white flowers in a tight circle. Kai watched, wondering why they skipped several spaces. Another group placed curved flat stones in the center, while others set a few seemingly random stones throughout the bed. Next came another circle of pale-yellow flowers, which blended into dark yellow.

"How goes the design, son?" Iver asked, handing Kai a cup of warm tea.

"Fast. It is amazing to watch. It is like watching an army of ants. It is hard to believe they will get it all done in two hours." Kai took a sip of tea, holding his focus on Linlou's green hat. She crisscrossed the design, refining the progress of each group. Always adjusting, stepping back for a broader view, and making modifications.

"It is good to be together today." Iver took a seat next to Kai to watch the activity. "Are you getting excited for your trip to Hamrin? You leave in three months."

Surprised, Kai turned to look at his father. "That soon?" He took a breath and looked up at the pale blue sky. "I believe I am ready, although I am unsure why I am making the trip." Kai looked away from his father, watching Linlou plant flowers. Still more flowers arrived.

"You will represent me to our people. I want to know how my people live. How their towns and cities progress. You've met most of the dukes and lords of the land. Make friends with them and their children, and they will be your allies in the future. The townspeople need to know we care. I want to know our borders are secure. Find out if our people are happy. You will deliver my letters and hear their complaints. Establish a dialogue. You are my emissary, and you will be their advocate when you return. You will also collect taxes while you are there. This is important work."

Kai thought about what his father said. It sounded like a tremendous responsibility. He wasn't sure he was ready. All he did know was he had no choice. This trip was part of his duty as a prince and part of his training. Someday he would be king of Milnos. "I will make you proud, father." He tried to put on a strong, confident face, even though inside, he was terrified.

"Son, come eat. They have much to do." Iver walked away, joining the others in the gazebo.

His father was right. There was still so much exposed soil, and they had less than an hour to go. They were currently planting flowers around the border, while Linlou pulled away stakes and string. Planting continued, and the design became tighter and tighter; each plant blended into the next.

Before joining the others, he saw a procession of men pushing carts with barrels. *Curious,* Kai thought as he joined the others. Inside the gazebo, he took a seat beside Seth and grabbed an almond cake to go with his tea. The bite sized cake melted in his mouth.

"Are they almost done?" Seth asked, yawning. He looked bored and ready to leave.

Kai shook his head. "I wish they were." He took another bite and savored the taste. He hadn't realized how hungry he was until now. He sip of tea and watched Nola pass baby Cordelia to Kendra.

Restless, Aaron kicked his legs back and forth. "What if they don't finish? What happens? Do we have to sit here until they do?"

Kai looked to his father, who bobbed his head. "See there, the horticultural society watches her progress. Though to be honest, we've never had anyone fail to finish." Iver looked to the lingering men and women doodling in their journals.

"Well, I don't see how they will finish," Kai added. "Moments ago, half the bed was still empty, and they had very few plants left."

"No worries, son." Iver clinked his glass and addressed the group. "Thank you, family and friends. We honor my son on the day of his birth. Given to us on this most sacred of days, the beginning of spring. The goddess Alenga gave us this world. In it, she encouraged life to grow. She raised the mountains, filled the seas, and gave us the sun and moon to light our way. We hold sacred the beauty of nature in all her grandeur."

"Here, here," Cazier cheered, and everyone clapped.

Loud sounds echoed up the stairs, and Kai dashed back to the steps, gazing down at the dwindling activity. His view from above had changed dramatically. The last group had poured white stones inside the remaining space. Barrel upon barrel had been emptied into the plant-less void.

Several men tamped the pebbles with flat boards connected to a post. They packed the ground into a white stone path. The rest watered the plants, filled birdbaths, and cleaned the space.

Instantly Kai saw a spiral design. The pebble paths flared larger and larger as they went around and out. The flowers formed a colorful starburst outward, and the seemingly random flat stones now held birdbaths. He was overwhelmed by the change. They were nearly finished with plenty of time to spare. Fewer and fewer men remained; each finished their task, removed debris, and left until all that remained was Linlou.

Together with his family, Kai marveled at the two different designs in one space. Linlou bowed to the royal family as they descended the stairs, stepping away so they could enjoy the area. Quickly, Kai followed the spiral path into the center, and Seth ran close behind. At the center was a round wooden bench with a large wooden box covered with tiny holes, tied with a royal blue bow.

Taking his time, he removed the ribbon and opened the box. Out of the box flew dozens of red and yellow butterflies. They flew straight up at first, then slowly descended around the garden. It was magical. He gasped at the sight. He had never seen so many in one place. To his delight, two butterflies landed on his shoulder, and one on Seth. They both stood together in awe. Not wanting to move lest they fly away.

"Thank you, Linlou. You have made a wonderful garden for my son. I look forward to your summer design on King's Day." Iver gave her a small nod, then walked into the newly designed garden behind Nola.

Linlou bowed and slowly backed away. The horticultural society awaited her. Although Kai could not hear what they said to her, he could see that they were smiling. Clearly, they were pleased with her design. Linlou bowed and left the gardens.

CHAPTER 21

Testing Limits

Every few days, Riome came for him unless she was away on a mission. They had been training for months. Today they took the long spiraling staircase to the old abandoned armory into the depths of the east spire. The stone, dirt, and wood smelled old and dank. Spiderwebs hung around every corner. Riome carried an oil lamp to light their way.

Riome reached the landing and led them through two iron doors to their training room. Within the dark room, she lit only a few sconces around the room. Fanciful flames danced their way into the high arched ceiling overhead. Along the walls were racks of weapons and various bits of beaten armor and padded targets.

It was difficult to fathom what she might teach him from one day to the next. She had mostly taught him a bit of street fighting. She wanted him to get used to unpredictability rather than teaching him choreographed maneuvers like the others. She insisted the unknown would challenge his wits.

Occasionally she added in knives or clubs to increase the intensity of their lessons. A few nights ago Riome gave him the thrashing of his life, but today she started teaching him a series of graceful movements. He was relieved by the break.

She told him the movements, once sped up, could be used

for defensive fighting and a few minor attacks. While he had wanted to learn, he'd had no idea what he'd been asking. This was nothing like what he thought. Not that he had any idea what it meant to be a spy or fight for one's life. He wondered if his father had done any such training in his youth.

One thing he was thankful for was Riome's patience. Kai's movements did not flow like hers. Often, he missed steps or motions as he tried to study her and keep up. Her movements were slow. The technique focused on precision and included deep breathing.

When he relaxed, her choreographed movements became a little easier, and he was a little less rigid. They moved silently, and each posture flowed into the next. She was not much of a talker some days. If she did speak, her words were direct. To Kai, she sounded like one of the captains drilling his team in the yard.

When they were done, Riome bowed, and they left.

Outside sunshine bathed the courtyard as Kai set out on a run, Smoke by his side. This was his time—time to think. Time to practice. In his mind, he connected to Smoke. Using his gift of sight, he gleaned his surroundings. Through practice, he had learned to maintain his focus regardless of the distractions.

Eyes wide, he ran. The life-emanating glow looked beautiful and soft. He was still amazed by the gift and the distance he could see in his mind. With each passing day, he could see farther and farther.

Connected with Smoke, Kai felt Smoke's wild exhilaration, his anticipation of running. They started at a nice leisurely pace as they passed the stables, training grounds, barracks, and kennels. The other side of the palace was more open until he reached the older cottages built near the wall. A few restricted his path; it was barely wide enough for Kai to run alongside Smoke.

Several places along the wall, there were other obstacles. Crates, barrels, and the occasional guard patrolling with a

Mryken. Spaces narrow and wide, each providing a challenge. Ever mindful of the unpredictable nature of others, he kept watch for the guard changes and people roaming near the wall. "On your left," he called as he passed a guard.

In his mind, he could see guards patrolling with their Mryken. The dogs were often excited by his running. He could tell they wanted to chase after him, but their training kept them focused. He had learned to connect with them as he did Smoke. Through the connection, Kai shared his nature and calmed their excitement.

Like with people, routine made the Mryken complacent. For the most part, they now ignored him. His daily run was now part of their typical day. As Kai approached the kennels, he reached out his mind to one Mryken. The dog approached the fence and sat. The others pranced after Kai down the length of the kennel yard.

The world around Kai became a blur as he ran faster. The wind pressed against his face. He leaped over a crate in his path and dodged a tall stack of boxes. A man converged on the next stack of crates. Smoke shot between the man and the crate on the ground and Kai leaped over, clipping the side of the man's container as he flew past.

"What was that? Prince Kai, watch where you're going, boy!" the man shouted, setting the crate down.

Kai laughed and kept running. He loved to run. It felt free to run. "On your left," he called to yet another guard. Still energized, he ran faster and faster. Again, he neared the kennel. With his mind, he called two more Mryken to the fence. Now three sat at attention while the others dashed along the fence until they could pursue him no farther.

He was quite surprised that he did not feel winded anymore. Months of daily running had made a big difference in his stamina. It made him wonder how fast he could run. *What are my limits?* He had to know. So, he ran faster, continuing around the wall. The sun broke through the clouds, warming his face. As he ran, he noticed more people set about their day.

Still, he continued to run, continued to push himself to go faster. Again, the kennels came into view. He used his mind to speak to the rest of the pack. Now every dog in the yard sat to watch him pass. None chased him.

The next lap, he ran faster still, Smoke still with him. He knew they could go faster. His thoughts connected to Smoke; he felt they both had more to give. With a smile across his face, he ran harder and harder. "On your left," he called passing another guard.

The obstacles came around faster, the guards more frequent. "On your left," he called, passing the next guard, leaping over crates and around barrels. The Mryken still sat waiting for him. Still, he felt he could go faster. When he passed the stables, he heard Haygan call out, but he did not stop. He was not ready to quit.

The gardens were ahead, and he ran faster. A few workers trimmed hedges and tended plants. "On your right," he called as he passed two gardeners. The orchard and the cottages came next. In his mind, he looked ahead. People were making their way about the grounds.

When he noticed a bright light ahead, he wanted to stop. It was a girl, leaving the palace and walking toward the cottages. He knew that light. He had to slow down. He would miss her if he didn't. He turned in her direction, and she came into view. He tried to slow down. He needed to stop. But he was going too fast. "Rayna, look out!" he shouted. With all he had he planted his feet and rolled head over heels, tumbling to the ground.

Exhausted, he panted at her feet. Hand on his chest, he looked up at the blue sky. The sun filled his eyes until a shadow crossed over him. Her smiling face came into view. "Someone's in a hurry this morning. Are you alright?" Rayna asked.

All he could do was laugh. What a morning he'd had. "Yes, Rayna, I'm fine."

She joined in his laughter and knelt beside him in the grass.

"I was headed to fetch my father's apron when I saw you running. I see you most mornings, up early. We are up before dawn to start on the bread."

Kai raised onto his elbows and looked around. "Can I see you later today? Shane is coming to the palace with his father. We had plans to go fishing, but I heard about a festival."

She looked over her shoulder to her family's cottage. "I will have to ask. There is much yet to do this morning. I doubt they would let me go alone."

"How about after lunch? Bring Julia. She is a lavender girl in the laundry service." Kai suggested.

Rayna offered her hand, and Kai hopped to his feet. "Julia is very nice," Rayna nodded. "We have lunch together nearly every day. I'll ask." Dusting off her dress, she headed toward her home.

"I'll see you after lunch!" he called out before heading towards the stables.

A few guards gawked at Kai. Their strange looks confused him, but he kept walking. The stables were a hive of activity.

Kai headed to Haygan's office, where the stablemaster hovered over stacks of paper. He quickly copied numbers from each sheet of paper into a large ledger and placed them to the side. "Good morning, Kai. Did you have a nice run this morning?"

Kai lowered his head. "Sorry, I didn't stop. I couldn't help it, the more I pushed, the faster I ran. The exhilaration was overpowering. I think I could have gone faster. Please don't be mad."

Haygan looked up from his desk. "Mad? You know why I am upset. Kai, you must be careful using your gifts. The older you get, the stronger you will become. I know you are testing your limits, and it is good training, but you can't do it here around the palace. People will notice. They noticed today. You put us all at risk. And release the Mryken. They still sit waiting for you." Haygan's tone remained level yet firm.

Kai took a deep breath, releasing it slowly. With a thought, he released the guard dogs from his suggestion to sit. "I didn't even think…"

He knew Kendra and Haygan insisted their secrets were crucial to their survival. Now he understood the strange looks. The guards were not sure how to process what they saw. His stunt could put them in jeopardy. "I am sorry, Haygan. I will be more careful."

Haygan leaned back in his chair. "If you want to run at those speeds, run at night or before dawn. I must be honest, at your top speed, you will someday be able to outrun Smoke. Technically, depending on how long you can hold out, you could run all the way to Port Anahita in less than an hour. Easy."

Kai noticed the tone in Haygan's voice had changed. For the first time, he sounded proud. Proud of their gifts. "Really? Can you outrun Shiva?" He already knew the answer, but he wanted to hear more.

"Yes, I can outrun Shiva. She is very fast, and it takes a toll. But I will say, the first time you beat an animal like a wolf or a lion, it is remarkable. There is little compared to running with a wild animal." Haygan smiled and leaned over his desk. "Now I have paperwork to finish." He sent Kai off with the wave of his hand.

Later that morning, Kai walked Smoke down towards the kennels. He wanted to continue to test his limits with his ability to connect with animals. Silence fell over the yard. The Mryken greeted him along the fence. Their thick white-and-gray fur shone brightly in his mind. Kai gleaned the pack and the surrounding area. The kennel and surrounding area were currently guard-free.

Kai sat cross-legged against a tree, and Smoke sat a few feet away. Within his mind, Kai connected to Smoke. He practiced directing Smoke to patrol the area while he reached out to the Mryken. His wolf complied. The guard dogs also did his bidding. He shuffled them around the kennel yard like chess pieces on a gameboard.

Dividing the pack into sets of four and then in twos, he

balanced sensing Smoke, directing the Mryken and scanning the yard. The more he divided his attention, the more difficult it became to maintain the thread to each group and Smoke. Pleased with his progress, he let the Mryken return to their own wanderings. In so doing, Kai's vision of the palace grounds expanded.

His exercise had increased his range. Within his mind, he saw the first few streets of Hightown Proper. People meandered through the avenues, darting in and out of shops into awaiting carts along the thoroughfare. Amazed at this expansion, he called Smoke to his side and returned to the palace to tell Kendra.

CHAPTER 22

Moon Blindness

Out of the family dining hall Kai chased Amelia. "Slow down! Where are you going?" When he caught up to her, he took her arm and spun her around. "We should talk. I know I have been busy."

Her eyes met his, and he could tell she was on the verge of tears. "Are you alright? What's wrong?" Over his shoulder, he saw Tolan take a step in their direction, then turn and walk away. "Does he have anything to do with this?" Kai's tone deepened, and he squeezed her arm.

"Ouch, you're hurting me." Amelia pulled her arm away. "You *have* been busy!" She pushed him away.

"Wait, I want to help. What's wrong?" Kai pleaded.

She glared back at him. "Why do you care?" The pain in her eyes echoed in her voice.

Her distress shocked him. Lost in her misdirected emotions, he withdrew. He knew he'd been busy, but this was not like Amelia. She continued away from him. There had to be something he could do to help. "Amelia, please, hold up." He dashed after her.

She stopped with her head down, but she waited. "You're right Amelia, I have been busy, but I am here now. The least I can do is listen."

Amelia looped her arm around his and carried on down the hallway. "There isn't really anyone to talk to about this, but you. Everyone else has their opinions and believe me they advise without my asking."

Happy to listen, he let her guide him. They had spent so little time together these past few weeks; he had no idea what was troubling her. Rumors crept through his mind. "What has Tolan done? If he hurt you, I will…" His voice trailed off as he watched a tear slide down her cheek. "Amelia, please tell me how I can help." He pulled her to a stop.

"He didn't do anything. Not really. He leaves today. And he will be gone for six months." Her voice wobbled. "I couldn't bear to say goodbye publicly." Her eyes filled with tears and gushed down her face.

He pulled her into a hug. He could not find the words to comfort her. Nola passed by, giving him a look. Not wanting any more attention, he pulled her into the music room and closed the door. "Here, sit. Tell me everything." Kai sat down on the sofa with Amelia, her hand in his.

"I am not sure where to start. Kai, you are my best friend. You're like my brother. I'm sorry, I know what our future holds." Tears began to fall again, and she pulled a handkerchief from her sleeve, wiping her face. "We didn't mean to…it just kind of happened." She stumbled through her words between sobs.

"Didn't mean to what?" He felt suddenly nervous.

Drying her eyes, she looked at him. "I know I am only fifteen, but I love Tolan, and he loves me. He told me yesterday after we…" Her hand touched her lips, and she blushed. "He kissed me for the first time—then he told me he loved me. I know it's a mistake." Tears welled in her eyes again.

Kai knew what she meant. It was wrong to feel for another when their duty would bind them together. They both had to grow up too fast. They were expected to marry and rule as king and queen of Milnos when they turned eighteen. She was like a sister to him. He could not change their future, and he could not change how she felt.

"Amelia, do you have any classes this afternoon? I want you to meet someone." He smiled at her and took her by the hand. Back on his feet, he pulled her up from the sofa.

"You want to introduce me to Rayna." Amelia smiled. "We've met."

Kai turned red. "When?" he asked, trying not to look concerned.

"People talk. They make up stupid rumors. The tales I heard I knew could not be true. I had to admit I was curious. If I was not your type, who was. I wanted to see if she was worthy of your attention. She is a lucky girl."

Amelia was right. Kai had heard things about her and Tolan. Things he knew could not be accurate. It made him crazy, the lies. He had tried to keep his moments with Rayna with her parents or in public areas. "I have heard stories too. Whispers around corners. None of them true, I know. Amelia, I respect both of you, and I would never want to tarnish your or Rayna's reputation, but I will not give up on what I want."

"Exactly. Which is why I wanted to meet her. Lizzy helped me arrange lunch. Since you spend little time in the gardens, it was the obvious choice." She chuckled at her own cleverness.

It was good to hear Amelia laugh. He had hoped to get her mind off Tolan. "So, what do you think of Rayna?"

Amelia tilted her head as if contemplating the right words. "I found her to be a most pleasant young lady. She is smart and charming. Did you know she is interested in plants? On our stroll through the gardens, she named every plant. She hopes to study herbs and their medicinal uses."

He swallowed hard. It was strange hearing someone else talk about Rayna. He had known desires to learn about plants. "We have walked around in the herb gardens near the palace. She knows a fair amount about them. I have brought her a few books, and I gave her a wicker basket at the winter festival," he exclaimed proudly.

She smiled and patted his hand. "Wherever we are going,

count me in."

"Great, change into your riding clothes. I will make the arrangements to have your black mare saddled and ready. Meet us at the royal stables in twenty minutes."

Dresnor waited for Kai in the breezeway. "Dresnor," Kai called. "Can you make the necessary arrangements for more guards? I want to take miss Amelia, Rayna, and her friend Julia out with Shane and me. We will all be riding to Henley. I heard they have a festival today, and everyone could use an afternoon of entertainment."

"Certainly, Prince Kai. I will see to the additional detail." Dresnor gave a small bow and backed away.

By the time Kai reached the stables, Ember was already being saddled by Weston. Finlee was happy to saddle Misty for Julia, leaving the selection of one more horse for Rayna. Meanwhile, Shane's white horse Winter trotted up the street. "What are you waiting for? Let's go." Shane questioned.

Kai kicked at a rock on the ground. "Small change in plans. I kind of invited Rayna." He started, folding his arms around himself. "And Julia. And Amelia." He waited for Shane to get mad, but no words came.

Winter cut to the right and Shane slid from his saddle. "I thought we were going fishing. Just us," he pressed. "Wait, did you say Julia is coming?" Shane's tone changed, and his expression beamed.

"She is." Kai nodded.

"Rayna seems nice. And you know I like…well, Julia is nice too." Shane added with a controlled grin. "Amelia. Do you mean the girl you're meant to marry? Awkward mix, don't you think? But what do I know? You know them best. I am just happy not to be working today."

Confident in his relationships, Kai knew this would be a good day. Amelia understood him, and she felt the same about Tolan. "Everyone will enjoy the festival. Trust me."

"Wait, where are we going?" Shane asked, confused. "I thought we were going to Baden Lake—fishing."

"We were," Kai responded. "But then I heard there is a festival today in Henley. I thought it might be more fun than going to the lake. We have all summer to fish and swim. The Henley Estate is only a short ride west," he assured his friend.

Inside the stables Kai found Weston inspecting the straps of his chestnut saddle. Rayna entered behind him with Julia. They were both wearing black pants and white shirts, ready for the day's ride. "Are you two girls ready to go riding?" Kai asked.

Rayna approached Ember. "Julia is. She's rides all the time." She looked up at Ember's large head and paused. "But I've only ridden a few times, on my father's pony. She is small and extremely stubborn."

"Julia, you will be riding Misty. Finlee is saddling her now if you want to meet her." Kai gestured toward the gray mare. Julia dropped Rayna's hand to spend time with her horse for the day.

"Rayna, would you like to pick your own horse?" Kai motioned down the long line of stalls. "You can ride any horse you choose. Riding a horse is not much different than a pony. The only real difference is size, and horses are not as stubborn. Usually."

"I thought there would be guards going with us." Rayna eyed the groomsmen.

Shane stood between the girls. "Hello, Julia. Rayna. The guards and Kempery-men have their own stables and should be down shortly. Why is Amelia not here yet?" He bent his neck around to search the doorway.

Julia blushed at Shane. "We didn't see her when we left, but then again, I wouldn't expect her to leave the palace through the laundry." Looking at her feet she pushed a clump of straw, avoiding eye contact with Shane.

Kai took Rayna by the hand. "Time to choose. If you pick the horse that speaks to you, you will find the ride more enjoyable. How about this one? Her name is Honey." He laughed. "Some of the names are not very original. Most are named for their coloring or temperament. He motioned across the aisle. I would never put you on Pepper; she has too much attitude. Bolt here, he is too quick to spook and requires an experienced rider."

Rayna slowly walked down the center of the stables, looking right and left at each horse she passed. She smiled at the names as she went. "Cinnamon, Scout, Brandy, and Blaze." At the end of the aisle, she read the name "Snowflake." She smiled wider. "Snowflake sounds nice. I can see how she got her name. I love the white spots across her ears and the white flecks across her hips. They stand out against her dark chestnut coloring."

Snowflake bobbed her head up and down. Rayna was delighted by the gesture. Kai eased Rayna forward and opened his hand for the horse to sniff his palm. "I think she likes you. Step a little closer."

"Kai, catch." Shane tossed Kai a large red apple. "Rayna should give her an apple. It will help them become friends."

Kai handed Rayna the apple. "Let her sniff your empty hand first. Then offer her the apple. You can stroke her head as she eats."

Rayna did as instructed. When Snowflake took the apple, she giggled. "That tickles." She ran her hands over the horse. "She is so gentle. I can feel her delight."

Kai opened the gate, clipped the lead to the halter and pulled Snowflake out of her stall. Rayna continued to fawn over the horse. He watched as the two melded together. The horse curled its head around Rayna, while Rayna rubbed her face, neck, and mane.

"I don't think Snowflake gets much attention," Rayna said, leaning her head in close.

He had never seen a horse take to a person in this manner. "Seems like a good match. Here, hold the lead, and I will get Finlee to bring a saddle."

When he returned with Finlee, Rayna still had her head nuzzled into Snowflakes dark mane. Finlee stopped short of the happy pair. "She can't ride her!" Finlee stammered. "You didn't tell me she chose Snowflake. How did you even get the horse out of her stall? Put her back."

"What do you mean?" Kai protested. "She has been fine. One would think those two were soulmates the way they are coiled around each other. Who cares what horse she chooses? I told her which ones are too wild. I have never seen anyone ride Snowflake, but she seems harmless."

Finlee hefted the heavy saddle onto a nearby barrel. "Look, all I know is everyone who rides her says she is high strung and anxious. She has good days and bad days. She will never let me put a saddle on her, let alone take her out of the barn. Haygan thinks she has a sight problem. She can't see far away, and he said her milky eyes are a sign of moon blindness. Haygan is the only person who can handle her."

While they spoke, Kai continued to watch Rayna. To everyone's astonishment, Snowflake knelt, and Rayna hopped up on her bareback. Still holding the lead, she squeezed her legs, and Snowflake stood and walked the length of the stables. Kai took note of her eyes. The faint cloudy layer over her dark eyes was there. He had not noticed it before.

Everyone gawked as Rayna rode Snowflake. Speechless, they ran outside to watch her confidently navigate the side yard. "Finlee, get Haygan," Kai instructed while he kept his eyes on Rayna. The pair slowly traversed the yard. Rayna continued to fawn over the horse, rubbing her neck and mane.

Haygan joined the onlookers. "Kai, come with me. I need to see how she is when you approach her now that she has a rider. Stay calm and reach out to Snowflake, let her sense your nature." Haygan kept his hands in his pocket and leaned against the nearest tree.

Connecting with a gentle horse was easy. Kai felt her nature, timid, and sweet. Palm up, he reached for Snowflake. Her soft nose nuzzled his hand. With a side glance, he inspected her eyes. The milky white cloud was definitely there.

Through the trees, Dresnor approached. The Kempery-man

moved at a fast pace, always on point. He went straight for Rayna and touched Snowflake's neck. "Miss Rayna, I see you've made a friend. I have never seen this horse before. Is she yours?" Dresnor looked over the horse and then up to Rayna.

"She is not my horse. I wish she were." Rayna looked over the moon with delight.

"You don't intend riding bareback, do you?" Dresnor pulled them towards the stables.

She laughed. "It is the strangest thing. She knelt, and I felt this overwhelming urge to ride. She has such a big heart and sweet soul—if you can know that about a horse."

"Great coloring. People call her pattern the dappled Moroka, which looks great against the dark bay. They are rare wild horses from the north. Didn't know we had one in the stables." Dresnor reached up to Rayna. "Here, let me help you down so we can get a saddle on her."

Kai stepped backward. Haygan leaned forward. "If she wants to ride her, it is good to know Dresnor can handle her. The horse seems to trust the man."

Rayna hopped down, and Snowflake allowed Dresnor to lead her back to the stables. "Did you see that?" Rayna skipped across the yard, wrapped in sunshine. "She is wonderful." Rayna looked back and forth between Kai and Haygan. "What?"

Haygan nodded respectfully. "We are happy to see you've bonded with Snowflake. You had better help get her saddled. Keep her calm." He directed Rayna to the stables.

"Kai, hold up." Haygan let Rayna get out of earshot and continued. "The Grand Duke asked me to replace Snowflake. He wanted me to turn her out since I was the only person who could get near her. Up till now, she was taking up space. I should inform him Rayna has a fondness for her. It is doubtful Dante will even remember. I will have the horse transferred with a saddle to the servants' stables with the Kendrick pony. Then Rayna can ride anytime she wishes."

"Do you want me to tell her?" Kai asked.

"Let me tell her father first. He should know he just acquired a horse. If her father is willing, I will make the arrangements, maybe even toss in food for a year to sweeten the deal. Let her father tell her tonight."

Slowly a large group of soldiers converged with their mounts at the royal stables. Kai could tell their rank by their uniforms; eight guards joined his three Kempery-men—Dresnor, Redmon, and Albey. The man bringing up the rear was a man he knew—Drew. His uniform indicated he would be their scout. It pleased Kai to see his old guard.

Amelia strolled out of the palace and joined the group. "Sorry it took me so long. Hello Rayna, Julia. It is a pleasure to see you both again."

"Miss Amelia. Good to see you today," Rayna said with a pleasant smile.

"Now that we are all friends, can we go?" Shane insisted.

While the others mounted up, Haygan pulled Kai to the side. "Keep an eye on Snowflake. Her eyes still have a thin haze, but I believe her sight has improved. Rayna's doing, no doubt." Haygan whispered.

The stablemasters words concerned Kai. "Is there any reason to worry? Should Rayna pick a different horse?" Kai hesitated.

"No, Snowflake will be fine. Like with me, I imagine she was fine with you and Rayna because you're able to share your emotions with her. She trusts you. I doubt Rayna even realizes she's doing it. You might not have noticed, but I believe Rayna is Katori. Her aura is unusually bright," Haygan confided. "And now this bonding, I would bet my life on it."

"What do we do? She must be taught to control her powers. We are the same age, so it makes sense she would only now be experiencing an awakening." Kai looked at Rayna.

"There is no time to speak to her before we leave for the summer. Kendra can keep an eye on her. Kai, you might be best suited to start the conversation. Find out what she knows about where she comes from. One look at her parents' energy,

and you know they are not Katori. See what you can find out.
You better join your friends before they leave without you."

CHAPTER 23

Cheese Pie

Cream-colored cottages and shops with thatched rooftops popping over short stone walls, came into view as they crested the hill above the town of Henley. Inside the tall gatehouse, Kai noticed the stone walls didn't completely encircle the city. Several sections were in various stages of repair, though nobody worked on them today.

Drew led the group around the outskirts of town to the Henley estate. Smoke leapt through one of the gaps in the walls and closed in on the group near the stables. Three groomsmen exited as they rode up and helped everyone dismount.

The lead groomsman took the reigns as Drew slid off his horse. "Master Drew, a pleasure to have you home."

"Hello, Eli. Good to be home." Drew responded.

"Prince Kai, I will inform my parents you are here," Drew said. "They will want to host you for a time. Say, afternoon tea in the park?"

How did I not know? Kai felt embarrassed he'd never asked about Drew's family. The guards and the Kempery-men formally addressed one another by their last names. He had always just called him Drew. "Drew, you are a Henley? Are you related to Kempery-man Henley?"

"I am. Kempery-man Marcus Henley is my uncle. Don't worry—everyone calls me Drew. It makes it easier not to confuse me with my uncle. I also avoid favoritism based on his reputation."

"Afternoon tea would be nice," Kai said, suddenly seeing his old guard in a new light. It was odd that knowing Drew came from money changed how Kai looked at the man.

"Follow this road back into the center of town," Drew said as he walked toward his family's home. "You will find the festival in the city park. Look for the gazebo with the Henley name on the post."

The estate road was paved with large flagstone and surrounded by large billowing oaks and rose bushes. Amelia looped arms with Rayna and Julia. "Ladies, we have a festival to attend!"

They walked down the road arm-in-arm, Smoke leading the way. Hands in his pockets, Kai trailed behind with Shane. He watched the girls giggle and chatter away.

What are they saying? Kai strolled behind them. "Today is not turning out at all the way I planned," he huffed.

With a small huff of his own, Shane looked at his friend. "I know what you mean. What was your plan again? Mine was going fishing."

"I wanted to spend the day with..." Kai trailed off; he couldn't finish. Shane was right. They were supposed to go fishing. But he'd been so caught in the moment when he saw Rayna. Julia simply came by default so Rayna's parents would say yes. Then he invited Amelia to cheer her up.

"I am sorry, it was our day. I saw Rayna, and my mind went sideways. Then Amelia was crying, and I couldn't leave her behind." He gestured to the girls up ahead.

"Don't worry, I'm not mad. You're a good friend. Besides, you also brought Julia." Shane paused, looking around. "I hear music. We must be close."

The road turned sharply to the left, and the trees ended. Music echoed through the streets. People were converging in one direction—the city park.

Dresnor placed his hand on Kai's shoulder. "Everyone, I need you to stop," he called loudly. "Each of you has an assigned guard. He rode beside you on the way here. They are personally responsible for your well-being. They go where you go. The remaining guards will filter throughout the crowd. I prefer you all to stay close together. Nobody should wander off alone. Do you understand?"

"Yes," they each answered.

"Prince Kai, we are going to an unknown event. It is my job to keep you safe. You and you alone. The others will also turn to protect you if necessary—over the others. Do you understand?"

"I understand, Dresnor. We will be fine. If we stay together, it will be easier for you and your men. So we will keep the group together!" Kai assured him.

The small town unfolded into a wide-open park. Colorful awnings and tents, tall trees and park benches dotted the area. People were everywhere, young and old. The presence of Diu guards parted the crowds. Their royal blue-and-silver uniforms stood out. Swords strapped to their waists and shields at their backs were a bit out of place in this quaint little borough.

Henley guards, dressed in gray-and-black leather armor stamped with a wolf, mingled with the crowd. While they patrolled, Kai noticed they did not have the same discipline and confidence that his men shared.

Desperate to keep them together and spend a little time with Rayna, he stepped up between her and Amelia. "I smell apple pie. Who wants some?" he asked.

Elbows out, he offered them both an arm. Shane offered Julia his arm, and together they approached a vendor. The sign over the red booth read: *Grandma's Fried Apple Pie with Cream.*

"Can we share a large bowl please?" Amelia asked. While Kai paid, a lady handed Amelia a large bowl and five spoons.

Kai held the bowl as his friends all took a bite. This moment would be something he would treasure for years to come. He took a heaping spoonful and then another. "This is wonderful. I love apple pie, but I've never had it with frozen cream before." Kai took a third bite.

Everyone else agreed it was magnificent. Shane took the last bite and handed the bowl back to the young lady. "Thank you, that was delicious. What's next?" Shane pointed to the next tent. The sign read: *Aunt Shelly's Custard Cream Pie.* "Not sure what custard is, but I'm willing to give it a try. Anyone else?"

"Five please," Kai said, handing the woman a few coins. In return, she distributed five small plates. The golden cream stood tall on the plate, held up by a thick pastry shell. He slid his fork through the pie wedge and took a bite. To his surprise, it had a hint of orange to the tongue. "I wouldn't have expected orange. Wonderful," he said carving off another bite.

The others all made yummy noises in agreement, enjoying their treat. While this was good, Kai still thought the apple was the best. Maybe because he knew his mother liked apple, too. Finished, they returned their plates and forks.

The next few stalls sold fruit, clothing, and trinkets. Julia pulled away from Shane to unfold a small quilt. Her hands roamed the floral and ivy pattern. The back was solid emerald green to match the ivy design on the front. "This is outstanding work. Fine stitching. Rayna, you have a look at this quilt. Isn't it lovely?"

"Julia, that is divine," Rayna agreed. "The rich green fabric suits you. Are you going to buy it?" Rayna lifted the other end to help refold the quilt.

"Oh no, I shouldn't. I only brought a little. My mother wouldn't approve of me spending all my money." Julia's fingers traced the fabric's stitching once more.

"How much do you need?" Amelia pushed in between them, inspecting the craftsmanship. One look at the sign and she pulled out a small change pouch from her dress. "That is not too much, I have enough." She handed Julia the money.

"I could never accept it, Lady Amelia. My mother would not approve." Julia pushed back Amelia's offered coin. "Thank you. You're sweet…"

Amelia cut her off. "Consider it an early birthday gift. Your birthday is next month. Surely your mother couldn't object to a gift. And call me Amelia. Formality sounds ridiculous between friends!"

"Lady Amelia…I mean Amelia. Thank you, I will cherish it." Red-cheeked Julia lovingly picked up the quilt and held it close to her chest. "This is the nicest gift anyone has ever given me. Thank you."

"What's next?" Shane interrupted, pointing to the next tent. "Lemon pudding? Not sure about this one. I like lemons, but what is pudding?"

Amelia pushed forward. "I've had pudding before. If you like custard, you will love pudding. They're very similar, only pudding is not as thick. Five cups please." She handed the man behind the table a few coins and distributed a tiny cup to everyone.

Kai hesitantly stirred the yellow mixture. He was not overly fond of lemons. Bravely he took the smallest taste. To his surprise, it wasn't bad. His next bite was a heaping spoonful. "Hmmm, I don't usually like lemons, but this is good."

"I disagree. I am not a fan at all." Shane made a face. "There is too much sugar in this. Lemons should be tart." He passed his cup back.

Rayna bumped Shane on the arm. "I can't believe you didn't like it."

Julia came to his defense, taking Shane's arm. "I agree, Shane. Lemons should be tart." She pulled him ahead of the group through the crowd.

Kai's eyes went wide, and he tossed his hands in the air. "Well, alright. What's next? I am getting full. We should find the Henley gazebo."

"Just one more," Amelia called out. "Cheese pie, that smells wonderful. It doesn't smell sweet at all. Miss, can you tell us what is in your pie?" She sniffed the row of pastry cups.

"Certainly, my lady. You are correct, this is not a sweet pie. Cheese pie is a savory dish. The outer shell is a flour pastry filled with a mixture of cheese, onion, herbs, and potato. Would you like to try a taste?" She cut a bite-sized slice from one cup.

Amelia took the offered bite. Thrilled, her eyes enlarged, and she swallowed. "It is wonderful, and still a little warm. You all must try this. Miss, can you cut the rest of this pie cup into four slices? I am afraid we've had a little too much before finding you." Amelia offered her a few coins and turned to the group delighted.

"Happy to, miss. Enjoy." She offered the plate.

Rayna sighed. "One last bite, and then I am finished."

Everyone ate their slice, and Kai nodded in agreement. "That was good, but I cannot eat another bite."

Six pavilions angled out like spokes on a wheel around one large gazebo, each filled with people eating. The Henley gazebo had eight sides, raised up several feet off the ground, and stood tall in the center. It was stained dark walnut, and it had two round tables beautifully decorated with white lines, flowers, sweets, and teapots. Drew sat with his father and stood quickly when he saw Prince Kai.

"Your Highness, Prince Kai, thank you for honoring us with your visit. I would like to introduce my father Lord Robert Henley and my mother, Lady Elizabeth Henley," he said, bowing to Kai as the group entered the gazebo.

"Drew, thank you. Lord and Lady Henley, thank you for having us on such short notice." They each shook hands.

Kai felt a little uncomfortable being the center of attention. He was used to his father being the focal point. He remembered seeing the Henleys at the winter festival, but he had not actually spoken with them. Seeing them once a year didn't make them exceptionally close.

"You have a lovely town," Kai offered. "I heard you were having a festival today. I hope it is acceptable we came unannounced."

Lord Robert shared Drew's pitch-black hair and blue eyes. "Your Highness. We are most humbled to have you here today. Drew speaks very highly of you. It is our pleasure to finally spend private time with the young Prince of Diu."

Kai blushed and quickly turned to his friends. "Allow me to introduce my friends. This is Lady Amelia Maxwell from Milnos." Amelia curtsied in response. "This is Miss Rayna Kendrick of Diu." Following suit, Rayna curtsied.

Next Kai gestured to his best friend. "This is Mister Shane Marduk of Diu."

Shane extended a hand. "Pleasure to meet you, Lord and Lady Henley."

"And finally, this is Miss Julia…" Embarrassed, he looked at Julia. He did not know her last name.

Julia did her best curtsy and added. "My name is Julia Blackwell, from Diu."

Lord Robert bowed to the group. "It is my pleasure to meet all of you. Please sit. I am sure you have tried many delicious treats around the festival. I doubt you have room for more."

Lady Elizabeth Henley offered a delicate hand to Kai. She also had black hair and blue eyes. "Your Highness, I am so happy you are here."

"Thank you, Lady Elizabeth."

Everyone sat. Kai surveyed his guards, staggered around the gazebo and staged through the park. Kai took a small sip of tea. "Lord Henley, this is a wonderful event. We have sampled a fair amount at the festival today. I could not eat another bite." He eyed the treats on the table and glanced at Rayna, who was quietly speaking with Amelia and Lady Henley.

With a nod, Kai motioned to the fortifications. "I noticed your walls are under construction. Honestly, I can't tell if they are being built or torn down. There is a rather large section missing to the west. I hope you've not had any trouble."

Lord Henley pursed his lips. "Well, in order to expand, we took down the west wall, and our plans were progressing on schedule. Unfortunately, this past winter we lost two large oaks near the east wall. The older section already had cracking issues, and the weight of two fallen trees was more than it could bear." He folded his arms around himself. "It is not a good feeling being exposed on two sides."

"I agree." Kai thought about what his father would do. "Would you be open to Diu offering aid? Either on the wall repairs or on the new buildings? The faster your new buildings are started, the sooner you can determine the new wall location."

"Thank you, Prince Kai. Any assistance you could provide would be most welcome." Lord Henley relaxed his arms and poured a new cup of tea.

"You are close enough, the very least we could do was offer additional guard detail. I will speak with my father and Grand Duke Dante."

This was a new feeling. Kai enjoyed offering support. He knew it would be his mission in the upcoming trip to provide this same support to the Hamrin Estate and its town if needed.

"Again, we greatly appreciate your provision. I hope it is not too presumptuous of me to mention, but I had heard you traveled with a wolf. I now see it's true. What did it take to domesticate such an animal?"

Taken aback by the question, Kai looked toward Smoke lying in the grass. A magnificent wild animal that he felt fortunate to know. "Smoke is still wild. I have not domesticated him. We share a mutual respect. Smoke is not dependent, unlike a dog who needs its human owner."

"Really? That is fascinating and terrifying at the same time. The Nebean black wolf is much larger than any other dog or wolf I have ever seen. Tell me your thoughts. We have a pack of black wolves to the west. My hunter says they are getting closer and closer each season. I would hate to put them down, but I have livestock and people to protect." Concern tightened Lord Henley's brow.

The thought of killing a wolf because it was too close to the town shocked Kai. Although he knew first-hand wolves were typically put down when they got too bold—for the safety of the people living nearby. Sadly, he remembered the day Hunter Marduk killed a wolf to save his life because he ventured out alone into the forest.

"Before you do anything, let me speak with Haygan our stablemaster," Kai implored. "He also travels with a Nebean black wolf. He may know how to keep them away or move them to another area."

Shane cleared his throat. "My father tends the base of Thade Mountain. We've had to put down a wolf or two over the years. They can get aggressive. They steal food and kill livestock. Although most are afraid and avoid people, a few get curious or desperate. Packs are territorial. They are either expanding their area or being pushed out by another pack. Even people can displace a group, cause them to get desperate for food."

Robert took a sip of tea and nodded. "My hunter still suggests we put them down, but I've been able to discourage the idea, at least for now. If you could assist us, I would greatly appreciate any advice."

Dresnor stood near the stairs. "My apologies, Prince Kai, but we should make our way back to the stables. We need to make it back to the palace before it gets too late." He motioned to a nearby guard. "See that the stables have our horses ready."

Drew stood. "I will go with him, see to the preparations. Father, it was good to see you. I will be back tomorrow. I have a few days off before summer. Mother." He offered her his hand and kissed her cheek before jogging after the other guard.

"Agreed, Dresnor." Kai stood and offered his hand to Lord Henley. "Lord Henley, thank you for a wonderful afternoon. I will send word when my father decides what aid we can offer. Your growth and security are important to Diu, and we will do what we can to assist. Also, I am most interested in finding a peaceful solution for the wolves. Expect a response within a day or two at the most."

"Kai. Can I call you Kai?" Lord Henley asked. "Call me Robert. Allow me to walk part way back with you. We should talk." Robert put his arm around Kai, escorting him into the crowd.

Robert was like an older version of Drew. Even though Kai was tall for his age, Robert was still much taller. "Sure. Robert, between us you may call me Kai." He wasn't sure his father would approve, but the Henley name had an honorable reputation.

"If you don't mind me saying, I notice you travel with ... well, common people, and you call them friends. My son Drew mentioned you're rather progressive." They started walking down the main street toward the estate grounds. "You favor your father in that respect. We were great friends when he was young. Even after you were born, we saw him quite often. Since he married Nola, we never see him outside the winter festival. The loss has been most unsettling for us."

"My father mentioned he spent a good deal of time here when he was younger. He said it was a picturesque place. I'd say your town has grown significantly over the years since his time."

Kai thought back. He could not remember Robert and Elizabeth from his youth. He was surprised to hear this man was so close to his parents. It was hard to believe they no longer spoke. "So, you knew my mother?"

"I knew your mother. Wonderful lady. Loved to laugh. She was all about you, her little man. My Elizabeth so loved your mother. They were very dear friends." Somber, Robert looked off into the trees. "You have become a fine young man. It has been my pleasure to get to know Iver and Mariana's son." Robert stopped at the entrance to his estate. "I should get back to Elizabeth."

"Robert, today has been a total surprise. I had no idea you were close with my parents. It is good to know they had loyal friends. I hope to return and get to know you and Lady Elizabeth." He turned to face Robert.

"You are welcome anytime. Should you ever need anything in return, you can count on us for support." Without asking, Robert embraced Kai. He let Kai go and looked up the road. "Your better catch up to your friends."

"Goodbye, Robert," Kai waved.

He approached Dresnor, who'd hung back. "Dresnor, I want to ask Drew to become part of my royal guard. I thought I owed it to you to ask if you agree. I know you have a few more men to select before our summer trip. Please consider my request," Kai said confidently.

Dresnor stroked his beard. "Normally they need to reach a certain rank to be in the regular detail. I will admit he is well on his way. He came with us today, recommended by his uncle. Your trip was short notice, and since Kempery-man Henley could not come with us, he felt it best if Drew, a local, take his place." They stopped and let the trailing guards pass them. "Look, Kai, if you want Drew in your service, I will do whatever you wish. Only, don't promote him before he's put in his time. That would not go over well with the other men. He should start as a scout; I will speak with the Grand Duke about the assignment. He oversees palace and royal security. Dante should not have a problem with your choice."

"I appreciate the advice, but I trust Drew. Provided it doesn't upset the natural order of his advancement, please consider him."

CHAPTER 24

Kodama

The late-afternoon sun warmed their backs as Kai's small group mounted up and left town Henley, behind the lead scout—Drew. Kai rode beside Shane. "I hope you had a good day. I know it is not what we planned."

"Like you said, we have all summer to swim and fish. Getting to know Amelia was nice. Especially considering you must marry her someday. Makes me wonder why you spend so much time with Rayna." Shane cringed at his words.

"You're not the first person to mention I should not spend time with her." He looked to Shane. "Be honest. If I said you could never see Julia, what would you say?"

"But I don't … well, maybe … she is very…" Embarrassed, Shane shifted in his saddle. "I hate to turn it back around on you, but what does Julia have to do with you and Rayna?"

"I am trying to prove a point. There's no need to say it out loud, but be honest, you like Julia. Every time we get together you enjoy her company." Kai let Shane settle on the truth. "Now imagine if you could not spend time together. Ever!"

Silence lingered in the air as they continued riding. Up and over the next hill they rode. Diu city was now in view. "Not being with Julia would be difficult. So, I ask again, why spend time with Rayna if it can never be more?" Shane pressed.

Kai knew Shane was right. Everyone was right, based on the information they had. Still, he could not let go. In his soul, Kai knew Rayna was meant to be his future. "Can I tell you a secret? One you promise you will not tell anyone, not even your dad?"

"Come on, Kai, you know I can keep a secret," Shane whispered. "I'm already keeping one. You can tell me anything."

Kai was afraid to say it out loud, and he held his breath, he'd only told Kendra. Haygan didn't even know. "I have dreams. Well, visions. Things that either have happened or will happen." Relieved, he let out a long sigh and looked to his friend. "Rayna is in my future."

"Not sure what to say to that. I think my mother had dreams. But then it is difficult to remember." Hesitating, Shane looked over his shoulder back at the girls. "I remember the day we met Rayna and how much you spoke about her on the ride home. If you believe she is important, then trust yourself. Trust Alenga. Whatever is meant to be will find a way."

Kai nodded. "You are my best friend. I appreciate your honesty."

Changing the subject, Kai asked. "Are you ready for our trip to Hamrin?"

"I'm excited, yes. This will be my first time east. We only ever go south to Porta Anahita or north around Thade Mountain. My dad said it will not be an easy ride. Unlike the gentle stroll today, we will ride much harder and faster. We must cover forty to fifty miles in a day—sunrise to sunset in the saddle. I'd say the better question is, are *you* ready?"

That was a good question. Honestly, he was nervous. He had never slept under the stars, and Hamrin would be two full days in the saddle. "I am as ready as I will ever be. Not much choice, really. My father wants to teach me responsibility. Between us, I am both excited and terrified."

Shane sat high in his saddle. "This will be the best trip of our lives. That is until the next summer when we go to Chenowith. Dad told me each summer trip we will go farther and farther. I can hardly believe we get to spend an entire summer together." He grinned from ear to ear. "Considering that we will be leaving soon, do you mind if I circle back and talk with Julia for the rest of the ride home?"

"I would like to speak with Amelia," Kai nodded. "See if she had a good day. I will ride back and send Julia forward." Kai pulled Ember out of line and circled back. "Julia, would you mind if I rode by Amelia for a while? You can take my place beside Shane."

Julia blushed, looking to Amelia, who nodded approvingly. Julia gave Misty a squeeze and trotted ahead to Shane.

Not wanting to remind Amelia of Tolan's departure, and make her cry again, he didn't mention the boy's name. "I wanted to ask, did you have a good day?"

"Thank you for inviting me," Amelia swayed with the movement of her horse. "You have kind friends. Rayna is a lucky girl."

Now *he* was embarrassed. Amelia meant the world to him. "Thank you."

He looked off into a nearby thicket and saw Smoke stalking something inside the tree line. In his mind, he connected to his sight and saw a small rabbit in the brush.

"No matter what, know that I am here for you. You are my dearest friend and my sister in spirit. We will find a way to make this work." Kai tried to reassure her, but deep down, he knew it was just as much for himself.

"Kai, you can say his name—Tolan. There I said it and no more tears. This morning his goodbye struck my heart. I will miss him dearly. Six months is a long time to be apart." She did her best to look happy. "Now since you leave soon, you better make use of this ride." Amelia pulled on her horse and circled around to Rayna. She said to her, "Trade places with me. I will ride with Kempery-man Dresnor. Spend some time with Kai before he leaves for the summer."

Rayna pressed Snowflake forward to join Kai and Ember. "Amelia said it is my turn." She smiled, her head held high, her back straight as a board.

How is it she could make him feel so happy and yet so nervous at the same time? "I hope you enjoyed the afternoon away. How are you and Snowflake doing?" He wanted to tell her he knew she had bonded with Snowflake and what that meant."

She paused, tilting her head to one side. "This may sound strange, but on the way here, I got a sense that she felt anxious. Lost, even. My dad told me when I learned to ride our pony that animals can sense your nature. Snowflake gives me such self-confidence and love. It is easy to give that back in return."

Her words were truer than she knew—without knowing how she had bonded with Snowflake. She was making a difference just by being herself. "That does not sound strange at all," Kai said. "Haygan told me something similar." How could he tell her? Learning her horse was going blind would break her heart.

They rode on in silence, his thoughts haunting him. Ultimately, he knew he had to be honest. "Rayna, I need to tell you something about Snowflake." He bit his lip, dreading how she would take the news.

Before he lost his nerve, he continued. "As I understand it, Snowflake has problems seeing anything far away. It makes her afraid to leave the stables. Today is the first time she has let anyone besides Haygan ride her. She has something called moon blindness, trouble seeing in low light, which could … or will … result in complete blindness." He had blurted it all out so fast that he felt sick. There had been no kindness, just facts. "I am sorry, Rayna. I could have said that better. I thought you should know, and I thought I should be the one to tell you."

Rayna closed her eyes, took in a deep breath, and folded down over Snowflake. She laid there for only a moment and then sat up. "Everything that happened before we left told me this horse was special. When I touched her, my hands felt warm, and she nuzzled me. With her neck wrapped around me, I felt connected. I could see her and me walking through a meadow. The one you showed me with all the wildflowers. She walked freely by my side without a lead."

"It is a precious gift to bond with an animal. I hope you understand why I had to say something." He glanced in her direction.

She nodded in understanding. "Given the terrified look on Finlee's face when I rode Snowflake, I do understand. But honestly, I don't think she has that problem anymore. Her milky eyes are clear now. I have not been directing her—she is walking all on her own." She held up her hands, the reigns resting on the saddle.

Kai pressed Ember forward to get a better view of Snowflake. He squinted at her, and to his amazement, Rayna was right. The haze was gone. "How..." He let his voice trail off.

The gift of healing freighted Kai. Haygan or Kendra had not mentioned this Katori ability. It was one thing to share your sight through the bond connection, but healing. He didn't know how Rayna had healed her horse. *How do I hide this secret?* "Don't tell anyone. Keep this between us."

Kai waved to Garrick as his group entered the outer gatehouse. Rayna lowered her head; he could tell by her expression she was confused and a little afraid. "What does it matter? If she is better now it is a good thing."

Conflicted, he rubbed the side of his head. "I was told to let your father surprise you." His tone hushed as they road through the city. "Dante was going to get rid of the horse, since blind and temperamental she is of no use. If she is healed, they may want to keep her, not to mention they will want to know how you did it. This is dangerous. If anyone knew you could heal, they might take you away from your parents."

Her mouth agape she whipped her head toward Kai. "I didn't do anything."

He reached over and touched her arm. "Relax," he begged. His eyes widened at her elevated tone. "For now, don't say anything to anyone, not even your parents. Haygan will take care of this before we leave," he assured her.

Entering the inner ward gatehouse, he needed to keep their conversation private. He raised his finger to his lips. "Shhh. When your dad tells you, act surprised and let it go. You trust me, right?"

"Of course," she responded, eyeing the others surrounding them.

With the stables in view, he relaxed into his saddle and fell silent. Bram and Finlee helped the ladies dismount and tied off their horses. "Bram, I need to speak with Haygan. Is he in his office?" Kai asked, dismounting and passing Ember's reins to Weston.

"I am sorry, Prince Kai, but he is not," Bram responded. "Should I tell him to find you upon his return?"

"I will stay and wait, Bram, thank you. Weston, hold up. I can brush Ember."

Hours later, Haygan entered the stables with a large black leather bag slung over his shoulder. Kai quickly explained the situation to Haygan about the wolves. "Send word to Lord Henley. I will move the wolves away. I will need Smoke and a few Mryken to push them back. Might take me a few nights. Dante should let me take the Mryken."

Kai felt suddenly uneasy. "What about our trip to Hamrin?"

Haygan tamped the air with his hand. "I will be back before it is time to leave. But it will take time to discover why they've ventured close to Henley. Provided they've not killed any livestock, it should be easy to push them out. If there is another pack pushing on their territory, it may take longer to move them to a new location."

The guilt over the wild timber wolf Hunter Marduk put down—while saving his life, no less— weighed on his soul. He felt driven to make amends. "How can you move another pack?" he asked, watching Shane and Marduk ride away.

"Same as you connect with the Mryken, although it is not polite to play with them." Haygan gave Kai a knowing look. "I understand you're developing your gift. I know you feel the timber wolf incident was your fault. But not all wild animals are created equal. Angry animals already in attack mode are difficult to confront for even the strongest Beastmasters."

"Beastmasters?" Kai had not heard Haygan use the term before.

From the look on the stablemaster's face, Kai knew the man cursed himself for using the term. "Knowledge is dangerous." Haygan stiffened." But to answer your question, a Katori person who can communicate with animals is called a Beastmaster."

This was interesting. Kai had so many questions. Before he could pick one, Haygan continued. "I can use Shiva and Smoke to push them away. I can connect with the wild pack. Encourage them to move. With, say, seven Mryken and two Nebean black wolves I can get them to move on." He dropped the heavy bag and sat on the edge of his desk.

Kai looked at the bag. "Where did you go? Were you making plans for our trip?"

Haygan ran his hands through his hair and smiled. "I went to see a friend."

Surprised, Kai tilted his head. "Who?"

"Her name is Simone. She is someone dear to me. I hope you will meet her someday. Now let me see about the Henley wolf problem." Haygan picked up his bag and headed to the stairs and the stable boarding rooms.

"Wait. There is one more thing. You need to look at Snowflake. I think Rayna healed her. Her eyes are no longer milky, and she let Weston brush her down this evening." Kai tossed his hands out to his sides. "I cannot explain it, but it's true. I have inspected her myself. Not sure what we should do, but I don't think you can go back to Dante and tell him a blind horse can suddenly see after spending the day with Rayna."

"Show me," Haygan insisted.

It didn't take long for Haygan to come to the same conclusion. "It would seem Rayna is Kodama." For the second time Haygan chastised himself, scrunching his face.

"Why do I get the feeling you wish you'd not said the word

Kodama?"

"A Katori-born child is taught from birth the secrets of our society, and the dangers, but you're a Half-Light. Our Katori elders don't want me teaching you anything. Even after I told them what you can do. Rayna, on the other hand, this is more than gleaning or bonding. She healed Snowflake. The Kodama are healers. Please don't ask me more. But back to the horse, Dante inspected her himself after I gave him the news. He had already told me to turn her out. I will tell Levi she is a gift for Rayna. He cannot refuse. I will move the horse myself tonight. Tell nobody about this. Do you understand?" His voice was firm and fearful.

Kai sighed with relief. "I do understand, which is why I have been sitting in the stables for two hours waiting for you to come back."

"This protects all of us, not just Rayna. Down at the lower servants' stables, they will have no idea." Haygan pulled Snowflake from her stall and climbed onto her bareback. "Goodnight Kai," was all he said as he trotted out of the stables.

In the family dining hall, Kai spoke with his father and Grand Duke Dante Carmelo. "Father, I wanted to let you know I spent the day in Henley." Patiently he waited for a response.

Iver stared at his plate. "How is Robert? It has been a long time." The words affectionately rolled off his father's tongue.

Kai could see the joy behind his father's eyes. "Lord Robert is well. Although he has a few security concerns. Seems two trees have damaged an old section of their wall, halting their expansion project. They now have three open wall sections. He needs help, either repairing the wall or additional men to secure the area. I trust it was acceptable to offer assistance." Kai waited again for a response, hoping his decision was right.

"Yes, son, fine idea." The king turned to the grand duke.

"Dante, see which men you can spare for security around Henley. They are only a few miles away. Until their walls are repaired, circulate your men back and forth. They can set up a camp outside Henley. Speak with Dean Biorne. See if he has any stone masons or carpenters he can spare to assist with the walls."

Pleased, Iver looked to Kai. "Well done, son. This is exactly what I expect from your summer trips. Find out what our people need. Dresnor can offer guidance—send word to Dante Carmelo if you need additional support. I will be leaving shortly after you for Bangloo." Pride filled Iver's eyes. "I would be pleased if you would compose the letter to Lord Henley, informing him of the support we offer."

Kai felt relieved that he had made the right decision, and a bit of pride that his father was pleased. "Certainly, father. I will write a letter tonight. Thank you."

That evening, Kai sat nervously at his desk, staring out the window. He had never written an official letter to a lord before. Where should he start? Robert Henley was a smart man, a friend of his parents—a Duke. Lord of his land and a keeper of people. This was not the same as writing a book report for Professor Greydon. This mattered. He thought about what the professor would tell him. *Keep it simple. Take the emotions out of the task. Write the facts, be concise, and tell what you know.*

Pen in hand, he stared at the blank paper.

Dear Duke Robert Henley,

It was my pleasure to spend the afternoon with you and Lady Elizabeth. Thank you for hosting my friends and me at your festival. Everyone enjoyed your kind hospitality and charming town.

Arrangements have been made with Grand Duke Dante Carmelo. He will be sending men to camp outside Henley. They will provide security on a rotating schedule until the wall repairs are complete. This should allow you to focus your men on repairs and internal security.

Dean Biorne will be sending stone masons and carpenters to pro-

vide aid in the repair effort. Use them as you see fit.

Our stablemaster, Haygan, has a solution to address your wolf concerns. He should already be on the outskirts of town searching for the rogue wolf pack. He is traveling with two Nebean black wolves and a large pack of Mryken dogs. He believes he can peacefully move the wild wolves away from Henley.

Again, thank you, for the beautiful day. My father sends his good wishes. I hope to visit again soon. I look forward to seeing you at the winter festival.

Yours Truly,
Prince Kai Galloway

He put down his pen and gently sprinkled the pounce powder over the letter. While he had used fine strokes, he didn't want to chance it would not be sufficiently dry before folding the paper. Gently shaking the sheet, he removed the excess, folded his letter, sealed it with wax and his royal stamp.

CHAPTER 25

Hamrin Bound

The rocky courtyard wall made for an uncomfortable seat. Kai contemplated his pending trip and his new responsibilities. Today, he would leave Diu palace and spend his summer in Hamrin, away from everyone he knew.

How am I ready for this? His nerves were making him sweat in the early morning heat. The sun was already beating on his back. It was going to be a long day. Smoke paced next to him eagerly. The wolf knew something was happening today.

The stables were a hive of activity. Everyone was saddling horses, loading supplies, and packing gear. Ember was all ready to go. Kai was not. He kept one eye on the assembling group and one eye on the bakehouse. Rayna had been up before dawn. He could see her working. She seemed rushed.

His heart raced. While his group waited for Iver, he waited for Rayna. If she didn't come out before his father came to see them off, he would not be able to say goodbye. They would go all summer apart. Hands in his lap, he stared at the bakery door. Twice she stopped near the entrance but did not exit.

The pressure was more than he could bear. Before he missed his opportunity, he would see her. Her face, not the wispy energy version within his mind. He marched straight toward the bakehouse door. Determined to see her, he reached for the handle. It swung open and there she was. The smell of fresh baked bread filled the air. "Rayna. I…"

Her navy-blue dress and white apron blew in the breeze. Her long brown hair had been pulled back into a tight braid. Flour smudged across her chin. "I am so sorry, Kai. There was so much work to be done today. I know you're leaving. We made your supplies yesterday. I have a moment, then I must get back to work. We are working on your father's supplies."

Dusting off her hands, she stood on her tiptoes to look over his shoulder. Her eyes went wide. "Oh, no." In a rush, she leaned in and hugged him. "The king just walked into the courtyard. You have to go," she whispered into his ear. When she stepped back, she held onto his hand. Her warm hand in his.

He glanced over his shoulder. Sure enough, his father was crossing the courtyard with Master General Cazier. She was right, time to go. "It will be a long summer. I will miss you. When I get back, I promise we will spend a day together. Kendra will look in on you." He squeezed her hand. It was difficult to let go, but he needed to beat his father to the stables.

In a flurry he dashed through the trees, making his way to the stables. He entered through the side door and made his way through the group. Next to Ember, he breathed a sigh of relief. He could hear his father talking with Dresnor. "Before you reach your first campsite, send a scout ahead. We have not laid eyes on this area in near a decade. They do not pay much in taxes, so they may have the most need of our support."

"Yes, Your Majesty," Dresnor answered in a level tone, his hands clasped behind his back.

Master General Cazier cleared his throat. "According to the maps, your first campsite should be an old hunter's lodge near Baden Lake. Make camp there. We don't know the conditions of the lodge. Your scouts should be wary. There used to be a few farms there, too. They may provide refuge."

Iver's face twisted with concern. "Dante, should you be going with him?"

Knowing everyone wanted to leave, Kai stepped around Ember and approached Dresnor. Next to his Kempery-man, he matched his stance, hands clasped behind his back. His eyes drifted from his father to his cousin Cazier.

Cazier's mouth curled into a smirk, and his eyes drifted down to Kai's midsection. He raised one eyebrow and nodded. "My king, they will be fine. You took the same trips at his age. He has three Kempery-men, Hunter Marduk and Haygan. They are all seasoned men. The prince will be fine."

Unsure why his cousin was smiling, Kai looked down at his stomach. It all became clear. There was a white dusty patch of flour on his dark blue shirt. Before his father noticed, he brushed his hand across his stomach.

Haygan stepped to Kai's right. His strong hand brushed across Kai's shoulders. Embarrassed, he looked up at Haygan. Kai was covered in flour. Rayna's hug left evidence he had seen her before coming to the stables.

Iver turned to address Kai. "Son, I know this is your first important trip without me. You will do well. Master General Cazier will be traveling home to Nebea. While I travel sail to Bangloo and Ahana, the Grand Duke Dante will remain in Diu. If you need anything, send a bird. A ship can cross Baden Lake in less than a day. Support can be to you quickly. This will be your first glimpse of the Katori mountain range. They are magnificent. Find high ground, and you should just be able to see their razor-sharp peaks stabbing the sky.

"Kempery-man Dresnor will guide you during your trip. Trust him. I have every confidence you will conduct Diu business with sensibility, understanding, and reason. May your judgment be decisive and fair." With a nod he offered his hand to Kai, pulling him into an embrace. "Take care, my son," he whispered in his ear. "I will see you at summer's end."

His father's strong arms held him tight. "Thank you, father." Kai stepped back out of the hug. "I hope your trip is a success, and I look forward to the new treasures you will bring back. Will Nola travel with you?"

"To her dismay, she will remain here with baby Cordelia. Between us, I relish my time at sea alone. It is time to think. Adventures aboard allow me to assert the might of Diu and make alliances. That is no place for a queen."

Iver clapped a hand on Kai's shoulder, turning him around to face the men. "Men, you ride out today to extend the hand of Diu to the people. Protect and serve, be true to all my people. Treat them as they were your own. And above all, protect my son."

Dresnor spoke for the group. "Your Majesty, we will protect your son with our lives."

Iver and Cazier stepped back. Everyone mounted up. As the group departed, Kai looked over his shoulder to his father. He was both excited and nervous about what lay ahead. He only hoped he could live up to his father's expectations.

When they traveled beyond the city walls, Kai stiffened in the saddle. Looking back, the sun glistened across the white stone of Diu city. He would miss his evenings with Cazier and Riome. And his time with Rayna. Three months felt like forever.

Focused on the road ahead, he could see the long bridge that spanned Stone River below the rock dam around Baden Lake's south rim. The bridge was a symbol in his mind. Crossing meant he was no longer a child. Responsibility lay in wait on the other side, ready to consume him. He knew embracing his duty would make his father proud. It would also bring him one step closer to Milnos.

Three scouts galloped across the bridge into the distant woods. They would check the woods along the road, ensuring all was clear. Each scout took turns riding ahead. When he came into view a new scout charged up the road. His men would become markers, proof that the route was safe. Kai was pleased to discover Drew had been selected as a scout on this trip.

The first of his group reached the bridge, four soldiers followed by Kempery-man Redmon. Pressure welled in Kai's chest. The closer he came, the harder it pressed. Next Shane and his father Marduk, and their packhorse reached the bridge. The clip-clop of horse hooves reverberated in the heat.

When Ember's hooves echoed on the stone bridge, Kai held his breath. Behind him, his city and his home. Before he knew it, the sound of Ember's hooves faded, they had reached the hard dirt on the other side. The click of tongues encouraged the horses to hasten their pace.

An extended sigh released the pent-up air. Kai rode between Haygan and Kempery-man Dresnor. Behind him was Finlee, their groomsman, and two pack horses, followed by Kempery-man Redmon and Albey, in addition to four other soldiers and three more pack horses. The gear was evenly distributed to avoid taxing the horses.

They were a large procession destined for the town of Hamrin, a wharf town on the other side of Baden Lake. Kai wished they were sailing a ship across Baden Lake, a journey that would put them in Hamrin before dinner. Instead, they traveled by horse. It would be a long twelve-hour day and half of the next day. They would ride nearly eighty miles around the great lake.

Kai knew their first night would be out under the stars if the lodge was of no use. While his father had offered to send tents, Cazier had suggested he would earn the respect of the men faster if he camped with them without elaborate luxury. Kai knew his cousin was right. Not that it made it any easier. He wanted to stand shoulder-to-shoulder with his men. He wanted their respect.

With the pressure easing in his chest, he watched the inviting ripples glisten across the deep blue water of Baden Lake. Perspiration ran down his back, and he imagined the others were feeling the heat. This made him feel bad for his men who were wearing heavy metal armor. The cover of trees ahead was a welcome sight.

Near the forest's edge, he saw Drew signal the all-clear before riding into the woodlands along the lake. Inside the cover of the trees, the temperature cooled. Even though the trees were sparse, they provided ample coverage and relief from the sun. It was a beautiful countryside. Ahead on the trail another scout waited alongside two riders and a cart. They were pulled over to the side of the road. They waited for the prince and his group to pass.

When they reached the third scout, he noticed the other scouts circling through the trees around them. They rode on like this for hours in the heat before Kempery-man Redmon halted the group and everyone dismounted and led their horse to the water's edge.

Haygan approached Kai and handed him a dripping wet cloth and a brush. "We will not remove the saddles at this stop, but we need to cool the horses down. We have been riding at a fast pace these past few miles. The cold lake water will help cool them in addition to the light breeze. Brush off the excess water and continue around the horse until he's cooled."

Kai took the cloth, and Haygan grabbed another and cared for his own horse.

"You can splash your face and neck after you finish." Haygan added. "We will rest here for a time before setting out again. This next portion will be a fair bit easier under the cover of trees, so we will continue to push the horses. The less time we spend on the road, the better."

Kai dipped the cloth into the lake and wiped down Ember's long legs, followed by a quick brushing. He could feel the gratitude through their connection. It would seem this trip would also be a test for his young horse. Finished, Haygan handed him a few pieces of meat, cheese, and bread. "Eat and cool off before we ride again."

Happy to stretch his legs, Kai ate the few scraps of food while he sat with Shane near the lake. "This is definitely different than traveling in early winter. Ember is much hotter than he was on the entire trip to Port Anahita. Even the short trip to Henley a few weeks back was not this hot."

Still sweating himself, he bent down and rinsed his hands

in the cold water of Baden Lake. The clear water felt inviting. Its glistening surface was nearly binding in the rising sun. After splashing his face with the fresh water, he ran his hands through his sandy blond hair. The cool water trickled down his neck.

"Shane, have you ever been on this side of the lake before?" he asked, wiping his neck with more water.

"This is my first trip." Shane responded.

"That's right, you told me that before. I had forgotten. I'm glad you are here."

A wave from Marduk told them it was time to leave. They had several hours more till they would reach their first campsite. Kai kept an open mind and tried to enjoy the experience. His father had done this, and now it was his turn.

Hours in the saddle made Kai's backside begin to ache. He wanted nothing more than to stretch his legs. The thick canopy of trees and cool breeze kept them cool. The longer they rode, the more everything began to look the same. Tree after tree, the rocky dirt road, and the glistening lake. He felt like he was in a foreign land. His only touchstone was Baden Lake.

The wind blew through the trees, carrying the scent of sweet flowering plants. The tree coverage began to thin, letting the warm sun beat down on their heads again. How he wanted stop, but time was precious, and they had a long way to go. He knew Dresnor was not keen to make a mistake on his first real trip. Protecting royalty was a serious responsibility for a Kempery-man.

CHAPTER 26

Three Wolf Night

Through the trees, they came upon a rundown hunting lodge. The lodge was a sore sight, long since abandoned. With no roof to speak of and a collapsed front porch, it was in desperate need of repairs. It would provide no shelter. The lack of care worried Kai. His father had mentioned the lodge, and all day he had hoped it would provide a respite for him and his men.

Compelled to earn the respect of his men, Kai found Dresnor leaning against a tree, picking his teeth after dinner. "I want to take guard duty," Kai insisted. "It is only fair I take a shift. In fact, I would like to take the late shift," he crossed his arms over his chest.

Dresnor pursed his lips but nodded in acceptance. "Your Highness, I recommend against the idea. I understand you may hope to gain the respect of your men. Admirable, but..."

"I must insist," Kai interrupted.

"As you wish. To ensure your safety, I must insist that Haygan and I take the same shift."

"Agreed." Pleased there was little argument, Kai shook Dresnor's hand.

"I will wake you when it's time. Get some rest. You'll need it." Dresnor smiled and walked away.

Excited, Kai laid down on his bedroll already waiting near the dwindling fire. Smoke slowly approached and lay at his side. Smoke's warmth beside him reminded him how lucky he was to have his wolf. It had been a long time since they'd slept this close.

High above, the starry black sky, the full moon beamed down. The crackle and pop of the fire brought his eyes down to the ground. Across the way, he looked at Ember, head down, nibbling at the grass. He felt a sense of deja vu. The memory struck him; this was the night he'd seen so long ago. His loyal companions. Happy, he let his eyes close and slowly fell asleep.

A nudge came all too soon. "Wake up, Kai. It's time." The voice sounded foggy as Kai opened his eyes. "Come on boy, time to wake." Haygan shook him again.

"Alright, alright, I'm up." He pushed Haygan away and scrubbed his face with his hands.

"Two men are circling around the outskirts. Dresnor is patrolling south near the lake. I will patrol north by the old hunting lodge. I want you near the camp and the horses. Do not wander too far," he cautioned.

"I will be fine," Kai assured him, stroking his hand down Smoke's back.

As they parted, Smoke ran out into the woods, happy to run wild. Kai knew just how he felt. To be free was his ultimate desire. Dictated by his father's decisions, Kai was here in the middle of the night—preparing for his future, to marry and be a king in a land he did not know. Far from everyone and everything he loved most.

Sticks and leaves crunched under his feet. He could almost hear Marduk now. *You make too much noise.* He chuckled to himself. With a change in his step he padded with purpose. The sound of his footfalls faded, and he moved silently between the trees. Only the night bugs and wind whipping through trees made a noise.

Ember and Winter rested inside the corral Finlee had

made. Through the trees, he could just see Dresnor pacing near the lake. Focused on his task, Kai continued circling the camp and the sleeping men, only pausing a few times to listen to the crickets and the frogs. The moonlight kissed the small camp. His men resting. He felt proud he was maturing and gaining respect. The fact they had stopped calling him the little prince said volumes.

Carried on the wind, he heard a wolf howl. The enchanting sound mingled with the stars and danced with the moonlight. Kai glanced around to determine his wolf's location. It came from behind him, high on the ridge. Smoke stood howling at the moon in a small clearing. From the campsite, Kai saw the moonshine highlight Smoke's ears and back. *Great spot, Smoke.*

The moonlight trickled through the trees, illuminating his way. The ground sloped down to the west, creating a clear path upwards. In his mind, he sensed this was the route Smoke had taken up. He ran through the woods, making his way along the slope. The smell of earthy moss and cedar lingered. Over large rocks he made his way.

The damp earth filled his lungs. He was surprised how the shade of the trees and the cool rocks changed the smell and the temperature. After a long, demanding climb, he stood with Smoke. "What a great view." He glanced at the full moon illuminating the camp below.

High above the trees, he could see far and wide. Layer upon layer of black rolling hills moved to the east. Above them were jagged white points: the Katori Mountains. Below, the vastness of Baden Lake sat aglow by moonlight, north of their camp. Kai gazed at the wiggly reflection of the moon. He had never expected it to be so soothing. He felt free, for the first time in his life. If only he could stay here forever.

Out of the corner of his eye, he saw something move across the sky. Focused on the trees to the east, he strained against the night. He saw something shoot out of the trees straight into the air. Whatever it was, it was close, and it was big. Again, he saw another. Their large black forms skimmed across the treetops.

Three large shapes shot up from the surface of the lake. Kai watched them flap their wings, climbing higher and higher. When they reached their peak, their true forms became clear —they were dragons. The bright white moon behind them revealed their massive wings, large horned heads, and long tails. One considerably larger than the other two. Its body, now illuminated by the moon, was silver gray. The smaller dragons were pitch black with only a few horns across the ridge of their faces.

For a moment they seemed to hang unmoving in the air. Then the dragons rolled and dove straight down toward the lake. Kai watched and imagined the speed they must be flying. Their dark bodies glimmered with moonlight.

Three forms converged, spiraling toward Baden Lake. Then they disappeared over the pitch-black water. Lost in the darkness, he heard a faint splash. The sound of something being dragged along the water's surface. Every now and then he could see a black mass break through the moonlight painted on the lake's surface.

He listened carefully. The night was still. Silence consumed the insects of the night; they too watched the dragons. His heart quickened. Never in his life had he been so close. From the Master General's tower in Diu, they were small winged beasts, floating over the lake. Their brilliance revealed only if they sprayed fire against the night.

Continuing to watch for signs, he wondered why they did not spray fire. How often did they really come out at night? They made no noise he could hear. Without the moonlight, he would have never seen them above the trees or skimming the lake's surface. Honestly, if he were not trying to see them, he would have dismissed the shadows as mere tricks of the night.

How he envied the freedom of their flight. His heart opened to their wild nature. Using his ability to glean, he reached out with his mind. Their brilliance beamed; he took a step back in awe. Focused on the silver dragon, he saw the outline of the creature's face and body.

Inside he felt the urge to fly with them. Then he questioned his feelings. How could he sympathize with these creatures? Yet at this distance, they seemed serene and almost beautiful. Could he be wrong about them? Was Cazier right? Had he condemned them all because of one bad dragon? Maybe there was more to them than he'd realized.

Kai scanned the camp. Their once roaring fire faded in the night. The shapes of his friends and guards resting after a long day's ride. He knew he should return to the perimeter of their camp before Dresnor and Haygan noticed he was gone. Letting go of his gleaning, he took one last look into the night sky. Their massive bodies passed through the glimmering moonlight and then disappeared.

Disappointed they were gone, he looked to Smoke. "Time to go back."

Smoke barked and Kai turned, glimpsing something above the treetops, getting closer and closer. "What is that, Smoke?"

Smoke growled into the pitch black. Still, the shapes got larger. "Is that the dragons?" he asked, squinting into the night, then his view burst with gleaning light. Kai stepped backward, it was obvious they were flying right toward him and his overlook. He took several more steps backward.

Panic filled his mind, and he held his breath, stepping back several more times. The lead dragon's nostrils began to glow with an orange-yellow light, and white gray smoked billowed out trailing behind. As its mouth opened, an orange-yellow ball of light grew and shot forth in a stream of fire spray aimed straight in Kai's direction.

Fear overwhelmed Kai, and he stumbled backward. Mindless, he raised his hands to protect his face while continuing to retreat. A blast of fire exploded over his head. His final step back met no ground. Falling, he saw the night sky light up above him. The curvy nature of the beasts was the last thing he saw before his shoulder caught on a tree limb, and he spun around.

Face first, he fell through the trees. Arms outstretched he reached for treetops. Thump! He struck the crown of a large pine tree. Thump, whack, thump! He hit branch after branch. Fear-streaked tears ran from his eyes. Prickly pine trees smacked him again and again. Moments later, he caught a branch in the chin. The blow spun Kai around before he crashed to the ground, landing on his side.

Winded, he gasped for air. This fall was all too familiar. His vision was coming true. Falling through pines was no longer just a dream. As his breath returned, he studied his surroundings. The smell of earth and pine with a hint of blood lingered in the air. Luckily, the dense pine trees had slowed his fall. Nothing broken, he tried to stand.

What just happened? One minute the dragons were flying over the lake, the next they were skimming the treetops soaring in his direction. *They weren't aiming for me, right?* Everything had happened so fast he couldn't be sure.

The surrounding cluster of trees blocked out the moonlight above. Kai ran his hands together and felt the sap, scrapes, and dirt across his hands. On his chin, warm wet blood oozed from a large cut. He pulled a kerchief from his pocket and pressed it against the gash. Lost and disoriented, he dusted himself off.

Through the dense trees he walked to the rocky cliff wall. Kai looked straight up. *There is no way I am climbing back up there.* Separated from the camp by a large sheer cliff, he recalled the steep hill he had climbed near camp to follow Smoke. He was now alone on the opposite side.

Sore from the fall, he leaned against the cool moss-covered stone. He had no idea which way would take him back to camp. Long deep howls echoed above—Smoke. There was no way up or down for either of them.

Heavyhearted, he decided to walk west. In his mind, he remembered the hill had slopped down to the west. West had to be his best chance. Maybe the cliffs would drop down, and he could climb back up.

Again, he thought about his dream. He knew what was coming. If his vision held true, the wolf was coming next. He tried to think of Haygan and what he might tell him. Show no fear.

Deep in his soul, he reached out to Smoke. *I am alright. Stay near the cliffs, walk with me.* He felt a sense of understanding and strength as Smoke followed above. Together they walked, following along the stone cliffs that separated them.

Hours later, exhausted, Kai desperately wanted to sit down, but he continued weaving through the trees. He knew his shift was long-since over, and others would be looking for him. Even if the others had seen the fireball above the camp, they would not have any idea where he was or where to start searching. Hidden by the dense stone cliffs Kai was well outside Haygan's ability to glean and search for him.

High above he felt Smoke keeping pace. He was glad he was not alone. Although the cliffs did seem lower, Smoke was still high overhead. Kai stopped to lean against a tree. If only he could sit for just a minute. Rest his eyes, rest his body. But he knew it was best to keep moving.

Ahead, the rocks jutted out in front of his path. Kai ducked under a pine limb and went through the trees, walking away from the cliff wall. He expected the mounded earth and rocks to fold back into the towering cliff. Instead, it opened into a small cave. A downed pine tree partially blocked the opening.

Curious, he stepped toward the cave, one hand on the stone and the other on the felled tree. Out of the darkness came deep growls. Startled, Kai backed away one step at a time. Five short steps later, his back pressed up against a large tree. Broken branches stabbed at his back.

There was no denying it. He knew what they were. They need not fear him; he meant them no harm. Eyes closed, he slid down the tree trunk and delved deep inside his soul. He connected to the spiritual energy within and became aware of the threads of life surrounding him. Eyes open, the world around him became illuminated in a soft glow. The pulse of life emanated from everything, even the dirt below him. The plants and trees felt more alive and welcomed his connection.

In front of him, the cave opening revealed three large adult gray wolves. Inside the cave, Kai sensed two young wolves and three little pups. The adults protected their pack. Their heads were cast down, leery of his presence. They waited. He could sense they were not afraid, only startled by his intrusion.

Exhausted, he tried to remain calm. Smoke was too far away to help, and Kai was in no condition to run. One dagger at his waist was not enough against three seasoned adult wolves. Not that he would want to hurt them.

The lead wolf stepped forward. *Alpha. I know you.* The final part of his vision had come to life. He opened his soul, his energy to the massive wolf. Eyes locked together, Kai lowered his head respectfully, peering into the wolf's soul. Kai felt the intensity. With a deep breath, he pushed his intention. *I mean you no harm. I need to rest.* He let his fear fade and leave his mind. He knew the wolves could smell the blood on his face and hands.

Now that he had a chance to sit, he noticed the cuts through his shirt and pants. All stained with blood. His body ached with pain. It had to be around three in the morning. He had hours to go before dawn, and he wasn't even sure he was going the right direction.

Once more he pushed his spirit to the wolf. *I mean you no harm. May I rest here till dawn?* he asked through the connection. High above he sensed Smoke waiting. A loud howl echoed through the trees; it was Smoke. Again, he howled. Kai touched his dizzy head.

The alpha wolf looked to the sky and howled back. Then all the wolves joined him. Kai could do no more. Exhausted, he slumped over, resting his head in the soft pine needles. His breathing slowed, and his eyes fluttered at the sight of the alpha wolf approaching. Unable to keep his eyes open, he fell asleep.

Low growls startled Kai from his slumber. The alpha stood

near his head. It took a moment to orient himself. Realizing where he was and what had happened, he rubbed the sleep from his eyes. The other wolves leaned into him, growling. Stiff from how he slept, Kai sat up. In the distance, he heard men calling through the trees. They were calling for him. The low light streaming through the trees told him it was just past dawn.

Still bleary, he reached out with his mind. He sensed Shiva nearby. *Shiva, I'm here.* The connection true, he felt her stop and turn in his direction. From another direction he sensed Smoke. *Here, Smoke, I'm here.* Relieved, he looked to the wolves guarding him. *They are coming to help me. Thank you for protecting me.* Gently, Kai touched the side of the alpha wolf. *You should hide in the cave. They're coming,* he encouraged with his mind.

The alpha turned, eyes on Kai. His intensity pushed against Kai's heart. Then he looked to his pack, and they retreated to their cave. Hidden in the dark, blocked by the tree, he felt them watching him still.

The sounds of leaves crunching and men calling were getting closer. Kai struggled to his feet, and half walked, half stumbled in their direction. Shiva found him first, followed by Smoke. Haygan hiked up the hill in his direction.

Stepping through the trees Kai called out, "You found me. How?"

Haygan handed him a pouch of water. "Here, drink." Relief filled the stablemaster's eyes, and he called for the others. "He's up here!" Haygan yelled through the trees.

Facing back toward Kai, Haygan continued. "When you didn't come back, I was worried. I woke Redmon and Marduk. We searched the forest surrounding the camp. Hours later, Smoke returned to camp. We have been following him ever since. I tried using my sight to find you, but you were too far away. Smoke brought us around the cliffs. You look dreadful. What happened to you?"

Kai knelt and stroked the top of Smoke's head. "Thanks,

Smoke." Through the trees, he could just make out the sounds of leaves crunching. He looked at Shiva. "Thanks, Shiva." He still felt exhausted, but the rest had done him good.

"I followed Smoke up the hill behind the camp. From the overlook, I watched the dragons over the lake. Then I fell from the cliff. Luckily the trees broke my fall. I walked for hours until I could walk no further. Smoke stayed with me, until … until I found some new friends to watch over me while I slept." Kai lowered his voice as the others approached.

Kempery-man Dresnor brushed past Haygan to inspect Kai's face. "Blessed be Alenga, Prince Kai, you look awful. Thank goodness you are alive. Your wolf has been leading us for hours. I was beginning to think we'd never find you."

Dresnor eyed Kai up and down. "You're covered in scratches. This gash in your chin will probably leave a scar." A look of pride gleamed in his eye.

The others exhaled in relief and led the way back down the hill. Dresnor pulled at Kai's shoulder. "Come with me, Your Highness. We have horses waiting at the bottom."

Thirsty, Kai drank. Marduk stood with the horses and offered another relieved look. Haygan shook his head, a small smirk lifted the corner of his mouth. "Friends, you say?" Haygan pulled something from Kai's shirt. "Anyone I know." He handed Kai a small tuft of gray-white fur.

"Maybe," Kai smiled back.

He closed his fingers around the small tuft and glanced over his shoulder peering through the trees. There, watching at the top of the hill, was the alpha wolf.

Haygan turned with him and smiled. "You've made a good friend. Don't be surprised if you meet him again someday."

Kai sensed the connection to the wolf, and he again pushed his soul to the alpha—a shared sense of gratitude.

"Let's get him back to camp," Haygan said. "We've lost half the morning. We will break camp just after lunch and hopefully make it to Hamrin before midnight. It will be another long day in the saddle."

Kai was so happy to see Ember waiting. Ember let out a loud whinny and shook his head. With his torn hands, he stroked Ember's neck and mane. "Good to see you too, Ember."

Back at camp, Shane and the rest of the group were thankful to see Kai returned to them. Dresnor wasted no time, however. "Finlee, see to preparing a meal. We have little time to waste. Drew and Redmon, see to the horses. Two hours at a heady clip has them in need of attention. Once they are ready to travel again, we depart. Albey, advise the remaining men to break down camp."

Drew took Ember and two other horses by the reigns and walked away. While the others busied about camp, Kai began to walk behind Ember until Dresnor pulled him back. "Not you, you need to rest." Releasing Kai's arm, Dresnor bowed slightly. "Sorry, Prince Kai. I need you fit for the saddle."

Kai let his arm fall to his side. "I understand, but Ember is my horse. All due respect, sir, I've rested. Each one of you spent a good portion of the night searching for me. I'll have all day in the saddle to rest. Let me tend my horse."

Dresnor nodded and walked with him to tend his own horse. No words passed between anyone while they removed saddles and cooled down the horses. It felt good to be with everyone. Kai let his mind relax into his task.

CHAPTER 27

Men or Monsters

Late that evening the group rode into Hamrin. The group split—two scouts and a guard rode ahead to announce Kai's arrival. The others rode for the stables. The hour was late, and everyone was dog-tired. Barely able to lift his arms, Kai insisted he could care for Ember. Dresnor took the brush from Kai. "We are all exhausted, Prince Kai. Let me escort you up to the estate. They are awake and mean to greet you. We should not keep them waiting. Their groomsmen will tend to our horses."

Kai looked at everyone. He didn't want them to think him weak. That he couldn't keep up. Six groomsmen swarmed around them, each pulling away horses. Happy to see his men walking down the hill, he relented.

Haygan laid his hand on Kai's shoulder. "You did very well today. Now get some rest. Finlee and I are staying here in the stables. They have made room for us."

"Goodnight, Haygan." He turned back toward Dresnor. "Where are we staying?" he asked, not really caring if he had to sleep on the ground again.

"We are staying in the Hamrin Estate. Kempery-man Redmond, Kempery-man Albey, Drew and I will sleep on the same hall as you. That was the request made by the Grand Duke's letter. Now let's get you through the gauntlet as quick as possible." Dresnor pulled him in close and whispered. "Listen to my advice, Kai. You have no questions. You have no needs. Say as little as possible, and I will see you to your room. Ask one question, say more than thank you, and Lord Hamrin will talk your ear off for hours. I've seen him at the winter festival. He is a talker. Do you understand?"

"Yes, Dresnor, thank you." He had no desire to be rude, but he could hardly stand. Each step they took was one more than he felt he could take. "What about Smoke? Do they know he is coming?"

"Dante informed them you travel with a Nebean black wolf and that you would not stay within the estate unless he could join you in your room. Though we are here within days of his letter, I am sure they are eager to make accommodations."

When they reached the final steps leading up to the estate, Dresnor paused and cautioned one last time. "Say nothing beyond thank you, Lord Hamrin. Speak only if spoken to and accept nothing."

Wanting merely to rest, he repeated the phrase in his head. *Thank you, Lord Hamrin. Thank you, Lord Hamrin.* At the top of the stairs, a long line of stiff servants waited. Their eyes focused downward; they made no attempt to look at him. Strange. They all looked tired, and he caught one man near the end yawn uncontrollably.

Near the doors stood Duke Hamrin with his three children, all dressed in exquisite clothing. Behind the duke's family, two broad-shouldered men towered. Dresnor placed his hand firmly on Kai's back and pushed him past the servants. "Lord Hamrin and Lady Hamrin, I am pleased to formally introduce his Highness, Prince Kai Galloway of Diu, son of King Iver and Mariana Galloway."

Lord Hamrin bowed. "Your Highness. Prince Kai, it is our honor to host your visit. My house is your house, my servants are your servants. You should want for nothing while you are here. If you would like some food prepared, anything, name it, and my cook will make it for you.".

Anxiously Lord Hamrin fidgeted with the long chain attached to a watch tucked inside his vest. He was a short, fat man with beady eyes, thinning gray hair that barely covered his scalp, and red blotchy skin that made Kai cringe. Kai stood eye-to-eye with the old man. "Thank you, Lord Hamrin."

Beside Lord Hamrin stood a demure young girl, with a kind smile, dark eyes, and flowing auburn hair. She looked just like her mother, the late Lady Hamrin. Kai had met her mother in Diu at the winter festival and was saddened to hear she had passed away. She had been a pleasant lady, but he always had the impression she was a simple woman putting on airs for her husband.

Kai knew he should not say it, but he felt moved. "Sorry to hear of your loss, Lord Hamrin." The glint in Lord Hamrin's eye unnerved him, and he instantly regretted opening the conversation. Before the old man could speak, he continued. "It has been a very long two days' travel. I must excuse myself until morning." Kai called for Smoke, who stepped up beside him.

"Prince Kai, you honor us with your visit. Allow me to introduce my eldest. Her name is Opal, the new Lady of Hamrin. These are my two boys, Ian and Darren. You may call me Lord Victor." Lord Victor pulled the young woman forward. She did her best curtsy, followed by the young boys offering bows.

Based on their height, he figured they were a few years his senior. Observing Opal, he noticed her nervous nature. Since they approached, she could not make eye contact and continuously fidgeted with the lace on the front of her pink dress.

In his head, Kai held to Dresnor's advice. Don't speak unless asked a direct question. He pursed his lips and looked back down the long line of waiting servants. He only hoped he'd not said too much.

Ignoring Kai's request to retire, Victor stepped toward him. "Prince Kai, can my servants get anything for you? They are most eager to please." With a wave of his hand, he motioned toward his people. They all looked exhausted and nervous.

Kai shook his head no. Lord Victor pressed again. "Are you sure, you look as though you could use a physician. I can send my man to you straight away," he offered. "Or a hot meal?"

"Thank you, Lord Hamrin, but there's no need." He turned to his Kempery-man. "Dresnor."

Dresnor's hand still firmly pressed into Kai's back, pushed him forward another step. "Please allow me to see Prince Kai to his room. Show us to our quarters." Again, he pushed Kai a step closer to the estate doors.

Dead set on ending the night, Dresnor ignored Lord Hamrin. It felt like a standoff between the two men with Kai caught in the middle. His authoritative voice and towering height gave Dresnor the advantage over Lord Hamrin.

Kai was surprised to see Dresnor handle the man so aptly. Lord Hamrin came every year to the winter festival, but Kai was unaware of how Dresnor had such keen insights into the man. "It has been a most arduous journey, and the prince needs to rest. I will tend to his wounds. Are we staying in the east wing?" With one more push forward, Kai was in front of the door.

Opal buckled first. "Prince Kai, you will be staying in the private east wing, please follow me." She gestured, stepping around her father.

Two butlers opened the doors wide. "You will use the room your father once used when he came to visit," Opal continued. "Your men will use the other rooms along the hall."

Without waiting, Dresnor pushed Kai through the door and kept pace with Opal. "Thank you for understanding, Miss Opal." The other Kempery-men walked swiftly behind Smoke, suitably blocking Lord Hamrin's ability to approach Kai.

Opal moved briskly through the vast marble foyer toward a winding gold and marble staircase. "We were a bit surprised by your early arrival. We only received word you were coming two days ago and did not expect you for another week."

Kai wanted to look at the tapestries and lavish decorations, but Opal moved too quickly. Too tired to care, he was glad Dresnor continued to push him along. When they turned down the last hallway, he noticed Drew, Redmon, and Albey stopped short and blocked Lord Hamrin's path. "Sorry, sir, that will be far enough," Drew commanded. "While Prince Kai is staying at the estate, we must insist that you refrain from accessing this wing. Is that clear?"

High on his toes, Lord Hamrin tried to look around Drew. "Prince Kai, we shall speak first thing tomorrow." With no response, Lord Hamrin huffed and left.

Kai hated to admit it, but Dresnor had been right. It was best to avoid conversation. It was best to allow his men to protect and serve. Miss Opal opened four doors before they reached the end of the hallway, each a moderate sized bedroom.

The last door she opened revealed a larger room. Windows filled one wall, and a large bookshelf filled another. Kai was pleased to see a nice desk and several chairs. The bed on the opposite wall called to him, and he desperately wanted to lie down.

"Prince Kai, thank you for gracing our home with your visit. I had the cook prepare a tray with bread and fruit should you feel hungry during the night." She motioned to a small table near the window. "There is water in this pitcher and linens in the drawer here, so you can clean your face. If you need anything further, please let me know, and I will see it done." Humbly she backed away to the door to give him space.

Again, looking around the room, the only thing he cared about was the large four-poster bed. "Thank you, Lady Opal. You have provided everything I should need. I will speak with you come morning when I am rested." Kai smiled half-heartedly.

She stared at Smoke, just short of trembling. "He is so large. Will he hurt me?" she asked, her voice trembling.

"Smoke protects me. Respect me, respect his nature. If I have nothing to fear on my visit, then neither do you." Kai gave Smoke a nod, and Smoke strode into the room and lay across the rug, his massive form exceeding its size.

Miss Opal quickly looked down and curtsied. "Goodnight, Your Highness." Then she turned and nearly ran down the hallway past his men.

Dresnor smiled and walked into his own room, leaving his door open. Redmon and Albey all went into their respective chambers. Remaining in the hallway, Drew stood guard, pacing the length of the hall to a back staircase. Kai felt bad that Drew would have to say up for his shift. He knew each of them would take a turn guarding the hallway, no matter how tired they were. "Goodnight Drew."

Eyes trained on his task, Drew nodded. "Prince Kai."

Kai closed his door, approached the bed, and lay atop the covers. He knew he should dust off his road-stained clothes and wash his face, but he didn't care. He plopped onto his bed, desperate for sleep.

Restless, he tossed and turned. He was over-exhausted. When his mind let go, he drifted off to sleep, and visions trampled through his mind. The scenes flashed furiously. A wild shadowy beast in the night tore through foreign soldiers. Their leather armor stamped with a serpent. Terrifying screams echoed around a grassy field as they were struck down. The glint of steel flashed in his eyes and rang through his ears.

The battle scenes were too quick to follow. Kai pushed the sounds away. A small boy tugged at Kai's shirt. Kai felt fear and looked up. Two blue eyes peered down at him through cracks in the ceiling. His heart pounded with dread. He fought the vision and pushed away the distress. *Wake up,* he yelled to himself. *Show me no more.* Yet he did not wake.

Unable to keep the visions at bay, his mind revealed a new image. Short frizzy blonde hair surrounded a woman's face as she begged for her life. Her frail form writhing against the grip of an angry man. Children cried. He felt their pain. He squeezed his eyes tight, the vision faded and twisted into another image. Dark blood pooled on old oak flooring.

Writhing against the nightmare Kai woke and bolted upright. Eyes open, he held his head. Unlike a dream, these images felt real. There was a sense of urgency in their delivery. There was no stopping them. He only wished he knew when and how to prepare.

He peered around his room, fixing the layout in his mind. The chamber smelled of roses. The small table near the panes held a large vase of roses, and the tray of food Opal had provided. Bright moonlight spilled in from the two large windows across from his bed.

He swung his legs to the floor and went to the window. The estate seemed very peaceful at this hour. No lights sprang from the other windows as he looked out into the gardens. The grounds were different from home. This bedroom was only two floors up, while it was far from small, it was nothing compared to his room in the palace.

He touched his chest above his heart. How he ached to be back home. He knew this was meant to be an adventure, to challenge him, but he couldn't keep up with all the changes that adulthood and responsibility were imposing.

He picked up the large pitcher and poured water into the washbasin. The water turned a muddy brown as he washed his hands and face. Hunger pressed on his stomach, and he snatched a few morsels and drank some wine. It was a little different than home but still good.

The star-filled night relaxed his mind, and he felt tired once more. Back in the soft bed, he was thankful they were no longer traveling the open road. Hands tucked behind his head, he lifted slightly to see Smoke resting on the floor. The wolf's breathing was steady and slow. How Kai missed his puppy days, Smoke sleeping on his bed. It was all he could do not to join his friend on the floor.

Tomorrow would be a big day. This Lord Victor had a

strange manner and he did not relish spending an entire summer with him. He only hoped there would be time with Shane and Haygan. Time to explore and enjoy the more leisurely pace this small town might provide. He closed his eyes and drifted back to sleep. No more visions chased him.

Kai awoke to a presence in his room and a low growl from Smoke. Disoriented, he looked to the door. A female figure stood holding a pile of clothes, her face hidden in shadow. "Put these on and come with me, Prince Kai. There are things you must see firsthand," she instructed.

Dresnor stepped up behind her. "Hurry, Prince Kai. We have little time to waste. This is Marabella. We can trust her." Dresnor pulled Marabella from the room and closed the door behind them to give Kai privacy.

Without question, Kai hurried into the rags she called clothes. They were threadbare, stained, and torn. He was relieved they did not smell. Through the open window, he could tell it was just before dawn.

When he entered the hallway, the low light illuminated Marabella's face. Her gaunt features shocked him, and he looked to Dresnor. "What is going on?" Another look revealed her clothes were also well-worn, the edges stained with dirt. She smelled of earth and waste. It was difficult to process, but he trusted his Kempery-man with his life. Whatever this woman had been through, Dresnor seemed invested. He too wore old, stained clothing—but Kai could see the daggers at his waist and one barely visible in his boot.

Dresnor motioned toward the back stairs. "Follow Marabella, she knows the way." He glanced down at Smoke and touched Kai's shoulder. "When we get outside, let Smoke roam. His presence might give us away. Do you understand?"

Suddenly nervous, Kai looked at Smoke and then back to Dresnor. "What's wrong?"

Marabella did not stop to offer an explanation. She moved quickly through the corridor, descended a narrow winding staircase, and exited through the library onto a terraced garden. The moonlight bathing the garden offered little concealment. She darted across the landscape, hiding in the shadows as they neared a large wall.

Shrouded in darkness, they waited under a large oak. Motionless, Marabella focused on one point—a wrought-iron gate. Silently they waited. Crickets chirped into the night, breaking the silence. She did not move. Kai had no idea where she was taking them, but he saw her determination and courage. Behind it all, there was sorrow and fear.

Using his natural sight, Kai observed their surroundings and saw no one. He wanted to know why they waited. To detect her concern, he needed to glean. Connected to his sight, he followed the wave of energy. Around the perimeter guards patrolled. In the distance, Kai discovered a person hiding in a tree. The guard turned the corner approaching the gate. Breathless, they waited as the man passed.

The *woohoo* of an owl, once, twice and a third time echoed from the man's position. He was her lookout. Marabella darted. She pushed through the gate, Kai and Smoke alongside. Dresnor secured the latch and ran after them. Under cover of the trees once more, Kai looked at his Kempery-man. Genuine concern crossed Dresnor's face. "Now can you tell me where we are going?" Kai persisted.

"Marabella has much to show us about the truth of Hamrin and its people. Seeing is believing." Dresnor fell silent as they reached the open streets in town.

Smoke stayed a reasonable distance behind. Without him near, Kai felt exposed. Through their connection, he sensed his wolf on the outskirts of town. The current streets were empty, but loud, angry voices echoed through the buildings, deeper into town.

Marabella crossed the street into a narrow alleyway. She stopped and pressed her fingers to her lips for them to remain quiet. Fear etched on her face, and her eyes welled with tears. They sneaked further down the alley before turning left between two buildings. With each step, the yelling and screams got louder.

Up ahead, a man yelled, "Wake up, bums. Move on. Get your belongings and go, or we'll burn it all and you with it."

In return, Kai heard men, women, and children crying.

"Please, we have no place to go."

The men showed no mercy. "You can't sleep in the streets. You live like filthy animals. Go sleep in the woods, or I will lock you in the mines with the other slaves. Either way, you can't stay here," the cold-hearted voice hammered.

When they reached the next road, Marabella pulled Kai forward and pointed. Soldiers were grabbing people and shoving them down the streets. "How many times must we run you off? You're worthless trash. If you can't work, get out. There's no free food here."

One soldier stood out, broad-shouldered. A man who took great pride in his work, smiling as he grabbed a woman and pushed her down the street. The man with her pushed the soldier in the back. He looked like a flea trying to move a mountain. "Leave my wife be, Tarren! You're the animal."

Angered, Tarren backhanded the man in the face. Knocked back, the older man hit the ground with a thud and his screaming wife scrambled to his aid. Barely able to stand, she pulled her husband to his feet, and they scurried away.

Tarren yelled after them. "Raise your hand to me again, old man, and I will have your head. How will you provide for your wife when you're dead?"

Shocked, Kai stepped from their hiding place. "We need to help them."

Dresnor yanked Kai back into the narrow alley. "No. Watch. Listen and learn."

It was agonizing to watch Tarren, and the other soldiers continue to harass the people. Each family roused in the darkness, gathering what they could before they were pushed down the road. Behind them, another group of men collected leftover belongings, tossing them into a horse-drawn wagon.

The man, Tarren, seemed strangely familiar. Then Kai recalled seeing him. He was one of two brawny men who stood with Lord Victor when Kai arrived. Tarren continued to bark orders. "Get this mess cleaned up. We need all the homeless removed and the streets cleaned before morning."

Marabella clutched at her stomach, unable to contain her own grief. She pushed between Kai and Dresnor back down the way they came. Tears streamed down her cheeks. Dresnor pulled Kai away from the oppressive display. Out of sight, the berating shouts and terrorized screams rang out down the alleyway.

Again, they crept through the cover of night across town. Off through the woods, they reached a tall structure where another man barked orders, and the cries of children were the only answer. This broke Kai's heart. "What is this place?" he asked Marabella.

No answer came.

Upon closer examination, Kai determined the two-story building resembled an old barn. Two glassless windows were lit brightly against the night. He followed Marabella closer and closer until they could see inside. This was indeed an old barn that had been turned into a home for children—an orphanage.

Relentless cries echoed inside as children were dragged from their beds. "Get up, waifs. Get this place clean, Miss Grimley. Get them clean. When the prince visits, they say nothing. He is here early. We warned you to get ready. You must cast some of them out—there are too many. Just one urchin per bed. Get rid of the rest."

Kai could not see the woman he addressed, but he could hear her freighted voice pleading. "Please, they are only children," she begged. "Please. I do all I can with what we have. Where will they go?"

Her frail, boney form came into view as she stepped

around the children. She wasn't much more than a child her-self. Frizzy blonde hair blocked her face from view, but Kai knew this girl—or rather, he'd seen her in his dream. His heart clenched with the thought of what was to happen next. From where he stood, he could only watch.

The man stepped forward, and Kai saw his massive stature. In desperation, she reached her trembling hands to calm him. Without warning, he struck her across the face. She dropped to the ground in a heap, clutching her face.

"Shut up, Alissa. You are here only by my grace. Know this —you can be replaced and sent to the mines." The soldier towered over the poor girl; his frustration curled his mouth into a snarl.

Cowering on the ground, Alissa whimpered. The brute grabbed her by the neck and pulled her to her feet. His massive hand clutched her throat. Alissa struggled against his mighty grip. The man lowered his face close to hers. His evil grin told Kai that the man enjoyed his work. "I will have what I want from you Alissa, or I will put you in the ground like the last girl. Are we clear? Even if I must continue to beat you, you will submit." Finished, he tossed her to the ground like a rag doll. "We do not have to tend to these unwanted children. It is by Lord Victor's mercy these children are not turned out into the streets to starve."

The children sobbed as Alissa grabbed at her throat, gasp-ing for air. "Please, Bevon, they are just children," she croaked. "Can Lord Victor not offer a little more food?"

Kai could now see her gaunt face. Her neck and cheek bloomed red by the assault, and a small stream of blood ran from her lip.

Near his limit, Bevon thundered at Alissa. "NO! Get rid of some of them, and you will have enough. Talk back to me again, and I will burn this place to the ground, with you and them inside."

The children muffled their sobs and cowered around Alissa. The door to the orphanage opened, and the light illuminated three figures. The men stormed out in force against the night. Bevon took the lead and bellowed. "A waste if you ask me. Why do we bother to keep this place? Nothing but unwanted brats. They serve no purpose until they are old enough to work the mines. When the prince leaves, I will deal with this new girl. She is too bold for her own good."

Devastated, Kai clapped a hand across his mouth. He dared not speak, but he wanted to have the man thrashed for what he'd done. Instead, they hid in the bushes. When the men were well away, Marabella silently led them back to the estate.

Kai had no words for what he'd witnessed. Heartbroken, Kai returned to his chamber. His Kempery-man followed him inside and paced the floor.

"Dresnor, what am I to do? I don't understand what's happening here. There is no real poverty in Diu. Rowdy areas, yes, but no starvation. I have never seen men like this Terran and Bevon. And the orphanage… I cannot even begin to understand what I saw there. How can this be happening in a Diu town? Why has nothing been done?"

Dresnor dug at his beard. "There is no way the Grand Duke would have sent us into this situation had he known. The people here are frightened. I am surprised Marabella was strong enough to come forward." Dresnor turned away, concealing his emotions.

"Unfortunately, if dukes pay their taxes and pledge fealty, they are often left to run their districts as they see fit. Kai, I respect your father. Before Iver was king, he tended these towns for his father. Once he became king, he made less time for his people outside of Diu city."

A pained look crossed Dresnor's face. "Forgive me for saying so, but the king stopped enforcing Diu law after your mother died. Even now, he travels the ocean searching for riches, building trade routes, and affirming allegiances elsewhere. He has forsaken his own people outside of the capital."

The words stung. How dare his Kempery-man blame his father for the atrocities they'd witnessed? But even though

Kai wanted to argue, he knew part of it was true. His father had stopped visiting their own country.

Kai leaned back, taking stock. "What is Diu law? I know from my history lessons you cannot own slaves. If these people are paid anything, they are not actual slaves. Mistreated sure, overtaxed probably, but not slaves. Although if they are locked up in the mines as Bevon said..." He let his voice trail off.

Lost by the horrors, Kai wanted to scream. Instead, he pounded his fist on the table. "We need people willing to give testament. This mine I heard them mention, what is Victor mining?"

"Marabella tells me there are two—copper and marble. Both dangerous, backbreaking work. If Victor is making money and not paying proper taxes, that is one charge against him. It seems he is also keeping the town visibly small and starving his people. That could also be a chargeable offense." Dresnor's green eyes glared with anger.

"So, you recommend we use the law to end this mess?" Kai asked.

"Victor is responsible for the orphanage. If he is aware of the mistreatment of the children, or aware of the men locked in the mines, he could face prison. All criminal offenses. This Bevon character, he may have committed murder. We need to know what Victor knows. We need the Grand Duke. In your father's absence, Dante can enforce the law of the land." Dresnor paused, shaking his head. "We only have a dozen armed men. Victor's men will not go easy. They enjoy their work and the life they've established. There will be a fight."

Dawn peaked through the trees and splashed through Kai's chamber window. A mix of fear and anger welled in his chest. "How can I face this duke? This Victor Hamrin? Am I expected to sit with this man and act like I know nothing?"

Dresnor shifted to the creaking door as Drew entered. "Drew, what have you learned?"

"Sir, for a small town, he has amassed a large force—over

a hundred men. Loyal men. He pays them well, and they do anything he says. They live like kings off the backs of the villagers. I had our men remove their Diu uniforms to learn what they could. Their men boast openly about thrashing the locals. They drink themselves into disgrace."

Drew clenched his jaw. "One of our men reported he found a tavern full of men drinking and fighting amongst themselves. They have no code. Best he could tell, most are unaware the Prince is even here. I have sent a bird with your note, but it will take time. And I have Finlee and a scout ready to board this morning's ship bound for Diu. They will take the letter you provided straight to the Grand Duke."

"Well done, Drew," Dresnor said. "You may go."

Kai crossed to Dresnor. "Now what?" He looked down the hallway after Drew, noticing Opal speaking with Kempery-man Albey. "Do we sit and wait until reinforcements come if they make it in time?"

Dresnor placed a hand on Kai's shoulder. "Our scout will inform Dante of the number of men required. Now we need to continue to gather information. Determine Lord Hamrin's culpability. Bide our time if we can. This town is on the cusp of breaking. Our early arrival has caused an unexpected storm. They were unable to properly prepare."

Hearing his Kempery-man's words, Kai felt a little better about their chances. "We simply need to make it through the day. Ask a few questions… I can do that. We need to change for breakfast. I am sure Victor is expecting us."

Dresnor shook his head in disagreement. "No. We need to make him wait. You need to avoid him this morning. I want to see how far we can push the old man. Become the spoiled prince he expects. When we confront him, I want him seething, disrespectful, and overconfident. Redmon is informing Haygan now. Together you should take your morning run. Get a lay of the land. Given what you've just witnessed, I doubt you are prepared to dine with Victor and play nice."

His man was right. It was best he take the time to process

all he'd witnessed. Relieved he could put off facing this duke, Kai breathed easier. "What of Marduk and Shane?"

"I will speak to them," Dresnor assured him.

CHAPTER 28

Childhood's End

Kai found Haygan waiting in the estate gardens with Shiva and Smoke. He leaned against a tree, dressed in black and gray. His shoulder-length hair was tied back. "Good morning, Kai. Kempery-man Redmon informed me we have a situation brewing. I am to keep you outside of town until late afternoon, buy us some time and allow you to calm down."

Kai nodded toward the gate. "We are to get a lay of the land. Dresnor believes things could go bad before help arrives. The longer we can avoid a confrontation, the better. There are well over one hundred men in town loyal to Lord Victor. He could easily turn on us. And yes, I need to prepare or I might punch the man in the face for what he's done."

Keenly looking around, Kai pushed through the wrought-iron gate. He couldn't help but notice how Victor's estate was rather large and opulent considering how poor the towns-people were.

Haygan closed the gate. "I get the impression the grooms-men are most fortunate to work within the estate. They would not speak with me about the conditions, but it is easy to see even they are struggling." Haygan quickened his pace and glanced over his shoulder. "We are being followed. Two men."

"I think we need to circle the town, work our way outward. We should see how many men patrol the streets." Kai used his sight to track the two men.

Their pursuers kept pace but hid in the early morning shadows. Smoke and Shiva trailed behind, forcing the men to keep their distance. Together they wormed their way around town. Remnants of half-constructed walls jutted up here and there; only completed segments surrounded the Hamrin estate. The next section of the buildings seemed newly built. Guards' quarters, three levels high, filled with rousing soldiers pouring out into the streets.

Farther around the town, Kai noticed the buildings were smaller and poorly maintained. While the estate had flat stone roads, and cobblestone surrounded the guards' quarters and homes, the roads in town gave way to dirt.

Near the wharf, the smell of decayed fish filled the air. The stench was nearly unbearable. About to gag, Kai looked to Haygan. "How disgusting." He picked up the pace, and Haygan matched his speed.

Smoke and Shiva drifted behind, keeping any who followed at a greater distance. Discarded nets, sails, and dead fish littered the water's edge. Only a few fishermen were loading boats with gear, preparing for a day on the water.

Kai hoped his men were on their way. It would take all day for them to sail to Hamrin. Help would not arrive until tomorrow morning, if they sailed overnight. Haygan urged him faster. "Let's pick up the pace, run faster, and widen our circle. After we pass the estate, we can run deeper into the forest."

When they increased their speed, the men following gave up. Haygan turned toward the forest, darting between bushes and leaping over felled trees. Three soldiers awaited them a few meters within the woods, but they were easily lost as Haygan and Kai climbed a steep embankment. Smoke and Shiva growled, and the men retreated.

Haygan scanned the area and took the steepest incline he

could find, weaving through the forest. Kai struggled to follow Haygan and keep his footing. After a few stumbles, Haygan slowed, allowing him to catch back up. "We need to get to the top of this ridge. It will level out, and there is an outcropping. You will be safe there."

They continued to run through the woods, climbing ever higher. Kai was glad that he ran daily, allowing him to keep pace. Over rocks and around thick underbrush they climbed. With two quick leaps they crossed a stream. Haygan made running look effortless. Even climbing over boulders and down trees, he bounded like a wild cat.

When they reached level ground, Haygan slowed and made his way through the trees. The dirt turned to stone, and the rock jutted out over the trees below. If they had not just spent the entire morning running away from an uncertain foe, this might actually be a pleasant day.

Kai scratched his head. "What did you mean, I would be safe there?" He ducked under a tree branch.

Haygan did not answer. Kai could tell Haygan was using his sight to survey the area. Following suit, he found Smoke and Shiva circling. The forest teemed with wildlife, but nobody followed them. His face stern, Haygan turned to Kai. "I saw this place from below. I need you to stay here. I can make better time alone." He stepped around Kai. "Follow me."

Back through the trees, there was a small cave. "Stay here. I will return as fast as I can."

"You're going to leave me here alone?" Kai's brows knit together, concern in his tone. "Why can't I go with you? I have made it this far."

"Please understand. I can make better time on my own, you're not fast enough yet. Shiva and Smoke will stay. It would take the average Katori man three or four hours to run north of Chenowith. I cannot afford to run as a man." He glanced away from Kai, looking to the woods.

Haygan's words ricocheted in Kai's ears. *What did he just say?* Before he could get clarification, Haygan continued. "The people I need to meet are uncomfortable around strangers. Half-Light or not, I need to leave you here. If I can bring back help, I will."

The stablemaster's words jumbled together in Kai's mind. If Haygan knew woodland people—Katori people—it seemed natural they might not welcome strangers. He also knew going too deep into any part of the Zabranen Forest was dangerous. This far west in Diu territory, they were near the Katori border. Given how high they had climbed, they were possibly already within its limits.

Several hours passed, and there was still no sign of Haygan. Smoke and Shiva lay inside the tree line, only occasionally leaving to scout around the cave and outcropping. Bored and unable to sit still any longer, Kai paced around the cave. Outside he walked to the edge of the overlook. He gazed over the trees. Baden Lake was a vast swath of blue in the distance. The afternoon sun was warm on Kai's face.

"How long are we supposed to wait?" Kai addressed his two companions. "What if Haygan never comes back?" he said out loud with a huff.

The wolves kept watch but did not respond. Kai thought about everything he'd witnessed; his blood began to boil again. He could wait no longer. "Let's go, we are going back. I can't hide up here any longer." Determined, he took one last look over the trees and started to climb back down.

He took the same way he'd come with Haygan earlier. Flanked by Smoke and Shiva, he scanned the hillside. Through the trees he noticed two white wisps moving in his direction. A voice called out. "Kai, hold up. Over here."

He recognized the voice. "Shane? What are you doing up here? How did you find me?" Kai called back.

When they came through the trees, Shane and Marduk were a welcome sight. Marduk, a seasoned hunter, surveyed the area. "We left an hour behind you, but we were not running. I doubled back a few times to hide our trail. Haygan only told me to pack for an overnight in the woods and which direction he planned to go. I've been tracking you ever since. The guards paid us no attention. Since we are staying at the inn, they were unaware that we were part of your entourage."

The concern on Marduk's face told him they did not have a clue as to why they had spent the better part of the day hiking. "Follow me," Kai said, "I believe Haygan meant for us to wait at this cave above." Leading them back, he gave them the condensed version of everything he'd learned.

Marduk shook his head in disbelief. Anger fumed in his eyes. "Why are we up here?" Marduk asked.

"I needed to get away, clear my head before I did something reckless. We are stalling. Dresnor sent a bird with a coded message and two men on the morning ship. One of our messages will make it. Dante will know we face one hundred men, maybe more. Help will come."

Kai could tell Marduk was unhappy about the situation. "It could all end peacefully if Victor tells the truth and surrenders. His men are the bigger problem. Bevon will not go down quietly."

Shane stepped around his father. "How long are we supposed to wait?"

There was no way to answer his friend's question honestly. He knew Haygan would need to run over seventy miles just to reach Chenowith. Plus, he had no idea where these Katori woodlanders might be. "I have no idea. Haygan left hours ago. Told me to wait. It would have been easier had I known you were coming."

With nothing else to do, Kai sat in the sun. Marduk opened his pack, and they shared a hunk of bread, dried meat, and some apples. Shiva and Smoke continued to patrol the woods, returning ever so often to the overlook.

When Haygan finally entered the clearing, Kai was relieved. "Marduk, you made it," Haygan called. "Good. I presume Kai has made you aware of the situation. We need every man we can spare, but I will not ask you to put your son at risk. The choice is yours. Shane can stay within the hills. He will be safe this far outside of town. Kai and I must go back. I hope you will join us."

Marduk looked at Kai, concerned. Kai knew Marduk saw Shane when he looked at him. "You mean to go back? There could be a fight. You plan to put the prince in harm's way?"

"The prince cannot hide. His presence may keep things calm long enough to get reinforcements. Once they are outnumbered, they will back down. I sent word we need help, but I am not sure they will come."

Marduk's eyes drifted from Shane to Kai. Haygan lifted his hand, tamping the air. "Look, we had no idea what we were coming into, but help is coming from Diu. We need to bide our time, and Dresnor needs the prince. I will not let anything happen to him."

Haygan pressed a hand on Kai's shoulder. "We must go. Stay here, Marduk, decide what is best for your son. If you choose to come back, go to the orphanage on the far side of town."

All the way back down the mountain, Kai pondered what he might say to this rogue duke. He hopped over a downed tree and weaved between several saplings. Unable to keep quiet, he tapped Haygan on the arm. "Can we walk?"

Haygan slowed. "What's on your mind?"

"You were gone for hours, and you came back with no help. Did they say no?"

"I don't know yet. I went to meet one person. She is going for help. If they say no, she will come alone."

The idea sounded ridiculous. "One person. A woman." Kai squinted at Haygan.

"I hope help from Diu arrives, but if all else fails, Simone offers the help of a dragon. We will not lose," Haygan assured him.

"So how did you make it all the way to Chenowith and back? You were gone a long while, but not *that* long."

A smirk pushed up Haygan's cheek. "Dragons fly, remember. She dropped me a little west of the overlook."

The thought of riding a dragon swirled in Kai's imagination. Before he could ask more questions, Haygan resumed a faster pace. Kai thought about the idea of a dragon helping him. He recalled Diu's history and the dragons that saved their city once before. Now one would come to save *him*. He really didn't understand these creatures at all.

Back at the estate, Kai changed into social attire and sat with Dresnor. "How did they take me leaving?" He asked as Drew entered his chambers.

"Victor has been fuming all day." Dresnor smiled. "He's near his boiling point because you made him wait so long. I assured him the prince spends his time as he wishes. I told him you'd return when you were suitably relaxed, ready for food and conversation."

Dresnor motioned to the hall, and they walked together. "When you were not back by lunch, I was a bit concerned myself. Victor has been irate for hours. If you don't come down for dinner, I think he will begin to question our delay." Dresnor's eyes narrowed as they reached the balcony.

Drew chuckled. "His men were none too pleased, chasing you and Haygan around the outskirts of town. Not to mention your wolves scared several men into hiding."

Opal waited on the bottom step.

"Well, let's get on with this charade, shall we?" Kai mumbled under his breath, descending the staircase.

By the time they reached the banquet room, Lord Victor was halfway through a glass of wine. A stern glance to a nearby servant, and it was quickly refilled. "Welcome, welcome Prince Kai, so *good of you* to finally join me. I trust your afternoon has you suitably relaxing." Victor's tone was snippy and verged on disrespectful.

Kai sucked at his teeth, nodding. "*Lord Victor,*" he said distastefully. "I hope I didn't tax your men as they lay chase after me most of the morning. I spend my time as I wish. I needed the quiet time to reflect. You've met Kempery-man Dresnor, yes?" He motioned to his left. "Allow me to introduce other Kempery-man Redmon and Albey."

"Nice to meet you all." Lord Victor gestured to the table. "Let's sit, eat, and relax."

Kai sat opposite Victor. Dresnor and Albey sat to his left and Redmon on his right. Opal sat beside her father, while Victor's two boys sat on the other side near Albey.

Beside Redmon, Kai noticed there were two additional place settings. Before he had a chance to ask who would be joining them, the banquet doors reopened. He nearly choked at the site of Bevon and Tarren entering the room.

Bevon was much larger than he realized. Kai's view inside of the orphanage did not do the man justice. A brawny man with long raven hair, a hint of gray speckled his temples and a short-trimmed goatee. When he stepped up beside Redmon, Bevon dwarfed his Kempery-man by nearly five inches.

Tarren was nearly as tall and also built like an ox. His black hair was cut short, and his youthful, clean-shaven face showed off his chiseled features.

"Sorry we are late, Lord Victor. We had … important matters about town. Prince Kai, it seems that your stable boy and scout have returned. Their ship did not quite make it to Diu. I hope they were not set on important matters." Bevon raised one eyebrow at Kai before he scanned the others, then offered a smirk to Victor.

Kai kept his composure. His mind raced with concern for his men, sent to get help. Even without it being said, he feared no help was coming. Their only hope was the bird carrying their news. He hoped it would reach Dante soon.

"Nothing that can't be resolved another way," Kai responded as casually as he could. "Where are my men now?" he questioned.

Victor cleared his throat, ignoring the question. "Prince Kai, these are my men, Bevon and Tarren Stratton." He tossed his hand in their direction. "Now let's eat."

Like bees to honey, servants swarmed the table, filling each plate as they went. Kai looked closer at the two men and saw the resemblance. *Of course, they're related. Like father like son. Monsters, not men.*

"Again, I ask…" Kai focused on Bevon. "Where are my men?"

Bevon glared back. "They are fine. My men will see they are returned to the estate."

Victor stabbed his meat. His fork screeched across his plate. "So, tell me, Prince Kai, how long will you be staying with us?" He eagerly took a bite.

Kai eyed Victor and considered his response. "We intend to stay the entire summer. I trust that won't be an inconvenience." Kai also took a bite.

Victor nearly choked as he glanced at Bevon, whose face twisted with disdain. Kai had apparently caught them off-guard. He watched their exchange. Victor swallowed his mouthful and coughed a few more times, trying to process this new information.

Opal handed her father his glass. "Drink, father. Are you alright?" Her kindness lost on the man.

Victor snatched the glass and took a gulp and exchanged glances with Bevon and Tarren. Kai continued. "I trust you will extend me the same courtesy you did my father in his day. A young prince out in the service of his king."

Kai leaned back into his chair and watched their discomfort. At least until he looked to Dresnor, who was clearing holding his tongue.

Meanwhile, Victor searched the ceiling, as if the answers to his situation floated above. "Of course, Prince Kai, we are honored to have you here. We would have preferred more time to prepare for your arrival, but we are here to serve." His response was insincere, and his eyes glared.

Both Bevon and Tarren seemed put out by the news and leaned back from their half-eaten plates. Victor's two boys were clueless about the mounting tension in the room and murmured amongst themselves. Opal kept her eyes focused on her plate, trying to pretend she was not listening.

Unable to control himself, Kai continued to poke. "Victor, I have seen so little of your charming town. Perhaps when we finish here, you would see fit to provide a tour."

Victor's face turned pale. If Kai didn't know better, he would have sworn he saw actual fear. Of course, the village held secrets, and Victor wasn't interested in parading through the middle of his mess.

The mines and its slaves. Kai had yet to find their location. Again, Dresnor's expression told Kai he was playing with fire. His Kempery-man pushed back his plate. Kai remained calm— he hoped he had not gone too far.

Bevon remained calm and pushed back from the table. "Lord Victor, if you plan to take a tour around town, I need to make arrangements. Please excuse us." Together the two men left, not addressing Kai in their departure.

A chill ran down Kai's spine. These men had no qualms about disrespecting a royal. They had no regard for human life. How far would they be willing to go? With the realization that no help was coming from Diu any time soon, Kai took a gulp of wine. Their only other hope was Haygan's plea to the Katori mountain people.

Victor downed the last of his wine. "Well, seems they are making the arrangements." With a glance to the window, he pushed back from the table. "I would be happy to provide a tour. Given the late hour, we should go now, before the sun sets." The man rubbed his belly and motioned to the door.

Outside they walked around the estate. Drew and four Diu guards, all wearing armor, joined the procession as they reached the gates, and Kai was relieved to see Smoke and Shiva sitting outside the estate. No Haygan.

By the time they crossed the second street, Kai had noticed Hamrin guards gathering to create a pathway through town. He cautiously looked for his remaining men and was pleased to find them advancing on his position. One man short, one less scout. *Where could they be holding Finlee and my scout?*

Concerned, Dresnor slowed and whispered to Kai. "I doubt Diu help is coming anytime soon. We are a dozen men, on our own. We must assume they've questioned our scout. He is an honorable man, but everyone has their limits. I am sure if given a chance, he disposed of my letter. If not, well, all my letter said is, the prince is bored and cannot be expected to suffer in these conditions for another one hundred days and asked for permission to return by ship.

"My note sent by bird said the same thing. Written in this manner, Dante will know we are in trouble and face one hundred men—we are desperate. We need to head west toward the orphanage. Haygan hopes to join us there." Dresnor ran his hand over the silver-and-gold wolf on his armor.

"These men are monsters," Kai responded, "and Victor knows it. He is living off the backs of our people. He needs to face his crimes and answer for what he has done."

"Just get us to the orphanage," Dresnor insisted as they reached the town square.

Victor motioned Kai forward. "Prince Kai, this is our humble town. It is small, but we are growing. My apologies, the fountain stopped working last autumn. We have yet to have it repaired."

Near the stone fountain, a few people stood trying their best to smile and look pleasant. "Please meet some local people. Your people." The old man wiped sweat from his brow.

The frail, frightened citizens waited for inspection. They were clearly hand-selected by Bevon, who stood close by. Nervous, they continued to glance from Bevon to Kai. They bowed respectfully but kept quiet. With Dresnor's approval, Kai stepped forward, extending a hand to each person.

"Pleased to meet you. I am humbled to visit your town. I will be staying the summer and hope to see you again during my stay." He held onto the last man's hand and clasped his other hand on top. "I am here to help," he added in a low tone.

Fearful and unable to do more, they all kept bowing and smiling until Victor dismissed them. Then Victor wrapped his chubby hand around Kai's shoulder. "Forgive my people. They are shy, you understand. They have not seen royalty in almost a decade."

The essence of the man turned Kai's stomach. The scene around the square solidified Dresnor's concerns. The entire town center was surrounded by Victor's men. Three rows deep, they stood shoulder to shoulder, armed to the teeth. A show of force. Nearly a threat, their foreign leather armor stamped with a serpent. Not the royal wolf.

"Lord Hamrin, I am here to help you and your people. Clearly, you need assistance." Kai kept his tone reserved; he'd seen that symbol before. The serpent from his vision. He could not help what he knew. Now all he could do was be brave and wait for the outcome to unfold. If only he knew how this would end.

Trying to sound genuine, he pulled Victor away from the others. "I know you don't want to ask for help, but let me help you. Your people will thank you for it, and I will look good to my father. I can request a few supplies and spend the rest of my summer sailing and hunting. Or better yet, go home early. I don't want to be here. This is boring." Kai tried to sound uninterested.

Victor's posture visibly relaxed, and he smiled over his shoulder to Bevon. "Yes, I think we can reach an understanding. Surely we can benefit each other. As you suggest, we can make a good show of this visit."

Kai pulled away from Victor and motioned to his men to fall in while he pushed through Bevon's men. He needed to get them to the orphanage. "Now let's see the rest of your town."

Victor followed while Bevon signaled his men, and they rushed ahead. Bevon sneered at Kai and whispered a few private words to the trailing duke. Visible anger swept across Victor's face.

Along their route, people ducked inside of their homes. Doors slammed shut. A rare few peaked through tattered window coverings. Nobody dared come out and greet the prince, less they tangle with Bevon's men. Each citizen was gaunter than the last. Their frail faces looked like ghosts peering through windowpanes.

The shoreline still smelled of decaying fish but had been cleared of debris. Beyond the wharf, the sun's final rays melted into the distance. "This is our shipping yard. It's not much, but we do with what we have." Victor nodded and walked away.

Kai gleaned the lake searching for a boat approaching. Nothing. Aid from Diu was not coming to save them. On the shore, Victor leaned against a tree speaking with Bevon. Kai hopped off the pier and looked through the trees as they neared the south side. He saw Haygan.

He tried to remember how to find the orphanage. Unfamiliar with the town, Kai attempted to recall his predawn scamper. Silently they walked until he caught sight of the lights illuminating the orphanage. Distant through the trees, it stood alone in the fading light.

Again, Kai slipped between the Hamrin guards. He hastened his pace and made straight for the orphanage. "Lord Victor," he asked. "What is this building used for?"

"There is nothing to see there, Prince Kai. It is only the town's orphanage," Victor stammered. "We have but a few children, abandoned by their parents. I do my best to provide a life for them. Let's go back to the estate. We have much to discuss," Victor pleaded, grabbing at Kai's arm.

Kai stopped and bit the inside of his lip. He pulled the old man away from Bevon. "Victor. Can I call you Victor? I hear you have found a copper mine and a marble quarry. I have yet to see that. Tell me, between us, have they been profitable? Maybe we can discuss how the profit of the mines can also be mutually beneficial—an understanding, just between us."

He let the old man go and marched up the path and pushed wide the two large front doors, followed by his Kempery-men and Drew. "Children, come out. I want to meet you. My name is Prince Kai Galloway. I am here to help you."

He noticed Alissa rise from her chair, holding a small book

as she stepped around a large wooden pillar. Slowly the other children scurried from their beds and clustered around her thin frame. Across her face, he noticed the large bruise she tried to hide with her short frizzy hair.

She patted the children's heads, softly reassuring them. "My name is Miss Alissa Grimley, and these children are in my care. It is an honor to meet you, Prince Kai." Nervously she pawed at the hair covering her cheek.

Appalled by the condition of the home, Kai observed the thin straw mattresses and dirty threadbare sheets. Rage fueled in the pit of Kai's stomach as he looked out through the window. It was the same window he looked through before dawn.

When he turned around, Alissa was swarmed by the cowering children, their eyes focused on Bevon and Victor near the doorway. Bevon stood arms crossed about his muscular chest, fiercely warning them with his eyes to keep silent.

Kai's three Kempery-men stood close by, hands on their hilts as they prepared to fight if things went wrong. Kai moved toward the children and stood beside his man Albey. Behind him, he felt Dresnor's warm hand nudge against his back. He knew they'd pressed their luck; they were surrounded. "Miss Alissa, it is a pleasure to meet you and your children. I think we need to be going. Perhaps I can come back another day before I leave."

Before she could respond, a small boy emerged from the pack. "You promise you can help us?" The little boy pleaded, eyeing Bevon. "Can you help all of us? Even my brother?" he begged in his frail voice.

"Certainly, even your brother. Which one is your brother?" Kai surveyed the group, expecting another boy to step forward. The little boy tugged at his shirt. Kai looked down, and the boy pointed up. Slowly Kai lifted his eyes to the ceiling, following the boy's gaze. Above in the loft through the cracks in the boards, he could see little blue eyes peering down.

Unfortunately, everyone else had done the same, Bevon included. Enraged, Bevon stepped toward the children and Alissa. "You deceiving little wench. I told you..." Rage boiled in the man's eyes.

Before he could continue, the boy near Kai rushed forward. "Stop it. Leave us alone," he yelled, pounding Bevon's leg, his little fists white with fury. "I hate you!" he cried.

Bevon turned his wrath on the child, sweeping his mountain-sized arm, striking the boy. The swat was violent and heavy-handed. Kai's heart pounded in his ears, and everything slowed. Everything crawled to a halt. He could see the look of terror on everyone's faces. His mind played out the scene; the boy's head striking the square post and falling limp to the ground. Blood spilling out around his little head.

No, this cannot happen!

Kai held his breath. In the next heartbeat, he lunged forward, his hand outstretched. Caught in the same time warp, his natural lightning fast movement felt slow. Outstretched, Kai's palm cupped the boy's head. With the release of his breath, time resumed.

The back of his hand struck the post, and it cut the skin. As he scooped the boy into his chest, he felt a warm trickle of blood run down his wrist. The pair slid to the floor against the post. Dresnor sprang to Kai's side, pulling his sword from its scabbard.

In a panic, Victor shook his head. "I will not give up my town, nor my fortune! This foolish boy means to blackmail me. Kill them all! If word gets out, we're all finished!" Victor stormed out and left Bevon to deal with Kai and his men.

Out of nowhere came a right overhanded punch to the side of Tarren's head, sending him into the wall. Bevon turned to see his son out cold slumped on the floor, Drew standing in his place.

Shocked, Bevon swung his cruel hand at Drew's head. Drew ducked and jabbed Bevon in the ribs with his left, then sent an uppercut into his throat. Bevon gasped and cupped his throat. Drew stepped to the side and gave a swift kick that knocked out the man's knee.

Drew pulled Bevon's arm tight behind his back, bent in an odd angle, his face pressed on the floor. Then he slammed his knee into the man's back and held a dagger to the base of his skull. "Yield or I'll run you through."

All three Kempery-men surrounded Tarren and Bevon—swords drawn. "Kai, is the boy alright?" Dresnor asked, eyes on Bevon.

"He'll be fine," Kai assured him. "What about Victor? He ran outside. His men will be on us." He helped the boy stand and shuffle to Alissa.

Outside in the night came the clash of metal against metal. Bevon squirmed. "My men will kill you all. Best let me up now, runt. Sucker punching my boy was devious. You got lucky with me is all. If I'd…"

Drew pulled back on Bevon's arm, and he winced in pain. "That's enough out of you," Drew barked.

Kai had always thought Drew was a large man, but beside Bevon… well, he was just happy it went the way it did. Glancing around at the children, he felt at a loss. "Now what?"

The yelling and fighting increased, and Dresnor braced the door. "I don't know how long we can hold out! Best subdue those two before we have a fight on our hands. We need to join our men outside. I can only hope Haygan was able to bring help."

Dresnor, Redmon, and Albey slipped outside, and Kai closed the door behind them. Several men grunted, and a few screamed. Kai watched Drew restrain the prisoners, desperate to join the action. "Go, Drew, they need your help." Kai motioned.

In agreement Drew opened the door and Kai got his first glance outside. His men were fighting the Hamrin soldiers. Dresnor and Albey fought back-to-back, a sword in each hand. Their metallic armor glistened in the moonlight. Drew sliced down two men and joined them.

Across the field, he saw three men dressed in black slicing through Hamrin men. They wielded double-edged battle axes, slicing deep cuts through the enemy's leather armor. They were swift, efficient fighters—one was Haygan. Their speed was unmatched by the Hamrin fighters, and together they ripped through a dozen men.

From the trees, he saw the occasional volley of arrows —Hunter Marduk and Shane. Beside them, a massive beast bound into the clearing. Kai gasped. "A black Shuk." Its massive jaws shook men like ragdolls. Three Hamrin men charged the creature. Its enormous body slammed two men to the ground and clawed the third across the chest.

He'd heard stories about a creature the size of a horse that roamed the Zabranen Forest. Large pointy ears, thick black fur that formed a dense ridge down its back, ending in a thick black tail. Its silver eyes flashed in the night, and its sharp fangs and claws continued to rip through men. Even with the Shuk and two extra Katori men, it was not enough. They were being overwhelmed.

Behind him, Alissa screamed, and Kai turned to see Bevon break free of his bonds. Alone, Kai stood face to face with a monster; a man who would kill him in an instant, should he get close enough.

They stared at each other. The moment lingered. Kai thought of Riome's training. He would need to be quick on his feet and attack, in short, clipped moves. His adversary was massive, but Kai knew size should not matter.

Bevon advanced.

Instead of retreating, Kai attacked. He landed several punches, and his superior speed kept him a move ahead of his opponent. Bevon countered, striking Kai in the shoulder, but Kai moved with the blow, lessening its force.

With Bevon overextended, Kai slid around behind the towering man. With all his might, Kai struck him in the spine. Bevon arched his back but swung his leg around and kicked Kai away. "You're not as weak as you pretend, little prince," Bevon sneered.

The children gasped. Kai's ribs ached from the blow. He

scrambled to his feet. It was vital he keep distance between them.

Bevon grunted and advanced again.

Kai twisted out of Bevon's reach and swept the man's bad leg. Bevon landed with a thud. Again, the man charged, a feral look burned in his eyes. Kai blocked the blow and landed another strike to Bevon's ribs before pivoting out of reach.

The next exchange sent Kai across the floor as Bevon's punch grazed across Kai's cheek and connected with his shoulder.

The taste of blood filled Kai's mouth. Again, he hopped to his feet. This time he pulled his dagger and took a stance, eyeing Bevon. There was no way to stop this man. He would continue to come at Kai until he was put down. He knew he would only get one shot with the blade, and he'd better make it count. Still, he hated the thought of killing this man.

Bevon stood, favoring his busted knee. "Your little blade won't save you, boy," Bevon hissed. "Don't worry, I'll kill you quick."

"You talk too much," Kai quipped, blade firmly in his right hand.

Bevon lunged. Kai charged—his only advantage was his speed. The distance shortened in an instant; Kai slid to his knees under Bevon's grasp. His blade sliced across the man's leg. Too low. Kai had missed the inner thigh. The sharp edge of his knife ripped through fabric and muscle. The wound gushed blood. In one continuous motion, Kai tossed the blade to his left hand and stabbed toward the man's lower back as he slid past.

Again, he'd struck too low. The blade held fast, stuck in Bevon's hip. Kai hopped onto both feet. Bevon stumbled forward, grabbing at the knife. "Nice move kid, but I've got your blade." Bevon pulled out the dagger; blood oozed and dripped on the ground.

The blade was now in Bevon's hands. Kai gulped. The children screamed. Bevon shook his head, dazed. Both strikes had been good hits, just not kill shots. Bevon was a strong man, and he would not go down so easy. Kai backed away. He knew there was no clean way to win a knife fight, especially against a seasoned man twice his size.

Riome would be disappointed Kai had not struck his mark. His unwillingness to kill this man put Kai at a disadvantage. He backed away toward the center of the room. The children cried and moved against the wall. The battle still raging outside, there was no one to help him. Even with his increased speed, he knew he could not disarm Bevon without getting cut.

If he did manage to get the knife, he would most certainly have to use deadly force. There would be no choice— Kai would have to kill the man, or they were all finished. The thought shook Kai's core. He did not want this burden.

Bevon regained his footing and wagged the blade at Kai. Then he cocked his head toward Alissa and the sobbing children. "Maybe I should cut them with your blade. Make you watch," he snarled.

A thunderous crash followed by a scraping sound rattled the barn's roof. The children screamed, and chunks of wood fell from above. Instinctively Bevon raised his arms to block the debris. Unsteady, he dropped to one knee.

This was Kai's chance. He dove for the knife, knocking it from Bevon's hand. It slid across the wooden floor under a nearby bed. *No. I missed the blade.* Kai clenched his jaw. He could not catch a break.

The timbers overhead creaked and shook under the weight of something massive. Loud screeching sounds penetrated the air. Through the holes in the roof, Kai saw flames fill the sky. One last scrape across the timbers and something shifted, followed by a loud thud on the ground outside. A mix of shrieks and screams filled the air. The ground rumbled and shook as a massive beast stomped and attacked the remaining men. *The dragon came!* Kai breathed a sigh of relief.

Bevon regained his senses. Shaking off the dust, he stumbled to his feet. Kai stood his ground, but his mind raced.

"Look at you, the royal brat has skill." Bevon moved on Kai, closing the distance.

Kai dodged the blow.

Bevon stopped frozen, blood gushing out his mouth. An arrow pierced his throat, and he dropped to the ground at Kai's feet. Blood spewing on the floor. Shock tremored through Kai's body. On the opposite end, Shane stood outside the glassless window, bow in hand. He nodded to Kai and disappeared from sight.

Kai looked to Alissa and the children. "Everyone alright?" He looked to Tarren, still secured to a wooden barn post, nodding in and out of consciousness. "Stay here, I will be right back." He called running to the door.

He opened one door to peek out. The fighting had stopped, and he caught the sight of a tree-sized black dragon. The scales glistened in the moonlight. A row of horns speckled its tail and spine. Amber eyes turned to glare at Kai before it took flight and disappeared into the night. *The dragon.* Again, Kai was unsure how he felt about them.

Outside the field was littered with dead bodies ripped apart by the Shuk and sliced down by his men. Arrows protruded out of legs, arms, and backs. Kai saw burning trees and bushes. Black, singed grass smoldered around a pile of charred bodies, and the smell of burning flesh was thick in the air. Near the tree line, Haygan spoke to two men. Through the trees, he caught a glimpse of the black Shuk just before it was enveloped in a gray mist.

Dresnor and Albey came to his side. "Prince Kai, it's over. We need to search the town for any stragglers." Concerned, Dresnor looked inside. Bevon's lifeless body lay in a pool of blood. "What happened?"

"Bevon got free. Shane saved us," Kai explained, scanning the yard for his friend.

Dresnor sheathed his sword. "If it weren't for Haygan and his friends, and Marduk and his son, we would not be alive. How Haygan managed to get that kind of help, I..." Dresnor let his words fade as he looked over the field.

Kempery-man Redmon approached. "Sir. We lost two men." He shook his head in sadness.

Marduk and Shane came around the side of the barn. "Kai, are you alright?" Shane ran to his friend and looked around him at the man he'd slain.

Kai extended his hand. "I am, thanks to you." The two boys clasped arms. "I am glad you came."

"You didn't actually think we would abandon you?" Shane's expression changed to excitement. "Did you see the dragon? It was enormous and fierce. We were lucky it came when it did," Shane exclaimed.

Drew, Albey, and Haygan approached the small group, bloodied but alive. Hamrin sustained devastating losses. Only a few wounded soldiers remained. Dresnor led the group toward the estate. "Prince Kai, come dawn we need to send for help. If there are any remaining Hamrin men, they need to be found. I believe we can fortify the estate for the night."

Kai nodded. "I agree. We also need to find Finlee and our missing scout. I fear for their safety."

"I have sent two men to search the Hamrin barracks. For now, I want everyone within the estate. Marduk and Shane, please collect your belongings and move into the estate. Haygan, you too."

"Understood," said Marduk. He placed an arm on Shane's shoulder, and the pair veered into town.

Kai desperately wanted to follow his friend. His mind raced with the evening's events. He had never seen a dead man before, let alone watch one die at his feet. He paused on the path, hesitant to continue.

Dresnor stopped while the others passed. "Kai, what's wrong? We need to get inside the estate."

Marduk glanced over his shoulder. "Prince Kai, you should come with us. Haygan and I need to speak with you and Shane."

Smoke and Shiva closed in around Kai. Dresnor huffed. Kai's

pleading eyes won out. "Go. I will see to the estate. Drew, Albey, please accompany them. Do not take too long."

Thankful, Kai darted down the path to catch up with Shane. Drew and Albey were quick to join them. Marduk walked between Shane and Kai. "Boys, no words can possibly help you make sense out of tonight. It is wrong to kill another, and yet tonight we defended our friends, and we did what was necessary. Shane, how are you feeling?" His voice calm and reassuring.

Shane walked head down, his bow in his hand. "I ... I saw the man's face. After. He lay in a pool of blood. The others, I did not see. I aimed—they fell. I did not see their faces. That man would have killed Kai. I knew it. I did not hesitate. I killed him clean. But ... it's not like killing an animal for food." Shane's voice was shaky, his eyes wavered. "I wish I hadn't looked. His face is etched in my mind forever."

Marduk put an arm around his son. "It is not easy to take a life. The men on the field, darkness hid their end. That man— no, that monster—he meant to hurt others, and I am sorry the fates placed the burden on you. I knew if we came to Kai's aid, some would fall. I prayed it would not be you, not be Kai. But without us, I believe the outcome would have been different." He cleared his throat as they continued in silence.

Heavy-hearted, Marduk turned to Kai. "How are you feeling?" Extending his other arm, he touched Kai's shoulder. "We are all here for you. Know you're not alone, and time will ease your soul."

Haygan held his chin high, his eyes lifted to the stars. "Heed your father's words, Shane. We were lucky to have both of you. It is a sad day when a life comes to an end—good or bad, all life is sacred. It is unfortunate that to save Kai and the children, you had to end another's life. I will pray for you. May Alenga bless your soul and give you peace."

Kai's heart ached for his friend's sadness, though he did not shed a tear for the man Bevon. "Sincerely, thank you, Shane. I feared for my life, I am not sure I could have beat Bevon." He let his hand fall to his side.

Smoke strode up and ran his head under Kai's hand. He welcomed his friend and ran his fingers through Smoke's fur. "I am sorry, Shane. We are children no more. Yet I'm thankful that you had the courage."

Shane dried his eyes. "I would do it again." His voice was resolute.

They were friends bonded for life.

CHAPTER 29

Town Hope

Kai had grown up fast in the past few days. He stood on the wharf, lost in the waves rolling over Baden Lake, the Grand Duke of Diu, Dante Carmelo, at his side. While the arrival of Dante and his men put him at ease, the burden of responsibility weighed heavy on his heart. "What am I to do now?" he asked, his hip pressed against a tremendous post.

Dante clasped a hand on the prince's shoulder. "Reassure our people. Talk with them, let them see you. I will appoint a new duke to be lord over Hamrin upon my return to Diu. Our men will secure the town. You will work with this new duke to get this town reestablished. This is good training for you as a future king."

Dresnor stepped up behind them. "Your Highness, I know this seems overwhelming. These decisions must fall on you. We can advise you, but you must lead. It is up to you to rebuild the people's faith."

Being brave made Kai think of Opal and her loss. First, her mother and now her father. "What of Opal and her two brothers? I don't believe they had anything to do with their father's dealings."

"They will be sent to Nebea. They have family there. It

is most unfortunate that Victor died in the battle." Dante huffed. "I would have liked to know why he betrayed us. Money and power corrupt the hearts of weak men."

"Doesn't matter. Now we rebuild. Bring the people back. Set everything right." Kai crossed his arms. "Dante, you leave on the next ship. I will do my father proud. I wish you could stay, but Diu needs you in the absence of the King. I hope it won't take long to find a suitable replacement for Lord Hamrin."

◆ ◆ ◆

Three arduous weeks after the battle for Hamrin, the town began to show signs of recovery.
Kai walked the streets daily to survey the restoration. Freed from the mines, people returned to their previous life. Shops and homes were being repaired. The homeless families and orphans were provided temporary housing within the soldiers' barracks, while a proper orphanage was under construction.

The wharf was a hive of activity, and the food shortage had been resolved. Men came by ships from Diu city and the northern town of Chenowith. They came to help their neighbors, and they all gave freely to those in need. New guards secured the town, and citizens walked freely, yet a few still cringed as these new men patrolled the streets.

Today was a big day, and it would mark the future of Hamrin. They all awaited the arrival of the new lord and lady. The boat reached the wharf, and everyone waited. Waited and hoped.

Kai watched the couple stroll down the long pier arm in arm. Lord Eugene and Lady Heidi Sknash. Eugene was a studious man with wavy chestnut hair, round spectacles, and a trim beard surrounding his jovial smile. *Well, the man certainly looks the part*, Kai thought.

Lady Heidi was a willowy figure with porcelain white skin, bedecked with tiny red freckles. The upsweep of her reddish-brown hair looked like a summer berry in the sun, piled high on her head.

Dresnor pulled at his beard. "The letter from Dante said this man was willing to move from Diu back to Hamrin. He left Hamrin as a young boy with his mother because his only prospects would be fishing or farming. He became an educated watchmaker in Diu, and he is friends with your Professor Greydon. A gracious man from what I understand. Lady Heidi is a teacher, and she is most excited to work with orphaned children. They currently have no children of their own. Dante believes they will be a good fit for Hamrin. Seems they can make anyone a Duke."

Lord Sknash reached the end of the pier, and the wary crowd pressed against each other trying to get a look at this new man come to save them. "A well-to-do man. One's the same as the next," one lady shouted.

"Out for themselves," another man shouted. "Time will tell if this man's any different."

Lord Sknash waited and looked at the crowd. "People of Hamrin. We don't know each other. I know I will have to prove I am not the tyrant that preceded me. Give me a chance, and we will make Hamrin great."

"NO!" shouted a young woman. "Hamrin NO MORE."

"Hamrin NO MORE," shouted a young boy.

The crowd joined in with the shouts. Lord Sknash raised his hand patting down the air to soothe the people. "What name do you give your fair town? Lord Hamrin is gone. Name your city," he called to the crowd.

Silence fell over the crowd. Kai watched most lowered their heads. Still afraid, they clung together. One man gawked at Kai. No one uttered a word. They looked lost, sad, and broken. Lady Sknash stepped forward. "For now, call it Hope. Until a better name comes to the people."

The crowd mumbled amongst itself. The word spread like fire through a dry field. The people looked to Lady Sknash. Whispers filled the crowd, low voices swelled. "Hope," agreed a young woman in the group.

"Town Hope," called another.

"Town Hope," Lord Sknash agreed. "Thank you, dear." He squeezed his wife's hand.

The matter settled, Lord Sknash removed his coat and hung it on the railing and rolled up his sleeves. "Good people. For now, food will continue to come from Chenowith and Albey. We are fortunate our neighboring towns are willing to give so much."

Lord Sknash motioned to the ships. "We have brought clothes, shoes, and books. There are linens, soaps, and other comforts. We will have everything brought to the center of town. Please come, take what you need. Diu city is sending more supplies tomorrow."

The crowd gasped as a line of crates began to spew from the two ships. Box after box made way down the wharf into town. The crowds parted and regrouped to follow the supplies. Bewilderment and joy lit the faces of the townsfolk. Kai nodded as they passed him.

In town, Lord and Lady Sknash personally saw to the distribution of every item. They laughed with people, played with children, and ate sitting in the dirt. Kai spent time observing this new man. Eugene did very little talking. He asked questions and listened.

Heidi cradled the young children in her lap. Their dirty feet soiled her dress. She bore each stain with a sense of pride and joy. Alissa and Marabella leaned on each other. Their faces eased into smiles as the children settled in around the new couple.

The next morning, Lord Sknash glanced over the mounds of paperwork on the dining room table. Flabbergasted, he shook his head and tossed down the sheets he'd reviewed. "I cannot fathom how this man managed to hide his dealings so well. The townsfolk must have been truly terrified."

He clasped his hands together and let them fall across his chest. "Well, the first thing we need to do is stop wage garnishments, levies, and undo these property seizures. My word, all these unbearable monthly payments. It's no wonder the people abandoned their farms and homesteads."

From his satchel, Eugene pulled a thick set of papers. "The town will be given a fresh start—we will offer a compromise for the people. I want this decree posted in town." He waved a sheet in the air. "It offers them three years to get their affairs in order before they pay any city taxes. Profits from the copper mine and quarry will easily pay for the town's security, building repairs, and new construction. At that time, I will extend flexibility as needed upon analyzing their ability to pay."

Kai listened intently. "That all sounds like an improvement, Lord Sknash. Has Grand Duke Dante approved your plan?"

"Call me, Gene, please. I've only been a duke for a day, and I already hate the sound of formality." He laughed. "Yes, Dante approves. I wanted longer, but he only gave me three years. That's not much time. Construction alone will take at least two years." He sighed a heavy breath.

Dresnor took a sip of tea and set down his cup. "You are fortunate this is early summer. The farms are being turned and will be set for planting within the week. Both Albey and Chenowith were most gracious in offering help. They've rebuilt two barns and plowed four fields."

"As I understand it there are more men and building supplies arriving over the next few days," Kai reminded them.

"True," Gene nodded. "We might be surprised at how quickly the town can recover. Although I must say, I don't fancy living in this big estate. I have set Heidi to the task of designing a new home."

"Lord Eu...Gene, are you sure?" Kai asked. "The estate is yours now. What do you mean to do with the property?"

"I mean to build behind the main estate. Near the stables

and the gardens. The current house and its three buildings will become a university and student housing." He reached for his tea and took a gulp, draining the cup.

Dresnor looked astonished. "Really, you mean to move out? When on earth do you mean to make this happen? How many projects do you intend to manage at one time?"

Gene waved him off. "I have already made arrangements. I sent word before I left. I have hired men from Port Anahita. They will be here next week. They assure me they will have the main part of our new house built before winter. Next summer, they will finish the remaining sections. Our home in Diu will bring a nice sum, and I will continue to design watches for the wealthy in Diu. That will provide me with a comfortable income."

This new duke sounded so sure of everything. Kai liked this new man, his humor in the face of adversity and his humble nature. He nodded his head, remembering his original thought —he certainly looks the part. Plus Gene had a mind for figures and a heart for the people.

For the first time in weeks, Kai ran alone. Well, relatively alone, with Shiva and Smoke at his side. Although he sensed Drew, Redmon and Albey kept an eye out for him as he circled the town. Many of the Diu soldiers also kept a watchful eye on the young prince as they patrolled the perimeter.

In town, it was a challenge to find time alone. The streets brimmed with new construction, soldiers, and townsfolk. There was no peace and quiet. People wanted to thank him and hug him. Although humbled by the experience, Kai was uncomfortable with the attention. Even with Smoke by his side, they approached him, always eager to say hello.

His hair dripped with sweat in the summer heat, and ever mindful, he scanned the area. The gleaning energy flowed around him. Through the trees he sensed Marduk and Shane, sitting on a large rock by the lake. Two wispy forms, Shane a little brighter.

Eager to see them, Kai turned and ran in their direction. He popped out through the trees a few yards away and waved. They waved back. "Shane. Marduk. Hot day." He rolled his eyes at the lake and smiled.

Shane lit up in agreement. "Can we?" he asked his father.

"You boys go ahead. I will go into town, find us some lunch. I trust you will be fine with Smoke and Shiva?" Marduk's tone was questioning yet confident.

Kai saw Shane's expression become fearful. Shane and his dad had been inseparable since the night of the battle. "I … I guess we will be fine." His face twisted in worry.

Marduk waved and left them alone. Shane began to fidget with his fingers. Kai watched his friend withdraw. He curled inward; his retreat was physically evident.

"Shane, now that we are alone, I want to share something Haygan told me. He said we don't have to live in fear. Yes, there are a few bad men in the world, but most are good. The town is now full of good men. Helpful, brave men. Also, bad things happen, and we must move on. We must live."

"I know you're right. But the images. At night they return. When I close my eyes, they are there. They seem harsh and loud, unyielding. I cannot escape them. I feel bad that I killed those men." Shane pulled his knees to his chest and wrapped his arms around them tightly.

"I know you feel bad, which makes you a good person." Kai climbed up on the rock next to his friend. "Close your eyes," he instructed.

Shane gasped. "Never! Why?"

Kai placed his hand on Shane's. "Sit with me. Relax. Focus on my voice." He put his hands on his knees.

Shane nervously relented, but he kept a tight grasp on his legs. His knuckles were white as he closed his eyes.

"Listen to the sounds around us." He paused to let the lapping of the lake and sounds of birds chirping dominate their ears.

"Focus on the water. Hear it lap against the shore. Hear nothing but the water. Push away the birds." Again, he let his voice fade away. He loved how peaceful the water made him feel. The cool breeze subsided, and the sun began to beat on them.

In the silence, his friend began to squirm. He wanted to touch his friend, comfort him, but he did not. Shane needed to console himself. Find the peace within himself once more. "I am here, Shane. Focus on the water, hear the water. Now see the water in your mind. Eyes closed, envision the water breaking on the shore. Let it wash away the memories. Let it cleanse your soul. Right now, it is just you and me listening to the water."

Kai saw Shane visibly relax his grip and let his legs lower. Together they sat in silence. Kai closed his eyes again and listened to the water. In his mind, he could see the waves splash on the shore, soaking the earth and receding back to where they came. Kai felt relaxed and content. "Now think about how the water would feel. Cool, wet, and refreshing."

Behind them, he heard voices, and he pushed out with his mind, seeing two guards patrolling a few yards away. Pleased his friend was improving, he focused again on the water. This was the first time he'd meditated since they came here. He had no idea how much he needed this; how much Shane need this.

Lost in the silence, he let the water wash away his own fears. His soul lightened, his mind refreshed, and his heart opened. Peaceful and happy, he sat. The sounds of water splashing opened his eyes. Shiva and Smoke romped in the water.

Kai looked to Shane. Shane smiled in return. The first real smile he'd seen in weeks. Happily, Shane slipped off his boots, jumped down, and stomped through the water. Kai laughed at his friend. His clothes were soaked through. Shane swung his leg through the water and splashed Kai.

"Hey, no fair!" Kai called, pulling off his own boots to join in the fun.

Together the two boys laughed and splashed each other. Carefree. Their clothes clung heavy and wet against them. Kai dove into the water and Smoke dashed after him, pawing through the water. Shane swam through the water, dove below and sprang up in front of Kai.

"This feels so nice. I missed swimming these past few weeks." Shane's face perked up as he looked to the shore.

Kai followed his gaze, and they saw Marduk sitting in the weeds, eating. Hunger welled in the pit of his stomach. Starving, he wiped the water from his face and hair. Shane licked his lips and grinned. "Race you."

The two boys swam and ran to Marduk. Soaked to the bone, they hovered over him. "Can we have some?" they said in unison, laughing at their identical words.

Marduk motioned for them to sit and opened the basket. It was filled with meats, cheeses, bread, and fruit. Each bite was better than the last. They sat giggling through lunch as two boys should. Then they laid back in the tall grass, shaded by the large oak watching the clouds go by.

Marduk watched over his boys, whittling a piece of wood with his knife. Shiva and Smoke sat nearby. The afternoon sun continued to strengthen, and it wasn't long before the two boys felt dry. Too dry. Practically together, they sat up and stared at the glistening water. Sweat had started to bead on Marduk's face, and the boys smiled.

He looked at them and smiled back. "I don't know about you two boys, but it's hot." Marduk kicked off his boots, ran and dove into the water, with both boys following him. It was good to laugh and play. It was especially reassuring to see Shane smile, the kind of smile that lit up the soul. They spent the rest of the afternoon at the lake. Kai even managed to get Drew and Albey to join them.

In the tree line, Kai saw Dresnor, leaning against a tree with Marabella. She had become a permanent fixture amongst the group. Wherever Dresnor went, Marabella was not far behind.

She was a brave young woman, and for a warrior like Dresnor, she was a good match. Kai wondered how they would take being separated in a few days.

Summer had come to an end, and it was time to leave Town Hope. Kai strolled through town with Dresnor across the new cobblestone streets. Newly added streetlamps flickered in the night, giving the area a cozy charm.

Dresnor looked around. "I am impressed by how much they've completed. I hear the new orphanage is done."

"I took a tour of it earlier today," Kai said. "Although many of the children have been reunited with parents from the mines, a fair few have nobody. The most significant change is the people. That makes it all worthwhile."

Dresnor stroked the end of his scruffy beard. "They have something to live for now. There are newcomers for the first time in years," he noted. "It doesn't hurt that Sknash is offering them a fresh start and free land."

"Lord Sknash gave the people a voice. Dante made a good choice. Gene and Heidi are good people, and the town welcomes his leadership."

When they reached the wharf, Kai noticed Marabella watching the men batten down the ships for the night. She approached one of the captains, spoke a few words, and handed him something. Finished, she walked in their direction.

Dresnor stopped to watch her. "Given all she's been through, she still has a strong spirit. Marabella is an amazing young lady. Lady Sknash has taken her into their home. She had no family left, and Heidi and Gene want to adopt her. They feel they have so much to offer her."

Kai cleared his throat, bringing Dresnor from his daydream. "Will Marabella be staying in Town Hope when we leave?" He thought he knew the answer but wanted to ask.

Dresnor did not respond. He closed the gap between himself and Marabella. "Good evening, Marabella. Have you made suitable arrangements?" he asked, taking her hand in his. He turned to walk toward the stables.

"I have," she responded, looking around Dresnor to smile at Kai. "Your Highness, are you ready to go back to Diu tomorrow?" Her big blue eyes sparkled.

"I am thrilled to be going home. Thank you for asking." Kai observed them together. Their proximity to one another told him a great deal. He knew very little about her. Alissa had told him Marabella was an orphan herself. She ran away after her brother died in the mines and was living in the hills these last three years.

"Are you coming to Diu by ship?" he asked presumptuously.

"I am coming to Diu. I leave the day after you. Although Dresnor tells me I will arrive before you." She squeezed Dresnor's hand, the affection in her eyes bubbled with delight.

"Lady Sknash would like me to stay in their home and help sell the furniture they no longer need. I will be moving in with her mother. She lives alone and could use companionship. I am very fortunate Heidi has taken an interest in my future. Although I am over eighteen, they mean to adopt me and give me their name." She leaned slightly into Dresnor's shoulder.

Kai was pleased Gene and Heidi were helping Marabella. "It will be good to have you in Diu. If you two would, please excuse me, I would like to catch up with Haygan before I retire for the evening." He waved and darted up the hill, catching up with Smoke strolling through town.

At the stables, he saw they were preparing to return to Diu come the morning, and he was happy to see Haygan had come back from his trip up the mountain.

"Haygan, how was your nature walk?" he asked hesitantly.

Haygan did not respond. He kept gathering supplies. Finally, Kai caught Haygan's eye. "Is everything alright?" His tone turned to worry.

An empty smile bloomed on Haygan's face. "Yes, yes, everything is fine. Just distracted, let me finish here. We can talk all day tomorrow. You should get some rest."

After everything they had been through together, now Haygan chose to withdrawal. Kai knew better than to challenge this man. Still, he could not let it go. "Please tell me what has changed?" Kai pleaded.

Haygan looked away. "I am struggling with some conflicting advice."

Unhappy by the short response, Kai backed out of the stables.

CHAPTER 30

Homecoming

Nothing could have prepared Kai for his summer in Hamrin. His father gave him the responsibility of spreading Galloway goodwill to the people to teach him accountability, but his trip turned out nothing like he had expected. He realized just how naïve he was about the world around him.

Home in Diu Kai sat at his desk, opened his journal, and wrote:

The battle for Hamrin, now Town Hope, changed me, changed Shane. Our innocence shattered, we can never go back. Maturity came at a steep price. My boyhood thoughts and concerns are all foolish nonsense to me now. I have so much to learn. My station has made me soft. Shane was right.

As a little prince, all I had to concern myself with was academics. To become a man and someday a king, I must set aside my fears. I must learn how to listen and serve others. Time to embrace the strength my cousin Adrian believes I have. I fear his disappointment most of all.

I am sure Riome will arrange brutal training sessions, given my less-than-stellar attempt to defend myself. I imagine they will leave every inch of me battered and bruised. Her methods are harsh but effective.

Let's hope next summer is not as taxing. Blessed Alenga, protect the budding Town Hope. Restore their faith.

Kai Galloway

My fourteenth summer.

Outside, Kai sat in the sun. Kendra entered his room. She strolled across his balcony to look over the sunbathed city. "You wanted to ask me something yesterday?" she said. "Cordelia is napping, and the twins are horseback riding. We have time."

He had wanted to speak with her about Haygan and Rayna. "On our ride home, I tried to talk with Haygan. He went away on something he called a nature walk, told me he stayed in the forest."

For Kai, Haygan's explanation was less than satisfying. Nothing explained the aloofness Kai now felt. "I don't understand why Haygan would spend two weeks alone in the woods, only to come back distant and removed. Did he spend time with two men who fought with him or the woman he claims brought a dragon to the Battle of Hamrin? I am extremely grateful, but why is he reluctant to share? Plus, I tried to ask him about Rayna. But you know how he gets when he refuses to discuss something. You and I never had the chance to speak about Rayna healing her horse before I left." He stopped to wait for her reaction.

"I know about Rayna," Kendra admitted. "And I watched her over the summer. We speak often, and she is pleasant, but she is very guarded. Her hesitation to trust me is a good sign she can keep a secret."

"Since we all agree she is Katori, I have questions." His brow knit together. "What can I tell her? What can we teach her? Have you seen her plants? They grow as if by magic. The path she walks each day is a streak of thick green grass. She shines as bright as you, maybe brighter," he persisted. "Need I go on?"

Kendra leaned against the stone balcony railing. Kai studied her posture and reserved expression. He knew the look. She was about to lie, or at the very least withhold information. Riome's lessons were paying off.

"Typically, there are two options. When we find a Katori orphan, we either take the child, or we keep our distance and wait to see what gifts manifest on their own. Orphans are rare since very few Katori choose to live outside our lands. Maybe we should not encourage her development." Kendra jutted her chin to the side, looking away.

"What? Why the change of heart? I thought we were to protect the Katori secrets at all costs. Teach her how to control her gifts."

"Do you want her taken away? Because that is our only choice. A full-blooded Katori must return home at seventeen or risk..." Kendra didn't finish her thought.

She turned away, and Kai knew—there was the lie. Or at least the omission of information. Why was she keeping secrets now? What had changed? Questions rolled around his mind, but he kept them to himself.

Eventually, Kendra continued. "Haygan did not ask about Rayna because he knows what they would say—leave her be or bring her to Katori. It is our best option not to spark her mind further. Let her potential fade away."

He could not believe what he was hearing. How could they deny Rayna her gifts? Although he could not bear to lose Rayna, it was not his choice to make. *Seventeen? What does age have to do with it?* This was the first time Kendra had mentioned that age mattered. *What else is she keeping from me?* He wanted to ask, but he was sure she would not tell. "What are you saying?"

"Maybe we made a mistake coming here—teaching you. Bonding with Smoke was your catalyst. If we had listened to our Chiefs and the Unie, stayed away, you might not have manifested any gifts."

This was news to him. He had no idea. If they had not awakened his gifts, he would be a normal child, only faster and stronger. Kai could not imagine his life without his connection to Smoke and Ember or his ability to glean. How could he possibly hide this from Rayna?

"Is this why Haygan has been distant? Because he does not want to teach her. Or… does he wish he'd never taught me?"

"He doesn't regret helping you. I tried to talk with him, but Haygan is a steel trap. If he means to keep a secret, you'll not pry it from him. I believe he asked too many favors getting help for Hamrin and word has traveled home to Katori. Our chiefs are not happy with him."

Kendra's expression changed. "I guess I should ask, what have you told Rayna?"

"We have only discussed her desires to learn about plants. But I've not really told her anything."

"Good. Let's keep it that way. I know it will be hard for you, but you must keep our Katori secrets from Rayna."

Torn by her words, he searched his soul for the solution. Kendra was not telling him the whole truth.

Kai spent days mulling over how to learn more about Rayna's past and how to tell her what he knew. Being Katori linked them together, and he hoped to share his secrets with her.

Back in Diu for eight days, he found himself avoiding certain people. First, Riome—he wasn't ready to tell her what happened. Second, Nola—he feared giving her the opportunity to brainwash him further. In both cases, he decided avoidance was a much better option. Everywhere he went, he gleaned. He was constantly on guard, altering his path to avoid the two of them.

No matter what happened with Rayna, today Kai was going to make the most of every moment. He sat leaning against a tree in the apple orchard, four botany books and two apples in his lap. The palace orchard was full of ripened fruit, and the sweet smell of apples filled the air. Eyes closed, he centered his mind and focused on his surroundings.

Through the trees he sensed Smoke padding around after Shiva. He saw their energy ebb and flow, a heartbeat of power pulsed within them. Eyes open, he gleaned, the light energy overlaid what his natural sight showed him, but in his mind he saw beyond his current surroundings.

His energy ripple went beyond the orchard. Among the dim wisps was one bright light. Her facial features became visible—Rayna. Happy to see her, he watched her walk through the trees in his direction. His natural vision beheld the curve of her face.

She plopped down beside him and stole an apple. "I've missed you. Tell me all about your trip. What are those?" she asked, thumbing through one book at a time. "Are these for me?"

He recalled his vision and this very moment in his mind. "They are for you. I borrowed them from the palace library. There are so many, I'm sure Professor Greydon won't miss them. Not for a while anyway."

In the back of his mind, he wrestled with Kendra's warning. "Rayna. Have you always lived in Port Anahita? Are your parents native to the area?"

She let out a frustrating sigh. "*Oh, Rayna, I missed you too. I had a great trip, can't wait to tell you all about it,*" she mocked, taking a bite out of the apple in her hand.

"Sorry, I did miss you, but there is too much to tell. I spent days in the saddle to get there. I fell off a cliff and slept outside alone one night near a cave. When we made it to the Hamrin Estate, I was so relieved, but then everything went wrong."

He shook his head, reliving that horrible night. The field of dead men and the beasts that saved them. Bevon lying in a pool of his own blood. A night he would never forget, but for now, he could not share it. It was still too raw.

"I am sure it did not go unnoticed when four ships set out across Baden Lake, nor when the men marched out of the city bound for Hamrin—now Town Hope." He paused to look at her kind brown eyes. "Maybe someday I will tell you about it. What I can tell you is the new duke, Lord Eugene Sknash—Gene—is a good man. I spent most of my time with Dresnor and Gene, rebuilding what Victor destroyed. I also got to spend time with Haygan, Shane, and Marduk."

He thought of the new Lord Sknash and his kind wife. "There was so much that happened. I don't know what news made it back to Diu. Back to the palace." He shook his head, trying to scatter the images that rose to the surface. "Please forgive me, I am not ready to talk about what happened."

He took a breath to calm his mood. Eagerly she waited. The trip had forever changed him, but it could not ruin how she made him feel. He let a smile tug at the corner of his mouth. "Dresnor advised me to keep a journal. He said it would make it easier to relay the information back to my father. Writing has also helped me begin to cope with the events. Over the summer, Haygan disappeared on a strange nature walk. Now he is distant. And now I am home."

Finished with the apple, she chucked it into the grass. "I'm sorry. I didn't mean to mock you. I had no idea," she softly touched his arm. "We don't have to talk about what happened. You're home now." She rubbed his hand. "It was hard not to notice Dante and his men set sail mere days after you left. No definitive news came back, only rumors. Ship after ship set sail, filled to the brim with men and supplies. I worried until the Grand Duke's return. I knew if something had happened to you, there would be some news." Sheepishly she pulled her shoulders in around herself.

"Rayna, I didn't mean to sound upset at you. It is a lot of responsibility, and it is on top of so many other changes. I have so many things vying for my time. You know, I wish I could go back to being casually unaware, sleepwalking through life, but I'm awake, and all I can do is face it," he said, realizing it felt good to share.

She nodded her head in understanding. "On to happier topics. You asked about my home. Well, I don't know where I was born. I've never really told anyone about this before. My parents know, but nobody else. This will sound strange, but Levi Kendrick found me on the docks in a crate, mixed with his baking supplies."

"What do you mean he found you in a crate? As a baby? Who would leave a baby in a crate?"

She shrugged. "If only I knew. I believe they only told me so I'd never get mad at them if my real parents returned. The man who unloaded their cargo said that he had no idea where I came from, only that he had no use for a baby, especially a girl. He said, taking care of me on the ship was more trouble than I was worth. So he dumped me with them."

"So I take it nobody ever came to claim you?"

She slumped to the side with her response. "Nobody ever came."

"It's hard to believe it's almost been a year since you moved to Diu. Are you sure your mother is alright with you spending the day away from the bakehouse? I know it is challenging work, and they depend on you greatly."

"Most of our work happens well before dawn," Rayna told him. "She is fine."

Before continuing, he hopped to his feet, offering Rayna his hand. "Let me collect our basket from Lizzie while you drop your books at home," Kai suggested. "Meet me at the stables. My men should be ready to escort us to the lake. They are very protective these days."

Dresnor led his group through the north gate, and they made their way down the steep hill toward Baden Lake. "Rayna, do your parents approve of me bringing you books about plants? I don't want to influence your interests away from baking if they disagree."

"Don't worry," Rayna responded. "We've talked about my future, and they understand where my interests lie. We moved to Diu to expand my opportunities. They have hired another girl to help cover my duties. Although I should tell you, my father finds our relationship unwise."

"I hear the same advice." Kai knew everyone was right.

There was little future for them given his betrothal to Amelia. Still, his heart was becoming attached, and he could not deny she was becoming more than a friend.

Kai's group stopped along the shore, south near their private dock. "Dresnor, I wish you had taken the afternoon off. I brought extra detail, and we are in Diu. I know you have someone else you'd rather spend the day with besides me."

"I thank you for the offer, but my duty is to protect you," countered Dresnor. "My place is at your side. I am your lead Kempery-man."

"I thought you might say that." Kai pointed up the hill. "Which is why I am having her brought to you."

Honey, a golden mare, strolled down the hill. Her rider was a young woman with long dark auburn hair. The wind fluttered Marabella's white dress. Dresnor could not take his eyes off her. The guard escorting her handed Dresnor a small wicker basket and rode away.

"Marabella, you look … lovely." Dresnor held up his hand. "Can you wait here for one moment? Prince Kai, we need to talk." He stomped off, and Kai followed.

"Don't get mad," Kai insisted. "I appreciate everything you've done for me. I appreciate your loyalty, but we are home. There are three guards here and three more by the docks dedicated to hovering over me. Way more than necessary. Stay here with us and enjoy a picnic together or go around the lake to the cove. But you're taking some time for yourself."

Dresnor glanced back at Marabella. "Thank you, Prince Kai," Dresnor nodded. "It is an honor being your Kempery-man. We will take the cove. By the way, call me Philip." Dresnor offered Marabella the basket and hopped up behind her. "I will be back for my horse."

With Dresnor gone, Kai spread out a blanket under the shady oak tree. The afternoon sun glistened across Baden Lake. The delicate breeze swept through the tall wildflowers around them. Rayna opened their picnic basket. They sat sharing tales of their summer and plans for the winter festival. Although the festival was four months away, Kai stressed about getting Rayna the perfect gift. He wanted to impress her with something she'd never be able to get for herself.

Daydreaming, Kai lay on the blanket with his hands behind his head. White puffy clouds drifted across the blue sky. "Kai," Rayna started, interrupting his thoughts. "Do you think I will ever find out where I come from?"

A lump formed in his throat. He knew where she came from, who her people were. If he told her the truth, would he lose her? Deep down, he knew the right choice was to tell her everything he knew. His faith in their future meant he needed to trust their connection. Honesty was essential to their relationship.

Over the next hour, he told her everything he knew about the Katori people. All the secrets he had, he shared. The power and light that emanated within everything—the ability to glean. And he promised to teach her how. He mentioned the Beastmasters and their abilities with animals. She was fascinated to learn she might be a Kodama—a healer and plant whisperer.

When he explained their gift for bonding with an animal, Rayna cried. She knew there was a special connection between her and Snowflake—now she had proof. It gave her comfort to know that the depth of her feelings were not just in her imagination.

Most importantly he warned her of the risks. The danger behind their gifts and need for secrecy. Before Kai knew it, they were sitting cross-legged with their hands on their knees. "I want to teach you how to glean," he told her. "Gleaning is a form of meditation. Only special because done properly, it will open your mind."

"Is that something I really want, to open my mind?" she asked. "What will that let in?"

Kai had never thought of it that way. What had he let in opening his mind? His visions of the future started when he learned how to glean. "Part of finding your potential requires a catalyst to open your mind to the world around you."

"I thought meditation was the art of doing nothing." She swept her long hair over one shoulder.

"Well, there is a little more to it. Close your eyes."

Together they sat facing each other. "Gleaning is about focusing your mind. First, focus internally on your breathing. Let it be your anchor. Let it draw you in while you let go of everything else in your mind. Be in the moment. Body, mind, and soul."

He paused to let her sit with his words, then he continued. "Free your mind. Search your soul and the energy that sustains you. Connect to the power and follow it outward. See the world anew."

Kai sent an energy ripple outward, bathing the world in light. In his mind, he saw Rayna sitting in front of him, a bright wispy light until he focused on seeing her physical form. Her face was clear but set aglow. Around them he could see the trees, the flowers, the lake. In the distance, he saw Shiva and Smoke lying in the shade.

Down the long dock, one guard paced. Behind him, more guards kept watch while the horses nibbled grass. With another push, he went further to the private cove. Dresnor and Marabella were beside Honey holding hands. Dresnor pulled Marabella into a kiss. Startled, Kai let go. He shook his head and opened his eyes.

Rayna sat meditating. Not wanting to disturb her, he walked to the dock. "Dresnor and Marabella will be back shortly. Time to go," Kai instructed the guard.

Back at her side, Kai touched Rayna on the shoulder. "We need to go."

Rayna's peaceful eyes greeted him. "I like this gleaning. I often sit staring out my loft window, now I can have a purpose. You know, I almost thought I saw a small light, but I couldn't make it grow."

Kneeling beside her, he whispered. "You must not force it,

let it flow naturally. Keep practicing," he said, pulling her to her feet.

The beat of horse hooves announced Dresnor and Marabella. "You two ready to go?" Dresnor called, riding through the trees.

"Yes, Dresnor, we are," Kai called back.

Dresnor transferred to his own horse while the rest of the group mounted up. "Thank you again, Prince Kai. It was the best afternoon I've had in a long while—no offense. And again, it's Philip, just between us."

"Fair enough, Philip. Then you best call me Kai ... just between us."

Their ride was short around the walls and through the city to the palace stables.

Kai stood with Philip as they watched Rayna ride toward the lower stables on Snowflake. "Are you making a mistake getting close to her?" Philip whispered.

Kai watched Rayna disappear down the hill. He wanted to disagree, he knew his duty would demand he marry Amelia someday. "I know," he said, leading Ember inside the stables.

CHAPTER 31

Future Predictions

The following days rolled one into another. When the bells rang out across the city, Kai bolted up from his chair. Professor Greydon's eyes halted his departure. The curve of his lips twitched the corner of his curly mustache. "Go—greet your father. If you hurry, you can meet him in the yard before he even dismounts. Take your brothers," the professor insisted with a nod in their direction.

Kai made an about-face. "Let's go, you two. We need to hustle."

All three boys rushed to the yard. They watched from the hilltop that led to the palace. High in the saddle, Iver bounced as his horse trotted up the steep incline, Kempery-man Ian Farwick at his side.

"Welcome home, father," Kai said as Iver slid from his mount.

"Ah, son. How you've grown this summer, look at your muscles. I have missed you." Iver swept Kai into a big bear hug and lifted him off the ground.

The sea had done his father good. He was stronger and clear-minded. "You should sail more often, father. The sea suits you. How was your trip? Did you go somewhere besides Bangloo?" Kai wheezed with the air being squished from his lungs.

Iver snickered as he lowered his son. "We also went to Ahana. Our trip was fruitful. Challenging but successful. I have many new wonders to share. The sea was refreshing. It's like a cloud has lifted from my eyes."

"Father, what about us?" Seth shouted, tugging at the back of Iver's shirt.

"We've grown too, father," Aaron insisted.

Iver knelt and scooped up both his boys in a display of strength Kai hadn't seen in years. His father's exceptional strength reminded Kai that Iver had distant Katori ancestry. "Come see the treasures I have brought home, boys. Jewels, fabrics, tools, and fruit."

Iver set the twins in the back of the cart and opened a crate. Iver hefted out a large yellow-and-green oblong fruit with large stiff green leaves protruding from the top. "They call this a pineapple. Inside this hard outer skin is the sweetest yellow fruit you've ever tasted."

From another crate, he held up a large round fruit, like a fuzzy brown ball. "That is called a coconut. It has sweet water inside and white flesh that is a pleasure to eat. Near impossible to open but worth the effort," Iver continued opening more crates.

He touched everything with the enthusiasm of a small child, enjoying every item with his sons. Captivated by treasure, they rummaged with their father. Impressed by the variety of fabrics, Kai stroked the soft material. "Father, why is this fabric so incredibly soft?"

"Ah yes son, they call it silk. They say it can be incredibly warm and cozy in winter and comfortably cool in summer. They would not share the secrets of how it is made, but I was able to acquire a great deal of it. There is more still on the docks of Port Anahita."

Sigry approached with his usual scowling face. "Sire, welcome back. I trust your trip was a success. Did you find a new suitable location … for your asset?"

"Yes, Sigry, the matter is handled. Though I am not sure why we keep it anymore. We've had no trouble these last few years," Iver assured him. "Here, stow this for me."

Iver handed Sigry a small item. Before Sigry could slip it into his flowy coat, Kai caught a glimpse of the golden box. The box with the crystal pendant. "Certainly, Your Majesty." Sigry nodded.

Kai desperately wished he knew their secret. Unable to ask, he watched Sigry cross the courtyard back to the palace.

Unstoppable, the twins dug through every crate, carelessly pulling out everything and then dropping it into the cart. "Children, we must be careful with some of these things," Iver cautioned. "They are rare collector's items and fragile."

"Father, what is this thing called?" Aaron asked. He held up a cylindrical metal device with a solid wooden handle.

"Son. No, don't touch that. Give it to me." Iver barked, snatching the strange device from Aaron's hand." Son, it is a dangerous weapon. Here, look in this container, I brought toys back for you and Seth."

Seth held his hand out. "There are toy boats and spinning tops. You place it on a flat surface like this and twist." Iver placed it on top of a large crate and twisted the wooden toy.

The top popped and spun on the crate across the uneven surface. Seth watched as it turned. The dark inlaid carving swirled, and Aaron took notice. Both boys beamed.

"I have four of these, each a different color." Iver handed one to Seth and one to Aaron. "This entire crate is for the three of you. I will have it delivered upstairs."

Kai desperately wanted to talk to his father about his summer. He had so much to share. "Father, I know you just returned, but I want to speak with you about my trip. About what happened in Hamrin."

Before his father could answer, their time was cut short. Queen Nola strolled through the courtyard. Her face pursed, her eyes crimped in a glare. "My dear, welcome home. Come inside, tell me about your trip. Let us catch up in private." She stepped between Iver and the boys.

"Yes, yes, my dear. Just spending time with my boys. You should see the wonders I have brought back. Where is my little princess? Did Cordelia not come out with you?" Iver asked, holding a small blue-and-gold vase he'd pulled from a crate filled with straw to protect, its fragile nature.

Impatient, Nola grabbed the vase and handed it to Warrick. She took Iver's hand in hers and caressed his bare arm. Her long fingers began to tap the back of his hand over and over. "Iver, my dear. You traveled far, imagine how it will feel to rest. The more you relax, the more comfortable you feel." She stared into his eyes.

The lilt in her voice was mesmerizing. "You are home now. You are happiest at home. Because you traveled far, you must rest. You want to rest. You talk about your trip tomorrow. Come, my dear." Her voice was rhythmic, soothing, and hypnotic in its tone.

Iver relented. Nola continuously tapped Iver's hand, speaking to him as they walked inside. Desperate to talk with his father, Kai watched his father walk away.

Left to sift through everything, Kempery-man Farwick barked orders. "Sorry boys, I've work to do. Come here, let's get you two down." Farwick removed both boys from the cart and sent them on their way.

Kai stayed to listen to the list of items—fabrics, food, weapons, and machines. Jewels, literature, and collectibles. His father had even acquired artwork and furniture.

As they set to distribute the loot upon Farwick's command, Kai returned to the palace. He spent the next three days trying to get a moment with this father, but Nola insisted he was unwell and needed his rest after his long journey.

Even Dante was turned away at the king's chamber. If Kai didn't know better, he would have thought her dismissive and cruel. Her eyes were ferocious, and her words were sharp. Unlike her usual self, her tone lacked sincerity and grace. She barked orders as if everyone should know better than to disturb the king.

Frustrated, Kai pressed the energy into his father's chamber. He had never pushed before. The air felt different, almost thick. Usually, the power flowed freely, and he need only follow and behold the essences of life. Now it pushed against him, resistant to being forced.

He relaxed and tried again. He let the light build in his mind, and he followed the ripple of energy. Within his father's room, he saw Iver's motionless body in a prone position. His chest rose and fell. Slow and steady. *What has she done?* His father had been excited upon his return. Now he was resting. This did not make sense.

From his balcony, Kai waited. The Master General's tower stood prominent in his mind, set aglow by the power of gleaning. A flurry of activity swarmed Cazier. Lines of people strolled up and down the tower, in and out of his cousin's office. Anxious to tell Adrian about Town Hope, Kai tapped his leg.

When the line of people dwindled, Kai made for the tower. Only Riome remained, as she often did. He could see their two forms hovering over Cazier's desk. He strained to see definition in their faces, but the dense layers of stone inhibited his sight. One thing he did notice was Riome's spirit was brighter than it should be for a regular person. Not full Katori bright, but Half-Light bright. How had he not noticed this before? Riome was a Half-Light. This certainly explained her strength and speed.

On the landing outside Cazier's office, Kai gathered his courage. Inside he could hear them arguing. He hated to add to their problems, but they needed to know what had happened. Kai knocked. The door swung open. Maid Mary greeted him. Her presence confused Kai. It had been Riome's essence he saw and her voice he heard through the door.

"Come in Kai," Maid Mary said, stepping aside. "Are your eyes playing tricks on you, Prince Kai?" Again, the voice matched the face—Maid Mary. "Look closer, Kai. Ignore the freckles, the fluffy black hair, and the lilt in my voice. Don't dismiss me because I wear a maid's uniform or even a familiar face."

He couldn't shake it. If he had seen this woman in the hall or heard her speak, he would have sworn this was Mary. Upon studying her, Kai noticed the shape of her eyes were a little off. The curve of her face too thin. Her frame a fraction taller. "Impressive, Riome. Makes me wonder how many times I have dismissed you for Mary."

Riome laughed. "More than you know. Too many, really." She teased, her voice her own again. "Why are you here, Kai? Do you have a story to tell?" she asked in a clipped tone.

He studied Riome. She was the same person he'd spent months with training before summer, yet somehow, he felt different about her, knowing she was a Half-Light. Now he was desperate to know her story. He wondered if she knew any Katori secrets, or if she was an orphan like Rayna.

"Part story, part confession. I have made a realization this summer, and I might as well tell you both together." He closed the door, and they took a seat. He told them about the horror Marabella had shown him. Bevon and his malicious son Tarren, and their inhumane treatment of the townspeople. And Lord Victor Hamrin—the man behind it all.

He mentioned the Katori men wielding their battle axes and the giant black Shuk's ferocious teeth ripping and shaking men apart. He told them how his men were barely holding their own until the massive dragon arrived. Favors begged by Haygan to save them all.

He recalled the volley of arrows Hunter Marduk and Shane launched from the trees. Which brought him to his own disappointing moment. Although he was honest about the description, he omitted how he felt in the fight.

The entire time Riome's expression was a mix of frustration and relief. "I told you I was not pushing him enough." She waved her hand at Cazier.

Cazier sat forward in his chair. "Kai, I am sorry." His expression turned hard. "Dante and I made a mistake by assuming our boroughs were safe and secure. I will not make the same mistake again." He sat back and looked to Riome. "You're right. I cannot always be there to protect him, no more than you."

"Of course I'm right," she spat. "Innocence is for the weak. I'm sorry he was afraid. I can't make him into me. I would not wish my life choices on anyone. Still, I should have trained him harder. He froze because he was not ready. Kai's instincts must be razor sharp. One must react instantly to take advantage of any situation. Hesitation gets you or someone else killed. And no, you do not always have to kill to stop your attacker." She glanced at Kai.

Cazier nodded in agreement. "I need to speak with Dresnor. We must double our efforts. His Kempery-man can teach him sword fighting, balance with a shield, footwork, and postures. Dresnor's hand-to-hand combat skills are the best I've seen. His style harkens to the old ways. He will make a valuable asset in Kai's training."

Riome gave him a glare.

"Second to you, my dear," he laughed. "This will cover your training, should he end up with any unexplained bruises." He looked at Kai. "Besides the standard means of defense, his Kempery-man's unique fighting techniques will give him an edge. Iver should have arranged training when Kai turned ten —he's now fourteen. His only training is a few months this spring with you." Cazier's voice raised in annoyance.

Kai listened until he could take no more. "I am right here, you know. Don't talk about me as if I am a project. I didn't freeze," he protested. "The man was bigger than me, he had experience."

"You froze," Riome barked. "Size doesn't matter. Skill matters. I taught you killing strikes, but you hesitated. I didn't need to be there to see the truth. Fear could have cost you your life. If you won't fight to save yourself, think of the others who may lose their life because you falter. See the moment and react. You must move and think faster. I will teach you. Learn to disable if you can, but you may have to put an enemy down."

It was difficult to take her seriously when she looked like sweet Mary. He sighed and refused to accept her words. How could he keep his innocence yet learn how to defend himself? It felt impossible to find the balance. The truth was he didn't freeze in fear—he was unwilling to take Bevon's life, even though he was an evil man.

She nodded at his reaction. "I know you are asking yourself. How can I be the hero and do what needs to be done? Sorry. You're not living in a storybook, Kai. This is real life. People are not characters in one of your novels. The hero does not always win, and sometimes, he has to make tough choices."

Her words were harsh but true. Books spared the hero, saving him from difficult choices. The events of Town Hope were living proof. He had been saved by Shane. Kai changed the subject. "Cazier, what about my father? Nola has him hidden away. I saw him when he arrived; he scooped me up like I was a feather. Steady and strong, he lifted both my brothers. His eyes clear and happy. Now all he does is sleep. Tell me, am I wrong?"

Riome looked at Cazier and waited. Cazier glanced from her to Kai. "Riome has not been able to get in to see him, even posing as Mary. Eavesdropping has also proven unsuccessful. She is the only one I trust with the secret tunnels other than you. According to Sigry, Nola requested something for a headache and a sleeping tonic for the king. We all know Sigry is loyal to your father. He would tell me if he thought something was amiss."

Kai wanted to believe this news. The nature of Nola concerned him, but he had no real proof. There was nothing tangible that revealed any wrongdoing. Only a feeling and strange behavior.

Cazier folded his hands together. "I will find a way to see Iver. I am sure he is as Nola says, merely resting after a long journey."

His cousin did not sound convinced. Kai stood and crossed the room. "Thank you both."

"Good evening, Kai," Adrian called after him.

Riome held the door. "I will look for you tomorrow evening."

Every other evening Kai walked Smoke and Shiva to the gates of the city. Tonight, Drew was his escort. From the torch-lit gatehouse, they watched the wolves dart away into the darkness before returning to the palace grounds. "Thank you again for everything in Town Hope. I am glad you were with us. We never really talked after..." Kai's voice dropped.

"We do what we must, Prince Kai. I've spent years watching you grow. You may be a prince to the others, but to me, you're a brother. Protecting you is more than my duty," Drew said sincerely.

Drew's words rang true for Kai. "Drew, I hope you know I feel the same. You are more than a guard." They stopped in the courtyard. "Again, thank you for the company."

"Anytime, Prince Kai. It was like old times," Drew replied.

Alone, Kai walked through the courtyard, thinking over the day. Out of the darkness, a sharp voice assaulted him. "All alone, little prince? Where's your mutt?" Landon mocked, stepping out from the shadows, shoving Kai in the back.

The force sent Kai stumbling forward, but he recovered and twisted around. "What was that for?"

Out of the darkness, another familiar voice challenged. "Well, well, well ... if it isn't the little prince? Having trouble walking?" Tolan laughed, pushing Kai in the shoulder.

Prepared for the shove, Kai held his ground. His attackers surrounded him. He knew he needed to get both boys in his line of sight. "What was that for?" Kai asked again, trying to sidestep Landon.

Kai wanted to run, but he refused to cower. Landon kept

Kai where he wanted him, between him and Tolan. "You're a spoiled little brat. You spend your summer socializing, while we learn to fight to protect your stupid easy life." Landon mocked as he stepped toward Kai and pushed him hard into Tolan's chest.

"We've got him now. What should we do with him?" Tolan asked as he grabbed Kai by the biceps.

"You think you're so special, but let me assure you, titles mean nothing," Landon sneered.

They had no idea what he'd been through this summer. Kai saw Landon clinch his fists. "What have I ever done to either of you?" Kai asked with a squirm.

"You breathe, boy..." Landon seethed, punching Kai in the stomach.

"Landon, stop," Tolan yelled. "That's enough, no need to hit him. We're just having a little fun." Tolan released Kai.

Kai stomped on Tolan's foot and jabbed him in the gut with his elbow, forcing the larger boy backward. Kai made sudden quick moves—he did not hesitate. One hand swung around and slammed Tolan in the sternum with his palm, sending the larger boy to the ground. Tolan gasped.

Landon swung, but Kai anticipated the strike. He sidestepped and grabbed Landon by the wrist in a heartbeat. Using Landon's own momentum, Kai tossed the older boy to the ground. Still angry, Kai climbed on top and punched Landon in the face.

Having witnessed their brawl, the Grand Duke ran to stop the fight. "What's going on here? Boys! Speak up."

"The little brat jumped me!" Landon yelled, wiping the blood from his nose and lip.

"I didn't start it, but I certainly finished it," Kai snarled.

Tolan hung his head low. "Sir, sorry, sir. Things got out of hand. Kai, I am truly sorry, I never meant..." Tolan stammered, covering his face.

"Tolan, you know better. You leave within a week for Fort Pohaku. This could ruin your reputation, lower your rank,

You know fighting is unacceptable. This will destroy your chances of becoming a Kempery-man." Dante stared Tolan down. "All three of you in my study, now."

Dante marched them through the palace and sat behind his desk. Dirty and bruised, Kai and Tolan waited for their punishment with their heads down. Landon stood tall and arrogant, hands behind his back. Dante stared at them. "What am I to do with you three? Acting like ruffians. You should all be ashamed."

"Grand Duke." Tolan stepped forward. "Sir, if I may speak. None of this was Kai's fault. We attacked him. I should have tried to stop Landon. I should have protected Kai, and I failed, sir. I understand this will be on my record, but I still wish to continue my service. Please, sir."

"Admirable son, but don't apologize to me. Prince Kai is the one who deserves your words." Dante motioned.

Embarrassed and red-faced, Tolan turned about-face. "Sincerely Kai, I know we … I give you a hard time. I should not be jealous of your position. I truly am sorry for my behavior, I never meant for it to go this far. I let you down—I let myself down. I will do better, that is my promise to you. Please accept my apology." Tolan extended his hand in a gesture of peace.

Kai felt the sincerity in Tolan's words and saw the regret in his eyes. He knew it would be better to make a friend than be at odds. He looked at the boy who'd bullied him, changed and was genuinely regretful. "I accept your apology, Tolan," he said, shaking the boy's hand.

Kai felt a twinge of regret in his heart, knowing he was not always gracious to Tolan, either. "Grand Duke Carmelo, sir. I too should know better. I should have walked away. And I have given my share of insults over the years." He paused to look at his two assailants.

Tolan, humbled, and genuine. Landon, filled with arrogance and loathing with no signs of remorse.

"Sir, regardless of what happened and why, could you give

Tolan a pass on this?" Kai asked. "I would greatly appreciate it if you could let him go to Fort Pohaku with a clean record."

"Landon, do you have anything to say for your actions?" Dante asked.

"Sorry sir, won't happen again, sir. I will report as ordered." Landon stood stiff, staring straight ahead, hands behind his back.

No apology came from Landon. Dante glared with disappointment at all three. "I will make my decision tomorrow. You are all dismissed." Dante motioned for them to leave and refocused his efforts to the papers covering his desk.

On their way out, Tolan slowed to walk next to Kai. "Kai, may I speak to you?" He stopped, putting distance between them and Landon. "I wanted to thank you for the kind words. I'm not sure I deserve them after the way I've treated you." Tolan hung his head low.

"You're welcome, Tolan. I'm not sure this makes us friends, but I am willing."

"I'd certainly like to try. Goodnight, Your Highness," Tolan said as they parted ways.

"Goodnight Tolan," Kai said, surprised with the turn of events.

Mind reeling, Kai fell into bed. After everything, who was he now? How could he find a balance between protecting himself and using his strength and speed? He could have seriously hurt Tolan and Landon. He shook away his frustration. He closed his eyes and hoped for answers.

His sleep shallow and fitful; he cringed at the visions that followed.

The smell of something foul caught in his nostrils and made him cough. His mind felt dizzy, and he fell to his knees. Toxic smoke rolled around him in the hallway outside the nursery. He felt helpless. The hall light illuminated the back of a man kneeling over Cordelia. Her small form lay limp on the floor. The glint of a blade flashed. Blackness loomed around the edges of Kai's eyes. Dizzy, he collapsed, unable to help his sister.

In his mind, he wrestled with his fears. In his bed, he tossed and turned and gripped his covers. His dream continued.

Battle sounds echoed in the wind. Swords clashed, metal against metal. Fires raged in the distance. The smell of burnt wood and flesh filled the air. Wrought iron curls and twists kept him out—the fence too high. Kai ran for the gate. His aunt Helena's garden was a battlefield. Men in black lay dead on the ground. Nearby, men in blue, Diu men, were covered in blood. Strange holes punched their bodies, which oozed with blood.

Around the hedge, he saw Drew slice down a man in black. The silver blade of Drew's sword now covered in blood. *Bang.* A foreign sound rang out. Drew twisted in pain, struck in the shoulder. Through the hedges, Kai saw two men in black, fidgeting with a silver weapon. He watched, frozen. *Bang.* Smoke, spark, and debris cut across the sky. Struck in the chest, Drew dropped to the ground.

Kai pressed the gushing hole in his friend's chest. Blood bubbled in Drew's mouth, his eyes fluttered, and he gasped. Drew's body went limp, his breath gone. "No, no, please," Kai screamed. Like grains of sand, Drew faded away.

Twisted in his covers, Kai woke his fists clenched. Sweat soaked his sheets. Alone in the dark, he wept. Was this his future? Could he save Cordelia? Could he change Drew's fate? Was he destined to watch everyone he loved die? The pressure was unbearable. Yet the facts were undeniable. This would happen. The only question was, would he be ready?

Bathed in fresh air and moonlight, he sat on his balcony. Smoke sat at his side, sniffing the air. Kai's hand glided over Smoke's ears. The autumn air offered the slightest breeze, drying the sweat on his back. He searched the night for his friends. Behind him, in the palace, Kendra slept in the nursery. Haygan slept in his room above the stables, Shiva near the door.

He searched for her through the inner ward. The little cottage was quiet and dark, nestled with the other private homes provided to palace workers. Rayna sat awake in her bed, her back to him. He focused on her long brown hair, pooled about her shoulders. He watched and wondered how her gleaning practice was progressing.

She turned her head toward her shoulder. He watched, as the side of her face, wrapped in the light turned to face him. He raised from his chair, crossed the balcony, and placed his hands on the stone rail. Anticipation made his heart pound.

She twisted in her bed. Her face raised up in his direction. He leaned forward, curious. *Can she see me?*

She tilted her head to the side, her neck strained forward. The moment lingered. He held his breath—Rayna waved. Astonished, he waved back. She covered her mouth. He chuckled and ran his hand down Smoke's back. "She is good."

For now, he found peace in the threads of energy emanating around him. Threads which connected him with Rayna and their future. Tired, he gave her one last wave and went to back bed.

The End.